"Tipping his hat to both
books, Chu delivers a
pounding, laugh-out-loud funny and thoughtful. Part
James Bond, part Superman, part *Orphanage*. There's
something here for everyone."

Myke Cole, author of Control Point *and* Fortress Frontier

"A totally original sci-fi thriller that will have you hooked
from page one with both riveting action and a sly wit. This
is a story of human history, the hidden powers that have
shaped it, and one man's transformation from complete
nobody to a key fighter in the war for humanity's future."

Ramez Naam, award-winning author of Nexus *and* Crux

"Just your usual 'I've got an immensely wise alien in my
head who wants me to become and international man of
mystery' story. Which is to say, page-turning homage to
other classic SF like Hal Clement's Needle. Recommended."

Steven Gould, author of the Jumpers series

"A fast-paced, high-action SF mix of Jason Bourne meets the
Hero's Journey, jam-packed with dark conspiracies, wild
romance, ancient aliens, and a secret, globe-spanning war.
Loved it!"

Matt Forbeck, author of Amortals *and* Hard Times
in Dragon City

"Chu's good-natured adroitness with character development
is matched by his thriller-style plotting, a fine blend of
gentle humor and sharp suspense."

Barnes & Noble Review

WESLEY CHU

The Rebirths of Tao

ANGRY
ROBOT

ANGRY ROBOT
An imprint of Waktins Media Ltd

Lace Market House,
54-56 High Pavement,
Nottingham
NG1 1HW
UK

www.angryrobotbooks.com
twitter.com/angryrobotbooks
Infinite lives

An Angry Robot paperback original 2015

Cover art by Stewart Larking
Set in Meridien by EpubServices

Distributed in the United States by Random House, Inc., New York.

ISBN 978 0 85766 430 3
Ebook ISBN 978 0 85766 431 0

Printed in the United States of America

9 8 7 6 5 4 3 2

To Amanda, Lee and Marco

CHAPTER ONE
REDWOOD RUSH

What is the meaning of this? Do you know who I am? I will have your skulls!

Huchel, Genjix Council – Eastern Hemisphere, when apprehended by Interpol Extraterrestrial Task Force while trying to flee Germany following the Great Betrayal

The problem Vladimir had with this damn country was that everything was too damn big. The cars were too big, the music was too loud, and the ridiculous trees in this forest were too tall. The raggedy group he led detoured around the giant redwood tree blocking his path. Blasted thing was big as a house. And the stupid trees weren't even red, though in this pitch-black darkness, he could barely see Alex clinging to his hand, let alone determine the color of tree bark. His eyes wandered up to the forest canopy. It was so thick he couldn't see the stars. That made it nearly impossible to navigate. Where the hell was south?

At least the food portions here were healthy. That was something Vladimir approved of. He'd never had such a large breakfast before, much less in the middle of the night. Who eats burritos with five eggs in the middle of the night, anyway? His little group did, and to be honest, it was pretty good. It was too bad the meal had been two days ago.

"I need to rest," Sachin said, leaning against the too-damn-tall tree. He propped his rifle against it and slid down to the mossy ground.

Vladimir reminded himself that the seventy year-old Indian man had spent the majority of his life in a classroom at the Institute of Technology, recruiting promising students for the cause. The professor wasn't used to running around the forest in the middle of the night, fleeing armed assailants. Vladimir looked down at his daughter and gave her a gentle nudge. She pulled out a canteen and walked over to Sachin, who drank his fill, pouring water down his chin and neck, letting it dribble down his shirt. Alex took out a rag and wiped the old man's brow. Vladimir shook his head. She was a good girl, so much potential. She deserved better than this.

Somewhere in the distance, the barking of dogs in pursuit pierced the otherwise quiet night. Vladimir closed his eyes and listened. Twenty, maybe thirty minutes behind. His gaze moved from his daughter and Sachin to the other refugees: Petr, a Russian colonel he had had dealings with in the past, Rin, the Japanese nuclear physicist, Marsuka, her research assistant, Ohr, the former South Korean Senator, and the remaining survivors of the Siberian Epsilon Shock team.

He grimaced. His entire life had collapsed in the blink of an eye. His fortune confiscated, his wife murdered, and now he was nothing more than a destitute refugee with a teenage daughter in a land unfriendly to his kind, a far cry from the affluent businessman and power broker he had been just a few weeks earlier. He looked back at Alex, still helping the old professor. Well, at least part of his wife escaped. Tabs would continue living in his daughter.

Move. Every second of delay is costly.

"Yes, Ladm."

"Break is over," he barked. "We go. Now."

He walked over, hooked an arm under Sachin's armpit, and lifted him to his feet. "Let's go, old man. You can rest when you're safe. Or dead." He looked over at his daughter standing on the other side of the elderly professor. "Alex, help him walk."

The small group continued south, following the twisting and winding paths when they could, and making new ones when they had to. Vladimir was sure they had missed the rendezvous. The coded message at the diner back in Portland had said to hit 42°, -123° and follow the river. However, they had gotten picked up by a Penetra net and had had to deviate from their course. The scanners the Quasing invented to detect others of their kind residing within a living creature were now used by the humans to hunt them down.

Now, nine hours later, the federals were closing in, and the group was completely lost. They passed another giant tree, this time so big Vladimir couldn't see its edge in the predawn darkness. The dogs' barking was getting louder and louder.

This group would be a prize capture. None of them would allow their Quasing to be taken, though. Vladimir looked down at his beautiful daughter. All except for Alexandra. Vladimir didn't care about sacrificing himself for Ladm, but no one was going to hurt his little girl,

Quasing or no Quasing. There had to be a way out for her.

Do not forget your place, Vladimir.

They picked up their pace and for a while, it seemed to keep their pursuers at bay, but soon enough, the exhausted group began to lag again, Sachin most of all. As the first rays of light peeked through the forest canopy, Sachin broke. By then, he was stumbling badly. He fell to his knees and rolled onto his back. He shooed Alex away when she tried to help him up. Instead, he leaned against a tree trunk and looked up at the lush leaves overhead, and then at the greenery of the forest. He closed his eyes and shook his head.

"Come on, Sachin," Rin urged.

He waved her off and kept his eyes closed. After a few seconds, his pained face changed. He nodded and looked at the rest of the group. "This place is beautiful and peaceful, like a painting. The air is clean and there is abundant life. Mawl would find serenity here."

"Shut up, old fool, we're all in this together," Vladimir growled. "We're not leaving you in the wild."

Sachin struggled to his feet and slung his rifle around his shoulder. "It's already settled. Mawl is at peace with this and by Brahman, I look forward to it. There are worse places to meet my maker, and for him to live free. Get moving. Go. I'll buy you time."

Vladimir moved to grab him. "I said we're not leaving…"

Sachin spun around and aimed his rifle at Vladimir, then slowly lowered it to point at Alex. "I mean what I said, you stubborn Russian. You have your little girl to think about. Now get out of here before what time I buy you doesn't amount to anything."

Do it. I have only known Mawl a short while on this planet when we fought together against the Bolsheviks. He will be remembered. I will return one day to find him.

Vladimir bit his lip. "Crazy fool." He walked forward and embraced Sachin roughly. "Until the Eternal Sea, my friend. Mawl, stay out of sight of humans. Your part in this is over for now. Ladm will return for you one day, if not this lifetime, in the next."

"*Mrithyur maa amritham gamaya*, my friend," Sachin said, then turned around and limped in the direction of the sounds of the pursuing dogs.

Alex took a few steps after the professor and made the traditional Hindu sign of peace. "*Phir milenge*, Mr Sachin. Goodbye, Mawl. Tabs says she'll see you in the Eternal Sea."

The sounds of humans shouting added to the increasingly loud barking of the dogs. By Vladimir's estimate, they were probably no more than a few minutes behind them now. He put his arms around his daughter's waist and hurried her along. "No time for sentiments. Let's go!"

Vladimir sprinted into the darkness, pushing Alex ahead of him. The others would keep up with him, or maybe they wouldn't. He had survived with them for weeks now, sharing food, sleeping in the same beds, fighting alongside them. But now that things were looking their worst, and the group was about to be captured, it was every man for himself.

All he cared about was getting his daughter to safety, even at the cost of his own life, or those of his companions, if necessary. Maybe if he outran the rest of the group, they would buy him some time to escape their accursed pursuers. Vladimir felt ashamed for thinking this, but when it came to Alexandra, nothing else mattered.

Do not feel ashamed. My only regret is involving her in this situation. Tabs should never have inhabited her when her mother died.

"I don't blame you or Tabs, Ladm. I blame those assholes that killed Marta and these damn Americans breathing down our necks."

Unfortunately for this plan, everyone else was in better shape than Vladimir, so they all kept up pretty easily. A few minutes later, the unmistakable sound of a Kalashnikov pierced the early morning air, its familiar peck-peck-peck joined by a chorus of higher-sounding rat-tat-tats. Flocks of birds took off, flying around trees as the forest came to life. The exchange continued for a few minutes, and then stopped. The forest settled and became silent again. The group stopped in unison and looked back into the thickets.

"Be well, Sachin," Rin bowed. "May you find a–"

"Later! We don't have time to mourn." Vladimir shoved her forward urgently. "We have to keep going."

Ohr looked at the others and then shook his head. "It's no use running. We're not going to outrun dogs and federals in their own country." He pointed at a small ledge off to the side. "That is as good of a point as we're going to get. I say we make a stand there and die fighting. I refuse to be run down like an animal, with my back to the enemy."

Vladimir shook his head.

He is right.

"No," he said, looking down at Alex. "We keep going."

There is no other chance. You have a day's worth of forest in front of you and the enemy only minutes behind. This will be the only time you can choose the battlefield. This ledge is an elevated spot facing west, your back will be against the sunrise. It is the right strategy.

Vladimir grimaced. He had hoped it wouldn't come to this, but it seemed the damn federals had forced their hand. He swung his rifle from his back and stomped toward the stone ledge. The others followed suit, climbing up the steep slant and stripping themselves of their gear. He watched as the surviving Epsilons attached their signature bayonets to their rifles and pistols, and then huddled together and prayed. Vladimir wished he had that sort of fervor. Over the past few months, his faith had been shaken.

A few minutes later, the group was entrenched in a defensive formation around a cluster of boulders elevated several meters above the ground. Vladimir hated to admit it, but Ladm and the others were right. By now, the sounds of the barking dogs were all around them, and he expected to see their hunters any minute. Hiding would be useless; no doubt the federals were carrying portable Penetra scanners.

Vladimir turned to Alex and pointed at a small crevice off to the side. "I want you to hide in there until this is all over. Don't come out until I get you. If we fall, you keep running, understand?" His daughter made a face and drew her pistol. Vladimir snarled. "Definitely not. You are not…"

She cocked the pistol in one smooth motion. "Don't be silly, Papa. I cannot escape the scanners. Besides, you'll need me. I'm a better shot than you."

Vladimir stared at his daughter, half with terror that she was about to wander into a firefight and half with pride. He dropped to a knee and drew her close. "Your mother would be so proud. Keep your head down. Shoot only when you have a clear target."

"I got movement," Marsuka hissed.

The others scrambled to the edge and took up position behind cover. Vladimir pressed his back to a boulder and unclipped his satchel of spare magazines. He placed three on the ground and handed the bag to Ohr, who was kneeling against the other side of the boulder. He looked over at Alex on the other side of him, positioned in between two smaller rocks. Dark figures emerged from woods, moving in between trees and brush, flanking them on both sides.

"They know we're up here," Petr growled. "Fire at will before they entrench."

He opened fire and the rest followed suit. Within seconds, the dark forest was lit up by yellow bursts of enemy muzzle flashes. The rattling exchanges punctured the previously calm dawn. The sky came to life as hundreds of birds took to the air, adding to the chaos and confusion.

The fight went well at first. Between the skill of the Epsilon-trained operatives and their elevated position, the body count initially skewed heavily in his group's favor. The federals had far superior numbers though, and as Vladimir's group's casualties began to mount, so did the enemy's ability to sustain the fight. Slowly, the tide changed.

To his left, Polski, one of the Epsilons, took a bullet to the head. Vladimir pulled Alex from the edge and pointed at the body. She nodded and scampered on all fours to rifle through the dead Epsilon's coat for spare magazines. She found four and tossed one to Vladimir.

He caught it mid-air and pointed at the other end of the ledge. "See if the others need some as well."

He glanced to his right as Ohr pulled back to reload. He only had one magazine left on the ground next to him.

All of them must be running low by now. Ammunition wasn't light after all, and most of their carry weight was reserved for food and supplies. He heard Marsuka call out that he was dry. He looked to his left as Alex slid another magazine toward the scientist.

No sooner did Marsuka pick up the magazine, than he stiffened, a bullet puncturing his neck. Alex dodged out of the way as his fell to the ground and rolled toward her. Vladimir's heart broke. She was far too young to witness such things. Then, if it was even possible, the situation took a turn for the worse. Just as Vlel, Marsuka's Quasing, rose into the air, a jet of flame shot up from below and consumed him. The small group watched horrified as the millions year-old being evaporated into the morning sky.

Their dwindling group fought on with renewed vigor. Vladimir shot two more federals before he had to reload, and then four more. By that time, only Rin had ammunition left. A few seconds later, she had run out as well. They had lost, and this ledge would become their grave. The gunfire became one-sided, until eventually, someone below ordered a ceasefire.

"Come out with your hands over your heads, aliens," a voice bellowed through a bullhorn. "We know there are five of you up there. We have scanners. There's no escape."

Vladimir held Alex tightly as he desperately prayed for an escape. The best he could hope for was the so-called Alien Containment facility, a top-secret prison where the Western countries incarcerated and ran tests on the Quasing. The worst and most likely outcome was torture and death, and with that, the death of Ladm as well.

The time has come to surrender to the Eternal Sea.

That was the logical thing to do. Give Ladm, Tabs, and

the others a chance, but Vladimir had never been one of those fanatics. He had come to Ladm later in life and had never developed the zeal that many others of his rank possessed. He looked over at Rin and Ohr; those two weren't hardliners either. All three were just smart, capable people who saw an advantage with the Quasing and took it. Now it had led them here.

His gaze wandered to Petr. He was as fanatical as they came. If his Quasing told him to kill everyone in the group to allow the others a chance to escape, he would do it. Right now, the man was praying with his eyes closed, preparing to sacrifice himself. That was the group's next move. That was the only move they had left.

Logically, it is the right decision. Make your peace.

Vladimir squeezed Alex tightly and knew he couldn't do it. She was an innocent; she had her whole life ahead of her. Surely, the federals would show mercy. Not even they could be so cruel.

"You have one minute before we gas your location, aliens," the voice from below called through the bullhorn. "I cannot guarantee your safety then."

Petr finished his prayer. There was going to be little mercy from either him or the federals, but as of this point, he knew on which side his little girl would have a better chance of surviving.

Before Petr could carry out that last deadly deed, Vladimir took his rifle and swung it with everything he had at the man's face, knocking him out cold. Before the others could stop him, he stood up and held his hands over his head. "There is a child here. We are unarmed."

This is unacceptable! You know what will happen to us.

"Shut up, Ladm," growled Vladimir aloud.

"Drop your weapons and come down off the ledge. Keep your hands over your head," the voice below said. "We can track all of you so don't even think about trying anything."

Vladimir grabbed the unconscious man's feet. "Ohr, help me pick up Petr." The Korean grabbed the colonel's arms, and together, they carried him down the ledge.

As soon as they reached ground level, they were surrounded by eight uniformed men. There were nine bodies on the ground. Vladimir grunted in satisfaction. At least they had put up a good fight. Still, only the end result was important. In this case, the result was defeat. Vladimir slumped his shoulders as all five of them were handcuffed and forced to kneel down. Even Alex. Seeing her like this brought tears to his eyes. How had it come to this?

"Agent Kallis, we have the group of aliens rounded up," the lead agent spoke into a small black box attached at his shoulder. "Bagging and tagging now."

"Good," a voice crackled back.

"We have a new signature," one of the federals standing near the back barked. "Just appeared out of the blue. Behind that tree." The team of federals standing out in the open scrambled for cover, leaving Vladimir and his people kneeling on the ground.

"How many?" the man with the bullhorn said.

"Just one. Stationary."

Six of the federals spread out facing the giant redwood on the western edge of the clearing. Two remained behind to guard their prisoners.

"Come out with your hands up," the leader yelled through his bullhorn. "You are outnumbered and we have the rest of your kind held captive. No one has to get hurt."

Two soft pings came from the east and the two men guarding Vladimir's group dropped. Then three more pings, and two federals on the outer edge of the clearing fell. The remaining federals, now believing themselves flanked, dove for cover.

"How many signatures," the leader yelled.

"Still one!"

"Damn it, they must have ghosts with them."

Another ping, this time from the west. The federal with the scanner fell.

"Drop your weapons," a voice called out from the forest, "and the rest of you can live."

The surviving four federals swiveled in all directions, trying to determine where the shots were coming from. Finally, one of them dropped his gun and held his hands up. Two others, after a second, followed suit. All eyes were on the remaining armed federal, the one with the bullhorn, as he considered his options. There was a soft ping from the forest and the dirt between his feet kicked up. He finally followed suit and dropped his rifle.

"Always a guy in the bunch a little slower than the others, almost ruining it for everyone else," a figure said, stepping out of the woods. He was dressed in camouflage and a hoodie, and carried a small assault rifle. He walked into the clearing, gun still trained on the four remaining federals.

Vladimir studied their savior. The man didn't look or sound familiar, at least not by the descriptions from their contact's dossier, considering their contact was supposed to be a woman. Most of his face was covered with a pair of dark brown aviator sunglasses and a scraggly beard, and the rest of his head was hidden by a skullcap.

"On your knees, folks." He squinted at the leader who had carried the bullhorn, who squinted back. "You know me, Boy Scout?" he said finally.

The now de-bullhorned agent scowled. "Yeah, you're a ghost."

"Not just a ghost. *The* Ghost." The man grabbed the comm from the agent's shoulder and lifted it to his mouth. "Hello. Who do I have the pleasure of speaking with?"

"Special Agent Kallis of the Interpol Extraterrestrial Task Force. Who the fuck is this?" the voice snapped.

"It's your favorite human traitor."

"Rayban Ghost? You bastard. What have you done with my men?"

"They're fine. How are you? How is the family?"

"Well, you shot my guys, so pretty damn terrible right now. And how many times do I have to tell you to never bring up my family?"

"Well, I used the electric tranqs on the guys I hit. They should be fine. You still got some live ones here, and they'll stay that way if you follow my demands. There's six North Korean Nationals at Guantanamo I need released within the hour. I also need fifty million dollars wired to a Swiss account."

"You know I can't do that."

"Okay, how about we compromise and you just donate four thousand bucks, a thousand for each of your surviving men, to the Eureka Animal Shelter. Then we'll call it square." He looked over at the kneeling federals. "Maybe one-point-five for that big guy over there."

"You better watch your back, Rayban Ghost. I'll get you one day."

"And my little dog too?" the Ghost grinned, clearly

enjoying this exchange. "Like you said, no one else has to get hurt." The Ghost turned to the men in front of him. "Face down with your hands behind your back. You know the drill. I got half a dozen others in the forest who I had to convince to not blow your brains out and toss your bodies into vats of acid."

A few minutes later, the federals made a neat little line of trussed-up bodies as they squirmed face down in the dirt. The Rayban Ghost took the time to tie up the unconscious ones as well. Vladimir wondered why the man was using non-lethal force. Satisfied with his work, the Ghost spoke into his own throat mic and then signaled for Vladimir and his group to stand and follow him.

"Thank you, uh, Rayban Ghost," Vladimir said as the stranger hauled him and his group to their feet. Unfortunately, their skin did not touch through the thick layers of clothing, though by now, he was pretty sure this man wasn't a vessel.

"Hey, what about us?" the de-bullhorned agent shouted. "You can't leave us here. We'll die like this! Why even bother sparing our lives then?"

"Rayban Ghost, we had a deal," Kallis's voice shouted over the comm.

The Ghost picked up the receiver. "You'll get your men back. I told you before, Kallis. We're the good guys. I'll call a forest ranger for them later on." Then he tore the comm unit from its cord. He turned and gestured to Vladimir's group. "Shall we?"

The Ghost marched them fifteen minutes deeper south into the forest. When he was satisfied they were far enough away from the federals, he called for a stop and studied the group.

"Thank you, brother," Vladimir said.

"Authenticate yourself."

"To advance without the possibility being checked…" Vladimir began saying.

The passphrase died in his mouth when the Rayban Ghost cut him off. "Shut it, Genjix. I don't care about that."

Then Vladimir realized who had saved them. At this point, he wasn't sure if they were better off being prisoners of the Interpol Extraterrestrial Task Force than with this man. At least with the IXTF, his people had a chance of being released by their people on the inside. With the Prophus, he expected nothing more than a quick death as soon as they got whatever they wanted out of him.

"I want names; you and your Quasing's," the Ghost said. "Full names and origins. Now."

Both Ohr and Rin looked to Vladimir for direction. He shook his head and spoke in a clear and loud voice. "Vladimir Mengsk. Ladm. I am a businessman from Moscow, and this is…"

"I can speak for myself, Papa," Alex said. She took a step forward and lifted her chin. "Alexandra Mengsk. My job is to be my papa's daughter, betrayer." She jutted her chin out at the Ghost as a challenge.

Vladimir stiffened as the Ghost approached his daughter and dropped to a knee. "Feisty little one, eh? And what's your Quasing's name, Alexandra Mengsk, Papa's daughter?"

Alex shook her head, refusing to speak. The Ghost looked up at Vladimir.

"It's all right," Vladimir said. "Go ahead and tell our friend here."

"Tabs," the name came out of her reluctantly.

The Ghost smiled. "Thank you, child. I hope she guides you well." He stood up. "What about the rest of you?"

Petr, unsurprisingly, refused to divulge any information. The colonel clamped down and looked away, refusing even to acknowledge the Rayban Ghost's existence.

The Ghost sighed. "Like I said, always someone screwing it up for everyone." He grabbed Petr by the shoulder and kneed him in the stomach, doubling him over. The Ghost knocked him to the ground and drew his pistol, jamming it into his forehead. He looked over at Rin. "His name and Quasing. Now."

"Petr. Coruv," she said reluctantly, eyes down on the ground.

Petr glared. "Weak runt."

His name must have meant something to the Rayban Ghost, who took a renewed interest in Petr. "Coruv. Russian by your accent." He looked down and saw the bayonet holster on each side of Petr's boots. "You're one of Vinnick's dogs?"

"What's it to you, betrayer?" Petr snarled.

"There's little I can do with a rabid animal." The Ghost took off his aviator sunglasses. "The Russians killed thirty Prophus refugees escaping the Chinese Inquisition two years ago. I had some friends there."

"I took great pleasure partaking –" Petr said.

"My name is Roen Tan, you mass-murdering asshole."

"You! You and your bitch were the ones that betrayed us to the humans!" Petr lunged at him and collapsed from a single gunshot through the chest. His sparkling Quasing rose from his body and fluttered about as if a wisp among these giant trees.

"Get out of here, Coruv, and consider yourself lucky I

don't have a flamethrower on me." Roen Tan turned and faced the rest of the group. "Anyone else want to release their Quasing? I'll be more than happy to oblige." He stared each of them down before finally adding. "Here's the deal. I can kill you now so your Quasing can find a host among the redwoods for a few centuries, or you can cooperate and come with me. Oh, by the way, if you were expecting your contact, sorry, but I think her Quasing is now living the good life in an anteater. What will it be?"

The small group exchanged looks, and the rest of them looked to Vladimir. He stepped forward. "We will cooperate, Prophus."

"Good." Roen gestured to Ohr. "Authenticate yourself."

"Excuse me, Mr Uh...The Ghost," Rin asked. "Why don't you just use the vessel the Penetra scanner had detected earlier? He can just identify us through touch instead of going through this charade."

Roen Tan shook his head. "I had to send him off ahead. His mom's going to kill us. He's already late for school."

CHAPTER TWO
DOMESTICATED

The Prophus, and I am sure the Genjix as well, had watched the Senate hearings very closely. Senators Mary Thompson and James Wilks, along with Haewon, Mary's Quasing, were interrogated, prodded, and tested extensively by the Military, CIA, FBI, and every other branch of the government.

In the end, three months following the Great Betrayal, the Extraterrestrial Sedition Act was passed. That marked the beginning of a new era on Earth. The governments of the world, one by one, began to recognize the existence of aliens. The game had changed for everyone.

Baji

Jill Tesser Tan used to hate cooking. The truth was she never learned how to cook growing up, because both her parents were too busy with their careers to ever step foot in the kitchen, other than to heat up the occasional late-night carryout. Unlike for most families, their kitchen was the least-used room in their home.

Now, in her forties, Jill had finally discovered the joys of making food from scratch. That was fortunate, because now, she had a kitchen in her quaint farmhouse that was about as big as her entire condo in Manhattan growing up, and she loved it. Over the past few years, she had found comfort in the constant warmth of their working brick oven and the aroma of home-cooked food wafting throughout the entire house. This kitchen was the heart of her home and the place where she conducted all her business.

She adjusted her headset as she mixed a batch of pancake batter. "I don't care if it takes three hours. I want a full count before we exchange the currency. No more weights, since he shorted us 30k last time, and damn it, Hite, make sure that rate is three quarters. If Moyan flubs it again, you tell him we'll wash it elsewhere in the future."

Moyan will know you are bluffing. There is no one within a thousand kilometers who can move this much volume.

"On second thought, don't tell him that. Just frigging count the money."

Jill switched over to the second channel as she turned the stove on and sprayed oil onto the griddle. The perimeter alert on the map of her property began to blink orange. Jill looked through the kitchen window and saw an armed figure emerge from the thickets. She stared at the orange light until it turned green, and then went back to working on her pancake batter.

She switched over to the next channel. "Kate? Oh sorry, Harry. Ping me when you receive an update on the registry. We need to get the Patels working during the trip, so make sure they have upgraded accommodations." She switched again. "Kate? Good. When you meet with the Hillmans, see if they have a couple extra cases of .45 bullets. Untraceable, of course. And some incendiaries.

Preferably nothing older than the Korean War this time, please."

"Hi, Mom." Cameron Tan, wearing a ghillie suit with a SCAR rifle slung around his back, waved as he walked through the kitchen doorway. He had wiped his feet before he walked in, but the rest of him looked like he had just come out the losing end of a mud-wrestling contest. She waved back, instinctively checking for any signs of injuries as he leaned in and kissed her on the cheek.

Jill took one sniff and shooed him away. "Go take a shower. You've already missed the bus, and you smell like you waded through sewage." She paused. "Did you and your father go…?"

He shook his head. "No, we did not go dumpster diving again."

Jill grinned at her gangly teenager. Cameron had floppy hair that she disapproved of because it covered half his face, which was a spitting image of Roen. His skin was dark from the many hours he spent outdoors every day. He was going through his growth spurt right now and at fifteen, much to the chagrin of his father, he was already the tallest member in the family. The perfectly fitting long-sleeve shirts, sweaters, and pants she had bought him just last winter were already showing too much ankle and wrist. She also noticed during their many sparring sessions that he had gotten noticeably stronger as well, whether from puberty or because the t'ai chi was finally clicking. She'd have to watch out for that; pretty soon, they wouldn't be able to spar anymore, and strangely, that made her a little sad.

She shooed him toward the stairs. "I'll have breakfast ready by the time you're not stinking up the joint." She held up a finger and turned away. "Comm Ops. What do you mean they can't support the Patels? There's a very specific reason we paid for board on a research vessel. It's a damn waste of money otherwise. Tell them we want our money back then. No, screw them. Get a refund or I will peel it from their hides."

Jill continued running Prophus operations for the entire Pacific Northwest while she poured the first batch of pancakes over the hot griddle. As she spoke, she noticed that Cameron had not moved. She clicked on the mute and looked at him. "Is there something else?"

"Mom," he said. "Dad's on his way back. He's radio dark, but wants you to know he's bringing a group of Genjix in."

She nodded. "Got it. Tell Ines to have the quarters in the dungeon prepared. The ones with the external locks, please." Cameron still looked like he had something else on his mind. "What is it?"

"There's a girl with them. My age. Kind of. I think..." he paused. "I think she's a host."

That gave Jill pause. She saw the confusion in his eyes and the hesitation when he spoke. God, she hoped the girl wasn't cute. As a mother, she just wasn't ready for that yet. If this girl was a host and attractive, his fifteen year-old brain might explode.

Your worst fears realized?

"Up there with Roen grocery shopping carte blanche without a list."

Jill pointed at the stairs. "Shower. Now." She watched as her son slung the rifle off his shoulder and put it in the weapons closet, and then scampered up the stairs. This was probably the worst time for a host girl to come into his life, especially a Genjix.

Trust me, we hate humans going through puberty too.

Cameron was a good son; his three parents saw to that. Between Roen and her putting all their energy into him and Tao's constant mentoring, he had little choice but to grow up the way they molded him. However, due to their special circumstances, he also had a worryingly unusual childhood, and hadn't grown up with many children his age.

They had had to pull him out of the second grade when the new administration ordered the IXTF to sweep all of the schools in the Washington DC area with Penetra scanners during the government purge. He spent most of his childhood either constantly on the move with Roen and Jill, or living with her parents in San Diego, only finally returning home after Jill's operation in the Pacific Northwest was up and running. Even with Tao to guide and keep him company, it had been a very lonely childhood.

The family had settled down on the outskirts of Eureka, California, four years ago, and this was the longest they had stayed in one place since the Great Betrayal, when humanity had learned about the Quasing. Now, Jill was responsible for Prophus operations from Vancouver down to San Francisco. Her job was especially critical, since the Quasing Underground Railroad ran directly through this region.

The tension between the Eastern and Western hemisphere had been ramping up for years, with diplomats on both sides predicting the breakout of World War III soon. The extensive naval blockades on both sides made transportation by ship dangerous. Traveling by plane was near-impossible, since there were Penetra scanners at every airport.

That left the thin stretch of ocean between Siberia and Alaska the safest option for refugees fleeing Asia. The overland path across the Bering Strait, through the North American continent toward safe havens in South America was one of the most trafficked and dangerous routes for the thousands fleeing Genjix domination in Asia. Interestingly, the refugees fleeing the continent were nearly equal parts Prophus and Genjix.

The Council Power Struggle had taken a toll on many Quasing and their hosts. For over half a century, Vinnick with Flua, and Devin with Zoras, had been the most powerful on the Genjix Council. Ever since the upstart Enzo succeeded Devin and became the leader of China, Enzo and Vinnick had waged open conflict, now known as the Genjix Power Struggle, that had spilled over across many other regions.

In recent years, the United States had tightened their borders, and the job of smuggling Quasing refugees had become more dangerous. These days, Jill half-expected the IXTF to burst into her farmhouse at any time. Couple that with raising a teenager...

She looked down and cursed. The first batch of pancakes had burned. She slid them into the garbage with her spatula and started over. She had thought taking command of the Pacific Northwest region would be a quiet change of pace from undercover work in the dense metropolitan cities of Chicago and Washington DC. Boy, had she been mistaken.

The work she did now was more important than any work she had done on the Hill for Senator Wilks. Back then, she had just helped create policy that might or might not have trickled down to the people she was trying to help. Now, she was on the front line. If Jill made a bad decision or her team failed, people could die or get captured by the IXTF. She directly saw the consequences of her failures. It was a sobering experience.

Jill switched over to Roen's channel. "This is Hen House. What's your location? Heard you're dark. Can you talk?"

"For you, darling, any time," his voice piped across the comm cheerfully. "We're just outside of the perimeter, a little over a klick out."

"I hear you went grocery shopping. Scrambled?"

"Roger. Five bad eggs. One scrambled. Four live chicks. Will need to incubate."

"Already on it. Hey, Bad Seed mentioned one of the eggs was..."

"...his age. Yes ma'am, she is."

"Is... is she pretty?"

There was a very long pause.

He finally answered. "Is this a trick question? Because to be honest, I can't think of a good way to answer this without getting busted by you, the girl's father, or some higher power. Therefore, I'll let you be the judge of that."

"I see. Are their feathers clipped at least?"

"Affirmative. They look a mess. Probably haven't eaten in days."

Jill looked down at the small stack of pancakes she was building and went to the pantry to get more flour and eggs. Fifteen minutes later, a red light on the screen came on. Roen must have reached the entrance to the tunnels. They would be at the main safe house shortly.

Jill wiped her hands of the pancake mix and removed her apron. She pulled back her hair and checked herself in the mirror. She left her pile of pancakes, snapped her holster around her waist, and walked into the pantry closet.

On the far wall, behind the five-pound cans of tomato paste, she punched a code on a number pad and waited as part of the floor next to her swung down to expose a spiral staircase. She trotted down the metal steps and went to meet her new guests, as any good host would.

The farmhouse, an old converted lumber mill near the Pacific Ocean, looked run down and decrepit from the outside. The interior reinforced the exterior image and looked perfectly ordinary. Under the farmhouse, however, was a fortified bunker prepped with enough supplies to last several years. The house stood on top of a mined-out gold plot with underground tunnels that snaked for several kilometers in either direction. At one point, back when most of the land here wasn't part of the United States, this was the Prophus command center for the entire western half of the country. Now, it served an even more important job.

There were two escape routes carved deep into the ground: a hidden tunnel that led westward two kilometers to an underwater cave where one of the remaining Prophus submarines – a tiny unarmed commercial submersible once used for tourism – served as their escape vehicle. The other tunnel was a straight shot east into the Redwood National Park to the edge of a cavern mouth. A dozen mountain bikes served as their getaway vehicles for that route.

Roen had corralled their new guests into the main open area of the safe house. It had roughly the same footprint as the farmhouse above it, except the ceilings were low, which made the space feel claustrophobic. That wasn't a problem for people like her and Roen, but for some of their guests – that Russian in particular, who had to tilt his head to the side when he stood up – it looked decidedly uncomfortable.

There were half a dozen cots and couches lining the sides of the room and a large square table in the center. A television was attached to the wall on the far end, a stack of free weights stood in the near corner, and a Ping-Pong table was opposite it. The very first person Jill trained her sights onto as she came down the staircase was the girl.

"Crap."

She is striking. The girl will be beautiful when she grows up. Definitely an Adonis Vessel.

"Nothing worries a mother more than a pretty girl. I have a bad feeling about this one. Maybe I should forbid them from showering."

The fair-haired girl looked to be about Cameron's age, though most likely a little younger. Jill could tell that the girl was agile; she moved easily when she walked and carried the grace of a dancer, though in this case, she was pretty sure the dances the girl performed were of the more deadly variety. Her gaze wandered back to the tall, gaunt-looking man standing protectively close to her. That had to be her father.

Ladm is a pragmatic Quasing and has always played the role of financier. His hosts never got their hands dirty. Vladimir is high on Vinnick's roster of rainmakers. Last recorded net worth was around four hundred million.

"A big fish. Why can't we have guys like that on our side?"

We did. They either lost their fortunes or are already dead.

"Is he soft? Just a rainmaker?"

Unlikely. No one operating in Russia is soft, especially those under Councilman Vinnick. Since the war began, no Quasing has maintained a more stable zone of control than Flua.

"Where does Vladimir rank on the fanaticism scale? If the reports are correct, many in Vinnick's regime are almost as crazy as in Enzo's."

Unsure. We will cover that during the debriefing.

"There're less of them here than I thought. Who's our VIP?"

The woman.

"What about ours?"

He is not there.

Jill looked over the group, identifying and detailing each Quasing and their host's role before clicking the safety off her pistol. She was sure there was no danger; Roen would never let his son get close to them otherwise. However, a show of force often proved the best deterrent for trouble. Just because both factions faced a new enemy in the IXTF didn't mean the Prophus and Genjix didn't still despise each other. Even years later, memories of Sonya, Paula, and Stephen were fresh in Jill's mind.

Jill stopped at the bottom of the stairwell and waited until everyone in the group noticed her, then walked deliberately slowly through them until she was at the far side. She turned around, keeping her hand close to her firearm. By now, the group had fallen silent.

"My name is Jill Tan," she said tersely, watching the recognition on each person's face. She was used to being the bogey-woman of the Genjix. More than a few had tried to attack her on the spot after she announced that, something she highly recommended against with Roen in the room.

She drew her pistol and kept it in plain view. "You are under Prophus protection as well as detainment. Try to escape and we'll kill you and your Quasing. Be disruptive and endanger my operation, we'll kill you and your Quasing. If you do not obey instructions, we will kill you and your Quasing. Do you understand?"

The girl's father put his arm protectively around his daughter's shoulder, but she was eying Jill without any hint of fear. In fact, she looked like she was seething. Jill hoped the girl wouldn't do anything stupid. Killing a child twisted her insides into knots, but no one lived in a civilized world anymore.

"We're going to interrogate you separately. Think very carefully over the next few hours about the words you'll say. Your life could depend on it." Jill looked at Roen. "Quarantine them."

"Excuse me," the father said. "My daughter. She can stay with me?"

She shook her head. "You, Vladimir, should think doubly seriously about your words. You have two to think for."

"She's only fourteen!" He raised his voice. "What sort of a monster are you?"

Two meters distance. Aim for his lower left leg to avoid the girl.

"I'm not going to shoot someone in front of his daughter, Baji."

Jill cocked her pistol and pointed it at him. "Take another step, Genjix, and I'll show you exactly the sort of monster I am."

Roen had his rifle pointed at the man as well. "Vladimir, step off. Nobody wants this; most of all you."

The large man held his hands up. Jill noticed that his daughter continued to look at her, no, study her, without fear. The girl was used to having guns pointed at her. She didn't flinch at all. This child was dangerous in more ways than one.

Jill holstered her pistol and walked back toward the stairwell. "You'll be given your own rooms with hot showers and a bed for now. I suggest you get some rest." As she was leaving, she saw Cameron standing halfway down the staircase looking at her.

Her heart twisted a little. Her son had experienced a lot since Roen and she had reconciled. They had done their best to shield Cameron from as much of the ugly parts of their work as possible, but it couldn't be helped. Then she noticed the pistol in his hand. Their eyes met and he looked abashed. He crept back up the stairs and was gone.

Jill shook her head sadly. Even with everything that had happened, he was a good kid. Reality was a harsh master, but in this case, it was also the best teacher. He was almost a man now. Pretty soon, he would need to join the network and fight alongside them. Not quite yet, though. Not if she and Roen could help it. At least not today.

CHAPTER THREE
WANTED GUESTS

Timestamp: 2566

They told me I was in a medically-induced coma for three weeks. Truth was, that was probably the best nap I'd had in years. When I finally woke up, I realized that something was wrong. I couldn't move and felt as if my body was floating on water. I knew that couldn't be, because I can't tread water worth a damn. I tried to call out, but could only moan.

A nurse came in and turned the lights on. She pulled this tube out of my mouth and asked if I could hear her. Asked if I was hungry or needed to take a shit. I nodded to all three. I looked down and saw that my entire body was wrapped in plaster like a mummy. My eyes focused on my exposed toe, and I wiggled it. Seeing it move felt pretty glorious. The pain that followed, not so much.

The first thing Roen did after he locked up the Genjix refugees was to walk Cameron to the end of their long driveway. It was already half past eight, so his son being late to school was a foregone conclusion. Roen handed him a typed-out tardy excuse; they kept a dozen of these in a tin box for these sorts of occasions. This time, according to the piece of paper, Cameron was needed to deal with coyotes that were stalking their chicken coop. He was pretty sure coyotes lived in these parts. Now if they only had a coop, or chickens, for that matter.

The high school was used to his tardiness, and he was a straight A student, so the teachers were willing to look the other way. Besides, his parents – actually just Jill – spent an awful lot of time volunteering for the PTA, so that earned Cameron a decent amount of slack in this small community. Still, best not to push their chances.

"Hey, Roen," Cameron said, walking the bike down the gravel driveway toward the asphalt road.

Roen nudged him on the shoulder. "That's Dad to you, pal."

"Sorry, just voicing Tao's words. He wants you to be careful with this group of Genjix."

"He says that about every group of Genjix."

"This one in particular."

Roen shrugged. "He says that too. They're in my home with my wife and kid. If that bald Russian so much as looks at you and your mom sideways, I'll put a –"

Cameron said, hopping on his bike, "It's not Vladimir he wants you to watch out for. He'll talk to you about it later tonight."

"All right, son, have a good day. Come home straight after school and don't run into any trees."

"Dad, I was six and the tree had it coming. It was between me and the sea lion pen."

Roen watched Cameron pedal away until he was only a speck disappearing down the road. He wondered what Tao meant. Wait, no, he bet he could figure out what his best friend and mentor was going to say.

The only good Genjix is a dead one. Usually followed by *shoot them* or *stab them through the heart*. That was regular Tao wisdom, second only to *get your ass out of bed*.

Roen chuckled as he walked back toward the farmhouse. The climb up the hill always reminded him of his age. His right knee ached again and both of his hips were flaring up. His lower back hurt. His left shoulder was starting to lose its range of motion, and he caught himself slouching more and more these days. Other than that, he was the picture of health. Now that he thought about it, he needed to take a piss more often, too.

Roen walked through the front door and found Jill in the kitchen, sorting out several plates of food. Either she forgot to tell him about the squad of agents coming in, or she was going to use blueberry pancakes for advanced interrogation. He opened the fridge and pulled out a container of orange juice.

He sniffed it and looked up. "Where's the good stuff?"

Jill shook her head. "Out of the non-concentrate. You're stuck with that until next week. Did you get confirmation from our VIP guest?"

Roen nodded. "She's our girl, and by all indications, a whale."

Jill lifted an eyebrow. "A real one?"

"As real as it gets. She smuggled some documents on this chip." He held it up. "Harry is skimming the download now. If it's legit, I'm shooting it off to Command for the brain boys to break down. I'm keeping her in the locked cells until we find out the other three's intentions. No need to blow her cover unless necessary."

Jill nodded. "What about the others?"

"Unknown. About to hit them up next." He motioned to the humongous stack of pancakes. "Are we using these as an interrogation tactic or are you pregnant again?"

"That's not funny." Using the spatula, she flicked a pancake at him. Roen caught it and put it in his mouth. "I'll come with you to talk to them."

"You know, instead of feeding them," he made a twisting motion with his hands, "I could just tighten screws into their thumbs."

She picked up the plate of pancakes. "Hearts and minds, dear. Hearts, minds and stomachs. Nothing speaks to a bunch of refugees like pancakes with mounds of syrup. Have they been separated?"

He nodded. "Block D. I gave the Russian and his daughter the last two rooms with the connecting door. We can separate them during interrogation."

"What about our man on the inside?"

Roen shook his head. "Sachin didn't make it. He sacrificed his life to buy them time, and he initiated a firefight with IXTF purposely in order for me to pinpoint their location. I wouldn't have reached them in time otherwise."

Jill cursed. "We are rapidly running out of agents in Asia. Do you think anyone will turn?"

Roen shrugged. "I don't see why not. Moderates on the run. Lost everything but the clothes on their backs. What do they have to gain dying by the sword? The line has been blurred since the Council Power Struggle enveloped all of Asia. Everyone's loyalty is flexible. It's just too bad the Prophus are so weak, we can't take advantage of the chaos."

Jill exhaled. "It's a shame. Even with their Council at

odds, everyone is more powerful than us. But as long as Rin's turned, we might finally have found a way to win."

"Ohr should turn as well." Roen tried to pluck another pancake with his fingers, only to be rewarded with a slap on the wrist and a stern look from his wife. "The interesting one will be the Russian. We'll have to play him close to the vest."

"Rats scurrying off the sinking ship? His network files had both him and his wife pretty high up in Vinnick's hierarchy. In fact, Alexandra is Vinnick's goddaughter."

"Fleeing that psychopath Enzo for sure." Roen paused. "The girl's a host. We could use her as leverage."

"Have we sunk so low we use children now?"

"Pfft. Pretty sure we kicked down that threshold four hundred years ago. It's a burden I'll gladly live with if it means getting the upper hand."

"Doesn't mean we should give up civility." Jill handed him the plate and picked up a bottle of maple syrup. "Let's go feed our guests."

The two of them went down the secret staircase to the main safe house area and then into a series of single-file corridors. Most of the tunnels here predated the farmhouse, a veritable maze of old mining tunnels, except now some of the walls closer to the main living space were plastered with rough and uneven drywall, courtesy of Roen's handyman skills. He had spent much of their first year here excavating and making the mineshaft functional for their needs by building everything out with nothing more than power tools and a do-it-yourself manual he bought from the Internet.

He admitted the hallways and rooms looked hideous, but they were *his* hideous hallways and rooms. He swelled with pride every time he led anyone down here and was always sure to let them know about his handiwork, even the prisoners. Especially the prisoners.

"Remind me to call the IXTF office after this meeting," he said, as they walked toward the doors at the far end.

"You tied them up and asked for animal shelter ransom again?"

"Might as well go to a good cause."

"You know, you're not helping any of these shelters by putting so much heat on them. I bet every charity you force a donation upon has gotten their books audited with a fine-toothed comb. One day, it's going to catch up with you."

"If they do, I hope they remember all the living IXTF agents that could have been dead IXTF agents."

They unlocked the door on the right and entered a small cell. There was a bed against the right wall, a small table with chairs on the left, and a toilet and sink on the far end. There was also a door that connected to an adjacent room. Vladimir was sitting at the table with Alex, whispering with their heads close together. The two stood up, and he moved his daughter behind him as Roen and Jill walked in.

"If you have any decency," Vladimir said, "do what you must, but not in front of Alex. Send her away. I beg you." He looked down at the plates of food in their hands and took on a sheepish look. "Perhaps I spoke too soon."

"Oh no, you were right," Roen quipped. "We just like to eat while we torture."

Jill slapped him playfully on the shoulder. "Vladimir Mengsk, would you like some breakfast? I'm going to take your daughter next door."

Roen watched as she coaxed the girl out from behind her father and ushered her into the next room. She looked back and nodded before closing the door. He gestured for Vladimir to sit before joining him. Roen watched as he dug into the pancakes, and waited a few minutes to let the guy swallow a few big bites. After all, the man had been on the run and hadn't eaten for a while. Not to mention that Roen still might have to shoot him, and he'd hate to execute someone without a last meal.

After he had polished off five pancakes in less than two minutes, Vladimir wiped his mouth and studied him. "The famous Roen Tan."

"Famous?" Roen perked up. "I mean, my exploits are pretty damn awesome, but I wouldn't go that far. What's my rookie baseball card worth these days in Genjix circles?"

The reference must have been lost on Vladimir, who looked puzzled. "Exploits? Sorry. I wasn't even aware you were an operative. You're only known as the human who survived a Quasing transfer. That was thought to have been impossible."

"Wait, you mean you've never heard of me? I'm pretty sure my Quasing was on several of your most-wanted lists."

"Tao, yes. You, not so much." Vladimir shrugged. "Don't take it the wrong way. Most vessels are not recognized; only their Holy Ones matter. However, the Genjix did name a project after you."

This was a first. Roen would have thought information of this kind would have reached his desk by now. After all, how many people could claim having secret programs named after them?

"So," he asked, "how did the project go? I'm assuming it's not anything cool like saving polar bears or bringing clean water to people in the desert."

Vladimir scooped another pancake into his mouth and spoke with his mouth full. "It was called the Tan Transfer Initiative. Body transfer research. The Council wanted to see if what happened to you could be replicated."

Roen grinned "Ooh, I even get a fancy name. How did the me transfer go?"

"Three hundred human deaths in the process. Then they decided to move the experiment to primates. All complete failures before the program was scrapped."

"Three hundred!" Roen had trouble processing that staggering number. In a way, he kind of felt bad. He couldn't help but think he was to blame for those deaths. After all, the project was named after him. "Leave it to your stupid Holy Ones to experiment on humans first, and *then* go to primates. I guess the bright side is three hundred Genjix agents died."

Vladimir grunted. "Anyway, you have questions, Prophus. Ask."

All right," Roen began. "Let's pretend we're both smart guys and we won't lie to each other. By now, you've probably surmised that I didn't find you in the forest by accident."

"You knew we were traveling through North America? How? The Prophus surveillance network is in tatters. A traitor then?" Vladimir furrowed his brow. "Couldn't be the Epsilons. I would wager my daughter's life on their loyalty. Couldn't have been the two Pakistanis we lost before crossing into Alaska. We deviated from the original plan by heading south..." His voice trailed off. "The professor."

Roen nodded. "Professor Sachin was a good man, and Mawl was not a traitor. He had worked as a Prophus agent since the beginning."

"Ladm always said Mawl never seemed to have his heart in the war," Vladimir said. "So you have me now. What do you want? You must know by now that I am powerless. My Council faction has lost most of its influence."

Roen chuckled. "We really don't care about you, Vladimir. You're just an added bonus."

Realization dawned on the Russian's face. "Rin. She's the one you are after all along. You want to capture one of the architects of the Quasiform program."

"Capture? She defected."

"I see. And the rest of us: Tabs, Ladm, and Brep, along with the vessels. Are we now expendable?"

Roen stopped smiling and leaned forward. "That remains for you to decide. You see, you have a lot of information we could use. Baji still remembers Ladm fondly from the Decennials and believes accommodations can be worked out. Admit it, as part of Vinnick's faction, you're not really down with Quasiform, are you? What kind of life do you think your little girl will live if it happens?"

"I am also not that disagreeable to it either. We are just instruments of the Holy Ones. If I say no?"

Roen pulled out a pen and notepad and slid it forward. "You won't, Vladimir, because you're out of friends. Enzo already killed your wife and won't hesitate to gun you and Alex down. You're in a hostile country where the government will go to great lengths to incarcerate you, and frankly, no one else in the world will help you. We won't threaten you any more, because blackmailed allies make poor allies.

"Think it over. If you wish to leave on your own, we'll cut you loose. If you wish Prophus protection, I expect everything you know about Genjix operations under your financier network written down by this evening. Then we'll lead you and your little girl through our Underground Railroad to one of our safe zones in Greenland or South America. So what will it be? Prophus help or risk your daughter's life and be hunted by both sides and every government in the world?"

Vladimir reached for the pen and tapped the notebook with it several times. "Those are my options? Hardly a choice."

"It never is," Roen grinned as he stood up and went to go retrieve Jill next door. "No one ever picks Greenland."

CHAPTER FOUR
SCHOOL DAY

So you wish to learn something besides ancient history? Well, we have already gone over my entire time here on Earth. How about we try something different? I have never told this to any of my hosts before. It is sort of an unspoken rule among the Quasing to not divulge our history before we came to this planet.

However, it is a mostly harmless truth, and I would like to wade through the memories of my home world again.

Tao

Cameron Tan stared at the history exam question on his computer screen: Was the Alamo the greatest tactical defeat in the history of the United States? If not, then name another.

This one took him a few seconds to mull over. "I'm going to have to say *yes*. That could also be the dumbest celebrated event of all time."

Except that Texas did not become a state until a decade later.

"Sneaky, Ms Federlin. What do you think then, Tao? Pearl Harbor?"

That or Chosin Reservoir.

"What about just overall dumbest?"

This is a difficult one to choose. I do rank the Alamo right up there with Napoleon's invasion of Russia for pure asinine decision-making, alongside maybe the Maginot Line. The level of dumb you humans can achieve is quite mind-boggling. However, I will have to go with your mother telling the world about the Quasing's existence.

"Someone reminds her every month."

And Jill still says she would do it again.

Mom had heard it thousands of times by now and had tried to always let it slide, but Cameron knew that it haunted her. She was just better at hiding it these days. Still, it pissed him off when people brought it up. Hundreds of refugees and agents passed through her region constantly, and someone inevitably mentioned it.

When he was a kid, he used to get mad for her and yell at them. She would scold him for raising his voice. Now, he just ground his teeth and kept his mouth shut, though then Tao would scold him for grinding his teeth. There was just no winning between all his parents.

He had arrived to school forty minutes late, drenched with sweat as he hurried to first period. The class was taking an exam on the United States wars up to the fall of the Soviet Union. Ms Federlin had looked at him with disapproval when he rushed to his seat with ten minutes left in class. She had told him that he could either wait outside or take the hour-long exam in the last nine minutes of class. It was an easy decision; Cameron couldn't stay after school, so he just tore through the test.

He had to admit he did lean on Tao a bit more than usual. Still, a minute before the class bell rang, he had finished the last question and hit the submit button. History was easily his strongest subject. Sure, having an older-than-dirt alien who had had front-row seats to the past helped just a tiny bit, but Cameron didn't think he leaned on his mentor as much as his parents thought he did.

Keep being delusional, pal.

As the students were leaving class, Ms Federlin beckoned him over. Cameron held in his sigh and he walked over to her desk. She held up his note. "I know for a fact, Cameron Tan, that you used the same note last month." She opened the drawer and pulled out an exact copy of the one he had just handed her. "That many coyotes?"

Oh Roen.

"Damn Dad. How did you ever survive in his body, Tao?"

Moving into you is like upgrading from a tricycle to a motorcycle.

"Really?"

No. Not really. Your father is a good man. He just tends to have more mental lapses than other humans.

"Is there something you want to tell me?" Ms Federlin asked. Her eyes wandered to his bruised neck, courtesy of his Brazilian jujitsu training.

Cameron shook his head. "Just coyotes, ma'am."

We need to work on your lying.

"Mom and Dad yell at me when I practice lying on them, and it's impossible to do that with you, so I blame you guys for my lack of preparedness in the fine arts of fibbing."

Ms Federlin obviously didn't believe him either. "Next parent/teacher meeting, I want both your parents here. Do you understand, Cameron? I'm going to have Ms Janice with me. I think we need to have a talk."

How many times is she going to try to send you to the school counselor?

"Yes, ma'am."

Cameron fled the room before she made him make another promise he couldn't keep. Getting both his parents away from their operation at the same time would be like trying to get the Capulets and Montagues to set a wedding date.

That reminds me. Why are you doing so poorly in literature?

"I'm getting a C, and you're not much help. You're obviously not a very cultured Quasing, are you?"

Sorry. I was too busy fighting the Genjix and trying to prevent the Thirty Years War from happening to attend much theater.

"So uncouth."

This coming from the guy who puts steak sauce on every single dish, including ice cream.

"Don't knock it until you've tried it."

"One more thing, Cameron," Ms Federlin called as he walked out the door. "This exam is forty percent of your grade. I know you took it because you never stay after school, but in this case, it might not be a bad idea."

He shook his head. "No, I'm good, ma'am." He walked out of the door into the crowded hallways of Eureka High School. At a little over twelve hundred students, this was by far the largest high school in the area, though his parents considered Eureka the smallest town they had ever lived in.

Cameron kept his eyes on the ground as he navigated the maze of other kids, careful not to bump into any of them with his bulky backpack. Eureka was a tight-knit community. That made it difficult for an outsider like him to fit in. He had stayed with his grandparents, Louis and

Lee Ann, down in San Diego, while his parents had gotten their operation up and running, and was home-schooled for most of his childhood. It was only after he had begged his parents every day for almost a year that they finally relented and let him come to a public school. After they were sure there were no Penetra scanners installed, of course.

The lesson was: be careful what you wish for.

High school was nothing like he had imagined. Tao had warned him ahead of time that it was its own insular, cruel world, but Cameron had longed for normalcy. Besides, he had been going out on dangerous jobs with Roen since he was thirteen. How much worse could high school be? Boy, was he wrong.

Cameron was stunned to find how difficult the transition from home schooling to the public high school was. He had a hard time communicating with his classmates. Sometimes, it seemed like they were barely speaking English, as if they had their own language.

For the students at Eureka High School, Cameron was an enigma as well. He was too socially awkward to fit in with any of the cliques. He just didn't understand many of their jokes or cultural references or social behaviors. They knew he was smart, though. Many of the cooler kids tried to partner with him during lab experiments but would ignore him in the hallways.

He was also very athletic, a physical specimen who had the football coach drooling the first day he walked into gym class. Couple that with his years of martial arts training, Cameron could have made any of the sports teams, but didn't sign up for any of them. In a small school, almost everyone was on at least one of the sports teams. Most of the athletes were on all the teams. It was the only way the school could fill an entire roster. Cameron's lack of participation and his quiet demeanor had earned him the scorn of the jocks, while his frightening intelligence, due entirely to Tao – at least according to Tao – made him the subject of gossip among the faculty.

Basically, school sucked, and it sucked hard. The worst part was, when Cameron had tried to talk to his parents about it, begging his parents to home-school him again, they flat out refused. Unfortunately, Pandora had opened the box, and it couldn't be closed again.

His dad just shrugged and chuckled. "Ahh, the good ol' days. Don't use your super powers to hurt anyone."

"I don't have any," Cameron had responded. "Tao doesn't do anything special."

Hey now, Tao had said.

"That means you're not using him right," Roen had replied. "What's for dinner?" As usual, once the topic moved to food, the conversation was over.

Cameron floated from class to class: math to English to Chinese (Tao insisted). Then lunch. Then gym class, and last was biology. Most of the classes just blended together. Tao was merciless with his education, making sure to teach him above and beyond what the teachers even knew. He was studying at a much higher grade level than what was being discussed in class, and for the most part, could teach the classes himself. He had learned, however, that no one liked a smart-ass, so he tended to keep quiet.

In his final class of the day, he was partnered with one of the prettiest girls in school. Well, more like she was using him to get a good grade while he did all the work. As unfair as that sounded to Cameron, it suited Tao fine, since his mentor somehow turned every dissection into a lesson about combat anatomy.

Do you see that ligament? Humans have something similar. Cut it and they lose all control of their lower extremities.

"Yeah, but if I can get a blade there, why not just slice upward?"

Because I guarantee that part of the anatomy is armored, at least too much for a blade. That ligament portion cannot be armored without hindering range of motion.

These fascinating lessons would sometimes go on for an entire hour, to the point he forgot why he was in class to begin with.

"What are you doing?" Heather, his lab partner, said from her seat at the end of the table. She detested getting the formaldehyde on her skin. "You're supposed to be cutting into its chest, not playing with its legs. Come on, class is almost over, and we didn't get any of the steps done."

Cameron looked up at the clock; school was ending in five minutes. In the next four, he got through all fourteen steps of dissecting and pulling out the frog's heart and lungs.

He slid the tray over toward her. "There you go. You can take this stuff away."

Before Heather could protest, he grabbed his bag and walked out of the room. Cameron was fully aware, after all, that she needed him more than he did her, and that most of the people who wanted to partner with him didn't really want to be his friends.

They were just using him; they were temporary relationships, like almost everything else in his life. Even his parents. Cameron remembered his earlier years, when it seemed like there was always only one parent around. Sometimes, he remembered not seeing Roen for months, or his mom would have to leave him with his grandparents for long stretches at a time.

The only real permanent thing he had was Tao. Tao was always there. Tao never left him. Not that he could, but his Quasing was his best friend, teacher, and the one soul Cameron knew he could always rely on. Sure, he was a snarky bastard sometimes and a taskmaster to boot, but Tao was the rock, the one stable presence in a sea of constant change.

Cameron navigated the crowded hallways and made his way toward the bike racks. While most of the other kids had team sports or glee club or student council or some other after-school activity, he knew he had to be home as soon as possible. He had promised Roen he'd help with the new guests. Besides, he was intrigued by that girl. He had never met a host his age before.

Oh dear.

"I'm just curious."

About what? There are dozens of girls your age at school you can be curious about. Why a Genjix, of all people?

"Because..." He stopped in his tracks. "Because she might understand what it's like. These other kids don't. They couldn't."

Mutual attraction through shared alien experiences. How positively romantic.

Cameron left the building and proceeded toward the bicycle racks next to the stadium. He wandered down the hill and noticed the football players lining up one by one, working on blocking drills and rushing techniques. He watched with an expert eye as the players' hands slashed at arms, knocking each other off balance. The pulling and pushing; it was all very t'ai chi. Cameron caught himself reflexively mimicking their actions and improvising on how he would have done it instead. He was just as big as these linemen, but just by seeing them move, he knew he could take them. Well, most of them.

"Having thoughts about trying out this year?" Coach Wannsik walked up next to him carrying a pile of orange cones. "You know, we could use another guy on defense."

Cameron blushed. "Thanks, but I don't have the time. I have chores to do at home."

"He thinks he's too good for us, coach," one of the players coming up from behind snickered. "Has to protect that smart-ass brain of his."

"It's a good thing you don't have anything to protect," Cameron shot back.

Well done. Point to you.

"Stow it, Bill." The coach turned back to Cameron. "You too, Cameron. Think about it. You know, colleges love students who are balanced academically and athletically. If you like, I can chat with your parents at the parent/teacher meeting."

Cameron hurried off before he had to make another promise he couldn't keep. The last thing he needed was to rope his parents into another meeting. As he unlocked his bike, he noticed several of the varsity guys pointing at him. As always, once those guys knew they had his attention, the catcalls came and the taunting got worse. Cameron turned his back to them.

"I could kick the crap out of all of them."

It would not even be close.

"All at the same time I bet. I don't care if they're football players."

You could do it without even breaking a sweat. In fact, if you sweat, I would be disappointed because it would mean it took you too long.

"Maybe even with one hand behind my back. Maybe with no hands."

Yes. You will head-butt them to death.

Cameron was treated to a montage of every one of Tao's previous hosts who had ever head-butted something, from several instances when he was a Triceratops, to the hundreds of times in Cro-Magnon hosts, to during the Roman Empire's Golden Age when one of his hosts was a bare-knuckle brawler, all the way to the one time Roen head-butted a wall by accident and broke his nose.

Cameron laughed. "Man, are you sure Roen is actually my dad?"

To be fair, he was undercover in Mongolia and they brush their teeth early in the morning with vodka. He was playing a drinking game with a local mobster he was trying to pull intel from and he lost.

Cameron thought about his father as he rode his bike back to the farmhouse. He didn't know much about Roen's time as a host; his dad didn't like to talk about it. Cameron knew losing Tao was painful for him and digging up those old memories hurt, so he didn't ask. Still, he wondered. Knowing the life expectancy for the line of work they did, Cameron would rather learn Roen's story now, before it was too late.

As he fell into his pedaling cadence, his warm-up for his three upcoming workouts, his mind wandered to the girl.

He knew she was Genjix, but at their age, did it matter? Of course it did. Cameron had been spoon-fed stories of the Genjix ever since he was a kid. He'd bet she had been told the same about the Prophus.

I know you wish to meet her. I approve of that, but be careful. She is pretty and a Genjix host, a deadly combination for any teenager. I get inklings of her being an Adonis Vessel as well, or at least one in training.

To be honest, Cameron didn't notice her looks. He had fixated more on the fact that she was like him. That meant she might understand things he couldn't talk to anyone else about. Also, from the few glimpses he did get at Redwood National Park, she looked a mess, sort of like how his dog Eva used to look after she had romped through the stream near their home. He couldn't blame the girl for being a little messy. She had been on the lam and had just pulled through a firefight.

Half an hour later, he saw the farmhouse in the distance. While the other kids were at football practice, Hsing Yi Quan was on his agenda today, then t'ai chi, then SWAT maneuvers, and then strength training. After dinner, weapons. Then his daily early morning free-running sessions with Mom, and then Ba Gua Zhang. Then back to school.

Cameron sighed. It sounded a lot more glamorous than it actually was. Somehow, playing football seemed so much more appealing. Oh well, Tao had always told him that a host carried heavy burdens. Cameron just wished he could shrug the responsibilities off once in a while and act his age. Roen appeared as he wheeled his bike into the garage.

"There you are, son," Roen grinned. "We're going to need to push your Chinese buzz-saw fighting" (Roen's nickname for Hsing Yi) "back an hour. I need you to help me out with our guests. We're still screwing some thumbs down and getting some answers. It'll be fun."

Cameron flashed his dad a weak smile. "Sure. I'll be right there."

CHAPTER FIVE
KREMLIN'S HEIR

The Conflict Doctrine is the foundation of all Genjix philosophies on Earth. Conflict breeds innovation. Innovation is what will take the Quasing home. That was our original intent. Though our primary objective has now changed, the principles of that foundation remain true and still apply.

I have been at the heart of the doctrine's inception and shall remain so until it comes to fruition.

Zoras

Today was a good day. A historical day, even.

Enzo, flanked on both sides by his entourage, took his time walking through the tall arches and rust-colored gates of the antique fortress, long the symbol of empires, and proceeded down the wide pathway, past the famed gigantic green Tsar Cannon, on his way to the church.

He could have met Vinnick at the Federation Council building in front of the entire Russian government, but instead, he had decided to show some manners. After all, no need to embarrass the old man in front of the humans. They were still Genjix, after all. His enemies and critics could say many things about him, but never that he was uncivilized. Besides, he enjoyed basking in history, and there were few grander, more historically significant places than the Church of the Disposition of the Robe nestled inside the Kremlin.

This country had seen its share of foreign invasions over the centuries. Their people tended to ensconce themselves with their own. Enzo would have to break them of this relationship with Vinnick, especially the high-ranking officials with whom Vinnick had long-established connections. The Russian politico class was in a frail state, and their allegiance could go either way. They recognized his power and influence as the accepted leader of not only the Chinese government, but the Genjix; yet they also considered him an outsider. Vinnick, while Genjix, was also Russian, and one of them.

Flua has spent hundreds of years building his power base here, and Vinnick has his hands in nearly every aspect of the current government. It is your responsibility to break their bond and take his place.

The next few hours would be delicate, but really only a formality. Unless Vinnick offered total capitulation, there was nothing to negotiate. The government had so far shown a surprising loyalty to the hundred-and-four year-old Genjix Councilman, but his influence and power, as his recent health, had finally waned.

It was Enzo who had chosen this location inside the historical church. It was he who had determined the date and time. These were his agents who secured the area around it. In other words, this was Enzo's party, his coronation, and Vinnick was here to deliver the crown. In many ways, he compared today's event to the Second Armistice at Compiègne.

It had taken over a decade before Enzo could establish this foothold within Vinnick's domain, but with the Russian president's invitation to hold talks, he could finally achieve dominance over his hated rival. The Russians had long proven to have more loyalty to ethnicity and money than they had to power. In both those matters, Enzo was at a distinct disadvantage and did not have the same resources as the Russian billionaire.

"Perhaps we could replace the president with someone more friendly to us."

Replacing the president by force will be messy, most likely escalating the situation toward a civil war and only reinforcing already negative world perceptions.

The Council Power Struggle had taken longer than anticipated. Much longer in fact, to the point that it had not only weakened the Genjix, but had hindered the Holy Ones's divine plans for Quasiform. Enzo placed that responsibility squarely on Vinnick. After all, it was clear by the fourth year of their struggle that the old man would lose. However, the stubborn fool dragged on their fight, only conceding ground when he had to.

Even now, with Enzo on the verge of victory, Vinnick had fought him tooth and nail, causing delays to the Genjix's most important programs. That delay was a sin Enzo could not forgive. What was he trying to prove? If he had only done the right thing, Enzo might have been merciful and let him live out the rest of his life peacefully.

A lesson had to be taught, and not just to Vinnick, but to anyone else who dared oppose Enzo. If he allowed his opposition pardons for their crimes, then he was simply inviting others to challenge his rule. No, even at his age, Vinnick must be shown swift and harsh punishment.

Those who did not bend to Enzo's will now, would only challenge it in the future.

Enzo nodded at several of his agents who had cordoned off the area. As far as most Genjix were concerned, he was the most important human alive. That was another thing he had learned from Vinnick. While all the Holy Ones were divine, not all their vessels were. Some were closer to divinity than others. In this case, Enzo's brothers from the Hatchery were the true vessels that the Holy Ones deserved. Those found outside were nothing more than shells, empty, unworthy containers that were meant to be used and discarded. In the end, most from outside the Hatchery were unworthy.

Enzo stopped just inside the church entrance and studied the long tunnel of arches that spanned the length of the building. Zoras was right to have cautioned that there were many places here for assassins to hide. However, Enzo wouldn't let such cowardly tactics dissuade him. He had already survived a dozen assassination attempts over the years, and his inner cadre was on alert.

He walked down the long corridor, his steps on the marble floors echoing. They were soon followed by two more pairs of footsteps. Austin and Matthew, brothers from the Hatchery who had been raised to full vessels.

Enzo loosened the straps on his holster. "Is he here?"

"Yes, Father," Austin said. "With only two Epsilons."

"And our strength?"

"Twenty inside the church. Forty on the perimeter."

"We could end it here," Austin added. "Be done with this charade and focus on more important matters."

Breaking your word to your enemies is sound strategy, but not so when it is to your own people.

"Of course, my Guardian."

Enzo shook his head. "Too much collateral risk with the rest of the Genjix. We can ill-afford the heat. Our credibility within the Council is already precarious. We will maintain the honor. Leave it to Vinnick to do otherwise. What about the perimeter?"

"Akelatis has eyes on two of Vinnick's extraction teams," said Matthew.

Enzo nodded. "Guess it's a standoff then. First side to shoot takes the blame. Make sure it's not us. And if they do shoot first, make sure we get the last shot."

They proceeded to the end of the hallway and walked up a set of stairs to an atrium. After several more turns down narrow passages, they entered a large circular room, empty except for a table and a chair placed in the center. There were two exits, one at the far end and one to Enzo's right. There were tall windows on his left. As instructed, the curtains were pulled closed to prevent the possibility of snipers.

The old man was seated in his wheelchair at the small round table in the center of the room, drinking delicately from a white teacup. Two large armored men stood guard at both sides of the door at the far end. Enzo recognized their suits and the bayonets attached to their holstered pistols.

Matthew leaned into him. "Confirmed Panell and Corisa. Non-blessed."

Enzo studied the face of the man who for over ten years now had prevented him from fulfilling his destiny of assuming the full mantle of Genjix leadership. This was the first time the two of them had ever met face-to-face in all those years. In the past, they had always sparred either across a video screen or through intermediaries. It felt momentous, if a bit anti-climactic.

After all, his sworn enemy looked positively awful. At a hundred-and-four, Vinnick was barely more than a bag of bones and blood, held together by tight, cracked and blotched skin, reinforced by thick wraps that covered most of his body. Half his head was bandaged, except for the white tufts of hair on top of his head. Enzo wondered what had happened to him. Was he sick? Was it safe for Enzo to be around him? Why had he even tried to stand against Enzo? The old man was on his deathbed!

The old man sipped tea as Austin and Matthew took their positions at the door. Enzo made sure to look carefree and charming as he sauntered toward the table. "Hello, brother."

Vinnick snorted in a way only old men could without seeming foolish. "Boy."

His voice sounded different than over the screen. It was weak, high-pitched, and tired. It had also been months since they'd last spoken. Months for a hundred year-old man might as well have been a decade.

Enzo reached out and picked up the teapot. He first filled Vinnick's cup and then his own. "Sugar, brother?" The old man met his gaze with a contemptuous glare. Enzo shrugged and added two spoonfuls. Old men liked sweets, didn't they? And if it wasn't good for him, maybe it would kill him quicker.

Touch him.

"Zoras?"

Identify him.

Enzo studied the face again. It was possible. With those bandages and his wrinkled visage, it wasn't out of the realm of possibility for this to be an impostor. He reached out for Vinnick's arm.

The old man snatched his hand back. "Don't touch me, boy!"

"I insist," Enzo snapped, reaching forward and gripping the old man's frail wrists.

Impostor. A non-vessel! Get out of the room now.

Enzo lashed laterally with his opened palm and smashed the old man's throat with his bare hands. To his right, several men burst through what must have been false panels and opened fire. Enzo felt a sharp pain in his arm as he dove to the ground. Before his assailants could get another shot off, four of them dropped. Matthew and Austin charged forward, pistols out and shooting. The table exploded into splinters as automatic fire shredded it. Enzo felt another bullet pierce his left shoulder as he rolled to his feet, pistol in his right hand and knife in his left.

Thirty and twelve degrees right. One hundred left. Six degrees above eye level. Now!

Two quick pops with his gun and one flick of his wrist later, two assailants lay dead by his hand. He ducked and spun just as a spray of bullets splattered the walls behind him. He felt another sharp pain in his thigh, a grazing shot that just missed his knee. By the time he had gotten his bearings, Matthew was hovering over him, while Austin, having shot two of the survivors point blank, was about to execute another.

Then Austin dropped, shot down by the Epsilons at the far door. Both Matthew and Enzo engaged, hitting their marks. However, the two heavily armored Epsilons shrugged off the shots. Another gunshot felled Matthew. Enzo didn't spare him another glance as he charged forward. The Epsilon got one more shot off point blank at his face. Enzo saw the bright flash of the chamber as he ducked to the right, the bullet nearly touching his cheek. He charged across the room and was on top of the man in half a second. He avoided a slash of the bayonet and shot an upward spear-hand into the soft tissue of the man's chin, killing him in one blow.

Enzo threw the limp body toward the other Epsilon and grappled with the man's pistol. Then he broke the second Epsilon's wrist with a sharp twist, took the pistol from him, and jammed the attached bayonet into the base of the man's neck. Enzo casually tossed the body aside and went to check on his brothers. They were both still alive, though Austin was injured badly. He had suffered a gunshot wound to the stomach that had gotten under his armor. Matthew, fortunately, took one to the chest where his armor had withstood the impact.

This entire church must be a trap. Get out. Now!

"I'm not leaving my brothers."

"Help me with Austin," he said, dragging Matthew to his feet.

"Brother, go," Matthew grimaced. "Your safety is paramount. We gladly serve..."

"Quiet and help me."

The two of them, dragging Austin with them, fled the room through the door they had come through. Austin's face was pale, and he was leaking a river of blood. If he died now, there was a chance his Holy One might not find another vessel in time. The three of them made it halfway down the hallway when an explosion rocked the church, blowing them forward as a rush of hot air lifted them off the ground.

Everything went black under a rolling cloud of dust. When Enzo came to, fire raged all around, the old church with its many priceless relics burning and melting in front of his eyes. Ignoring the sharp pain in his leg, Enzo pulled himself to his feet and picked up his two brothers.

Austin was unconscious, having taken the brunt of the explosion, the left side of his once-beautiful face now marred by burns. Matthew came to a second later, in only slightly better shape. Together, the two of them picked Austin back up and carried him down the stairs. They were met halfway by Enzo's perimeter security, who helped get them outside to safety.

A few minutes later, as the doctors checked on the three Adonises, a veritable army of fire trucks and ambulances swooped in. They were soon accompanied by fifty Genjix operatives, who canvased the area.

Enzo pushed the doctor fussing with his shoulder aside and struggled to stand as Akelatis, the Adonis who was responsible for securing the church, approached and fell to a knee. "How did Vinnick get those men in there?" he thundered. "How did we not detect them?"

Akelatis looked ashamed. "I'm sorry, Father. I have failed. They must have planted those men into the walls for over five days."

And the extraction teams that were in wait?

Enzo repeated Zoras's question.

Akelatis shook his head. "They never moved in. They pulled back as soon as the explosion happened."

Enzo swore. It was ruse all along. The worst part was, Vinnick had made the entire meeting seem like it was Enzo's idea, and he had fallen for it.

See to your men.

"What about our casualties?" he asked.

"Fourteen dead. Nineteen injured. Six missing as of this moment, Father."

Enzo balled his fists together. So much for this being a Genjix unification. The stubborn bastard was intent on fighting to the very end. Very well, if that's the way he wanted to play it, Enzo would treat him as he did everything else that stood in his way.

"Call the Assembly," he said. "We're going to war."

CHAPTER SIX
ROEN

Timestamp: 2571

It took me a while to realize that my head was empty. Tao was strangely silent. At first, I thought he was – I don't know – sleeping or something. Maybe he was just letting me rest. I tried to speak to him; asked how he was doing. He didn't answer.

After a day of silence, I thought he might have been injured as well. I did get busted up pretty good after all. At no point did I ever think that my best friend was no longer with me. That would have to mean that I was dead, right?

Roen brought up the evening dishes and found Jill and Rin relaxing over a glass of wine. The scientist was the only one currently allowed in the farmhouse. Sachin had vouched early on for her, and the scores of documentation she had already handed over were one of the first things the Keeper had verified. Her defection was the real deal, and now an army of Prophus scientists were poring over each and every file.

Roen grimaced at the mound of dishes piled up in the sink. He and Jill had an agreement; if one of them cooked, the other cleaned. One of the stark realities of being a secret agent that people never realized from movies and books was that there was no cleaning service on secret bases. It was great that they lived hidden on the edge of a forest, but acquiring monthly supplies for the operation without attracting attention required a feat of logistics that Nathanael Greene, who incidentally had been a Prophus, would approve of.

The worst part was, even though the rest of the refugees were still technically his prisoners, Roen was currently acting as the prisoners' butler, bringing them food and sundries upon request. While all had agreed to turn to the Prophus cause, they hadn't earned his trust yet. The information they had provided him could prove valuable, but their intel had to be checked and cross-referenced before he really believed they had changed sides. If verified, Roen and Jill would have scored a trove of sensitive intelligence. Until then, he couldn't be sure the prisoners weren't double-crossing the Prophus, so they had to stay in their cells. There was no way he'd let them near his family, so for now, he was relegated to butler duty.

Jill finished her glass of wine and shook it at him. Roen obliged and brought over the eight-dollar container of chardonnay they had stacked by the crate in storage. "Madam," he purred in an exaggerated fashion. "Your box." He motioned to Rin who raised her glass as well.

"Thank you, Alfred," she answered, craning her neck up to kiss him. "Now, my grapes."

"We're fresh out, but I believe we have a box of raisins." He put the box down and headed out of the kitchen.

"Hey, what about the dishes?"

"Cameron's training right now. I'll do it after he goes to bed. I want to talk to Tao for a bit."

"Likely excuse, mister."

As he left the kitchen, he heard Jill tell Rin, "God, I love that man." It made him feel good. The two of them had gone through a rough patch years back when things had really turned south for the Prophus. Roen had left Jill and newborn Cameron to follow the rumors of the secret Quasiform project, and though his suspicions were proven correct and the scale of the secret Genjix project was even larger and more terrible than anyone could have expected, Roen knew he had been wrong listening to Tao and abandoning his family.

He had spent the next few years intent on repairing their damaged relationship, and now, even in these dire times, they were stronger than ever. It was a massive hole in his heart that he had finally filled. That left only one other hole, one that had no fix.

He went to the attached garage, where the gym and training room was located. There, in the center of a padded area, his fifteen year-old son was flowing through a complex Chen t'ai chi straight sword form more smoothly than he ever could, even at his peak. Roen couldn't help but smile watching the motions. Cameron was a prodigy. Tao's ego must be bursting at the seams.

"Hi, Roen," said Cameron.

"How many times do I have to tell you to call me Dad?" Roen growled.

"Sorry. Tao's words," he replied, not breaking form at all. White-snake-spits-out transitioned to black-dragon-swings-tail. "We've been working on getting better talking as one person." Luo-Han-subdues-dragon flowed into black-bear-turns-backward.

Roen wasn't sure if he liked the sound of that. Tao

inhabiting his son was a prickly point. He had dreamed of passing Tao along to Cameron, but had thought it would happen when he was at the ripe old age of eighty something, preferably on his death bed.

It took him a long time to reconcile with the reality that his old friend was no longer with him. He still hadn't gotten over it, and while he loved his son more than life itself, he couldn't help but feel robbed of his years with Tao. Being jealous of your teenage son felt wrong, but Roen couldn't explain it any other way. He longed to have Tao back in his head, not only for the friendship, but for his mentor's wisdom and assurance.

When he was with Tao, Roen remembered being decisive. He never second-guessed himself and always felt that he, with Tao's input of course, made the best possible decisions when presented with difficult choices. There was an empowerment to that confidence, and he loved feeling that way every day he lived his life as a host. Now, it was missing, and like a recovering addict, he longed to find and feel that confidence again.

When Cameron had still been figuring out who this new voice in his head was, Roen had tried to be there to smooth the transition. However, as with most young children, Cameron had taken the new change in his stride. Within a few months, Tao speaking in his head had felt as natural as everything else in his life.

Now, Roen was pretty sure that he was only the third most important person in Cameron's life, after Tao and Jill. How could he compete, after all? With Jill, it was the way it should be. She had been there for Cameron when Roen had had to leave them. She had always been the better parent, anyway. She deserved to have more of the boy's love. Tao jumping in front of him for his son's affection and priority hurt. The truth was, though, how do you compete against a voice in his head with him all the time?

By the time Cameron was five, against the wishes of both of his parents, he began training to fight, first in boxing, then in Shaolin Fist and Fanzi Fist, and then in t'ai chi, Ba Gua Zhang, and Hsing Yi Quan. Basically, his son had learned more martial arts in a few short years than Roen had in a lifetime. By the time he was six, he had shot his first gun. Now, at fifteen, Cameron was well on his way to becoming that rare Prophus equivalent of an Adonis Vessel, and it worried his parents. This was the last thing they wanted for him.

Even worse, his son being a host so early made him a very vulnerable target, especially with the invention and miniaturization of the Penetra scanner. Not only were the Genjix after them, but most of the advanced countries on this planet were as well. These days, their enemies flanked them on all sides and numbered greater than they had at any other time in their history.

"Let's see what you got," Roen said, lunging halfheartedly with a stick. Swordplay was not his strong suit; there wasn't much call for that in their line of work. Still, Tao insisted that it was an important part of the boy's training.

Cameron switched out of his form, parried Roen's thrust with his sword, and pressed the attack. Roen danced out of the way, circling to his right and beaming with pride as his son moved with the skill and instinct of a master swordsman. They clashed a few more times, each blow just short of hitting its mark.

Roen was always surprised at how fluid and natural his

son's movements were. In a few years, when he grew into
manhood, Cameron would become one of the finest hosts
the Prophus had ever had, his father had no doubt of that.
That fact also terrified Roen. Cameron already acted much
older than his fifteen years, and he carried a seriousness
that was eerie for someone so young. Blame or praise for
that could be squarely put at Tao's feet.

"Not like you came out so well-adjusted yourself," he
muttered under his breath.

Then the unthinkable happened. Cameron slipped
under his guard and jabbed Roen in the thigh. It didn't
sink in deep, but a sword was a sword – Tao believed in
training with semi-sharpened weapons – and a moment
later Roen found himself sitting on the ground, trying to
stem the flow of blood trickling down his leg.

"Sorry, Dad," Cameron piped, not sounding sorry at all.
"Tao says you should pay attention when there are sharp
objects about and also that your footwork has gotten
sloppy."

"Well," he replied, "you tell Tao that maybe teaching
kids to stab their parents is a bad idea."

"Tao says you shouldn't be such a sore loser and a big
baby."

"Big baby?"

"And sore loser," said Jill, joining in on the conversation.
Roen and Cameron turned to see Rin and her standing at
the doorway, wine glasses in hand. "And bleeding all over
the floor."

"Tao wants to know if you feel old now," said Cameron.
Then he added, "Because he says you should."

Rin walked up to his son and stuck out her hand.
"Hello, Cameron."

Cameron took her hand. "Hi, Chisq. Tao and you crossed paths shortly before the original Inquisition. He was surprised when you took the side of the Genjix."

Rin smiled. "It was a difficult time for us all. I didn't realize the Prophus had an Adonis program."

Roen scowled. "Yeah, the entire program is standing right in front of you." He stood up and tussled Cameron's hair. "All right, Lizzie Borden, time for bed. Fall asleep fast; I need to talk to Tao."

Cameron sheathed his sword. "Sure thing, Roen. Just give me five minutes and I'll be out."

"Stop calling me by my name!" He watched as Cameron put the sword away and exited the garage. He turned to Jill. "I swear that damn Quasing has too much control over him."

She arched an eyebrow. "Really? Sounds familiar."

Roen's face turned a shade of red. "That was different."

"Yes, the fifteen year-old seems more mature."

Jill had long ago forgiven him for the years in which he had abandoned her and newborn Cameron to go chasing Genjix rumors. In the end, even though he was credited with blowing the lid off Quasiform, he realized the price his family had paid for his absence was still too high. She took satisfaction in watching him squirm every time she brought it up, more so for his own guilt than anything else.

Rin's eyes trailed after Cameron until he was out of the room. "He has the presence and the demeanor, though I don't think he would have made it into the Hatchery."

"Why not?" asked Roen

"To be honest, he's not beautiful enough. The Adonises at the Hatchery are physically exceptional." Rin blushed. "Sorry, no offense intended."

"You just called my son ugly. How do I not take offense to that?"

Jill pointed at Roen. "Well, look at what genes Cam had to work with."

"That is true," Roen acknowledged with a shrug. They both chuckled. He pursed his lips at Jill and she patted his butt. Rin rolled her eyes.

A little while later, Roen went upstairs into Cameron's room. The lights were on and his son was reading *The Phenomenology of the Spirit*.

"That's some dry bedtime reading," he said.

Cameron put the book aside. "Just passing the time until you get here." He lay down on the bed. "Okay, I'm going to sleep now."

"I'll come back in a few," Roen said.

"No need. Like you and Tao always say, a good agent knows when to sleep." And just like that, he closed his eyes and was out.

Roen waited for about a minute until he was sure Cameron was deep asleep. His son had learned from an early age to fall asleep right away. "Tao?"

Cameron sat up and blinked. Right away, Roen could tell by his son's face that he was no longer in control. Roen knew both his son and his best friend well enough to tell which was which. It was the many small things that changed. There was stiffness to his movements, and his face became more solemn. When he looked at Roen, his eyes lingered as if he was staring at something far away.

Tao threw the blanket off him and stood up. "I know what you're going to say. I had nothing to do with the selection."

"Really? He decided he was going to read Hegel for the hell of it?"

"Ask Faust. Hegel was Galen's host after all."

"Go figure. A stuffy Quasing was in a stuffy German philosopher."

Together they walked out of the bedroom and headed down the hall toward the second-floor balcony. Roen stopped by the mini wet bar just inside the door and pulled out a bottle of scotch and an empty glass. Together, they went to the deck. It was a daily ritual between them, one they had seldom broken over the last decade. Roen poured himself a half glass of the peaty scotch and inhaled the scent of smoke and wood. He held it out for Tao to smell and then took a sip.

"You should just let me drink it," said Tao. "I miss the complexity of a good scotch."

"Sorry, Tao. Cam isn't allowed to drink until he's thirty. Maybe forty."

"You know, many of my hosts drank young, even as children."

Roen took another sip. "And look how they turned out."

"Do you want to compare?"

"Not really." Roen changed gears. "How's his training coming along?"

"Exponential as always. He stabbed you in the leg today, did he not?"

Roen lifted his glass up toward the sky as a toast. "I knew my son would one day surpass me. I just didn't realize he'd do it before he could drive."

"What can I say? I am good at what I do. He is ready to join the network as an operative. He has been for a while. You know that, right?"

"Over my dead body, Tao. I mean that, like, literally – my dead body."

"You can only hold him back for so long. Remember, he is a host and technically outranks you."

"And I can ground him until he turns thirty, so I guess we're at an impasse."

"We shall see. Do you have Sachin's intelligence report?"

Roen pulled out his tablet and handed it to him. "The good professor gave the data fob to Rin the day he died. I filtered out the info on Quasiform and the Council Power Struggle before sending the rest off to the Keeper."

Tao read through the reports, graphs, and summaries in only a few minutes, faster than Roen could ever go through them any more. When he finished, he flipped through a few more screens, then looked up. "What about Vinnick's faction? How bad a shape is it in?"

"Vladimir says he doesn't think they can last the year. The old man's just old. Last he heard, Enzo was taking a contingent up to Moscow. He thinks Vinnick might be throwing in the towel. That or laying a trap for Enzo."

"Shit," Tao muttered as he finished reading the data. He put the tablet on the small table between their chairs.

Roen nudged Tao on the side of the head. "Hey, watch your language. Don't forget whose body you inhabit."

"I am the one saying it. Do not take it out on him."

"Well, I'd appreciate a clean mouth from my son. What's the shit about anyway?"

"According to this report, the power struggle has just about run its course."

"So what? Vinnick was almost as big a threat as Devin during his prime. Good riddance."

"Good riddance, yes," Tao said, "but he has distracted Enzo for the past decade. With Vinnick out of the way,

Enzo can refocus on completing Quasiform and destroying the world. Their little civil war bought this planet a few years. Now, you know that psycho is going to try to sprint to the finish."

The two of them went over the rest of the daily reports on Jill's operations. By the time they were through, it was way past midnight.

"We'd better wrap it up," Tao said. "Cameron is going to be exhausted in the morning. I promised to take him to the forest to teach him tracking before he free-runs with Jill. He wants to be able to sneak up on deer."

"It's your fault for keeping him up way past his bedtime."

"Roen, fifteen year-old teenagers should not have bedtimes."

Roen, who was putting the stacks of documents away, made a face. "Yeah, about that. I think that's something we should probably pow-wow about. His mother and I think you're pushing him a little too hard."

"Funny. I thought I was going a little easy on him."

Roen got serious. "Tao, you're pushing him harder than you ever pushed me, and he's just a kid."

Cameron's face looked equally serious as he stood up and towered over the sitting Roen. "That is because he has more potential than you will ever have. Do not take that the wrong way."

"My teenager has already outstripped my abilities. How should I take it?"

"He is from your loins. Must be getting that potential from his mother's side."

Roen held back the urge to shake Tao. "I mean it. Let him have a childhood."

"No, you listen, Roen," Tao said, hands on Cameron's

hips. "You of all people should understand. If the Genjix win and succeed in Quasiform, humanity dies this generation. Cameron will be lucky to live to forty. If the human governments succeed, he'll be hunted for the rest of his life. Either case spells certain death for your son. Your family has been amazingly fortunate the past few years in lying low while all our friends and comrades have fallen. These few precious years are the only ones where we can train him in peace, because otherwise he will train by fire." Tao reached out, grabbed a fistful of Roen's shirt and tugged. Jill was right; his son was getting strong. "I almost lost you because you were not good enough. I will not lose Cameron."

Roen scowled. The encounter with Jacob was a sore point for him. It had taken him years for the nightmares of that night to end. Now, he was conflicted between revenge on that psychopath and fear of crossing his path again. "Just… try," he said finally. He headed back into the house, but paused to look back at Tao. "By the way, I wasn't not good enough. I had already gone through a lot and wasn't one hundred percent."

Tao shook his head. "I can spot talent and skill, Roen. He will beat you nine out of ten fights. You will win the tenth because he caught food poisoning, and even then, you will barely win. Jacob is that good."

CHAPTER SEVEN
STATUS CALL

When the full scope of our actions came to light, humanity's fury knew no bounds. At the time, we felt that if our existence was going to be revealed, we might as well come clean and tell them everything. Perhaps that was a mistake.

When the truth got out, the Quasing were painted as manipulators and conspirators who had a global agenda against all humans. The Prophus and Genjix factions were treated as one evil. I cannot blame them for believing that. After all, we have preached a more peaceful solution with the humans, but have the Prophus's action shown that to be true?

Baji

"Are you sure Rin will not come to Command? The heart of our research division is here, and the facilities are much more secure. She can continue her work uninterrupted with all our resources at her disposal. That won't be the case elsewhere."

Jill, leaning back in her chair with her feet up on the desk, shook her head. "Sorry, Keeper, I don't think she cares if you're offering a gold-plated swimming pool filled with six-packed pool boys. Greenland's a hard sell."

The Keeper and her host, Meredith Frances, was the leader of the Prophus, and the only Quasing from the original Grand Council to join the splinter faction during the Spanish Inquisition. Meredith's family came from a long line of Prophus and was one of the large financial backers of the faction. Now, even in her old age, she ruled with a firm hand and at times seemed to keep the faction together with glue, rubber bands, and sheer force of will.

Many worried about what would happen once she passed. Meredith's heir to the Keeper, Hubert, had died on a mission fifteen years earlier. Coupled with the death of both Field Marshal Stephen and Admiral Abrams, both lost right before the Great Betrayal, there was a huge hole in the Prophus leadership. The Keeper's new host heir was currently only six years old.

Jill, a rising field commander within the ranks, was considered a longshot for assuming that mantle because of the three crosses she had attached to her name. The first was that she refused to join the rest of Command in Greenland. Jill had refused to transfer there for a promotion, since she didn't think Cameron could have a good childhood there. Most of the Prophus there were hidden either underground or lived in remote villages.

The second problem was more serious. She was married to Roen, whom most within the organization detested. That suited him fine, since he didn't think much of them either. Both he and Tao had developed reputations as mavericks during his tenure as a host. His subsequent flouting of authority did not help his case, or hers, any.

Her last and most serious offense against the Prophus was that she was the one responsible for the Great Betrayal.

Most Prophus disagreed with her decision to expose the Quasing and would probably never forgive her for it.

All this suited Jill fine, because no one had ever bothered to ask her if she even wanted the job. If someone had only posed the question, she would have gladly told them she'd rather be shot out of a cannon than head the Prophus from Greenland.

There wasn't a week that passed without one of the Underground Railroaders bringing the topic up. She was not just the commander of the Pacific Northwest Conductor, she was infamous for being the host who made the decision to reveal the Quasing to the world, and she continually found herself defending her position, not only to strangers, but often to herself. Her usual response when asked was that she would make the same choice again. However, as the years went on, with the situation deteriorating day by day, even she found it difficult to believe her own words.

Stop beating yourself up over it. There were no good decisions that day, Jill. For what it is worth, I still feel it was the right choice.

"That makes you and me the only ones, then."

Remember, the war was over; we had lost. You snatched victory from the enemy.

"If we can't win, no one should. Nothing like being a spoilsport, eh?"

In this case, yes. I cannot even imagine what the world would be like now if we had allowed them to succeed. For one thing, we would all be living in caves in Greenland, or dead.

"Most of our people already live in caves in Greenland, or are dead. Also, if you had allowed the Genjix to win, maybe your people would already be swimming outside bodies having babies like crazy, while we humans suffocated from toxic air in blistering heat."

Ah, paradise.

"Moving on," the Keeper was saying. "If that's Rin's choice, then so be it. As long as she's working against her own abomination, I don't care where she is. I assume her escort to the next segment of the Underground Railroad has been arranged?"

"I didn't want to send just anyone, so I thought I'd have my husband run the route."

As if on cue, Roen walked into the room, going on about how he'd need to make a run into town tomorrow to stock up on salt blocks and gasoline. Jill turned away from the monitor and put a finger to her lips. She pointed at the screen and waved him away. Roen craned his head around her and saw the Keeper staring back at him. He scowled, the Keeper scowled, and then they both looked away pretending the other didn't exist.

One day, she will forgive him for Hubert's death.

"One day meaning when Meredith dies?"

I was thinking more like when he dies.

Roen, now out of view of the webcam, was miming. She had no idea what he was trying to say, though; he always did suck at Charades. Jill tried to ignore him, but a small smile crept up when he began to make faces. Then he started to dance. She suppressed her broadening grin.

"Excuse me, Keeper," she said, putting the channel on mute. She turned to Roen and hissed. "Get out of here."

He leaned in and kissed her on the lips. "Just wanted to make sure I can still hold your attention." Roen looked over at the screen and waved. The Keeper, looking like she was etched out of stone, did not wave back. He held onto her hand until the very last second as he left the room.

"Apologies, Keeper. Please continue."

The Keeper's face looked a little more sagged than usual. "Jill, my dear, I'm amazed he was ever able to land you, and even more so that you two are still together. Please tell me he has redeeming qualities that he hides from the rest of civilization."

"Probably not, but I wouldn't have him any other way."

The Keeper shook her head. "No matter what, you are *not* assigning that man to someone as important as Rin. I forbid it."

"Keeper, he's the best I have."

"I don't care if he's the last human being under your command with legs. You are not placing the linchpin to stopping Quasiform in his care. Send someone else. Yourself if you have to."

Jill furrowed her brow. "Sorry, but my operative days are over. I was never really good at being an operative, anyway. Besides, you do remember what happened last time I was put in a position to make a decision that affected all Quasing, don't you?"

"Of course I do," the Keeper snapped. "I was there. Dumbest decision I've ever made."

Jill cocked her head to one side and sighed. "Meredith, you can't take the blame for my – "

"You bet your ass I can, girl." The Keeper's voice took on a softer tone and for a second, she almost looked warm and affectionate. "Listen, Jill, regardless of what happened afterward, that was one of the bravest calls I've ever seen. You showed me something that night. That's why you head the West Coast. It's one of the toughest regions in the world. Things could have been different if we had played our cards right. We didn't handle it like we should have, so don't beat yourself up over it."

"I appreciate that but –"

"And I won't handicap your career because of that either. Good or bad, that call lives and dies with me. When I'm gone, girl, we'll need more people like you keeping things together."

"Yes, Meredith. And thanks."

"Don't thank me, yet. Consider it a possible punishment." And just like that, Meredith was back to being the ice-cold Keeper. "There's one more thing you need to pay attention to near the Oregon border. One of our clandestine operations has run red near your territory. For the past few months, we've been tracking the flow of money to that region. Supply logistics, bribes, raw materials, building machinery and such, all allocated in massive amounts to a small town in the middle of nowhere on the far eastern edge of Oregon named..." The Keeper looked off-screen. "... Ontario."

Jill nodded. "I'm familiar with the town. It's on the border of my region, but I'm not aware of anything going on there."

"Correct. It's actually Wohlreich's. He sent a scout team to investigate."

"It's still near my zone of control," Jill said, sticking her finger into the monitor. This ground her gears to no end. The Keeper was an old-school leader, having honed her skills during the Cold War, and still believed that the only person who needed to know everything was her. Everyone else had to know just enough to stay out of trouble or help in a pinch.

"Typical Keeper. How infuriating."

There is a reason why clandestine ops are called that.

That wasn't how Jill ran her operations in the Pacific Northwest. She made sure all her people had high-level information about what everyone else was doing, and those within a hundred kilometers of each other were updated every three days. It was an administrative slog that led to long meetings, and several of her operatives had balked at first, thinking the tedious intel unnecessary. They changed their minds when they realized the usefulness of being interconnected, knowing what a team nearby was doing, or even calling for support if a problem arose. Jill's region eventually became one of the most well-run on the planet.

"I would have appreciated Wohlreich notifying me as a courtesy," said Jill.

"Well, you're being informed now," the Keeper continued. "It should have been a pretty standard mission. They've been surveying the town for a few weeks. Their host commander, Prie, was detected and injured in a firefight. Unfortunately, Wohlreich has most of his resources occupied right now dealing with the fracking sites in Montana and Wyoming, so it falls upon you to help the team out. I'm transmitting the details now."

Jill skimmed the mission report. "Looks serious. Need an extraction?"

"No. We are sending in a new host commander to finish the job. You'll need to send escorts to accompany the new host commander and reinforce the scout team's ranks. Also, the last report yesterday was that Prie was too injured to move. Send your doctor as well and see if we can stabilize and prep him for transport."

"All right," Jill said slowly. "I'll look over the breakdown."

She checked a list off to the side. "My guys are stretched kind of thin right now. If you need a couple guys for an extended period of time, I'm not sure how many men I can cobble together, especially if we need to get Rin moved safely to the next Underground Railroad station." She looked up at the Keeper. "I can assign Roen, my doctor, and maybe one more. That's it."

The Keeper nodded. "Make it a priority. We don't know how long Prie will last, and the nearest Prophus medical facility is two days' journey from Ontario. The new host commander will fill you in when he arrives at your base. He should be there by this evening."

"Who is he?"

The Keeper paused, and then began to chuckle. "Oh, I just realized. This is just too good. Sometimes, karma's an absolute bitch, and her name is Meredith."

Jill didn't like the sound of this. "Excuse me, Keeper?"

The Keeper told her the rest of the mission parameters. Jill's face turned sheet white as she added one and one and came up with "oh, fuck."

"Oh fuck is right," the Keeper chortled. "Personal issues aside. Get this done. These are the two most important operations on your slate. I know I can depend on you. Command out."

The screen turned black. Jill sat there for the next few minutes and tried to piece together the right words to say. Then she examined her personnel and tried to reassign agents or pull someone, anyone, off a job. In the end, there was only one clear way forward, one that she was not looking forward to.

"Fuck it, they're professionals," she muttered. "It'll work. I hope."

"Hey, Jill," Roen's voice popped over the comm. "Freezer two's broken down. Everything inside's melted."

Jill clicked over. "Move what you can to freezer one and three, and I guess we'll have whatever is in two for dinner."

"Hot damn, twenty pizzas for dinner tonight. I've died and gone to –"

Jill closed the channel and rubbed her temples. "We are so screwed."

She couldn't even figure out how to break this to Roen, let alone send him on this job. The whole thing was a disaster waiting to happen. At least she had a few hours before this evening. Maybe if she framed it in such a way that he could calm down before…

The external perimeter alarm dinged. Hurley, their next door neighbor and agent manning the surveillance grid, buzzed over the comm system. "You've got company, Jill. Single signature inbound. Pass phrases accepted."

So much for giving him an early warning. Well, at least the pizzas were already thawed.

CHAPTER EIGHT
CLANDESTINE OP

Timestamp: 2622

Not gonna lie; the realization that I lost Tao broke me. I was distraught for months. Angry. Moody. So in shock that I questioned if I was even alive. After all, a Quasing couldn't leave a host until death. So how did this happen?

When I found out that he had moved to Cameron, I was thrilled and mortified at the same time. At least my friend was still close. I had feared him dead. On the other hand, I was angry at him for choosing my boy. I wanted better for my son than this war. I wanted him to grow up and live a normal life where he wouldn't get shot at. Instead, he was going to follow in my footsteps, and it made me hate myself and Tao for it.

The stack of thawing pizzas in Roen's arms was taller than his head. It made walking up the narrow staircase from the safe house to the farmhouse a little tricky. He wondered how many of these pizzas he could handle by himself. Tao had weaned him off this food-of-the-gods early in his tenure as a Prophus, but like a first love, pizza would always be near and dear to his heart.

He whistled as he bounded into the kitchen and piled the pizzas in two neat stacks. With only four ovens, it would take a while to cook everything. That suited him just fine. For once, in the name of not wasting food, he was honor-bound to eat pizza for the next three days. Two if he tried really hard.

"Roen," Jill called over the comm. "I need you in the living room."

Jill was using that voice again. She had used it once in a while before they were married, much more often after they were married and had separated, and all the time now that they were back together and she was his direct superior. Well, if there was one thing he had learned over the years…

"Happy wife, happy life," he chirped cheerfully, strolling out of the kitchen. The house was divided into small rooms, intentionally compartmentalized to create choke points in case of an attack. He walked through the living room, family room, sitting room, and finally to the room Roen referred to as the coating room, where the front door was. Jill and Hurley were already there, speaking to their visitor, who had his back to him. Roen walked closer and extended his hand, and then his mouth fell.

The man turned and exclaimed. "Oh hello, Roen. My, there seems to be a lot more of you. Are you well?"

"Marco!" he choked.

At that very moment, he nearly drew his sidearm. He had to remind himself several times that they were on the same side. This was one of the few instances that Tao not being in his head was helpful, since Tao hated Marco's Quasing, Ahngr, more than he hated most Genjix, and Tao's hatred for the Genjix was legendary.

"It'd be a lie if I said it's good to see you, but no need to be uncivil about it, eh?" Marco smiled with those oh-so-perfect teeth.

Roen wound his immediate instincts to punch the guy in his perfect teeth into a tight ball and stuffed it deep down into his gut. "What are you doing here?"

Marco took off his jacket and held it out to him. Roen was perfectly content standing there, not taking it, until a glare from Jill gave him second thoughts. He accepted the jacket and hung it on one of the coat hooks lining the room. It must have been raining outside; the thing was soaked all the way through. He pulled his hands away and noticed that they were stained red.

With newfound concern, Roen tapped on Hurley's shoulder. "Wake up Ines. She's down in the safe house. Tell her we have injured."

Hurley hurried off. Roen reached forward to help Marco, but was waved off.

"Don't worry about me, old chap," Marco said. "Most of it isn't mine." He grimaced. "Ran into those fine Interpol folks coming in from Vancouver. That border of yours is like the Thirty-eighth Parallel now."

"You fool," Jill berated Marco, ushering him into the main room. "Why didn't you tell me you were injured?"

"Really, hardly that." Marco winked. "I couldn't by any chance trouble you for a drink?"

Roen led him into the sitting room and noticed the Brit wince as he sat down on the couch. He also limped, though that might have been an old injury he had sustained protecting Jill several years back. The reality was, Roen owed Marco for that one. The man was responsible for her still breathing today. However, as much good as he had done for Jill, he had always equally been an ass to Roen.

When the Great Betrayal swept across the world, Roen was smuggled from the Queen's Hospital to the Cook Islands to the same remote Prophus-run recovery facility at which Marco was staying. Roen had tried to thank the guy for keeping Jill safe. Instead of being gracious about it, Roen received a good-natured lecture from the egotistical jerk about how he should have been at her side instead of gallivanting around the world like a bachelor, and how she was too good for him. He might have let that slide, if Marco hadn't continued on about how once he recovered from his injury, he would teach Roen how to act like a real man. And somehow, the Brit had had the audacity and glibness to say all of that in an affable manner.

The two had exchanged harsh words while both were wrapped up like mummies. It was a sad spectacle. Nothing looks more pathetic than two recently near-dead men getting into a fight. The two pushed a seventy-four year-old nurse to her limit when she had to restrain them both at the same time. They got into it three more times before Roen was finally well enough to leave and rejoin his family.

God he hated that guy.

The worst part was that Jill and Marco had kept in touch. The truth was, Roen was to this day jealous of Marco, not only because of the man's close friendship with his wife, but also his suave ways, money, and charm. The damn guy had been dealt all the good cards in life. And now he was good friends with Roen's wife. To top it all off, Roen had to grudgingly admit that Marco was better than him at just about everything.

Jill went to the infirmary to retrieve the necessary

supplies while Roen and Marco sat across from each other in the living room. She shot them a worried glance before disappearing around the corner. They sat in silence for a few awkward moments, Roen staring intently at Marco, and Marco acting like he was alone in his own house. They began speaking at the same time.

"So how's our bird holding up?" Marco asked.

"What's going on out there?" Roen said.

Another awkward pause followed.

"Well, you first," Roen said.

"A gentleman gladly waits," Marco replied.

Do not bite on everything. Let it go, Roen. You have bigger things to worry about.

That's what Tao would say if he was here. His friend's phantom voice in his head came across loud and clear. He took the imaginary voice's advice and elected to remain civil. "Jill's good. She's prospering in her command post."

Marco nodded. "I don't get to catch up with her as much as I'd like – or as much as you think I do – but I hear good things about her when I drop by Command. By the way, old chap, could you hand me a glass of water? I'm parched."

Roen looked at the red stains on Marco's shirt. He went to the kitchen and returned with two cups, a pitcher of water, and a bottle of scotch. He found Marco limping around the room, examining the cheap knick-knacks they displayed to make the house look homier without actually giving away any personal information. Of course, none of the pictures were of the family.

"You're dripping blood all over my imported carpet," Roen said, putting the tray down on the table.

Marco looked down at the floor. "Swedish?"

Roen nodded.

"I hope you didn't pay for it."

"Cheap. Moving sale."

"You paid too much, then."

Marco brightened when he saw the bottle of scotch, the glass of water now forgotten. He gave the twelve-year a nearly imperceptible upturn of the nose before taking a glass.

"Do you need ice?" Roen asked.

Marco sniffed. "A touch of water will do."

Roen poured them both a drink. They sat back down in awkward silence, both raising their glasses only slightly to acknowledge the other.

"So how's the boy?" Marco continued. "Rumor mill says he might be the second Prophus Adonis."

"Who's the first?"

Marco raised his glass again and grinned.

Roen rolled his eyes. He had walked straight into that one. "He's doing very well, but I don't want him to be an Adonis."

"Aren't you too old now to still be full of self-loathing?"

"I just want what's best for my son, and being a hardcore Prophus agent isn't it. If I could get him away from all Quasing and have him live a normal life, I would. Unfortunately, fate has other plans for him. How is the war going in the rest of the world?"

Marco took a sip and shook his head. Roen wasn't sure if it was because of the bad news or the bad scotch. "Well, old boy, the world is in a bit of a jam. Seems aliens as a whole are just a step below taxes on the world popularity scale."

Roen grunted. "At least the Quasing are still above politicians then."

"I would put them about even," said Marco. "Right now, Asia is a total loss and Europe a powder keg."

The bad news continued to pile on. Between Asia solidly behind the Genjix and most of Europe and North America hunting all aliens, the only relatively safe zones for the Prophus were South America and Africa, both of which had so many problems they couldn't care less about millions-of-years-old visitors from outer space.

The rift between the two factions had precipitated tensions across definitive lines, and now countries were picking sides and preparing for global conflict. The world was on the cusp of World War III, which played right into the Genjix's hands, and the Prophus were smack dab in the middle of it all. The worst part was that nobody wanted the Prophus on their side. They were their own little island about to be crushed between several juggernauts trying to crack the planet in two.

"A little histrionic, no?" Roen said when Marco finished.

The Brit shrugged. "Well, while you've been playing Lost Boys in your forest, I've been out on the front line." For the first time, Roen noticed the man's overly confident facade crack a smidgeon. "It's rough out there, Roen. Consider yourself blessed for having this." He gestured at their surroundings. "I haven't had a place I could call a home for more than five years now."

"What about your estates?"

Marco shook his head. "All under my sister's name. Haven't seen my family either. Wasn't able to make mother's funeral. Couldn't risk having my family linked to an alien." Anguish flashed across his face. He picked up his glass of scotch and raised it to Roen again. "But that's the life we lead, right, old boy?"

Roen nodded. It seemed not even someone like Marco could avoid the new Quasing-hating landscape. At least Roen's parents had been completely insulated from his extra-terrestrial activities. He didn't realize how easy he'd had it compared to the others. Marco was right, though. They had been blessed here in the Pacific Northwest, partially because of the tight ship Jill ran, and partially because the only sort of action that ever happened here was refugees passing through.

"Are you two behaving?" Jill asked, coming up the stairs.

Marco held up his glass of scotch. "I have my remedy right here, love. However, I'd like to get to that scout team post haste. Those Interpol boys are – how do you say it out here – circling the wagons in Ontario. There's no time to waste."

"The Keeper considers your operation high priority," Jill said.

Marco struggled to stand. "Very well then. Here's what I need. Weapons, ammunition, unmarked cash, a crate of the finest whiskey you can drum up here in the backwaters, six operatives, and a vehicle. Preferably a German convertible but I'll settle for a Jaguar if I really must suffer."

"That's a large operation." Roen frowned. "What are you guys running? Six is a tough order to fill. We can't spare those numbers. Do you need incendiaries?"

Marco shook his head. "Small arms fire will do."

Jill ticked off her fingers. "I can send my doctor, Ines, and two bodies. Roen, what cars can we spare?"

"I got that Oldsmobile in the back, which should – big emphasis on should – get him to Ontario."

Jill smiled. "There you go, Marco."

He sniffed. "At least it's not another old Fiat."

Roen ticked off the head-count in his head. "I don't count three. Ines, Hurley, and you? I don't like this at all."

"No," Jill said. "Not me. I need to run Ops. You're going, Roen."

"No!" both Roen and Marco shouted at once.

"I… this is unacceptable. Disastrous," Marco sputtered.

To Roen's surprise, it seemed Marco actually disliked Roen more than Roen disliked him. This was a rare display of outright outrage. In a way, Roen was glad he got under the arrogant man's skin. After all, the guy went out of his way to offend Roen every chance he got, while at the same time pretending to do it innocuously.

"Jill, be rational," Marco raised his voice. "You know what happened the last time we had to be in the same room together, not to mention Egypt."

Roen scowled and stood up. "You want to bring that up again?"

"Yes. Yes, I do, you stubborn oaf," Marco said.

The two of them stared at each other across the coffee table. Marco threw back his half-full glass of scotch. Not to be outdone, Roen did the same. He was almost successful at keeping the burning climbing up his throat from showing on his face.

"Shut it, both of you," Jill snapped. "I don't like this any better than you, but that's our orders. I have a lot more to babysit than you two, so figure it out."

"I'm no longer running missions away from my family. At least not for more than one night." Roen shook his head stubbornly. "We agreed on this after DC."

"Keeper's orders," sighed Jill. "I don't like it either,

Roen, but we're low on manpower. It's been over ten years since she's made this sort of request. Make an exception, hon. It's important; lives are at stake."

"I still don't like this," Roen growled.

"That makes three of us," Marco growled back. "Ahngr thinks this is a shit idea."

"Well, live with it," Jill snapped. "Roen, Marco's the host. He holds command." She stuck a finger in his face. "You follow orders." She turned to Marco. "If word gets back to me that you're mistreating my husband, I will rain holy hell upon you. You two got it?"

"Yes, Jill," they both answered grudgingly.

"Good. Get to work." She reached out and gave Roen a kiss on the mouth. "Thanks for being understanding. Now behave, mister. I mean it."

He grunted as she walked out of the room. Finally, Roen sighed and looked at the Brit. "Guess we're stuck with each other."

Marco gnashed his teeth in a very ungentlemanly way. "Just follow my orders, Roen. Remember, you're under me."

"Kiss my ass, Marco. What's the plan?"

Marco sighed. "It's a twelve-hour drive to the Idaho border. Why don't you ride with me and I'll fill you in?"

CHAPTER NINE
THE RUSSIAN CAMPAIGN

I first came to standing among the Quasing in India when I, along with Chiyva, laid the foundation for Hinduism. After that, sensing opportunity with the unrest in the Median Empire, I moved west and joined a young prince named Cyrus who rebelled against his father.

Together, we overthrew the Medes and ushered in the first Persian Empire. The region was wracked by strife, though, and his empire was short-lived. However, with this experience, the Council hypothesized that humanity's conflicts were a great catalyst for their innovations.

Zoras

Austin died three days after the cowardly ambush at the Church of the Disposition of the Robe. Any time an Adonis Vessel passed, the loss was widely grieved. Any time it was someone from Enzo's Assembly, his inner circle, justice demanded vengeance. Any leniency he might have given Vinnick was now off the table. To strike at one of his Hatchery siblings was a personal affront to him. To strike at Enzo himself was treason.

It was one thing for them to play at Council Power Struggle. That was expected and even approved of by the Holy Ones. However, the attempt on his life changed the game. It broke the unspoken rules among the Council. Now, Enzo was going to treat Vinnick as he did all enemies.

This meant war.

The death toll had risen to twenty-six, and Enzo intended for Vinnick to pay for every single one of them. An entire wing of the Botkin Hospital was cordoned off for its fourteen newest patients. His entire security team had swooped in and locked down the building, and now the entire city block was a veritable fortress.

Vinnick's desperation will not go unnoticed. However, restraint in this case will curry more favor than recklessness.

"I won't stand for it, Zoras."

You will not have to. I may need to speak with Flua directly. We cannot tolerate a delay to Quasiform at this important stage of the project.

"Impossible. You already saw what he attempted when I tried to parlay in good faith. Besides, it would lower my standing if I put myself in that position again."

See to it. I do not care how.

Enzo grimaced. "As you wish, my Guardian."

Amanda pushed her way through the gaggle of doctors fussing over his wounds and whispered into his ear. "Azumi and Jacob have arrived, Father. The Assembly is complete."

Enzo waved off the nagging nursemaids. He had suffered worse injuries during training. Still, Amanda, the only non-vessel he allowed within his Assembly, insisted. She had previously been Devin's aide and continued to serve Enzo faithfully. No one knew the daily operations of his vast holdings as well as she did. He had been meaning to bless her, but her standing was far too low for any Holy One to accept. Still, loyalty, much like treachery, had to be rewarded.

"Get out." He pushed the doctors aside and hopped out of bed. His shoulder ached and he would need to walk gingerly for a few days, but otherwise, Enzo couldn't waste his time with rest. Amanda helped him into his shirt. "Clear and assemble in ten minutes."

She nodded and left the room. He could hear her shout through the hallways to clear the floor. A few minutes later, Enzo and his most trusted lieutenants squeezed into one of the small hospital meeting rooms. Amanda, who was sitting next to him, activated a small machine on the table. The group waited as a low-pitched resonance in the room got higher and higher until it got imperceptible to the human ear. She looked over at him. "The room is soundproofed, Father."

"Praise to the Holy Ones," he intoned.

"Praise to the Holy Ones," the rest of the room repeated.

"Vinnick's on his last legs," Enzo began, looking each of his Hatchery siblings in the eye as he spoke. "He's desperate. His last cowardly act has proven that he is unworthy of the Council. However, it is our duty not to destroy his operation, but to take it intact in order to continue serving the Holy Ones's end goals. Our primary objective will be to unseat him from power in Russia. With the old snake so embedded, we will be under constant threat. Austin has fallen and Matthew is injured. Therefore, Palos will take point on my security detail going forward."

Palos, an older operative and the only non-Adonis Vessel in the group, stood up and bowed. "Your will, Father."

Enzo looked over at Azumi at one point, a close second to Enzo at the Hatchery. "Where are we on the Russian Parliament?"

"Father," she said, "all from the Federal Assembly can be leaned on, except those with close ties to Councilman Vinnick."

"And the State Duma?"

She paused. "They might prove problematic. United Russia can be bought. However, all the other minority parties have been non-committal."

"Salvageable?"

"Possibly, with the exception of the Liberal Democratic Party of Russia. They consider our influence an encroachment on Russian nationalism."

You must consolidate quickly. The delay of Quasiform has already reached unacceptable levels. Tighten your control and move on to our real goals. Do not get bogged down with the meanderings of Russian politics.

"How strong is the LDPR currently?" he asked. "And how many are vessels?"

"Eighty-four seats and none, Father. The LDPR uses Penetra scanners on all their ranking members. They are hardline xenophobes."

Enzo scowled and recalled his education from his Hatchery days. "Sacrilegious animals. Fifteen percent of the Duma. Very well. Organize a shade team and have it stand by just in case. If we cannot coerce them, we will find more direct alternatives. Coercion first."

Azumi hesitated. "We cannot guarantee the Holy Ones's safety in the event of discovery."

"Then use the newborns."

This will be frowned upon.

"Times are too critical for half-measures, my Guardian."

Shade teams were a relatively new branch of Genjix operatives. With the ability to procreate under their control now, Quasing extinction on this planet was no longer a threat. Initially, Enzo had planned to just overwhelm the entire planet with Holy Ones. What better form of invasion could there be than one from within? However, his plans were derailed when the first batch of Quasing were born. They discovered that the incubation process was woefully inadequate.

On Quasar, new births had a near-infinite number of other Quasing to interconnect and share knowledge with. This allowed them to grow and mature rapidly by quickly merging and transferring thought. Because of the limited size of the ProGenesis vats, the newborns on Earth required a much longer period of time to incubate.

This was a difficulty the Genjix scientists had not anticipated. They determined the only solution was to speed up Quasiform. At this moment, the Quasing could only procreate and allow the new Quasing to gestate slowly. His scientists estimated that it would take centuries before these incubated Quasing were mature enough to truly join the ranks of the Holy Ones.

For Enzo, it had become an expensive and frustrating process. His initial plan of creating a vast vessel army was destroyed. Not only that, maintaining even the current vats was a drain on their resources. Currently, over fifteen percent of their expenditures went to maintaining the housing facilities for the two million Quasing birthed in the past half-decade. That was two million Holy Ones who would be ineffective for the next couple of hundred years.

However, that was also ten times the number of Quasing

estimated to be alive on Earth just ten years ago. It was progress, not the sort Enzo had hoped for, but progress nevertheless. There was another advantage to this: shade teams. Because the threat of extinction was no longer as relevant, the Genjix could afford to take greater risks with their Holy Ones, using them more and more as weapons and spies against their enemies.

Furthermore, as in the instance of the LDPR, the Genjix could use the currently barely-sentient newborn Quasing to inhabit humans not amiable to the Genjix. After all, how could they object if they themselves were vessels, even if it was forced? Most of the Holy Ones disapproved of this process, but they saw the value of it. This was war, after all, and sacrifices were expected, even from the gods.

There were side effects to using the non-sentient newborns though. Much like a human baby, the newborns tended to be vocal and uncontrollable. Several of the early vessels who had taken on these newborns were driven to insanity from their constant mewling. It took several years before medication was developed to allow the vessels to filter those sounds out. Even then, they would be dependent on it for the rest of their lives.

Those Holy Ones are the future, not expendable tools. Do not set a poor precedent and dip into this well too often.

"Everyone has their place in achieving victory, my Guardian. Myself, the original Holy Ones, the newborns. We will do our best to ensure their safety. However, I believe blessing those in the Russian government who oppose us will help keep the country under our control."

We will not tolerate unconcerned casualties among our kind, regardless of whether they are still too young to have become sentient.

"Your will, Zoras. I will do my best to see to their safety. However, as in the case of all wars, casualties are necessary, regrettable as they may be.

"All targets blessed by a shade will require twenty-four hour surveillance," Enzo added.

The rest of the meeting went more or less as planned. Enzo's teams were outnumbered badly here in Vinnick's home region, but this was never a war of numbers. He would defeat the old billionaire at his own game by buying the right people and assassinating the rest.

"I want a bio of all Federation Council and State Duma members we can purchase," he said. "Those we can't, we blackmail. If that's not possible, we assassinate. Give me a list by the end of the week. As for the LDPR, work the same angle, and then use a shade team if necessary. Is there anything else?"

The room was silent. Then Amanda looked up at him. "Father, we just received a communication from Councilman Vinnick. He wishes to parlay. This time, while the Russian Parliament is in session. At your convenience."

The room was still, with everyone watching what Enzo would do next. He made a fist and cracked his knuckles. The safest thing to do would be to reject any overture and grind out a war of attrition with Vinnick, either politically or through clandestine means. However, it could also be a wasted opportunity. The old man was near defeat anyway. Maybe that assassination attempt was his one chance. When it failed, he realized he had no other alternative and was now truly trying to negotiate peace. Or maybe he was going to try and take Enzo out again.

How would his people react if he allowed Vinnick to ambush him like a coward, and then give the traitor the privilege of another meeting? No, it would just tell all the Genjix that there were no consequences to attacking the greatest Council member. Enzo's reputation was more important. He couldn't show any weakness. There were hundreds of other vessels who would kill to assume his position. He glanced around at the faces looking at him expectantly. How many here in this room?

None of your Assembly has given you cause. Trust should be rewarded. Distrust likewise. Wandering down that dark path will only make it a self-fulfilling prophecy.

Zoras was right. The ones in this room were the only ones he should trust implicitly. No one else. Enzo stood up abruptly, masking his grimace and ignoring the pain shooting through his body. "No meeting with the traitor. Set up my first meetings with the State Duma in four days. By that time, I want the names of those in my pocket, and a list of those I need to buy. Warn Vinnick that the State Duma building is mine while I am there. Wander there at his own risk. Get to work."

Enzo watched as his Assembly dispersed. These days, it had become almost as dangerous to be part of the Genjix as it was to be an enemy, though he wouldn't have it any other way. With a world war just on the horizon, and Quasiform nearing its final stages, everyone on the Council was maneuvering for higher standing.

Conflict bred innovation, after all, and that was doubly true of conflict within. In preparation for the upcoming world war, the aggressive Genjix war machine built up over the past five hundred years had turned on itself, especially now, with the Prophus nearly dormant. Of course the two strongest factions within the Genjix went head to head, and now victory was near for Enzo and his

Asian stronghold. However, rules still had to be observed and Vinnick had broken them.

"Jacob, a moment," Enzo ordered as the rest of the Assembly filed out. He watched as Jacob walked up and knelt before him. The grandson of a prominent vessel, he had lost his patronage when his grandfather, Sean Diamont, was murdered by the Prophus. He attended the Hatchery late in his youth and was not chosen to be blessed with a Holy One. Instead, he had joined the ranks of the officers and distinguished himself in the war. Eventually, Sean's Quasing Chiyva, thought to have been lost to the Eternal Sea during the debacle at the Capulet's Ski Lodge, found his way back to the Genjix and had chosen to bless Jacob.

The Adonis was a blunt-force instrument, more fanatical than most and possessing a singular devotion rare even among vessels. No one else under Enzo exhibited the same intense will in hunting the Prophus. He blamed the Prophus for Sean's death and carried a personal vendetta. While that was a useful trait to leverage, the man was often blinded by his hatred. However, give that dog the trail and he would follow it until the ends of the Earth.

"I have another task for you," Enzo said, beckoning Jacob to follow him out of the room. "Did you find out anything else regarding our lost Quasiform architect?"

"Yes, Father. Vinnick was intent on taking Rin to the loyalty haven in Canada. I dispatched a team to intercept her, but she has evaded capture and disappeared."

"The Prophus have her."

"I had guessed as much. How can you be sure?"

"Seems some of Vinnick's faction is still loyal to the true Genjix after all. I want you to take a team to the United

States and retrieve Rin personally."

That command surprised Jacob. "Father? Have I done anything to displease you?"

"Not at all, my son. Consider it a favor."

"Why would you task me with such mundane work?"

Enzo pulled up the information in his tablet and showed it to Jacob. The blood drained from his face. "Because it seems Roen Tan is alive, and he has our scientist."

CHAPTER TEN
ALEX

The entire surface of Quasar is covered by a vast ocean, a primordial soup partially like your ocean and partially like the insides of your bodies. The ocean – I use that term loosely – is thick, almost like quicksand. Quasar is further away from our sun than Earth is from yours, but our sun is nearly twice as large.

I cannot flash an image to you because sight is a foreign concept on our home world. Quasing inherently do not see. We feel. We absorb. We touch. We merge with each other to create a larger, more singular entity, powered by our individual ideas and experiences.

In a way, we are not unlike the cells of your bodies that form your whole.

Tao

Cameron thought mud-walking was stupid. It was the very first Ba Gua Zhang move that Tao had taught him when he was six years old. Deceptively difficult, Cameron had practiced mud-walking counter-clockwise in a circle for two hours a day every day. After three months, Tao felt that his mud-walking was decent enough to move on to the next step, which was having Cameron mud-walk in a clockwise circle for the next three months.

Nine years later, Cameron mud-walked with the best of them, flowing through the eight diagram boxing movements as if they were second nature. By now, he had walked this circle thousands – no, hundreds of thousands of times – feeling the energy move up from his *dan-tian* to the tips of his fingers and then back down through to the ground. He could run through this form unconsciously, in his sleep in fact. He had to, because right now, Tao was lecturing him on Matroid theory.

If one is invariant, does it have the same or different polynomials?

"Does it matter if it's chromatic?"

Not at all.

"Tao, I don't understand why I need to know this."

Advanced mathematics opens doors to many fields of study. More importantly, it expands the way you think.

"Who cares? It's hard and I suck at it."

One day, you might need to draw upon these skills. A good operative must know many things.

"I'm not going to need to do hard math while on a mission. You even said your Prophus job is to be a secret agent and not someone researching in a lab."

In this case, our natural talents are aligned. I think that will be a large part of our success. However, calculus is still basic knowledge you must master. By the way, that was sloppy footwork on that third palm roll body-back.

"Sorry."

What is with that left arm movement?

"Sorry!"

Do not apologize, Cameron. Fix it. You are not focused at all. What is wrong with you today?

Cameron glanced over at Alex leaning on the front porch railing studying him. He looked away, his face turning red. He re-ran that part of the form again, this time with even more force. However, the harder he actually concentrated, the worse he got.

Stop. We are done for the day. Is that what is bothering you? Alexandra?

"She keeps looking at me. I don't know. It makes me nervous."

You really are like your father.

"What does that mean?"

Never mind. If you want to tell her to stop staring, you should talk to her.

Cameron stopped in the middle of his form and looked up at her. "Is there something you need?"

Alexandra, looking inquisitive, walked across the lawn to the edge of the circle where Cameron was tracing. She swept her foot across the worn-out lines. "What are you doing?"

"I'm training," he said, suddenly feeling hot and getting the urge to get rid of her as soon as possible. "You're interrupting me."

"That doesn't look like training to me. You look like you're doing a funny dance."

"I'm running forms, Genjix," he snapped, saying the last word as if it was an insult.

That is one way to get her attention, though probably not the kind you wanted.

"Okay, betrayer Prophus," she shot back.

You will never get her to like you if you act so insolent.

"I don't like her, Tao!"

Why do you bother trying to lie to yourself, or more importantly, to me? Ask her what her style is.

"How do you fight then?" he asked Alex.

"Samozashchita Bez Oruzhiya," she replied. "My dad says it's the best."

"No, t'ai chi is the best. My Quasing invented it. It's the Grand Supreme Fist."

"You're just waving your arms and walking funny."

"That wasn't t'ai chi. That was Ba Gua, and I bet it's better than Samoz... samsoz..."

The known name for it is Sambo.

Their squabble degenerated into a shouting match on the front lawn until Jill and Vladimir appeared from the kitchen. Both of them just stood there and watched as Alex kept making fun of Tao's style. Why did his mom look amused? This girl was a Genjix! What was she doing here, anyway?

Things are a little different these days. It seems not all Genjix are bad anymore.

"That's not what you always tell me."

I do not agree with that assessment either, but it does seem the lines between the two factions have blurred somewhat.

"I'm going to go finish my training elsewhere," he said lamely, his ears burning. This wasn't how he imagined his first conversation with her would turn out. For some reason, since those Genjix came, he had been thinking about her a lot. He hadn't had a chance yet to talk to her, because the Genjix refugees had stayed locked up in the safe house until this morning. Mom had decided that it was time to trust the refugees and let them upstairs to the farmhouse.

Now with his dad gone with Uncle Marco, and his mom always running ops, this girl had no one to bother but him.

Ten minutes after he had stomped off, he caught sight of her still watching him while he tried to rerun his form. Something about the way she looked at him made him squirm.

Cameron eventually called it quits and climbed the large tree in the middle of the open field. This was his favorite reading spot. It reminded him of his father. Roen had tried to build a tree house when Cameron first moved here. Cameron had had to remind him that he was no longer eight years old. Still, it made him feel a little better that his old man had made the effort. His father was like that guy whose aim was always a few centimeters off the mark, no matter how hard he tried. But the thing was, he never stopped trying. Cameron appreciated that, even if Roen embarrassed him to no end.

Out of the corner of his eye, Cameron saw her walking back to the house, and his blood boiled. The worst part was, he didn't know why he was so mad. For as long as he could remember, Tao had always emphasized being calm and in control. When they were constantly on the run, Tao was there to soothe his many crying nights. When he got pulled out of school, Tao had assured him things were going to be okay. When he was lonely with no one to play with, Tao was there. He had learned to just be calm. His training demanded it. Tao demanded it. And he was good at it. But somehow, this girl – this Genjix – made him so mad just by saying a few words.

Cameron, it is all right. Perfectly natural, even.

"I don't like feeling like this, Tao."

Maybe that is what has been missing in our training. I have spent so many years suppressing you. Maybe it is time I try another approach. Stand up and do your form.

"I'm on top of a tree branch!"

No kidding. Just do it. Old-frame-Chen. This time, I do not want you to push your emotions down. I want you to keep them close to you. Lift them to your head and let those emotions flow with your qi. *Be here but also find the calm in the storm.*

Cameron had no idea what Tao was talking about; he had just proposed Cameron do exactly the opposite of their training. Still, he had been with Tao long enough to know to just follow directions, or at least try to. Standing on the tree branch that was barely wider than his two feet side by side, Cameron began to run through the old form, stumbling a few times on the rough and uneven surface. His form was awful, since he was distracted by his still simmering anger, and the fact that he had to try to maintain his balance high up off the ground.

After nearly falling off the branch a couple of times, he settled down and worked through the movements. Three-quarters of the way through the form, something unexpected happened; Cameron reached out and grabbed a small branch adjacent to him, except he wasn't the one to do it. Cameron stopped and stared at his hand.

"Tao, was that you?"

Yes, Cameron.

"How is that possible? I'm totally awake."

I think you and I might have found something out, something significant in human and Quasing relationships. This could be a breakthrough. We will need to experiment more. However, this is enough training today. I have another lesson to teach you, something possibly even more important.

"Yeah? What is it?"

I want you to climb down and talk to Alex. We are going to practice talking to girls.

"I don't –"

Just go.

Cameron found her in the living room a few minutes later. She sat on the floor with the pieces of his father's sniper rifle scattered all around her. She was using a washcloth and a bottle of gun oil to methodically wipe down each of the components. She obviously knew her way around that rifle. He felt a tinge of jealousy when he saw that. That sniper rifle was strictly off-limits to him.

"Hey," he said. "What are you doing?"

Alex didn't bother looking up. "It's filthy. You should take better care of your guns."

"I…"

Go ahead. Just like we talked about.

"Hey, I mean, I think we got off on the wrong foot."

Alex stopped what she was doing and looked up. There was a long pause. She grimaced, much in the same way Cameron did when Tao told him to do something he didn't want to do. Finally, she spoke. "Tabs wants me to…" She stopped again. "I'm sorry, too, for calling you a betrayer."

He sat down next to her. "Do you know how to put the rifle back together when you're done?"

Alex held up the barrel piece. "Your bore is filthy. You have copper fouling." She held up a rag. "The dagwood sandwich here is bad."

For the rest of the morning, Alex helped him clean the family's entire rifle cabinet. He learned right away that it was one of her pet peeves. She had this urge to always keep guns clean. Cameron thought it was a strange habit, since he always considered gun-cleaning a chore he had to do when he got into trouble.

"Tell me about your t'ai chi and Ba Gua thing," she

asked after they had finished taking apart and cleaning the last gun. "Tabs says it's really hard."

Cameron's chest puffed out a little. "It is. Tao says I learned it faster –"

Easy there. That will not get you anywhere with her.

"Cameron, lunch," his mom called from the kitchen. "Get Alex, too."

"I mean I can show you after lunch. Maybe we can spar a bit."

"I would like that," she said.

The two got off the living room floor and moved their conversation to the kitchen. Jill, Rin, Ohr, and Vladimir were already there. His mom was setting out a plate of meatloaf and potatoes while Ohr and Rin were setting the plates.

Pull the chair out for her.

Tao flashed an image of a Victorian formal dinner party. He pulled out a gold trimmed chair for a lady wearing a funny white wig and made a grandiose gesture to her. She flashed him a smile and sat down.

Cameron dutifully complied and tried to imitate that same gesture. He caught his mom looking at him funny and he blushed. He waited until Alex sat down before he took the seat across from her.

Good. I think this is a good time to teach you a new game. It is called how to act like a gentleman and impress the girl…

CHAPTER ELEVEN
TWO PEAS IN A POD

Timestamp: 2666

Let me tell you, if you ever have to stay at a hospital for an extended period of time, the Queen's Hospital in Honolulu comes highly recommended. Sure, the food sucks; the best thing there was the jello, but there's something about perpetually sunny days that's good for one's health.

The very best part of my stay, though, was the time I spent with my family. Jill and Cameron were with me every day. After being separated for so long, we had a lot of catching up to do. I can honestly say that it was the happiest time of my life, all things considered. I did break nineteen bones in my body, after all.

The first six hours of the drive from the safe house in northern California to the fringes of eastern Oregon was downright pleasant, mostly because Marco was driving, and Roen had fallen asleep as soon as the farmhouse was out of sight. There was an unspoken rule somewhere about people riding shotgun having to keep the driver company, but Roen was a trained agent, and he slept every chance he got.

After all, who knew when the next time he could get a solid block of rest in would come? It was one of the first tenets that Tao had hammered into him. Rest whenever you can, be ready to wake at a moment's notice, and never fall asleep on the job.

Early during their partnership, it had taken Tao a tremendous amount of effort to wake a slumbering Roen. Once Roen embraced his life as a Prophus agent, Tao was his constant alarm clock. These days, he had perfected the art of sleeping lightly. Somehow, whenever he needed to wake up, a phantom Tao would yell at him to wake up just like in the old days.

At around the six-hour mark, Marco nudged him awake and they traded places. Roen took the wheel while Marco settled into the passenger seat and promptly returned the favor. Except this time, the Brit snored. Loudly.

Roen preferred a snoring Marco to a talking one anyway. For him, chatting with the guy ranked somewhere between his yearly checkups with his proctologist and having a guys' night out with Louis, Jill's dad. Though the old man had sort of forgiven him by now, he still took a sick satisfaction in torturing Roen, usually with a combination of bourbon and not-so-subtle insults.

Still, by the fourth hour of his shift, the drive was getting old, and as much as he'd hate to admit it, a little company would have been nice to keep him alert along these long winding mountain roads. He welcomed hearing another person's voice when Marco woke up around the fifth hour. That welcome respite lasted a whole five minutes into their conversation.

"Before we begin," Marco said, "let's get a few things straight. We don't want a repeat of Egypt, right? We didn't have a defined chain of command last time. This time we do. Are we in agreement?"

Let it go. Just let it go.

Tao's voice repeated itself over and over in his head. Roen felt his guts twist into pretzels but held his tongue. Marco had a point, and this time, the chain of command was very clear. All hosts outranked non-hosts. The Prophus command structure was set in such a way that all hosts automatically were ranked at the Commander tier and had the ability to take control of any operation at any time, regardless of their capacity. The reason was that most Quasing were privy to more classified information.

Roen was in the unique situation of being the world's only ex-host, but there were several consequences to that. Even when he had operated as a rogue, he had had the authority as a host to leverage Prophus resources. Now no longer a host, coupled with the fact that most of Command – the Keeper most of all – hated his guts, he was effectively the lowest of the low. In fact, he was pretty sure the Keeper had created a new sub-rank just for him. Stephen was the only guy high up in Command who had ever championed him. Now with him gone to the Eternal Sea and Camr missing somewhere in Tibet, Roen had no one backing him up.

In fact, if it hadn't been for Jill, he was pretty sure they'd have just kicked him out of the organization altogether, which to be honest would have suited him fine if it hadn't been for the fact that the rest of his family were chest-deep in Prophus operations. Well, that, and he honestly didn't possess any other skills to make a living these days. After all, there weren't many job opportunities for secret agents, and he sucked at his previous career.

"You got it… sir," he said, trying to appear as un-sullen

as possible. After all, why give Marco the satisfaction?

"Excellent," Marco continued. "Now, because of your history as an ex-host, you're my second."

Roen grunted an affirmative. To be honest, this was a little better than what he thought Marco would do. "All right, what's our objective? I'm still in the dark on what's going on."

"First things first." Marco ticked off on one finger. "We bust our scout team friends out of the jam they're in. The host commander is in a serious condition. Ines stabilizes him and we move him to safety."

Roen nodded. "Sounds easy enough. And?"

"That's just the warm-up," said Marco. "The bean counters have been tracking various raw materials being shipped by the Genjix to this region. We think they're building a base or a manufacturing facility here. It's our job to help the scout team finish the job. Then we send the information to Command and let them decide what the next action items are."

"Sounds fairly cut-and-dry. We can swing in, show those amateurs how two pros do it, and be back in the morning for more of Jill's pancakes."

Marco nodded. "I appreciate your optimism, old boy."

"Who is the injured host?"

"Prie and his Quasing Pri."

"Prie and Pri?"

"He had it changed legally when he became a host. He's French and very much in love with his Quasing."

Roen made a face. The presence of hosts on this operation definitely complicated matters. However, most missions involving the Genjix required at least one host to identify other Quasing.

A small yellow light a little ways up the mountain caught his attention. "What's that?" Roen asked. He realized what it was as it became a bright streak shooting toward them. He punched the acceleration and swerved the car, but it was too late. The ground behind them exploded into a column of flames. Roen lost control of the steering, and gravity abandoned them. Then it came right back as the car crashed onto its side and rolled down the hill.

Fortunately for Roen, this wasn't his first rolling car. Tao was with him the first two times, and he had learned, albeit the hard way, how to handle the chaotic impact. He hugged the steering wheel tightly and closed his eyes. The car felt like it was bouncing forever, but it finally came to a stop after crashing down a line of trees on its side.

It took a few seconds for his brain to reboot his bodily functions. He groaned as he moved his arms and wiggled his toes. Nothing seemed broken. He opened his eyes and looked over at Marco, who was hanging limp above him. Was the guy dead?

"Oh no." The thought of Ahngr occupying him gave Roen the chills. He whacked the guy in the chest. "Dude, wake up. You better not be giving me –"

Marco groaned and opened his eyes. He looked down at Roen. "We're alive? Brilliant." He twisted his head back at Ines and Hurley sitting in the back. "You guys all right back there?"

He was rewarded with a soft affirmative.

"No time," Roen said, unfastening his seat belt. He climbed out the driver's side window, barely squeezing his frame through the opening. He grabbed tufts of grass and pulled himself out of the car until his legs were clear. He moaned as several parts of his body complained about moving so soon after an accident. For a second, he considered giving his body a rest.

You are in danger. Keep moving.

Tao's phantom voice echoed in his head. Roen looked up the hill and saw several shadows against the moon's backdrop move toward them. He drew his pistol and looked over at Marco, who was still struggling to get out of his seat belt.

"Stay behind cover. You have company coming," he said, retreating into the thickets.

"Where are you going?" Marco hissed, still working his way out of the window.

"Don't die," Roen called back and, keeping his head down, rushed into the brush.

"Thanks a lot, arsehole!" Marco shot back.

Roen crawled ten meters into the thick foliage, cut a hard left and doubled back toward the road. The sounds of gunfire erupted, sharp banging noises from Marco's pistol and the more rapid tick-tick sounds from their assailants' automatic rifles. Roen hoped the guy could hold out for a little while longer.

He reappeared out of the woods thirty meters from the crash. Hiding behind a large tree, he glanced over the top of a branch and assessed the enemy's strength: three, no, eight spreading out to flank the car. Roen set his sights on four of them, moving through the rotation a few times. Then he exhaled and unloaded five shots, two of which found their marks. He was able to take down another before he had to duck behind cover.

The branches shuddered as a stream of automatic fire tore into them. He felt the heavy thud of bullets as they punched into the tree's trunk. Then he heard pistol fire again. Well, at least one of his people was still alive.

Roen turned to the other side of the tree, but was rebuked by a stream of gunfire. They had him sighted. Grimacing, he flattened to the ground and dragged himself to the adjacent tree. He shot off another grouping and took down one more of the assailants, and then he was out of bullets. Roen reached down to his side and realized he wasn't carrying spare magazines on him. He smacked his forehead.

Duffel bag front pocket.

That left one thing to do. As much as he hated Marco, there was no way Roen was going to leave his guys to take on a group of heavily-armed men just because he was out of bullets. Roen picked up a baseball-sized rock, moved a bit further down the tree line, and sprinted up the bluff, scrambling against the steep incline and loose soil. Over seventy meters from the enemies, it was dark enough and he was far enough away that he was a difficult moving target to hit with an automatic rifle. Hopefully, he could draw some heat away from those guys in the car without getting shot. Then he remembered he wasn't wearing any armor.

"Crap," he muttered as dirt kicked up nearby. He reached the top of the hill and dove onto the road as more gunfire trailed after him. Peeking over the edge, he saw one of the enemy giving chase. Well, that was one less attacking his teammates. He hoped Hurley and Ines were all right.

The exchanges continued below as Roen lay in wait for the guy scrambling up the hill. Just as his head came into view, Roen lunged forward and tackled him. Together they rolled back down the bluff, the guy struggling to push

Roen off so he could get a shot off, and Roen desperately trying to keep the rifle muzzle away from his chest.

They were halfway down the slope when Roen found himself on top. He swung the rock in his hand at the man's night-vision visor, once to knock it off his face, and then two more times against his skull. The guy stopped moving. He wasn't surprised when no Quasing left the man's body. The Genjix didn't assign Quasing to scrub missions. Even if it had been a host, though, Roen didn't care. Most Quasing would only move into an enemy's body as a last resort. Joining with someone from the opposite faction was practically suicide.

Gasping for air, Roen pulled the body up in front of him as more bullets flew at him. He grabbed the assault rifle, noting its strange make and model, and then returned fire. After his magazine ran out, he dug through the man's pockets to find more magazines, and then continued to pick off the shadows one by one. The battle seemed to go on forever, until finally there was a lull, the echo of the last round hanging in the air.

"Roen," Marco's voice pierced the calm. "You alive, old boy?"

"I think so." Roen peered over the bullet-riddled body he was using as cover and watched as Marco came out from behind the car and checked the bodies. He scampered to his feet and made his way back down the slope.

Marco was checking the Oldsmobile when he got down there. He looked over at Roen and shook his head. "Hurley died in the crash, and Ines took one in the chest during the exchange."

Roen slammed the rifle on the ground. "Damn it!"

He had feared that one of his people might not make

it out of this ambush alive, but losing both hurt. Badly. It had been years since he had lost an agent, and it still tore at him just as much as the first time.

"Come on," Marco said. "We have to get going. How far are we from town?"

"Five, maybe ten klicks. By the way…" Roen picked up the rifle again and tossed it to Marco, who flipped it over and studied the markings. "Chinese CS variants. Interpol in the US uses M variants."

Marco grimaced. "Genjix, and they knew we were coming. We have a leak somewhere."

Roen's blood froze at those words. Jill and Cameron's well-being immediately came to mind. All it would take is one dropped word or a giveaway, and they could have the IXTF or the Genjix at their door. Images of the IXTF hauling Jill away and putting Cameron in… where do they take host children? It wouldn't be juvenile detention, would it? Certainly not the black ops alien containment prisons that were rumored to be all over the country. He was only a kid! Roen's hands balled into fists.

Marco gestured at the bodies. "Come on, grab our gear and get our friends out. I want them buried by dawn. We've got a bit of walking to do. I want to be in town by first light. Let's move."

CHAPTER TWELVE
FEDERAL ASSEMBLY

From the Persian Empire, the cradle of civilization, I moved west to Greece through a satrap, a Persian governor. It was my vessel who negotiated the alliance with Sparta, shifting the balance of the war from Athens to the Peloponnesian League and escalating the conflict. It was also there that my satrap vessel was assassinated for being a Persian spy.

I stayed in the region for nearly five hundred years, studying human philosophy, culture, and government until a new opportunity arose. I moved further west and joined with several other Quasing as they began to expand their influence from a new empire based in Rome.

Zoras

"Finland can get quite cold," Vitaliy Laminick mused as Enzo laid out his offer. "And you only offer me the northernmost province. Lapland feels…" he held his hands out in a shrug, "…not enticing. Beautiful, yes, but lacking in useful resources, and I already experience enough harsh winters here in Russia."

Enzo personally adored Finland and thought the land

not only beautiful, but its residents easy to manage. However, when it came to its climate, the country did tend toward the cooler end of the scale.

However, Vitaliy, though on the Federation Council, was not one of the more prominent members in the upper house, and Enzo would be damned if he was going to offer him prized real estate near the Mediterranean. Those parcels were reserved for important people. Besides, Lapland was a relatively large territory. Who did this human think he was?

Dangle the carrot. Vitaliy carries six, but has some influence over a larger caucus. Possibly twenty. That would be significant.

"There is some flexibility, Councilor." Enzo leaned back, legs crossed as he drank his tea. "However, I am told you can bring six votes. Show me you can bring me more, and I can definitely see opportunities for... an upgrade."

Vitaliy stiffened. "One vote or six or fifty. I am a member of the upper house."

Massage his ego a little harder, but offer a threat.

Enzo wiped his hands and stood up. "You are an important man, Mr Laminick, but you are an important man among many hundreds of important men. Your support will be appreciated and rewarded, but know that there are others who would gladly take your place and reap the rewards I offer. Think it over." Enzo stood up. Just like that, the meeting was over. Vitaliy looked like he was about to protest, hoping to finagle a final concession, then, reluctantly, he stood up as well.

When the councilor left the room, Enzo allowed his body to slump a little. This was draining. He had spent the entire day speaking with over two dozen members from both houses of the Federal Assembly. These small, near-sighted men wanted small things for their support: money, land, positions. Most, Enzo was happy to offer, though he had to be careful about how much he conceded.

Once Quasiform was in play, these small materialistic desires would be worthless. However, he needed their support first, and he certainly could not offer them all the same thing. If they were ever to compare notes, his takeover of Russia would fall over like a house of cards. If one got the scent of what another was offered, it could throw the entire negotiations into disarray. In truth, it didn't matter what any of these fools received in the end. So, as painful as it was for him, he would have to play these silly games. For now.

"Is there anyone else?"

Azumi looked down at her notes. "You had three cancellations. Tachkin from illness, but Polanski and Maximov abruptly at the last minute. I think Vinnick may have gotten to them first. I will check my sources and confirm."

Enzo nodded. He picked a pear up off the table and bit into it. He hadn't eaten since breakfast and his finely-tuned body wasn't happy. He had been neglecting it as of late, something he would have to rectify. He wished he could focus his time on real battles instead of these games. It was his duty as a vessel to maintain it for his Holy One.

One battle won in these halls is worth ten on the field.

Enzo gritted his teeth. That much was true, as much as he detested the fact. Once he established control over the world, he intended to end all political bickering, not that it would happen for much longer. Quasiform was at hand and would usher the end and the beginning of everything.

"All right, then," he said, "I want a fresh report on my desk by tonight with new trajectories. Put Polanski and Maximov on the list for blackmail or extermination. Verify first. With Tachkin, send him a request to reschedule. If he refuses, put him on the list as well. Let's get out of this cesspool."

Enzo left the room with his honor guard in tow. A full twenty of his Hatchery siblings – all vessels – spread out before him as he walked down the hallways of the Federal Assembly building. The usually crowded corridors were deserted. Everyone in the building, from the Chairman to the janitor, knew who he was and stayed out of his way.

As his group turned the corner, they were met by another group coming from the other end of the hall. A group of suited men, Epsilons by the look of them, surrounded an old frail man in a wheelchair. Azumi tensed and jumped in front of him, gun drawn out. The rest of his siblings closed ranks.

Enzo took a quick inventory. Approximately forty Epsilons to his twenty-one Hatchery-trained vessels. He held the advantage. No matter how well-trained Epsilons were, they were no match for vessels from the Hatchery. The narrow hallway would prevent Vinnick from utilizing his superior numbers as well.

He was waiting for you. Do not fight on your opponent's chosen field.

"Fuck Sun Tzu. I can end this bastard now."

Vinnick has obviously come to you. He would not accompany an ambush. Also, look at who is standing next to him. This is not a battle worth waging. Show him who is in control.

Enzo put a hand on Azumi's shoulder and gently nudged her aside. He took two steps forward and spoke in a loud voice. "You wish to talk now, old man? Now is your last chance."

The Epsilons standing in front of Vinnick parted, and one of the Epsilons – no, Sergii, Vinnick's adopted son and heir to his fortune – wheeled the man forward. Sergii was an Adonis Vessel from a previous generation and had spent the past twenty years waiting for the old man to die. He wondered about the Adonis's loyalty. If he was truly a Genjix, he would slit Vinnick's throat at this very moment. Sergii came to the middle of the hall, dividing the two groups, then he walked back to the group of tense Epsilons alone. Vinnick sat in the middle of the hallway waiting for Enzo to meet him halfway.

Enzo considered forcing the old man to come to him, but decided against it. After all, he could still show that he was the more magnanimous one in this conflict. Enzo walked forward until the two of them were face to face.

"You've aged some, boy," were Vinnick's first word.

"You're one to talk, brother," he replied.

Vinnick cackled. "When you get to be my age, you can say whatever you want." He motioned to his left.

Enzo looked and saw an open door leading to a courtyard. Obviously, this entire thing had been set up by Vinnick, just like the assassination attempt at the church. First things first, Enzo reached out and touched Vinnick's hand.

Flua is there.

Enzo drew his pistol, ignoring the tense movements of Vinnick's men down the hall, and jammed it into the base of the old man's neck. "Now I'm ready to talk."

Vinnick chuckled. "Do you think threatening someone my age with death actually means anything? Put the gun away. You're not going to need it. Why don't we take a stroll through the courtyard?"

Calculated. He wants you to know that he does not care about his welfare. He wants you to turn down this opportunity to talk. He is playing for sympathies from the rest of the Council.

"He tried to kill me the last time!"

You had set draconian terms previously. I warned you not to push your demands too far. The others on the Council took note.

And now he was pushing the old man into the courtyard, an area of his choosing. What would others think of this photo op? It would show Enzo serving Vinnick. Enzo squeezed the handles of the wheelchair tightly; his knuckles drained of blood. Again, outmaneuvered. Well, the trap has been sprung, and now he couldn't back out. Doing so would paint him afraid and insecure with his position. He had survived one of Vinnick's traps; he could survive another.

Enzo nodded to Azumi and wheeled Vinnick into the outdoor area. No doubt Vinnick had snipers at some of the windows. By now, Palos was having his people sweep the rooms. They entered a garden that had two cobbled paths intersecting in the middle. At the center of the courtyard was another small round table with one chair. There were settings for two and a steaming pot of tea welcoming them.

Tea; of course there would be tea. Enzo pushed Vinnick to one end and sat down at the opposite end. He reached out and picked up the teapot, first serving Vinnick a cupful and then pouring his own. Then he waited. The two sat in silence, neither moving as their stares became a contest of will. Ten minutes passed with neither taking any initiative.

Finally, Enzo gestured. "Your tea is getting cold, brother."

Vinnick smirked, picked up his cup with shaking hands, and took a sip. He placed the cup hard on the table, making a loud cracking sound and sloshing some of the liquid out. "There you go. Happy?"

Enzo smiled and took a sip. "I was just respecting my elders."

"I've seen firsthand how you've shown respect over the past ten years, boy. If you had only followed the natural order within the Council, things might have ended differently. Instead, you barged in like a bull and tried to run everyone over. So let's get down to business. What do you really want?"

"You've had a long and illustrious reign on the Council. You've served the Holy Ones well. Mostly. Why don't you retire to a nice villa in Nice or Belize? Call it a career."

"And let you slide right in here, eh?" Vinnick chortled. "Take control of my domain? Put a puppet on the Council who agrees with everything you say?"

"I'm sure the rest of the Council can find someone suitable to replace you," Enzo said. "I'm willing to offer very generous terms for your graceful exit."

"All right," Vinnick sighed. "Let's hear your shit."

Enzo placed his cup down on the table. "Let's begin with your robust estate. Allow me to compliment you on your financial health. I am prepared to offer you five million Euros to settle you into a life of comfort for the rest of your days."

"Five million?" Vinnick looked incredulous. "You're offering me five million of my own money out of my four billion net worth?"

"Well, you won't need it for much longer. The funds would be put to much better use in the service of the Holy Ones and Quasiform."

"Yes, Quasiform. We barely have enough catalyst facilities

for Quasiform. There is still much work to be done before the world is ready. Why not build a few more for redundancy in case a few fail or fall into enemy hands? This world will be ready for Quasiform in a generation or two, but not now."

Enzo scoffed. "Unacceptable. The critical path is the rods, not the facilities. Redundancy is meaningless if the supply of rods is insufficient. Not to mention the cost of building the facilities. It would be wasted billions. Also, if I may remind you, brother, time *is* running out. That so-called Interpol Extraterrestrial Task Force has been mostly incompetent until now, but they are getting their act together and getting organized. Every year, they grow stronger and bolder."

Vinnick waved that off. "The IXTF will end up like the United Nations. Impotent and useless. There is nothing to worry about from those fools."

"I feel you are wrong about this. It's only a matter of time before they discover our plans. If we do not start a world war and initiate Quasiform within the next decade, we will be found out and won't be in a position to protect our interests. We cannot afford to dawdle much longer."

"Still in such a hurry to blow the world up." Vinnick shook his head and picked his teacup up again. "Several of the leadership feel more loyalty havens are needed to ease the transition when the transformation begins. Otherwise, there will be dissension in the ranks."

Enzo sniffed dismissively. "You must know this is a non-starter, but let's talk this out."

Enzo detested the concept of loyalty havens. It was a recent concept that had sprung up from many of the lesser believers, if they could even be called believers at all. Self-serving bastards, more like it. They should be embracing Quasiform and the new Holy Ones home world. Instead, these petty Genjix, who had probably only joined the cause for selfish reasons, weren't prepared to face the destiny the Holy Ones had always intended.

These havens were proposed ten years ago by several on the Council, when the inevitability of Quasiform within the next half-century became clear. The proposal had quickly gained popularity among the unblessed ranks, as well as a large percentage of the vessels. After all, why wouldn't they? It would give loyal humans and vessels the ability to survive through the Quasiforming of Earth into the new Quasing homeland. From a practical standpoint, it made sense, except for those who did not embrace the change.

Enzo was vehemently against building havens. He considered them outright sacrilege. What sort of true believer would beg to delay Heaven in order for human bodies to survive longer? It would be like Christians refusing the Rapture, or the ancient Vikings refusing to enter the halls of Valhalla. All true Genjix should embrace their bodily deaths as Quasiform takes over the planet and ushers in a new beautiful world where the souls of the blessed and the Holy Ones stand side by side in harmony and peace. Because at his core, Enzo was a man of peace and pursued this vision of paradise for the good of all.

Your devotion is to be commended, but I would not go that far.

"When there is no one else left to fight, then there will be nothing left but peace."

In the end, Enzo suffered a rare defeat on the Council, and the Genjix began Operation Gardens of Eden, a hundred-billion-dollar waste of time and resources. Since then, twenty-seven of these havens had sprung up, with the total capacity of safekeeping forty percent of all the existing Genjix. And because Vinnick himself put much of his fortune on it, the entire project fell directly under his control.

There was a political consequence to the project that Enzo had not foreseen. Since Vinnick was in control of all the havens, he was the one who determined which haven was allocated to which Council member. This had greatly raised his standing with all of the Genjix.

The political fallout from that battle had heavily hurt Enzo. It was a direct slap in the face that he, the councilman with the largest faction, currently had only one haven under his control, while all the others had several. Vinnick himself had ten. Many had rushed to curry the Russian's favor, which made the Council Power Struggle even more difficult for Enzo than it had to be. In fact, he attributed Vinnick holding on to power for this long to that one crushing defeat. If it hadn't been for the loyalty haven project, the old man would have been finished five years ago.

It didn't bother Enzo that he was only allocated one haven. In fact, he had no intention of using it, nor would he allow any of his faction to delay their ascension. It was for their own good. One positive that came out of all of this was that now he knew who the true believers were and who was just riding the coat-tails of the Holy Ones for personal profit and gain. He reminded himself that once the Quasiform cycle began and could not be stopped, he would turn his attention inward and root out all the weak-willed and non-believers. In the end, only the pure would witness the final ascension.

Moving the conversation to these havens set the tone for the rest of their negotiations. Enzo knew why people who were in no position to negotiate still tried, but he never understood why they almost inevitably felt insulted when he didn't budge. Whoever said a good agreement was a compromise neither side was completely happy with just had poor negotiators. For Enzo, the only time to bargain was when there was only one resolution. Everything else was details.

Unfortunately, Vinnick didn't see things the right way. After an hour, the old man broke it off. "As expected, you've wasted my time, boy," he said as he motioned for Sergii to come retrieve him. As Sergii wheeled Vinnick backward out of the courtyard, the old man stopped and looked back. "I gave you one chance to talk sense, and you blew it. You want Russia, you little prick. You come fucking take it from me."

CHAPTER THIRTEEN
TEENAGE LIFE

Quasar is a living being. The planet itself is not alive, but the entire surface is interconnected as if it is a giant organism, with shared memories and experiences from billions of voices and minds mingling at all times.

It is that whole, that collective, those trillions upon trillions of Quasing merged together that allows us to evolve and advance, and eventually seek destiny beyond the boundaries of our planet and our solar system.

Tao

Cameron, wake up.

Cameron was out of bed before Tao finished the sentence, moving confidently in the dark. The sun had not risen yet, and the woods outside looked as pitch dark as they had when he had gone to bed just a few short hours ago. His window shutters rattled from a light breeze, but other than that, the entire house was still. Those signals told Cameron all he needed to know about what to wear this morning. He brushed his teeth, slipped on a long-sleeve shirt and running pants, and was out the door within two minutes.

To his surprise, his mother was still in bed. He tapped the door twice and walked in.

Give her one nudge and then let her sleep. She has had a lot on her plate lately; she deserves the rest.

"Mom," he whispered.

She reached under her pillow. He knew she kept a pistol stuck to the wall behind the mattress. She had one in the drawer of the nightstand too, and a knife wrapped inside the pillow as well. Dad, on the other hand, was armed to the teeth. Cameron and Mom used to joke that he could accidentally discharge a shotgun if he just rolled in his sleep.

Both parents had worried about having so many guns around him when he was young and considered removing them entirely from the house. It took Tao, controlling a four year-old child, giving them an hour-long lecture exhibiting how much influence he had over Cameron before they acquiesced. They were in the middle of a war, after all.

His mother yawned. "Oh, yeah, I promised, didn't I?"

"If you need rest..."

"No, no." She sat up. "I could use the workout."

A few minutes later, they were stretching against the wooden fence leading down to the main road. She wore several layers of clothing that covered every part of her body except for her face. She looked disapprovingly at his thin long-sleeve shirt and running pants.

"You'll catch a cold."

"You'll overheat," he responded.

She chuckled. "I don't know how hard you think I'm actually going to go. I'm just here to instruct."

You have two hours. Make the most of them.

They started jogging down the dirt road leading into the forest. Once they reached the wooded area, Jill tapped Cameron on the shoulder. "Tag, you're it."

She took off, barreling through the thickets and hurdling over logs, weaving in and out of tree trunks. He gave chase, following her not at a direct angle, but just a bit off to the side. The truth was, he was much faster than she was these days and could catch her within thirty paces. However, this was an old game and easily one of his favorite pastimes. It wouldn't be right if he spoiled it too quickly.

Adjust to the elevation.

Cameron watched the dip as his mother jumped feet first into a ditch, only looking at the ground while she was in the air. She bounded to the side right as she landed, turning sharply away from him. He switched angles to follow. She grabbed a tree branch overhead and flipped herself smoothly onto it, then disappeared behind the trunk. He followed her up, but by the time he got onto the branch and looked around, he had somehow lost her. It took him a second to locate her again, but, by that time, she was already several meters away, running in another direction.

Seems Jill still has tricks up her sleeves. Careful with the soft mud on the right.

Cameron leaped off the high branch and rolled out of his landing. Within seconds, he had split the distance between them. One moment, he was twenty meters behind her. The next, she had disappeared again. Cameron maintained his trajectory for another fifteen meters before he came to a stop and listened. Nothing.

Watch out!

It was too late. Jill, lying in wait on the ground, tapped

him on the foot with her hand imitating the shape of a pistol. "Bang." Grinning, she tousled his hair as he helped her up. She held up one finger and then took off again.

Cameron gave her the requisite five seconds before going after her. This time, she headed toward Melon Hill, a series of mossy boulders and rises that looked like a giant watermelon patch. She scaled a boulder twice her height in two bounds and disappeared over the top. Cameron followed, taking a few more tries to claw up before he was able to get a solid handhold on the ledge.

"Use angles, dear," she called to him. "You went a little too vertical that time." Then she jumped off another boulder and was gone.

Use your core muscles more when you lift your feet.

Cameron leaped from boulder to boulder and ran parallel to her as she dove around the side of an old collapsed stone wall. He took three big jumps across two rocks and a hill, and landed on the wall. Again, she had disappeared.

"I think she's cheating," he said, perplexed.

Did Jill invent an invisibility cloak in her spare time?

He sped down the length of the wall, balancing on its narrow ledge. He still didn't see her. He backtracked. "Where the hell did she go?"

Watch the language. I promised your dad. Here's a clue. Look at the ground.

Cameron noticed it a second later. There was a footprint in the mud. He jumped down and checked the bushes. A pebble bounced off his shoulder. He spun around and saw Mom coming out of the opposite bush on the trail, a ghillie cover wrapped around her shoulder. She held up two fingers.

"You did cheat!"

She shrugged, a smile from ear to ear. "I'm triple your age. I'm allowed to cheat."

She has a point. There is no such thing in reality as fair play.

They continued the game for another hour. Jill was able to rack up a four-to-one advantage before she began to tire. Cameron was eventually able to catch up before they finally took a break. Next, she worked on his balance, both on his feet and while standing on his hands. She had him jump from rock to rock, always landing on only one foot. Then, she had him do handstands while on the stone wall, knocking one of his hands off, forcing him to quickly shift his weight.

By the time they were done, he was exhausted. Cameron looked at his mom as they walked back toward the farmhouse. Even at her age, she was able to keep pace with him. How could he ever fight the Genjix? He felt that he should have put up a better fight. His frustration boiled up. He didn't feel that he had improved much over the past six months.

She is in her forties. Hardly an advanced age.

"Well, relative to me. I should be in my prime."

You are fifteen. Easily ten to fifteen more years before your prime.

He wasn't convinced, though. He would have to just practice harder.

Maybe your father is right. I put so many expectations on you. I am pushing you too hard.

"Obviously not hard enough. I suck."

You are starting to sound like your father more and more every day. Have a pity-party on your own time.

"Has Roen called in?" he asked.

She shook her head, looking a little distracted. "Not yet. Your father should have reached Ontario by now. I'm surprised he hasn't pinged me yet. I'm sure he's just running a little late." She emphasized the "your father" part of her sentence. He took the hint.

"Mom, why does Dad push me so hard but doesn't want me to join the Prophus?"

She sighed. "Your father has a very complicated relationship with all this." She gestured all around them and then tapped his forehead. "Especially that alien in you."

"He doesn't like Tao?"

"Oh, he loves Tao. He had always just hoped for something more for you than becoming an agent."

"Well, it's not his decision."

She nodded. "That's true. It's yours. Or is it Tao's? In either case, his way of coping with your becoming an agent is to either make you the best agent possible, or dissuade you from becoming one altogether. Why do you think he bought you that cello?"

"I'm tone deaf."

"Yes, dear, we are all painfully, painfully aware of that."

They reached the house and Cameron rushed upstairs to wash off the grime. If he could get ready in the next twenty minutes, he could take the bus for once. He had tried to skip the shower, but Jill would have none of that. He guessed it was for the better. Most of the other kids thought he was weird already. Stinking up the class wasn't going to earn him any more points. He rushed through the shower, and then rushed out, throwing on whatever clothes he had readily at hand. He came down with five minutes to spare and saw Mom staring out the window, coffee in hand.

"Okay, I'll see you tonight." He hesitated. "Mom? Everything all right?"

She tore her gaze away from the window. "Have a good day, Cam."

Something has happened to Roen. Press her on it.

"What is it?" Cameron asked.

"It's nothing."

"I'm old enough now."

Jill hesitated, and then exhaled before finally speaking. "A forest ranger found a bullet-riddled Oldsmobile on fire off the side of the road."

Check for bodies.

Cameron's heart skipped a beat. "Did they find anyone inside?"

She shook her head. "No. They also noted that someone had built a fire ring around the car."

The site has been cleaned. The Genjix.

"We have to find him and Uncle Marco."

She shook her head. "I don't have anyone to spare at the moment. I just... I just have to trust that your father is all right."

Cameron felt his heart slam against his ribcage, as if it was trying to break through his chest. His legs buckled, but Jill caught him before he could sit down on the floor. She looked at him with a renewed intensity. "Your father is fine, and you are going to school. Do you understand?"

"But Dad..."

"I will not operate under the assumption that my husband is dead until I have proof. For now, we have jobs to do. Yours is to go to school."

"No way!"

"Tao, talk some sense into him."

She is right. Anything could have happened. No need to jump to conclusions. A good agent continues his mission no matter what the cost.

"Get your butt to school, young man," she said, grabbing him by the arm and leading him to the door. She looked up at the clock. "You've missed the bus. Bike to school and then bike straight home. I don't want to get a call from Ms Federlin that you were late. Do you understand?" Then she pushed him so hard toward the door he stumbled.

Stone-faced and numb, Cameron turned around and looked at his mother. "Will you... at least let me know if you hear anything? I need to know."

She shook her head. "Your mission today, as a Prophus agent, is to go to school. I will update you when you've completed your assignment and are safely home. Not before."

Cameron curled his hands into fists. He felt his eyes well with moisture and his vision swim. "That's so messed up. He's my father!"

Jill kicked him out of the house before he could protest any further.

She is right. Otherwise, you will waste the entire day waiting for that message. Nothing you do right now will make a difference. Go to class. It is too early to panic. Now! Start moving your feet, Cameron Tan.

The rest of the day was a haze. He received a B+ on his History test, his first this year, but he didn't care. He walked through the hallways like a zombie, numb and oblivious to what was happening around him. He didn't notice the usual glances or the snarky laughs. When a group of the football jocks called him names, it didn't register. All Cameron could think about was whether his father was alive or dead.

Cameron was sure this wasn't the first time his father had been in danger. After all, the two of them had taken down the remnants of an IXTF squad just the other day. However, this was the first time that he could remember being unsure of Roen's wellbeing. In all the previous missions, it had never even occurred to him that his father could have been injured or killed. Maybe it was because he was too young to realize it, maybe he thought his father was invincible, or maybe now that it had actually happened, all of a sudden it felt far too real. The waves of worry and fear were overwhelming.

Cameron, get ahold of yourself. Jumping to conclusions is the fastest way to drive yourself insane. What do I always tell you about intel?

"Three times a lady."

Once you know she exists. Twice she has your attention. Three times a lady. Wait for confirmation of facts or lack of facts, and determine actionable items before you start to panic.

"I can't help it, Tao. I can't stop feeling this way. He's my dad."

If it helps, I am concerned as well. Roen is more than a friend to me.

"I don't know how to deal with this."

Focus on what you can control, and trust that your Roen is all right. In fact, I am sure he is.

"Really?"

Of course. I trained him.

Cameron was in gym class, standing far back in the outfield. No one ever hit the ball this far. It afforded him the privacy he needed to process all the conflicting emotions and try to tame his out-of-control imagination visualizing his father dying in a ditch or a prisoner of the

Genjix. A hundred scenarios ran through his head, each one worse than the previous.

"Hey, Tan, heads up. Stop screwing around!" a voice yelled.

He looked up just in time to see a pop ball fly toward him. It made a lazy arc toward the center of the field. If he had been paying attention, he could have run and caught it. Heck, if he tried now, he might still be able to. However, this stupid gym class game was the last thing he could give a crap about. He stood there while the ball bounced off the grass and rolled toward the wall.

"You suck, Tan!" someone catcalled.

"Get your head out of your ass!" someone else joined in.

"Fucking loser!"

"Watch your mouth," Coach Wannsik yelled. He looked over at Cameron. "Get the ball, Cameron. You're not here to daydream."

Cameron saw the white baseball poking out of the grass. What was he doing here anyway? This was all so stupid. His dad was missing! He had the urge to just walk away or kick the damn thing or throw it out of the field.

You are better than this. Get a hold of yourself. Find the calm.

Cameron closed his eyes and breathed. In. Out. Like how Tao had taught him, he tried to keep his wild emotions present, embraced them even, but still tried to find that calmness. Controlled. Manageable. This time, it didn't work. He snarled and stomped to the ball. He picked it up and hurled it as hard as he could back at the group of students. The ball traveled long and fast, easily reaching the home base and bouncing off the back fence. Well, no one said his aim had to be good.

Nice throw.

"I surprise myself."

Throwing a ball is nothing more than good t'ai chi.

"I could kind of see that."

The rest of his day flashed by. All he could think of was getting home for some news about Roen. It wasn't fair that Mom wouldn't let him know. What if she had heard something by now? She was wrong. He deserved to know right when she found out. Well, nothing he could do about it now. He had to get home.

After the last bell rang, Cameron hurried to his locker and ran through the gym toward his bike. He bet he could cover the forty-minute ride in fifteen if he pushed himself. He nearly bowled over Coach Wannsik on his way out.

"Hang on," Wannsik said, blocking his way. "Watch where you're going, son. You're going to hurt someone. Hey, Cameron, that's quite an arm you have there."

Cameron's first two impulses were either to shout at Wannsik to get out of his way or to just bowl him over.

If I was cruel, I would teach you a hard lesson right now about spiting yourself with stupidity. However, knowing this situation, my advice would be to speak softly. Anything else will simply delay your trip home.

"Thanks, Coach," Cameron said breathily. He tried to find the calm. Embrace it. Squeeze the calm. Truth was, he wanted to tear that damn calm apart into little pieces and stomp on it. However, he bit his lip and flashed Wannsik a smile.

"Why don't you try out for the baseball team? With an arm like that, with a little work on control, we can use that. You know, a lot of Division One schools offer great..."

Cameron stood there for five minutes as Wannsik

continued on about the merits of college scholarships. That wait hurt him worse than the one time Roen broke his collarbone when he was twelve years old in a freak sparring accident. Finally, when the coach was done with his sell, Cameron politely declined and bolted for the sports field.

When he got to the bicycle racks, he unlocked and pulled his bike out of the rack, and jumped on. He had already begun pedaling when he realized that something was wrong. He looked down; his tire was flat. He looked behind him. Both of them were.

Cameron jumped off and checked the treads. Someone had slashed them. With a snarl, he threw the bike to the side. Several mocking barks came from the field and he saw a group of those jocks laughing. He began to stomp toward them.

No, Cameron.

"I'm sick of them. I'm going to teach them who they're messing with. I'm going to break –"

No. You will not.

"They've been picking on me since I moved here. I'm going to make sure they never pick on me again!"

You are more powerful than they. Direct your power up, not down.

"It's not fair!"

Things rarely are, son. You have more important things to deal with right now.

Cameron shot them one more glare and stomped back to his bike. He picked it up and threw the frame over his shoulder. If he ran the entire time, he could make it back in about two hours. Three, maybe, with this bike.

Behind him, he heard those jerks throw more insults

his way, taunting him with chicken noises and baby crying sounds. God, with humans like these, it sometimes made him want to be a Genjix.

Stop! You will take that thought back, Cameron Tan.

"Like hell I will, Tao. Those fucking kids are the scum of the Earth."

Do not judge an entire species based on the actions of their worst few. That is the trait of the Genjix. The Prophus choose to look at the best of humanity. That is our difference. If you cannot learn this, then you cannot be my host. And watch your language; I promised your father.

At that moment, no matter how hard Cameron tried, he couldn't stop it. He began to cry. Tears streamed down his face as he lugged the bike over his shoulder and jogged home. He was so embarrassed; he probably looked ridiculous too.

It is all right, Cameron. There is nothing wrong with what you're feeling, though you are right about one thing.

Cameron sniffled. "Right about what?"

You do look a little ridiculous.

Cameron caught himself chuckling in spite of how he felt. A little of the pressure bottled up in his chest was let out. "You're supposed to make me feel better, not worse."

I know. I sometimes suck at this job. Now, get home and see if we can find some good news about your father. How fast can you run?

CHAPTER FOURTEEN
ONTARIO OREGON

Timestamp: 2712

Before the ESA passed, the Prophus depended on commercial air transportation to move around the world. We were getting our butts kicked financially, politically, and literally, so Command had decided to scrap our meager fleet and fly everyone coach.

Luckily for us, that crappy law damaged the Genjix far more than it did us. Ironically, as much as we despise it, it probably saved the Earth from total destruction.

Roen and Marco must have looked like a dirty pair of homeless hitchhikers by the time they limped out of the mountains to the outskirts of Ontario, Oregon. It had taken them a lot longer to cover those ten kilometers than they had originally planned. Both of them suffered several minor and not-so-minor bumps and bruises from rolling down the hill in the car. Fortunately for them, the antique heavy steel-framed Oldsmobile was built like a tank, and they had come out of the accident a little better than the casual observer would have expected just by looking at the wreckage.

Burying Ines and Hurley was a no-brainer. Neither Roen nor Marco even considered leaving their comrades unburied. Still, it took three hours to dig the two plots with their entrenching tools, so they didn't start on their journey to town until well past dawn. Roen had wanted to call Jill, but both of them had had to go dark. Between the NSA, IXTF, and now confirmed Genjix involvement in this area, any use of a cell phone or Internet was an invitation to have a SWAT team knocking at the door. The only way to safely contact her was to utilize the crypto key, and they couldn't do that until they set everything up and got on-line.

What compounded the difficulty of their journey was the fifty kilos of gear they carried on their backs. Marco had insisted they bring all the weapons and ammunition they had had with them, and Roen did the same with the medical supplies and the cash. In the end, they decided to just suck it up and bring everything. Add the thick forest, the rugged terrain, and Mother Nature deciding to toss in a shower to boot, the two made a pair of miserable-looking dogs by the time they reached the Mountain Border Roadside Inn.

Roen checked in at the front desk where a bored attendant handed him two sets of keys. He paid with cash and came out a few minutes later to see Marco staring disapprovingly at the entire establishment. The motel was just a run-down two-story building with doors opening out to a parking lot through balcony hallways. The awning was a combination of lime green and brown, and the building looked like it was designed sometime in the early seventies to serve as a drug or prostitution house that charged by the hour.

"Well, it was only thirty bucks a night," Roen said when he noticed Marco's scowl.

"Thank goodness Mum isn't alive to see this." Marco shook his head. He held out his hand. "Very well, give me my keys. Were you able to get us adjacent rooms at least?"

Roen made a face. This might get a little ugly. "Well, actually, we're in the same room. It's a queen-sized bed, though." If his heart had been any weaker, the look Marco gave him might have struck him dead.

The Brit's face turned red and his eyes went all sorts of stormy as he threw his four bags over his shoulder, walked five steps away from Roen down the side of the building, and kicked the ugly brown-and-green brick wall. He walked another few steps, and then repeated the action. Again, Roen wasn't sure if he should be more insulted or amused by Marco's reaction to being stuck with him. In this case, he decided to be amused, so he grinned as he trailed after the pouting Englishman.

Roen had specifically asked for the upstairs corner unit. It offered them some privacy, though he was fairly confident anyone who patronized this establishment would probably prefer to keep to themselves anyway. More importantly, this unit offered them multiple exit points for a quick escape.

The two settled into their new room, negotiated sleeping arrangements – Roen left side, Marco right – and then he set up shop while Marco hopped in the shower. This was when he found his new Marco pet peeve: the guy liked to take long showers. Thirty minutes after he came in, after Roen had finished doing all the work breaking down and taking inventory of their supplies, Marco came out of the bathroom dripping wet with a towel around his waist. He began to comb his hair.

"You might want to hold off a bit, chum," he said. "I think they're out of hot water."

Roen, with the mud on his outer layer now caked dry, but his underwear still soaked through from the rain, took in a deep breath and counted down from fifty-one. Long gone were the days when it took him less than a minute to keep his cool. And when it came to Marco, his countdown might have to go into three digits. At this point, he could smell himself, he was so dirty.

Eventually, though, he got his shower in and came out looking like a civilized human being again, though they did have to wash their clothes in the communal washer and dryer before they had anything to wear. They had decided a few hours into their walk that they needed to unload some of their luggage. After some negotiations, they finally agreed that their spare clothing was the most logical choice. Now, with one change of clothes and down two operatives, they were finally ready to begin their mission. First things first, though.

Roen opened the duffel bag with the comm units and scowled. "We have a problem." He held up a small bullet-ridden bag. Inside, the crypto key had broken in two.

"We need to re-establish communication with Command another way, then," Marco said. "It'll be a problem getting in touch with the scout team as well."

"I think food is the more pressing matter at the moment," Roen said. "We haven't eaten in a whole day."

"See if we can find an up-to-date map of the town," Marco continued. "The scout team should have left markings in case of this happening."

"Food is more important," Roen repeated.

"I'll look into finding a secondary base of operations as well. There's no way we can run this from a sex motel."

"But first food. Really, I'm starving."

"And maybe buy a change of clothes," Marco said.

"Food. Food. Food, before I chew your arm off." Roen pounded a fist on the bed. He was not ashamed to admit he got petulant when hungry.

Marco looked over at Roen as if he had just noticed him talking. "Well yes, dinner would be fantastic as well. I'm quite famished."

"I'm going hunting," Roen growled, heading toward the door. "I think I saw a General Tso's Chinese restaurant and a convenience store across the street."

"Try not to get anything with MSG," Marco called after him. "It gives me indigestion."

Roen didn't bother looking back as he raised his hand and gave Marco the middle finger. Twenty minutes later, after being tortured by the aroma of his cooking take-out, Roen came back with a pile of food. He plopped the five containers on the table and begun to dig through them.

Marco, sitting on the bed, going through a map of the town he had found, looked up, puzzled. "Are we expecting guests?"

Roen ignored him and began to shovel the Singapore noodles into his mouth with a pair of chopsticks. He picked up a box of General Tso's chicken – their specialty, unsurprisingly – and unfolded the container into a plate. Then Roen busted out a twelve-pack of beer and tossed Marco a can. The two ate in silence for the next fifteen minutes, polishing off two beers apiece.

"You know," Marco said, tossing an empty box into the

garbage can. "This Tso chap makes a damn tasty dish. He must have been a fine soldier."

Roen spoke with his mouth full as he kept stuffing himself to make up for a day of not eating. "Pretty sure this dish was invented in New York City. Besides, I didn't know a general's skill was reflected by the dishes named after him. That would make Napoleon a great general."

"Napoleon *was* a great general, one of the finest in history."

Roen grunted. "That's not what Tao told me."

"That's because Tao's host, Lafayette, hated Napoleon's guts. Oh, trust me, Ahngr was there. He saw firsthand. Anyway," Marco said, standing up, "now that your stomach has had its fill, let's get down to business. We have to assume that all communication and Internet usage has a higher possibility of being monitored. The only crypto key available is with the scout team. But we can't contact them without a key.

"First thing tomorrow, head to the main streets and look for any IXTF or Penetra patrols. Keep an eye out for Prophus scout team markings. I don't know what dozen they're rotating through, but you should be able to catch the signals."

Roen looked dubious. "That's the plan? You want me to walk around town all day until I find something?"

Marco nodded. "No one said you have to walk. Go purchase a vehicle if you like." He pulled out some cash and tossed it on the bed.

Roen picked it up and counted through it. "Five hundred bucks? What kind of car do you think I can buy with five bills?"

"No one said it had to be a car. You seem like a fellow

who can make a dollar stretch."

"Well, what are you going to do then?"

"The thing I know you positively can't be trusted with," Marco sniffed. "I'm going to buy us some clothes."

The next morning, right after sunrise, following a breakfast of leftover Chinese food, Marco and Roen headed to town. Their sleep the night before had been both blissful and uncomfortable. Blissful in that it was the first time either had slept in over twenty-four hours. Uncomfortable in that Marco liked to roll around in his sleep, and that he was a hugger.

Roen woke up to find the Englishman draped over him. It made for a very unsettling morning, especially knowing that they were probably stuck in the same bed for the immediate future. He thought about putting a rifle down between them, but decided against it, given neither of them were small men, and bed real estate was at a premium. It was just going to have to be a burden he had to live with.

They reached the outskirts of town and split up, Marco to shop for clothes and groceries, and Roen to explore Ontario and search for the scout team. They had decided that with the threat of the Genjix and IXTF, Roen should be the one to do most of the work around town, since getting dinged by a Penetra net was a very real possibility here.

The first thing he intended to do was buy a car. Somewhere in this small town, someone must be selling a car for cheap. Roen had two thousand dollars in cash on him. Marco had given him the clearance to only spend the five hundred, but Roen decided he would give himself a little flexibility. After all, a car could be a valuable asset; splurging a little made sense.

Roen spent most of the morning wandering around town until he found a salvage yard. He had stopped by all the car dealerships earlier, but was laughed out when they found out how much he wanted to spend. The salesman at the last dealership took pity on him and directed him to this place, which was hardly more than a junkyard.

The owner of the yard noticed right away that something was a little strange about him. After all, in a town of twelve thousand people, everyone was bound to know everyone else. When a complete stranger walked up to his lot looking to buy a car, the guy had to know that something was off.

In the end, with Roen's pitiful budget, he only had three options: a 1978 dark green Rabbit, a rusty, mustard-colored 1982 Bug, or a 1970 light-blue station wagon with the fake wood panels on the sides. The station wagon won the beauty contest, because it had room to stow their gear, a roof rack, tinted back windows, and because he drove it off the lot for a measly three hundred and seventy-five bucks.

"If Tao could see me now," he grumbled, feeling the engine twitch and pop as he made a right turn out of the lot onto Verde Road. Screw it; Tao would be proud of him for his tough negotiating skills. The guy originally wanted four hundred bucks for this damn thing.

You drove a hard bargain, his friend would have said.

Actually no, Tao would say something sarcastic about all the fine vehicles he had driven while working for the Prophus. That much was true. For some reason, ever since he had first become a host, he was allocated crappy car after crappy car. He initially thought it was simply because he was a new agent and had to work his way up. It wasn't until a few years into his service that he realized that someone, or multiple someones, or everyone, for all he knew, working within the quartermaster division hated Tao and was purposely allocating Roen really pathetic and embarrassing cars. Even now, when he got to choose his car, he somehow ended up with a wagon with wooden panels.

Lunch was at one of the local pizza joints. It seemed most of the restaurants here fell into one of four categories: Chinese, pizza, steak, or burgers. That suited him fine.

By mid-afternoon, Roen had identified all the important landmarks, from the combination police and fire station to the local sporting goods store to the grocery store and restaurants. It was by chance while going over the map of the town that Roen noticed one more thing. It seemed all the hotels and shopping areas here in Ontario were located in one place, just east of the highway. The town was only eight kilometers long, after all.

He parked himself in one of the main intersections and spent the rest of the day watching traffic. Surveillance was one of his worst skill-sets as an agent. He didn't have the patience, he got distracted easily, and everything seemed to blur together after a while. However, he was experienced enough after all these years to power through it, and by nightfall he had noted, tracked, and followed four promising leads. In the morning, he would follow up with these leads and hopefully find this scout team.

As he was crossing the bridge of the river that passed through town, he noticed a gray unmarked van that hadn't been there earlier. There were many vans in town, but this one was slightly different. It sported a hump on top of its roof, just a slight elevation followed by three protruding fins not unlike that of a shark. These vans were pretty common in many major cities all over the country, but rare in such a small town. It meant the shark had smelled blood. The IXTF were here and hunting with Penetra vans.

CHAPTER FIFTEEN
THE PRESIDENT

Though it was more extreme than most civilizations, the Roman Empire followed the usual cycle: it grew, prospered, and then stagnated. It was a shining beacon of civilization, and also an example of their need for forced change. The two-hundred-year Golden Age saw little for the Quasing in terms of the advancement we required from the humans.

Therefore, we worked tirelessly to corrupt what we had built by injecting several tribal ethnicities into the Roman armies. Near the sunset of the fifth century, we succeeded, and the Western Roman Empire fell from within. Chaos ensued, and the wheels of change continued to turn.

Zoras

Today was an important meeting for Enzo. It was probably a good idea to not make the Russian president wait for too long. The man was important if Enzo was to cinch this entire continent for his faction. However, it was also important for Enzo not to show the man that they were equals. Far from it. Enzo was bestowing a favor upon a raised underling. The president must be made aware of that.

There are some lessons that should be taught now and some later. In this case, it is better for them to have their delusions now and disappointments later.

Enzo looked up at the clock and cut his workout short. He had been lax over the past few months, and needed to beg forgiveness and rectify his sins. However, today was not the day, and his Holy One understood, commanded it even.

He tossed his towel to the waiting Amanda. "Have the escort ready for the Grand Kremlin Palace."

The look of relief on her face was palpable. She had the difficult job of shepherding him through his daily schedule and worried constantly when he pushed those constraints. One day, he reminded himself, he would find a Holy One for her.

Enzo was twenty minutes late meeting with the president. However, he considered it a wash, considering the president had insisted on meeting him at the Grand Kremlin Palace, which was nothing less than a grandstand on his part. Still, he had to remind himself that he was not only buying the man as well as the country, but also taking him out of Vinnick's grasp. Most importantly, the currency he was purchasing with was illusion.

For now, Enzo would have to play these games. He walked into the office and nodded. "President Putyatin, thank you for seeing me."

Putyatin looked up, then down at his watch, and then up again. "Ah, Mr Enzo. I apologize. I forgot we had an appointment today. Please, sit."

Again, the grandstanding. There was no way the man didn't know that Enzo was coming. He was the most important person on the continent, and the KGB had twenty-four hour surveillance at Novo-Ogarevo, the guest complex where he was staying. If Enzo so much as tripped over a rock – not like that would ever happen – it would light up half a dozen intelligence reports.

"I am here now. That is all that is important," he said, taking the invitation and sitting in the chair across from the president.

"What can the Russian people do for you?" asked Putyatin.

He is fishing. Putyatin believes he has the upper hand.

"As we've discussed earlier, Germany."

Putyatin looked unimpressed. "What would I do with that? It is a people I do not identify with, a land I do not care for."

Enzo was surprised at the answer. "It is a land you would rule. One in which you could create a dynasty. To pass down to your sons and daughters."

"So you wish to make me a king?"

"An emperor. A tsar. Whatever you wish to call it."

Putyatin stood up and turned toward the large map of the world behind him. He looked at Germany. "You ask for a lot, and offer not little, but I am a patriot as well. What would you do with my country after I align its interests with yours?"

"There are enemies to both of our people," Enzo said. "I would see them crushed."

"To war then," Putyatin nodded thoughtfully.

This is a ruse. Well-rehearsed. His decision has already been made.

"Let me ask you, Mr Enzo," Putyatin continued. "Tell me why it is in my best interest to hand over my beloved country, just so you can lead her to war, in exchange for a small piece of the Earth. It seems you have much more to gain from my cooperation than I would receiving a land of good beer and little oil. It is too much risk, not enough reward, and frankly, no guarantees."

"Are you doubting the Genjix, Mr President?"

Putyatin shrugged. "I doubt anyone who offers the world to me on a platter. Besides, I know Mr Vinnick. He and I have had business in the past. I know what he is offering. I can see and touch it. You offer me nothing but platitudes and dreams, Mr Enzo. Dreams that require I risk my country."

Enzo stood up and sneered. He was tiring of these constant games. "Dreams? Mr President, the Genjix are currently in control of a power bloc of nineteen countries, including China, the second largest economy and military in the world. You think all we have is wishful thinking?"

Putyatin stood up as well. "Good day, Mr Enzo. I wish you and your people the best. We are done here."

Enzo, in a controlled rage, turned to leave. Right before he reached the door, he stopped.

I would not advise playing this card. Not yet.

"How is your mother doing in Sochi? The Black Sea is beautiful this time of year."

Putyatin stiffened. "A threat, Mr Enzo?"

Enzo turned around. "Or Boris, your brother, the General currently in charge of retooling the Eighth Army in Stryi? Your daughter, who exactly seven minutes ago went to her skating practice just off the Varvarka? I hear she is fantastic and has a good chance of qualifying for the Winter Olympics next year. You'll see to that, won't you?

"But that's all public information. How about your son, currently attending the Lundsbergs boarding school in Sweden under the pseudonym of Karl Pschuenko? Your youngest daughter, currently at the Humanitarian Classical Gymnasium? Your mistress, the twenty-two year-old daughter of your loyal ally and friend, the Prime Minister? Not that I blame you; she is quite a beauty. She is currently in Paris attending Fashion Week.

"And your wife's nephew, the one you detest for being a bumbling simpleton, Captain Lieutenant Masorin. Ah, he has risen in rank quickly. Nothing to do with his aunt's influence, of course. I believe as of oh-four-hundred this morning, his battleship *Martynin* had just embarked for the White Sea on a nine-day patrol over concerns of United States submarine incursions in the Arctic Circle. I believe that mission is classified."

Enzo relished the stunned look on that arrogant Russian's face as he walked back to the desk. He leaned forward. "You see, Mr President, we Genjix have been running the world for a very, very long time, and we've been guiding humans toward what is best for them for almost as long. I encourage you to reconsider our offer. It's really the best scenario for everyone."

A little over the top, but effective. I would have held back. It could backfire.

"I am through with these games, Zoras."

Then Enzo walked away and stopped at the doorway once more. He turned and smiled at Putyatin. "By the way, I am going to do you a favor. Good day, Mr President." Then he walked out of the door.

That night, the Russian Battleship *Martynin* sunk under

mysterious circumstances. There were no distress calls, signs of battle, or indications of a collision. All hands on deck were lost.

CHAPTER SIXTEEN
FIFTEEN CANDLES

My people were explorers. Over the course of millions of years, we colonized planets, moons, and asteroids, expanding our vast civilization to new solar systems. We created a vast network of living planets, each individually unique, yet part of a larger collective.

Earth would not have been an ideal candidate for colonization. Too much would have had to be cleaned and altered for the planet to become suitable. You see, we prefer planets without atmospheres, because we can apply our own onto prospective colonies and eventually grow our red ocean until it covers the entire surface. That is true Quasiforming.

Tao

The three-meter-long spear with the heavy-edged metal point flickered through the air, bending and slashing like a snake's tongue, its waxwood shaft, soaked in water for weeks, making it malleable, like a heavy whip. Cameron swung and twisted it around his body as if a dance partner, using it as an extension of his arm to skewer, cut or, in the unlikely case of this happening, stop the charge of mounted cavalry. Tao called it the king of weapons, but his mentor was always a bit of a drama queen.

Hey now.

"Considering you named the fighting style you created the Grand Supreme Fist, I think drama queen is a pretty apt description."

One day, after you have single-handedly defeated the Genjix and are crowned high protector of the Earth and Heavens and all the little furry animals in between, I will not begrudge you such a lofty title. For now, I would say I have earned that title for t'ai chi.

Lower the shoulder. Watch your leg work. Your right leg. Your other damn right leg. How many times do I have to tell you to not dangle your left hand out like that? Keep it closer to your stomach.

The instructions and corrections came fast and furious as Cameron flowed through the form, striking with precision and keeping the long spear a blur as he slipped through the motions as smoothly as water. Many of these moves he had learned when he was barely old enough to walk. Now, they were second nature, and he could do them without thinking.

That was a good thing, because right now, his mental state was a torrential mess. His constant worry about his dad was now a dull pain that lingered just outside his consciousness. Tao had been pushing him extra hard during his training in order to keep his mind off his father. However, Tao regularly red-lined his training anyway, so it was something Cameron was used to. It didn't help that he wasn't talking to his mom right now either. Jill was usually his calming influence and his current tantrum – he knew it was misplaced – just made things worse.

You are sloppy.

"I can't help it. I keep wondering if my dad is dead right now."

Worrying will not solve anything. Training will.

"It won't mean squat if he's dead."

It will if you have to avenge him, but we are getting ahead of ourselves. Roen means a lot to me as well. He is my friend, too.

"I don't want to avenge him. I just want him to be okay."

Cameron's feelings welled up again. Usually, these forms and exercises calmed him, but Tao was experimenting and didn't want him to suppress his bubbling emotions. He wanted to keep them on the surface of his thoughts as he ran these forms. It was the opposite of what he had been trained to do all his life. Now, Tao wanted him to wade through his chaotic thoughts while trying to find the calm at the same time. It was very frustrating.

Let go.

Cameron began to run through the form faster and more powerfully than he ever had before. His body reacted differently than he was used to. Then he began to deviate from this form, running through new sets of movements that he had never learned before. Cameron began to observe himself move through his own eyes, feeling detached from his body, as if he was having an out-of-body experience.

Tao had taken over his body.

An image flashed into Cameron's head of a Chinese man wearing dress-like leather garb weaving through this exact form, kicking up a storm of dust in a circle. He was surrounded by a crowd of rough-looking men studying him. Then another image flashed. This time, he was fighting a skirmish against Mongols surrounding his party. Cameron gasped as the Chinese man took out an entire group of cavalry with those exact same moves.

"What's going on? What form is this? I don't recognize it."

An old one. I have never taught it to anyone before.

"Then how –"

I am accessing your movements directly through your conscious thoughts using a combination of our link and your training. This is extraordinary.

"It's weird, Tao. Do you have control of my body now forever? Can I even get it back?"

Go ahead. Try to regain it.

Just like that, Cameron was back in control. Immediately, the spear flew out of his hands and thunked into the tree in the middle of the field. The physical exertion that Tao was putting his body through swept over him. A headache came out of nowhere and blindsided Cameron in the back of his brain. He fell to his knees and groaned.

Interesting side effects. I am exhausted as well.

"I feel like I just sprinted a marathon while discovering cold fusion."

You know how to produce cold fusion? We are going to be rich.

"You know what I mean."

It seems this process takes a severe mental and physical toll on both the host and the Quasing. We will have to monitor this carefully. Rest a bit.

Alex found Cameron relaxing at the base of the trunk with his arms wrapped around his bent knees. The sunset was bathing everything in a rather angry red glow, which matched the twisted feelings in his guts at the moment. The spear was still stuck into the tree next to his head.

Alex poked the spear with her hands and watched it wiggle back and forth. "Where's the rest of your phalanx?"

Cameron tried hard not to smile; he was enjoying

stewing in his misery, but he couldn't help it. The edges of his lips curved upward, and the rest of his mouth followed. He looked up at her and tried to say something smart. "Wrong kind of spear," was all that came out.

Oh dear. We have our work cut out for us.

"Of course," Alex said, picking up the spear and showing that she knew how to handle it. "This toothpick wouldn't stop a charging Russian Don. Maybe one of those puny Western ponies."

Cameron let that slide. She was goading him, either because she could or because she had seen him mope all evening since dinner and was trying to break his malaise. Cameron's heart just wasn't into it today.

Your father experienced something similar after a tragic event.

"Did his dad die, too?"

No, he killed someone.

"What? I did that when I was eleven when those Genjix were after Mom and Dad in Vancouver."

You and Roen are of a different mettle. Remember, you have been trained for this since you were four. At the time, your father was just into his first year as a host.

"How did he handle it?"

Very much like you are now. He moped.

"I am not moping!"

Then get your ass up.

Intent on proving Tao wrong, Cameron got up and brushed the dirt off his pants. He looked up at the still-setting sun and figured he had maybe an hour until nightfall. He held his hand out to Alex. "Want to go to the forest?"

She didn't take his hand but nodded. "Lead the way, capitalist pig."

"Says the billionaire's daughter."

"My father is only a multi-millionaire," she sniffed. "My mother married down."

"Funny, Tao says the same thing about my mom."

"That is another similarity we share."

The two walked away from the house, down to the tree line and into the forest. There was a small grove of large trees a hundred meters in that had several intertwining branches. At some point, these trees had grown close together. However, instead of the larger trees pushing out the weaker ones, they had learned to grow harmoniously.

The result of this outgrowth was a network of large branches that Cameron discovered made a very natural tree house. Last summer, he had hauled up some wooden planks and made it his own personal safe house when he needed time alone. It was his fortress of solitude.

His parents knew about this hiding place, though they pretended not to. Cameron knew they knew, and they knew he knew they knew. However, everyone pretended to not know, so whenever he needed some time alone and came here, they would know where he was, but wouldn't bother him just to keep up pretenses. This arrangement suited everyone fine.

"Did you build this?" she asked as he grandiosely gestured at the primitive structure.

He nodded and pointed to the small wooden stick nailed to the trunk as a step. "You start there and climb that way." He pointed to a winding path that went from the trunk they were climbing over to the one on the right. "And then once you get to that branch…"

Without another word, Alex was scaling the branches as easily as he ever did. Impressed, Cameron followed her up, noticing that even though this was her first time climbing this tree, she looked comfortable moving among the branches.

They do have trees in Russia, you know.

"I was just surprised. Most girls I know don't climb trees."

That is because you do not know any girls.

Within a few minutes, they were cradled in a little nook of branches two stories up. Cameron had moved several large pieces of plywood here and stolen some of the deck furniture pillows. He pulled out two bottles of water from the emergency pack he hid here and handed one to her.

The family had several of these emergency packs all over the place. One was at his school, another nestled between a couple of large boulders at the south end of town, and two more on each end of the safe house tunnels. He had enough experience early in his childhood to know these survival packs were often the difference between life and death. This one had a 9mm pistol, several magazines, flashlights, water, and dried rations.

"So how do you like your Quasing?" he asked. "I hear you're a new host. I'm sorry about your mom."

Alex shrugged. "She was a vessel to a Holy One. It was a great honor." She paused. "It is a great honor now."

"How are you adjusting to someone talking in your head? I've been a host for as long as I can remember. If you have any questions, I can help."

Stop trying to show how smart you are.

Alex rolled her eyes, and then she took on a thoughtful expression. "Is there really no privacy anymore? Ever?"

Cameron shook his head. "Tao can hear everything I think. I can't keep a secret from him. He can tell when I'm lying."

It is because you are as bad at it as your father. However, I think you hit a nerve.

Though Alex had attempted to seem like the perfect host for her Quasing, she looked troubled. "I had only had Tabs for a few weeks before we had to run, but my friends… the ones I used to have before I became a vessel… Everything is different now. I do not see the world the same way they do. Not anymore."

Cameron leaned forward, his head bobbing up and down. "Yeah. I get the same way at school. All the kids my age, it seems like they just don't know anything. But I'm not allowed to say anything either. It's like, they're so…"

"Stupid," Alex said.

"… sheltered," Cameron finished.

They both laughed nervously and settled into several seconds of awkward silence. On one hand, they had just formed a connection, no matter how minute. Whatever this bond was sent tingles down his spine and scared him stiff. After all, she was just like him and understood what he was talking about, but she was also Genjix. Cameron didn't seem to know what to make of such an awkward relationship. After all, all their lives, they'd been told the other side was the enemy. It was all very confusing, but exciting.

Something is off. I think Tabs is trying to play us.

Cameron wasn't listening to Tao at all, though. They both blushed. Then he noticed her face for the first time, really studied her face, with her blonde hair, startling blue eyes, sharp nose and chin. She looked like a doll, with perfect features, as if she were etched out of marble. She was hard and soft at the same time, and for a second he wondered if she was from the missing Romanov bloodline or some other Russian royalty. Or something. His face felt hot, his palms sweaty. By this time, he had no idea what was going through his head right now. The words he was thinking didn't even make sense.

Really? I think it is time you two head back to the house.

"Why? I like it here."

Just do it. Now.

"Tao thinks we should head back," he said, hating every word that came out of his mouth. He began to get up.

Alex leaned forward and put her hand on his wrist. "A few minutes more. It's nice here. Tell me, do your parents treat you differently? I feel like I have this weight on my shoulders and Papa treats me like a glass figurine."

And just like that, Tao lost control of his host for the rest of the night. The dam between the kids had sprung a leak, and suddenly they were sharing their feelings, fears. They spoke about being hosts, but it was more than that. While Cameron had experienced loneliness all his life, he also knew nothing else but Tao and this loneliness. For Alex, it had come as an even greater shock. She had been popular with the other children in the Russian upper social circles before becoming a vessel. Now she had no one.

The sudden collapse of everything she knew in life was so oppressive, it hurt her physically. Yet, as a young Adonis, she knew that it was her destiny to become a host, or a vessel, as they called it. The only reason she had not gone to the Hatchery years ago was because of the Council Power Struggle. Her father had elected to train her closer to home as opposed to at the Hatchery, which fell under Councilman Enzo's control.

Questions and personal thoughts he had of the Quasing and the war dribbled out of Cameron like a running faucet. It was the same with Alex. The two of them viewed the Quasing civil war from an entirely different angle than the adults, and they both had a desperate need to talk to someone who might understand. Before the night was over, way past the time they were supposed to be back home, Cameron felt like he had never known someone so well as he knew Alex.

"We should head back," he said, standing up and helping her to her feet. Together, they climbed down the tree and made their way back toward the farmhouse. This time, as they made their way through the pitch-black forest, Alexandra held Cameron's hand.

"Hello, Tabs." Tao stood at the doorway to Alex's room.

Jill had offered to move all the refugees up to the farmhouse. Vladimir and Rin, feeling more secure underground with escape routes, declined to come up to the civilized world and stayed in their cells. Ohr and Alexandra had leaped at the chance. The old Korean senator complained about how the dank underground made his bones ache, while the girl just wanted a little space between her and her father.

"Tao," Tabs said, sitting her sleeping host up. "I was expecting you."

"Oh?" Tao moved Cameron into the room and sat at the end of the bed. "I honestly never thought I would be in this situation."

"And which one is that?" Tabs said. "The one where you and I, two extremes of our faction, are talking through slumbering vessels, or that we are actually talking and not trying to stab each other."

"You still have not forgiven me for the Mexican War, have you?"

"You buried my vessel neck-deep and left him for the vultures. I am pretty sure I never will."

"Sorry." Tao shrugged, not sorry at all. "War is hell. What did you end up inhabiting next anyway?"

"A vulture."

"Ah, makes sense. How long did that keep you out of the war?"

"Part of the reason I will never forgive you."

"Excellent."

"So to what do I owe this pleasure, then?"

Tao squared up Cameron's body so it faced Alex directly. "There are some things occurring between our two hosts that I do not approve of. What are you trying to pull?"

Tabs gave an innocent shrug with a mischievous glint in her eye. "I do not know what you are claiming. After all, are we not on the same side now?"

"Maybe. I can believe Ladm would find a conscience. You finding one would be a surprise."

"I do not care what you think of me, Tao. I do not think much of you. You are as rabid an animal as Zoras and Chiyva. They just seem much better at it than you. To be honest, if our sources are correct, most Prophus do not think much of you either." She held up a finger. "First of all, my previous vessel was killed by Enzo and his minions. I take offense to that. You should know how much I take offense to that." She held up another finger. "Secondly, I am not sold on this planet being ready for Quasiform. Perhaps next century, but certainly not now."

Tao processed Tabs's words. Knowing Tabs's history and personality, it made sense. Tabs was just as attached to her host as any Quasing was, and Enzo had had Marta assassinated. Her motives aligned with her actions. Maybe his judgment was just being clouded by their centuries of animosity.

"What will you do for the Prophus, then? What do you plan next?" he asked.

Tabs smiled. "Nothing. I will not lift a hand to help the Prophus. However, I am going to take a rest from the war and spectate from the sidelines. And since Enzo does not believe in neutrality..." Tabs made a magnanimous gesture with her arms. "Here I am. I would like to raise Alexandra in peace until she can fulfill her potential as an Adonis Vessel. Is that so far a stretch?"

He leaned in, shaking a finger. "What you say is plausible, but I will have my eye on you. Do not even think about betraying us. You know my reputation."

"And a vicious reputation it is," Tabs said mockingly. "That is what makes you so unbearable at Decennials."

"And if you think I will allow your host to have sway over mine..."

Tabs puckered up and blew him a kiss. "Oh Tao, she already has."

CHAPTER SEVENTEEN
SCOUT TEAM

Timestamp: 2788

Sadly, my vacation in Hawaii came to an abrupt end. In the middle of the night, a squad of Prophus transferred me to a secret long-term care facility to finish my rehab. It seemed the government wanted to haul me in for questioning. Thus, my life as a fugitive officially began.

After I recovered, I snuck onto a cruise ship headed for Mexico and paid a coyote to ferry me across the border to rejoin my family. Deciding to stay in the United States was a tough call. Sure, there were two Quasing with us, but this was our home.

And no, I won't tell you where the secret hospital is. Don't even ask.

Roen and Marco knocked on the door of the car repair shop. It was 12.05pm, and it was closed. The shop had closed promptly at noon. Roen had friends who were mechanics; it came with the territory when his job as a Prophus made him wreck cars on a daily basis. That and he was a pretty poor driver as far as secret agents went. One thing he had learned about the mechanics who ran their shops, though, was that these shops never closed early unless they'd already hit their daily quota.

In this case, this particular shop had closed at noon for two days in a row. It must be doing very well, even though it hadn't serviced any cars since he had first scoped it out. He knocked on the door again, harder this time. A stick-thin old man with disheveled white hair and nervous wandering eyes answered.

"We're closed," he barked.

Marco pointed at the parked station wagon behind him in the lot. "Sorry to bother you, good sir, but our car broke down. Could you by chance help us out?"

"I'm not open and too busy. Come back next week," the old man snapped, closing the door.

Marco stuck his foot in before he could slam it shut. "Come on, please, we're just passing through and we're stuck in this one horse town." He paused, glancing uncertainly at Roen, unsure if he got the reference right. "Just one look, and we promise not to trouble you further." Roen covered his mouth and snickered.

Old Crazy Hair gave them both a look and then sighed. "Fine, but if it's something I can't fix in a couple of minutes, then you guys are out of luck until next week." He walked out of his shop and toward the car.

"What's so funny?" Marco asked as he trailed after the guy.

Roen smirked and slipped into the shop while Marco kept the man busy. It looked like any other gas station in a small town. There was a little convenience store area up front, an office in the back, and an attached mechanic's garage on the side. He slipped into the office and checked the bathroom; nothing conspicuous there, either. Roen continued through the side door to the attached garage. There were three cars on lifts, three garage doors at the front, a door leading to the outside at the far end, and then a door to the back. It looked like any other automobile garage. Roen went out the back door and noticed a set of storm cellar doors in the rear locked by a chain and padlock.

He came back inside and scanned the room. He was running out of time. He could hear Marco speaking loudly out front, begging and imploring the man to fix a car that wasn't broken even though it was purring at the moment. Well, running as well as a car in its condition could run. Roen looked at the gaps under the ramps. Of course. There had to be a basement below this garage. It took another couple of seconds before he pushed aside a rolling tool cart and found a metal hatch on the ground. With a hard jerk, he pulled the hatch up and came face to face with the business end of a rifle.

"What are you prowling for, boy?" a voice said from somewhere down in the darkness.

"The gift is nothing without the gift," he said.

No reaction from the darkness.

"Give me chastity and continence?"

Still no response.

"Dang it," he stammered. "You may not be interested in war?"

He heard another voice down there say, "Just kill him and get it over with."

Roen ran through all the possible pass phrases. He was supposed to contact Jill to get the right pass phrase once he got here, since it rotated daily. Unfortunately, he had been unable to get a hold of her, so he wasn't sure which one to use. Finally, he tried one more time. "Only two things are infinite, the universe and human stupidity."

"And I'm not sure about the former," the voice said.

With a visible sigh, Roen slumped his shoulders and extended his hand. A hand appeared from the black void and Roen pulled him up. "Roen Tan," he said.

"The Pacific Northwest commander's lesser half," the man grinned. "Elias Roas, sir."

Behind him, Roen heard Marco raise his voice yet another decibel. Obviously, no matter how good the Englishman's charms were, it was wearing thin on Old Crazy Hair.

Roen nudged with his head. "He one of ours?"

"No," Elias said. "We're renting Ian's silence and his cellar down there. Come on, let's go get him before he tries to shoot your man outside. Guy shoots first, asks later. Elias and Roen walked through the garage to the convenience store and watched as Ian kept repeating that there wasn't anything wrong with the car while Marco kept insisting on paying for the station wagon to get a physical.

"Physical?" Elias asked Roen, who shrugged. He coughed a couple of times until both Ian and Marco looked their way. Elias and Roen waved lazily.

"Jig's up, Ian," Roen said. "We know you're harboring fugitives."

The blood on Ian's face drained. "Look officer, they just broke in. I swear…"

"Hey now." Elias frowned. "Way to stab us in the back first chance you get. Guess money can't buy loyalty after all." He turned to Marco and saluted. "We're relieved you're here, Commander. Please come with me. We have injured." The small group headed back to the garage while

Elias briefed them on their situation. The scout team had been based in the town for the past month, until Prie was caught rummaging through a cargo truck at the Genjix facility's loading dock and got injured during the escape. The team moved him to this concrete cellar to hide him from the Penetra nets.

The five-member scout team was holed up in a tiny crevice near the back of the cellar. The ceilings were low, and there wasn't a lot of room to move around. Roen was shocked they could all fit down there. Elias was currently running the show while Prie was incapacitated.

"Bullet through the stomach. Still inside. Missed his spine, though," Elias said. "We were just trying to keep him comfortable until you came. Which one of you is the doctor?"

Roen exchanged a hesitant look with Marco. "Um."

"Well, you see," Marco said, "we ran into a bit of a sticky–"

"She's dead," Roen said. "Ambushed by Genjix."

Elias and his team deflated when they heard about the events of the previous days. Upon closer inspection, Roen realized just how low morale on this team was. They were exhausted, having been operating around the clock for a month. Now, Prie's injury had compounded the situation.

"If there's no doctor, how are we going to get Prie out of here?" Sheck, one of the scouts, asked. "And when are we getting extracted?"

Marco shook his head. "We're not extracting, boys. Command believes that facility you've been checking out is important. We're here to help you finish the job."

There was a grumbling among the ranks. "What are you good for if you can't save the commander?" Chase, another scout, added.

Roen looked over the unconscious Prie and checked the wound. He looked up at Marco. "We need to get him to a doctor. He's not going to last much longer. What's the Quasing transfer plan?"

Elias looked around and leaned in. "Uh, I don't think any of the boys want to be a host." He looked over to Marco. "No offense, Commander."

"Oh, not at all," Marco quipped. "It feels lovely being a leper."

That startled Roen. Prophus operatives had always aspired to become hosts. It was considered a great honor among the ranks and automatically promoted the host to commander. It was amazing how a few short years had changed things. With the Quasing found out by the rest of the world and the continued advancements of the Penetra scanners, it seemed being a host now was toxic.

"I can't accept that," Marco said. "In the event of Prie's death, we need a host ready for the transfer. If no one will volunteer for the privilege, then I will assign one."

"We can't just let him die," Roen said.

"You can't force a Quasing on any of us," Helen, the operative tending to Prie, said, shaking her head.

"It's a death sentence to be a host these days," Chase growled, his hand moving toward his side arm.

"I'm not taking him," Sheck added.

"Seriously, am I the only one that sees an issue here with Prie still being alive?" Roen said, louder this time. He couldn't believe what he was hearing. The atmosphere in this small cramped room was getting ugly. The scout team looked ready to lynch Marco, and the crazy Brit seemed intent on taking them all on. To be honest, if that happened, Roen wasn't sure what side he'd take.

Marco pointed a finger at Chase. "You move your hand one inch closer to your pistol. I dare you."

"Woah, woah. Ow!" Roen said, standing up and banging his head on the ceiling. "Everyone chill out."

The entire room froze as Chase and Marco stared each other down. Gunfire in such a small room would be catastrophic. Besides the real danger of a ricocheting bullet, the sound of the discharge was a severe threat to all of them.

"I'll take it," Helen stood up. "I'll take Pri if there is no other choice."

"Thank you, Lieutenant," Marco nodded.

"He's not fucking dead yet!" Roen yelled. "What is wrong with all of you?"

He was met with another long silence as all eyes looked his way. Some looked angry, others ashamed.

Marco shook his head sadly. "You saw the inventory, Roen. They're low on morphine. No surgeon. No way to transport him. It's the humane thing to do. At the very least, we can save Pri. There's no other way."

"Like hell there isn't," Roen snapped. He surveyed the others in the room and then looked at Ian, who was standing at the entrance looking terrified. He walked over to the old man and put his hand out. "Give me your phone."

Ian looked over at Elias and then back at Roen and then back at Elias again. "What?"

"Now," Roen said, putting his hand on his sidearm. "Give me your damn phone." The old mechanic reluctantly pulled out a cell phone that looked like it was made in the nineties. Roen hefted the brick in his hand and pointed at the rest of the group. "Stow your gear and get ready to move."

"Who are you calling, Roen?" Marco asked.

"Someone who can help us take care of Prie." Roen dialed a few numbers and scanned the room while the phone rang. "You've got two minutes," he mouthed, holding up two fingers.

Someone on the other line picked up. "Hello, 911 emergency services."

"Hello 911," Roen said loudly. "I'd like to report a body."

Roen, Marco, and the scout team watched from up the hill as two police cars, an ambulance, and a fire truck parked on poor Ian Crazy Hair's lot. The excuse they had concocted was that Ian had found the lock on his back door broken, courtesy of Roen breaking it, searched his garage for vandals or thieves, and happened upon Prie lying unconscious in his cellar. Then he called 911.

"It's a Saint Alphonsus ambulance, all right," Elias said, handing the binoculars over to Marco.

"They'll find out he's a host once he checks into the hospital. It's standard protocol now in most Western countries to scan all patients," Marco said, looking at Roen. "I hope you know what you're doing, mate."

"I hope so too," said Roen. "At least we save Prie's life. We can worry about breaking him out of jail after he is stable."

"What if we can't? We risk Pri."

Roen shook his head. "It's a tough call, but I don't subscribe to the belief that a Quasing's life is more valuable than a human's. We'll get both of them back after they discharge him. Maybe bust him out of the hospital or intercept the transport when they move him."

"That's a big maybe," Chase said.

"Well, I made the call. It's a burden I'll just have to live with," Roen said. "You can worry about court marshaling me later."

"Weren't you already court marshaled once?" Marco asked.

Roen shrugged. "Yep. Lot of good that did, huh? Come on, let's get back to the motel." He looked at the rest of the group and sniffed. "We'll probably have to get more rooms. We only have one shower."

The group walked to the station wagon they had parked down the street. Roen was glad he got that old behemoth instead of the other options. Clown car-ing six people would be tight, but better than trying to do that with a Rabbit or a Bug.

"I'll need a report on what you have so far on that facility you've been reconnoitering," Marco was saying to the group. "The sooner we get caught up, the sooner we can make the assessment, bust Prie out of the hospital, and get back to a place that serves proper tea."

"We were infiltrating one of the recent shipments when Prie was detected," Elias said. "He brought a sample back." He handed Marco a windowed metal cylinder filled with clear liquid.

Marco hefted it in his hand and peeked through the window. Then he flipped it upside down and looked again. "It's like a Magic 8-ball with no fortune. What is it?"

Roen saw a hint of black and snatched it from Marco's hand. He stared at the smooth black rod swimming inside the container. He had seen this before. An image long buried came flooding back as if Tao had just flashed it into his head. His recollection of the mission in Taiwan was spotty. His injury on that freighter was so severe it had joggled his memory to the point he could only recall bits and pieces of what had happened. However, he remembered holding a similar-looking container with a black rod sitting in liquid.

"Oh shit. I know what this facility is."

Marco raised an eyebrow. "Oh? Well, spit it out, so we can call it a wrap and go home."

Roen closed his eyes and rubbed the bridge of his nose with his forefinger and thumb. This was bad. He faced the group and shook his head. "It's a catalyst reaction rod. That Genjix building you found is a Quasiform facility. They plan on using these things to blow up the world."

CHAPTER EIGHTEEN
TAKEOVER

The Black Plague swept across most of the known world, decimating half the known population. It was a world-killer, unleashed by us gods to usher in a new dawn of innovation and creativity. It was a resounding success, for the Renaissance was born from the depths of the Dark Ages.

It was then that I dedicated all my efforts to fulfilling the destiny of the Conflict Doctrine and feed that engine of change by constantly perpetuating war throughout the known world.

Zoras

Enzo helped himself to a glass of President Putyatin's vodka. Hard liquor wasn't his drink of choice, but someone of his stature only drank the best. If the Russians were renowned for their vodka, that would be what Enzo drank. He made a face as he sipped the spirit, then he walked across the president's office to the wingback chair in front of the fireplace. On the two televisions above the mantle, a rare joint session of both the lower State Duma and the upper Federation Council was convening.

Today would be a glorious day. Both chambers were

190

voting to extend a permanent alliance with Enzo's faction and declare Vinnick a traitor and enemy of the state. It had taken marathon negotiations by all his people, but through a series of bribes, blackmail, and threats, they had wrangled the votes they needed from both houses.

The tricky part was playing to the president's greed and fear, and then playing good cop, bad cop. It took a few more meetings with Putyatin before he came around. After he had played bad cop by sinking the *Martynin*, the man had dared summon Enzo to demand an explanation. He laughably threatened war. The next day, Enzo demonstrated his goodwill by having an agent give everyone in Putyatin's immediate family a Chinese red envelope, a symbol of luck, but mostly a demonstration of just how far Enzo's influence reached.

Enzo then played good cop by adding the regions of Calais and Champagne along with hereditary titles to the initial offer of Germany. Once the man realized that allying with Enzo would prove a much more fruitful relationship than the one he had with Vinnick, he acquiesced to the terms.

Once the Russian president was on board, the rest of the government fell in line. This vote tonight was nothing more than a formality. It was a *blitzkrieg* of sorts. Enzo wanted to sew them all up before Vinnick had a chance to counter his offers. The old man had moved too slowly, and now it was too late. The Council Power Struggle was finally over after all these years, and Enzo hadn't even had to fire a shot.

"Mr President," Enzo called, holding up his glass. "Why don't you come join me? It is a momentous occasion, after all. A victory for us both."

Putyatin, barely able to hide his disdain, didn't even look up from his desk. "No thank you, Mr Enzo. There will be many changes occurring in my country over the next few weeks. I have much to do for this transition to be successful."

Enzo nodded and turned back to the television. The man might not like him, but his friendship was unnecessary. All that was required was that he deliver Russia to Enzo. Once the continent was fully under his control, then maybe Enzo might even allow him to keep his station. No, that would be foolish. A vessel would be needed to occupy such an important position.

Azumi is the logical candidate.

"She has the most knowledge, but her skills are too valuable for the Russian presidency. I will put one of my brothers of lower standing. Matthew perhaps."

Conquering a kingdom is always the easy part. It is keeping it that is difficult.

"Azumi will be needed once we start the global war. Besides, we won't have to keep it for long once Quasiform is initiated. I will need her on the front line."

Again, your confidence will be a downfall. You cannot win a global conflict without Russia firmly behind you. A strong hand will be necessary.

Enzo put his drink aside as the voting began. Each television showed a live feed of the State Duma and the Federation Council respectively with a tally of the votes on the floor. As expected, the voting began with nine straight yay votes on the Federation Council and sixteen on the State Duma for the alliance with Enzo.

He grinned as he picked up his glass and toasted the televisions, and then threw back the vodka in one shot.

He was pouring himself another when the first couple of nays came in. Enzo frowned. That was to be expected; his people weren't able to get through to everyone. However, one of the Federation Council members who voted nay – the Krasnoyarskiy Krai – was someone Enzo had wooed personally.

The news became grim as more votes were tallied. Enzo stared at the screen in disbelief as the number of nays climbed. His pollsters had assured him that everything was squared away. In fact, they had confidently stated that the vote of the State Duma would be a dominating landslide. However, by the time both the upper and lower houses were done, he had lost by over forty points.

Enzo threw his drink at the fire, exploding the crystal into shards. He turned to Putyatin. "What is the meaning of this?"

This time, Putyatin looked up and acknowledged him with a smirk on his face. He took his time walking around his desk and sat down in the wingback opposite Enzo. The Russian president poured himself a drink from the decanter and sniffed the glass before taking a sip.

"Ah, Kauffman. My favorite Russian vodka," he said. "Do you know why I use a decanter? Because Kauffman might be seen as, how can I put it, not presidential. It is good vodka, but not the most expensive and unattainable, maybe only eight thousand rubles a bottle. I first discovered it when I was just a lower official in the army. High enough to buy decent vodka. Low enough not to be stupid about buying too nice a bottle."

"You could have had a kingdom. The world, you fool," Enzo snarled.

"Now that I am president," Putyatin continued with his

story, ignoring Enzo completely, "I could easily have…" he made a grand gesture with his hands, "… presidential vodka. Instead, I still ask for my Kauffman, because I like what I like, and I am not a greedy man. Kauffman was good enough when I was a soldier, it is good enough for me now."

Enzo growled. "We had an agreement. There will be consequences for double-crossing me." He considered reaching out and breaking the damn Russian's neck. A quick dart forward and twist, and he could drink all the vodka he wanted in hell.

No.

"Zoras, he taunts me."

You will not touch him. You might have lost him to Vinnick, but that still keeps Russia under Genjix influence. You kill him, and the country will fall out of Genjix hands. We cannot allow that.

"You see," Putyatin droned on. "You offer me Germany and Champagne and all these fancy things. No matter where I have climbed in life, I will always be that young officer at heart, albeit now fatter. I want my vodka, I want money, and I want to serve Russia, with none of your strings attached."

"And now you might lose everything," Enzo said, taking a step forward.

Putyatin wasn't cowed. He nodded to the side, and a dozen soldiers came in, rifles all pointing at Enzo. "And one more thing," he said. "I do not like fucking foreigners threatening my family. You might be more powerful than Vinnick, but he is Russian and will do what is best for Russia. That, and he pays with cash, not promises."

Four of the soldiers grabbed Enzo's arms. He considered

killing everyone in the room. It would be difficult, but not impossible. The key would be to prevent any of them from escaping to alert others. The two exits in the room would prove troublesome, though.

No. You are too valuable and the risk too high. Find another way to achieve my goals.

"Gaaah, fine. I will have his tongue one day."

Putyatin walked up to Enzo and jabbed him in the chest with his finger. "No one threatens my family, you son of a bitch. You are lucky you are an official envoy. Your delegation has two days to leave Russia. One minute past and I will have the military storm your compound and have you all dragged off to the gulag, diplomatic status or not. Now get out of my sight."

Enzo and his entourage were pushed and herded through Moscow under armed guard. His limousine was led by no less than four police cars and two Typhoon armored trucks. It would have been flattering if it wasn't so humiliating. When the convoy reached Novo-Ogarevo, they were met with an extensive military blockade. Obviously, both Vinnick and Putyatin had conspired ahead of time and were aware of the results beforehand. This made Enzo fume even more. They had made him look even more the fool.

Worry about your pride and revenge later. Vinnick has struck at you once; he may do so again.

The military blockade opened just enough for his limousine and one of the Typhoons to go in and then closed behind them. Enzo looked out the window and noticed his entire security on high alert. All of his brothers and sisters were armed and operating as if a force under siege. This complex was tactically indefensible. The drain on Hatchery talent would be immeasurable if they were killed. No, open conflict was not an option. However, Enzo was not ready to admit defeat.

He stepped out of the limousine and stared at the Typhoon transport that had followed him into the compound. "What is Putyatin playing at now?" he muttered. He pointed at a group of agents nearby. "Secure that vehicle."

He watched as a group of men and women stepped out and realized right away that they weren't regular military. All were uniformed, but he could tell these people were not just administrators. No, by the way they moved, and the look in their eyes, these were Spetsnaz or possibly KGB, or both.

The last to come out, an older woman with a long neck and sharp nose that reminded Enzo of a hawk, walked over and nodded. He noted the lack of respect in her demeanor. "I am Natalya Voznesenceva. By order of President Putyatin, I am the envoy assigned to oversee your withdrawal from Russia. I will have full access to your embassy and will accompany you any time you depart the premises. These terms are not negotiable."

One step would cover the distance. He could crack the woman's skull, get two shots with his pistol, and pull back behind cover before those Spetsnaz knew what happened. The rest of his brothers and sisters would follow suit and wipe them out within a second.

There are a thousand troops surrounding your complex.

"Do we have an alternate exit route?"

One established by your scout team before your arrival. We will have to check if the Russians have blocked it. For now, bide your time.

Enzo, in what he considered a shameful act, turned away from the Russian envoy and retreated into the main building.

Amanda met him at the door and bowed. "Councilman Vinnick is on the phone, Father."

See to his terms.

Enzo took the ear piece from her and stepped off to the side, noting the envoy following him every step of the way. He nodded to his two guards at the door to let the woman pass. The words being passed to her ears would be harmless.

"Brother," Enzo said into the ear piece, not willing to give Vinnick the pleasure of hearing his frustration.

"Threatening the president and trying to bribe the Federal Assembly with things that don't cost you anything?" Vinnick chortled. "As unpredictable as you are as a person, you are mightily predictable in your tactics, boy."

"Thank you for the lesson, old man."

"Listen, Enzo," Vinnick said. "I won today, and I do so for the good of all Genjix. You are the future. Surely we can accommodate each other. Together, we are stronger. The planet is still not ripe for Quasiform. It needs a few more years to incubate. Can we not agree on this?"

"Your greed betrays you."

Vinnick barked a sharp laugh. "You think it is greed that motivates me? I'll drop dead any day now. Stupid boy. All I care about is seeing Flua and the Holy Ones's objectives completed, but the risks you take are too high. Quasiform will fail if the planet's conditions are not within parameters. Right now, Earth is barely within range. The Genjix only have one chance to get this right. Even increasing global temperatures a few more –"

"The parameters are acceptable, and have been for years," Enzo snapped. "It is non-believers like you who drag your feet because you fear the evolution that lies ahead."

"God damn it, Enzo. What is the hurry? Time is all the Quasing have. Why don't we meet –?"

Enzo hung up on him. "Assemble," he said to Amanda standing at the door. He looked over at the envoy following close behind.

You can be assured this Natalya is fluent in most of the Chinese dialects.

"Portus Cale," he added to her.

Amanda nodded and stepped away, butchering the Portuguese language as she attempted to relay his orders. He was expecting too much from her, though. She was not blessed, after all; one could not expect too much from lower humans. As long as the message reached his siblings, that was all that mattered. Enzo would have preferred to use a dead language, perhaps Coptic, but most of his Hatchery siblings were not as learned as he was.

Fifteen minutes later, all from the Hatchery stood around him in his state room. The room stayed silent until Amanda gave the signal that the room had been soundproofed. Enzo looked over at Putyatin's dog standing at the doorway. She would get nothing from this meeting.

Enzo began speaking in perfect Portuguese. "What happened, and can it be resolved?"

Azumi, a chastised look on her face, shook her head. "Vinnick threw a third of his entire fortune into this vote. It seems the short-sighted Federal Assembly prefers money now rather than wealth later. Putyatin threw his support in with Vinnick right after your first meeting. They have been conspiring since last week."

"Recommendations," Enzo asked.

"Withdraw and wait for the Councilman's death," Akelatis said. "His heir will be weakened during a transition and will not be difficult to defeat."

Azumi shook her head. "Sergii is competent enough and the transition has been long-planned. He is not true Hatchery, but he is not weak, either. Flua will not lose much in the transition."

"Our situation is tense, Father," Palos added. "We are at a severe disadvantage politically and tactically. You stand to lose everything if we are defeated."

"But if we withdraw, we are back to a complete stalemate," Matthew said. "Worse, if Vinnick passes and Sergii consolidates his control."

The debate went on for another twenty minutes, but Enzo had already made up his mind. After everyone had presented their recommendations, he glanced over at the confused envoy, and spoke to his assembled. "No retreating. Prepare for the reckoning." He turned to Amanda. "Send scouts to survey the escape tunnel. Make sure it isn't blocked. I want full blueprints by this evening."

"What about our shadow?" Matthew asked, gesturing over at Natalya, who was studying the meeting with unabashed interest. No doubt she had recorded this conversation from somewhere on her person and was now studying their mannerisms.

Enzo turned to Azumi. "Summon a shade team."

"How many targets, Father?"

"All of them."

CHAPTER NINETEEN
NIGHT WATCH

In the years following the ESA's passing, thousands of Penetra nets were installed in every major airport, government building, and high-value facility. It became as common to see a Penetra scanner as a metal detector. Transportation around the world became extraordinarily difficult. Prophus operations were crippled.

The political arms of both factions were wiped off the face of the Earth in many countries. Governments confiscated properties, accounts, and even entire companies. Within weeks of its passage, the Prophus were decimated to a fraction of their original strength. Fortunately, the Genjix lost even more.

Baji

Nothing made Jill stew as much as being cheated. Well, except for maybe when Roen did something asinine, which was quite often. In his defense, though, once she yelled at him about it, he rarely repeated the mistake, though he had this unique talent for finding new dumb things for her to yell at him about. She had assumed he'd eventually run out of original ways to mess something up, yet he kept impressing her with his imagination.

God, she loved that man.

Right now though, she was pissed and ripping one of her agents a new asshole. "Six thousand dollars, Hite! What did I tell you about counting that money? Do you know how many cases of ammo I can buy with that? I'm taking the missing amount out of your salary. I don't care if you don't draw salary."

Jill clicked him off and briefly considered chucking her headset at the nearest wall. Then she remembered that she was running low on those and decided against it. She stopped layering the lasagna she was building, turned around to wash her hands, and saw Vladimir waiting at the doorway.

"Have you given consideration to my request," he asked.

Persistent, is he not?

"Great, just great. This is exactly what I need right now. I don't know how many ways I can say no before it sinks into his concrete head."

The rich rarely accept "no" as an answer.

She put on as apologetic a face as possible. "Of course. Unfortunately, the arrangement for your transport from Las Vegas to Cuba and the transport to Panama can't be rescheduled."

Not to mention the four connection journey from the farmhouse to Vegas, the forged passports with set dates for St Johns once they boarded the cruise ship, or the dozens of bribes for the workers and officers on duty the day they were being moved were already arranged. Oh no, all the Russian cared about was getting things his way because he wanted to leave two weeks early. Of course she didn't mention any of it, though she desperately wanted to take this cooking pan and hit him on the head with it.

"If it's a matter of money…" he began.

Typical of someone from Vinnick's faction. For a while, I thought their plan was just to buy their way to victory.

"Not a bad plan, to be honest."

True, but it has been proven again and again that money can only buy so much before brute force wins out. Look at Athens.

Jill shook her head and said aloud. "I'm sorry. You're set for two weeks from tomorrow, and that's that. You might as well sit back and enjoy the fresh air."

"You tell your boy to stay away from my Alex," he said, his face darkening. "I know how you Americans are."

She looked away and began to work on layering the pasta and cheese with renewed fervor, lest Vladimir see the scowl on her face. He was getting on her last nerve. This was going to be one glorious lasagna when it was done, fueled by her long list of irritations and constant worry for her husband's welfare. It had been four days now and –

"Jill," Shiloh, the new operative on comms loaned from Faust cut in. "We have a direct route request to Pacific Northwest command from a Mountain North Region secured encryption. Your eyes only."

Jill's heart rate picked up as she responded. "Double-check the crypto key as well as the route hops, then patch them through."

Keep a good head on you. The news could be anything.

The five minutes it took for Shiloh to perform due diligence on the comm route were some of the longest of her life. A dozen scenarios ran through her head, and most of them were bad. From the scout team telling her that Roen never made it, to them reporting him dead, to… she shook her head. Every subsequent scenario was worse than the previous. There was only one possible good outcome, and considering the luck they'd had lately, she wanted to pick up this stupid lasagna and smash it against something.

"Hey, babe," Roen's voice said through her headset. "Babe? Jill?"

It took Jill a few seconds to regain her composure. She fought back the swell of relief that rose from her chest, threatening to have her in tears in front of Vladimir. She looked at him and shooed him away with her eyes. He must have recognized the look, because he drifted backward out of the room sheepishly.

"Where have you been?" she demanded. "You were supposed to report in right when you got there!"

"Car got ambushed on the way there. Genjix patrol. Our crypto key got shot up in the process, and I didn't want to risk contacting you until we reached the scout team and used theirs. Why? Is everything okay? How's Cameron?"

She was never so glad to hear his stupid voice. "I was worried about you."

"We're fine, but I can't get into that right now," he answered. "Can you pull up the Keeper?"

Jill checked the time. "Are you sure? It's the middle of the night in Greenland right now."

"It's always night in Greenland. This is important. We need to pow wow right away. Don't worry, if she complains, tell her it was Marco who called the meeting."

"Can't you just take credit for this? She hates you already. Why do we both have to get in trouble?" Marco's voice joined in the call. "Actually, Jill, he's right. This can't wait. We're sending you the scout team's intel right now. Forward this on to Command."

"All right. Fine. Roen, ping me at twenty-three-hundred. You can tell me all about it, and I can tell you about Cam's new girlfriend."

"Sure thing. Don't worry about me, hon. No Genjix can bust your hubby up. Old Roen is as tough as rusty nails. Wait, what girlfriend? What are you –?"

Jill cut him off. It usually was time to do so when he started referring to himself in the third person. A few seconds later, Roen's report landed on her computer screen. She scanned the contents and switched over back to Shiloh. "Place a priority call to Command," she said. "Full route encryption. Yes, I know what time it is right now."

It took some finagling and some time to pull the elderly Keeper out of bed. As soon as she was on, though, they transferred all the photos and files the scout team had acquired. Roen and Marco didn't have visual on this call, but Jill watched the Keeper's reaction as she skimmed what they had sent over.

There were several moments of awkward silence as the Keeper read through the materials. Near the end, her eyes widened and she looked up. "How reliable is this information? If these estimates are to be believed, they have something along the lines of seventy thousand square feet of facility, and that's only what they can see on the outside, not including the underground and in the mountain."

Jill gasped. "That big? How did they get this cleared without being discovered?"

The Genjix must have spent an exorbitant amount on buying the local officials.

Several blueprints appeared on her screen. The first was

of a large rectangular facility nestled in a thickly forested region. The next was of a similar set-up on the side of a snow-capped mountain. Another was in the desert. There were nine facilities in total. Then, each of the blueprints changed into satellite images overlaying different parts of the planet.

If this is what I think it is, this is bad.

"Oh no," Jill whispered. "Are these…?"

The Keeper nodded. "Catalyst facilities. These are the ones that we're aware of. Five of them are operational, and four are still under construction. This new one makes the tenth."

"Why would they build one in Oregon?" Marco asked.

Jill felt a chill down her spine as she manipulated the map of the world. All the other known facilities – northern Russia, Pakistan, Botswana, China, Algeria – were located in firmly Genjix zones of control. They would be impossible to get to. They were aware of other hidden facilities in Sweden, Switzerland, Bolivia, and the United States, but they hadn't known their actual locations. Until now.

"How many would we have to take out in order to prevent Quasiform?" she asked.

"That is for Rin to tell us," the Keeper said. "We just don't know enough to know what it'll take to stop it. We don't know how the locations are chosen or how many facilities to disable to stop the chain reaction. How many of these facilities do the Genjix have? Do we need to just destroy one or two of them, or all ten? She needs to help us plan the strategy."

"I'll pass this information along to Rin right away," Jill said.

"Marco," the Keeper continued. "I need interior data

on the facility. Defenses, security systems, infrastructures, anything we can use to plan an assault."

"An attack on US soil?" Roen said. "That's dangerous."

"We have little choice," the Keeper replied. "Marco, I need full confirmation on this before proceeding. Get this for –"

There was a loud pop in her comm and then the line went dead. Jill clicked over a few more times before pulling Shiloh up. "What happened to our connection?" she demanded.

"All lines outside just went dead," Shiloh answered. "Hang on. The perimeter alarms just tripped. Multiple signatures. From north and west. Moving in quickly."

Assume the worst. Cut off connections with Command immediately and ready the wipe protocol.

Jill glanced outside the window and scanned the tree line. "This is Hen House. We are under attack. Prepare to receive. All personnel report."

The news trickled in in bits and pieces. The supply warehouse to the east and the residence to the south reported nothing unusual. The comm building to the west and the garage to the north were silent. Then Shiloh's line fizzled and went dead as well. That could only mean one thing. Jill punched the emergency master code on her terminal, setting the network on a thirty minute kill timer unless she entered the unlock pass-phrase. She tore off her apron, yanked a small hidden latch under the sink, and pulled out an automatic rifle from a hidden drawer just as the first sounds of gunfire punctured the air.

Ohr came running downstairs. "I hear gunshots."

"No shit," Jill said, pulling out a pistol from another hidden drawer and tossing it to him. "Get downstairs."

Eight more of her agents who were working at the farmhouse or down in the safe house ran into the room. She directed them to defensive positions. She wished she had a few more minutes to organize them. The houses were interconnected through the tunnels underground, but it seemed two of her buildings were hit at once. It was a coordinated attack. How did they even know about them?

"What is the commotion about?" Vladimir said, running up the stairs with Rin. The kitchen was positively crowded now.

Get Rin out of danger now. She is the priority. Relay a message to the outliers to go dark.

"We're under attack. Don't know who. Don't know their strength," Jill said. She pointed at the weapon cabinet. "Grab a gun. And for God's sake, Rin, get your ass downstairs. You're too important."

"Alex! Where's Alex?" Vladimir said, as he pulled out an older AK. "Where's my daughter?"

Cameron went to the forest with Alex after his practice. Do not tell Vladimir; the fool will just charge outside and get himself killed.

"Shut up and man the front door," Jill snapped. "Protect the house or get out of the way."

The truth was, she was as terrified for Cameron as he was for Alex right now. She knew he must not have been in the house, or he would have reported in by now. That must mean he was out in the forest, probably with the girl. They had been spending a lot of time together, often going out on their own.

A bullet shattered the window, followed by a dozen more that splattered against the back wall. Everyone ducked and took position under windows or to the side of the doors. Jill looked at Harry, who manned the dining room, and gave him a set of hand signals, which he communicated to the rest of her team.

On my mark. Now!

Jill pushed a button on her console and the exterior of the farmhouse was lit up by a series of large floodlights that shone outward in all directions. Jill stood up at the window and saw a dark figure temporarily blinded and caught out in the open. She pulled the trigger and watched him fall, then ducked and moved to the next window.

The farmhouse erupted with automatic fire as the defenders took momentary advantage of the confusion. Jill heard random shouts from her people, each calling out how many they'd engaged and how many they'd taken down.

"Kate's down," Harry said. "Haven't heard from Garrett or Sals either. Collin and Freeni are upstairs."

They manned the west side of the house.

Staying low, Jill moved to the dining room as small fragments exploded from her house, raining debris all around her. She saw the knick-knacks she had painstakingly collected over the years scatter across the floor. Sure, the house was staged and made to look generic, but she had put a small personal touch into each and every item. Her family had made it their home, and there were reminders of them everywhere.

From the scratches on the floor caused by Roen dragging the dining table across the room to the crack in the wall from Cameron playing baseball indoors, this was the home she had worked so hard to build to give her family a semblance of normalcy. It wasn't her house that these attackers were blowing apart, it was their lives as well. It pained her to see everything destroyed and blown apart, but mostly it pissed the hell out of her.

Jill peeked over the window and saw another crouched figure. She trained her sights on him and took him down. She swiveled to the left and saw another approaching. She took quick aim and fired. Something unbelievable happened. The second figure, whom she had dead in her crosshairs, dodged her shot, moving with a ghostlike grace.

An Adonis Vessel. Genjix attack.

"Crap."

There weren't any good scenarios here, but a Genjix attack was the worst. Add an Adonis Vessel, and the entire situation just took a hopeless turn. This wasn't a regular Genjix patrol happening upon her operation, but a full-scale, planned attack. Adonis Vessels never participated in minor skirmishes.

Evacuate now.

Jill signaled to Harry and called for the retreat. She ran back into the kitchen and yanked Vladimir back from the door. "We're getting out of here."

"Have you seen Alex?" he said, eyes wide and voice slightly crazed.

"She's with Cameron," Jill lied. "They're fine."

"If anything happens to my little girl, I will kill your son."

Jill grabbed a handful of his shirt and pulled him close. "Say that again and I will shoot you right now, you bastard." She pushed the stunned Russian back toward the pantry. "Get your ass downstairs." She waved at Harry to follow, and they were soon joined by Freeni and Garrett. That was all she had left. She had lost five good people in a matter of minutes.

You are going to lose more if you do not get going.

Jill made sure she was the last person down the trap door, locking it behind her as she clambered down the spiral staircase. When she got to the main room, she took a quick inventory: Vladimir, Ohr, Rin, Harry, Garrett, Freeni. She suppressed the scream in her chest. She had hoped against all hope that Cameron was here as well. He was upstairs still. Outside in the forest. Anywhere. Scared, possibly on the run, maybe even dead. It was too much for a mother to bear.

Focus on the task. There are others who are depending on you.

Jill allowed herself a split second to grieve, and then she was the commander again. She looked up as the sounds of heavy footsteps began to clomp on the ceiling. She heard faint sounds of "clear" being called out. The Genjix were in her home.

Vladimir still wore that desperate look on his face. "Please," he begged, moving up to her. "My Alex."

Jill pushed him back. She felt his pain as well, but she still had people to care for. "Everyone, silent. The trap door is barred and well-hidden. Maybe we can wait them out."

A few minutes later, they heard the high-pitched whine of a drill as it dug into metal. The entire room froze as the whirling sounds made the entire staircase shudder. They would break in within minutes.

How did they find the trap door so quickly? And how did they know to carry a drill? Something is wrong.

"Only one explanation."

There was no time for that, though. Jill pushed to the front of the group. "I'm taking our guests to the sub. Harry, you and Garrett go through the eastern forest exit and make your way to Mountain North base. Tell them what happened. Let the Keeper know we've been compromised. Tell them... tell them we have a leak." She motioned to the agent in the back. "Freeni, you're with me. Let's go."

"Sir," Harry said as Jill led the group down the long tunnel toward the coast. "Be safe, and if I don't see you, then to the Eternal Sea."

"None of that. We're still alive," Jill said, and then she turned to her wards. "Let's go."

CHAPTER TWENTY
NON-PARENTAL GUIDANCE

I was on one of those colony ships seeking new worlds to bring into the Quasing fold. The truth is, your solar system is not ideal. Too many gas giants, no planets within our Goldilocks temperate zone, and far too few resources. Earth was also a unique and particularly undesirable case. It was one of the few planets that had already evolved an atmosphere of its own. That meant we'd have to do extra work to transform it for our use.

However, when our ship was damaged by asteroids, it leaked the compounds necessary to catalyze the process, and we did not have enough to begin gestation for a desirable atmosphere. Fortunately, we were able to locate something similar on Earth. At the time we did not know that the compatible atmospheres we detected were the living creatures on the planet.

Tao

Cameron put his arms around Alex and pulled her close. The two froze in place as gunfire popped all around, bouncing and echoing through the forest. He heard screams, followed by more gunfire. Then he thought he heard rustling beneath them, footsteps crunching leaves and snapping branches.

He closed his eyes and tried to make out a pattern, a location, a direction, anything that could give him any clue as to what to do next or which direction to flee. Unfortunately, it sounded as if they were completely surrounded.

Three distinct groupings. Originally one directly north. One in the far north. Then directly northeast. They must have hit the communication building first. Then the farmhouse.

"Mom!"

Calm down. Remember your training. Assess your situation. Get to safety. Plan.

Assess your situation. Cameron tapped Alex on the shoulder until their eyes locked. He put a finger to his lips and then motioned for her to stay put. He slowly released her and made his way up the branch, inching toward the far end of his treehouse to his emergency pack. He pulled out the 9mm pistol and loaded one of the three magazines, wincing as it made a sharp cracking sound when it clicked in, and then again when he chambered the first bullet.

You need to get away immediately. Deeper into the forest.

"Come on," he whispered. "We need to get out of here."

The two of them climbed down the tree as fast as they could, landing and kneeling at its base. Cameron had slung the backpack over his shoulders and kept Alex behind him. The night seemed to have come alive. The sounds of battle still raged at the house, and wind was rustling the leaves. Cameron could hear the flapping of wings, the hoots of owls, and even the howl of coyotes in the distance. The darkness felt like it was closing in on him. He grabbed Alex's hand and pulled her south, deeper into the forest.

"You're going the wrong way!" she said. "We need to get back to the house."

He shook his head. "It's too dangerous."

"My papa is there."

"So is my mom," he said, his hands shaking. First his dad and now his mom.

Focus, Cameron. Find the calm. I know this is hard, but you must.

"I need to make sure my papa is all right," she said, pulling away. "He needs me."

Cameron clamped down on her hand and pulled her close to him. "We don't know who is attacking the house. It could be the IXTF or the Genjix. In either case, they will have Penetra scanners. It's too dangerous to go back. We need to get as far away as possible."

Alex's eyes were unfocused as she consulted with Tabs before she relented. The two of them continued deeper south. While the moon was out, most of its light was lost within the towering trees. It made for a treacherous walk through the forest. Cameron had a flashlight in his bag, but he couldn't risk giving away their position.

"What are we going to do?" Alex asked.

"I don't know," he replied.

"Where are we going?"

"I don't know!" The words came out of his mouth a little harsher than he had intended. He felt this weight on his chest as the familiar forest around him all of a sudden felt oppressive and imposing. The darkness felt blacker and more suffocating than usual, and he found himself taking short hurried breaths.

All right, Cameron. Let us get some things straight. First of all, do not say that again.

"Say I don't know?"

Yes. If you are going to lead, you have to be in control. Keep your insecurities and your doubts to yourself.

"But I don't know what I'm doing right now. In fact –"

It does not matter. Keep that thought to yourself. I will always be here to advise you. Second, relax. Find the calm. You have trained for situations like this. This is still your backyard. You know this area like the back of your hand. You have the advantage.

"But there are –"

Do not worry about that right now. Get your bearings. Stay in control.

It took Cameron several slow exhales before he got the urge to throw up under control, and then a few more moments to still his quivering hands.

Good. Now, get to safety and find shelter for the night. I suggest you head south, deeper into the forest.

"Follow me," he whispered, "I know where to go."

Some of the large roots created natural shelters and made for excellent hiding places. They could hole up there tonight. He looked up at the sky when a gap between the trees exposed the moon. The night seemed clear. That should mean no rain. That was comforting, at least. Cameron heard a sharp crack in front of him and froze. He looked back at Alex and motioned for her to get down. The two stayed still as he scanned the area.

Sentry just southwest of your position. Night vision goggles. Automatic rifle. You will need to take him out if you want to get past him.

"Shoot him?"

By melee if possible. He is fully armored and you could attract more.

"I don't know if I can get close enough before he notices."

Use Alex as bait.

"I don't know how she'll feel about that."

Again, not a democracy.

"I'm going to try to take him out," he whispered to Alex. "I don't think I can get close enough without him noticing. Can you divert his attention?"

Alex looked like she was about to protest, and then nodded. She crept away from their hiding spot and moved parallel to where the sentry was standing. Cameron went in the opposite direction, moving away from the man's viewpoint, going from tree trunk to tree trunk, ducking when the sentry's gaze swept in his direction. It was painstakingly slow, but eventually, he got within ten meters before he ran out of trees to hide behind.

Cameron must have made too much noise, because the sentry was scanning directly at him. He waited and waited for Alex's diversion, which never came. Then the sentry, suspicious of the noise, walked toward his tree. Something loud came rustling through the trees from the right. Then a girl's voice made a sharp cry of pain. The sentry immediately turned toward her.

Now! Take out the rifle first.

Cameron leaped out of cover and angled for the sentry's blind spot. He put one hand on the rifle and kicked the man's heel with his left foot, simultaneously whipping his free hand backward across the man's chest. The trip should have worked, but Cameron, in his anxiety, mistimed the move. That, and the guy looked like he was twice Cameron's size. The sentry stumbled, but kept his footing. Cameron tried again and followed up with a high head kick that snapped the larger man back. Somehow, though, the guy stayed on his feet.

He is armored all over, including face and arms. Watch for his sidearm. Hack the knees.

Cameron stomped down on the side of the sentry's knees, driving him to the ground. He followed up with a three-punch combination that seemed to just bounce off the man's body. Then the sentry backhanded Cameron in the chest, temporarily knocking the wind out of him.

Cover the distance before he can draw!

It was too late. The pistol was out in a flash and Cameron was a second late reaching for his. He froze, horrified as his very young life flashed before him. A shadow leaped out from the darkness. Alex appeared, smacking the pistol out of the sentry's hand with a branch. She distracted him long enough for Cameron to draw his pistol and take aim.

Do not shoot if you can help it. You will call attention.

Instead, he clubbed the guy in the jaw with the pistol handle. The sentry stumbled and threw a hay-maker, clipping Cameron just above his eye. The impact of the blow spun him around, and he fell to the ground.

Shake it off. Now!

Cameron ignored the screaming pain and the feeling of something stuck in his left eye as he picked himself up and charged, half-blinded by panic and fear.

Find the calm. Control yourself.

Alex was swinging the thick branch in her hand expertly, hacking and slashing at the sentry. He was able to block most of her attacks with his armored forearm, and she lacked the strength to bludgeon him and keep him down. Slowly, he got to his feet and threw a couple of awkward swings at her. She artfully danced away.

Cameron came in from behind and slapped the man on

his ears with opened palms so hard, he might have ruptured an eardrum. The guy staggered and dropped to one knee.

Alex was on top of him in an instant. She charged forward and kicked him in the face. The guy's head snapped up, and he fell onto his back. Then she pounced and swung the branch down at his head. Once. Twice.

"He's out," Cameron said. "Check him for anything we can use."

Alex wasn't done though. She planted a knee on the side of his face and pulled out a knife. Before he could stop her, she jammed it down into the guy's neck. She looked up at him, breathing heavily. "We can't take any chances."

Cameron was stunned, surprised at her ferocity. He had shot people trying to kill Roen before, maybe even killed some, but he had never done anything like this, especially to an unconscious opponent. It made him sick.

She is right. If he had been able to report you two to the authorities, the danger to you could grow exponentially.

He swallowed the bile back down his throat and nodded. "Take his rifle and magazines. We need to get moving. Grab his radio, too."

They searched the body in silence. He still wasn't sure what to make of what he had just seen. On the one hand, Cameron was ashamed that he had put up such a poor showing in front of her. On the other, the way Alex had so callously killed the man terrified him. The silence continued until it became uncomfortable. Finally, Cameron decided to break it.

"That was some interesting stick fencing you were doing," he said. He felt pretty lame as the words left his mouth.

"Cossack swordplay," she said, blushing a little. "Mama was a proud Cossack. Gave me my first *shashka* when I turned four."

He frowned. "I got a Lego set for my fourth birthday."

In a few minutes, they had taken his rifle, six magazines, and a wallet with only a federal ID. Cameron looked at the card and handed it to Alex. "IXTF."

She scowled and threw the identification on the ground. "Where to," she said, slinging the rifle over her shoulder.

Cameron, that identification was fake. The IXTF rotate their holograms on the cards every six months as a precaution. These are Genjix.

"Should I tell Alex?"

Not yet. Digest the intel later.

"What should we do now, Tao? I have enough supplies to last a day or two. I don't know where Mom is, or if she's even alive. Should we try to go to a motel?"

No motels. There is a good possibility the Genjix are operating out of Eureka. They will be watching the few hotels there are in town. Staying in the forest is your best bet. For now, get some distance from the farmhouse.

"I hope Alex likes camping."

Somehow, I doubt it. As long as it does not rain, you two should be fine for a few days.

Cameron looked up at the sky. It was clear now, but it rained around these parts more often than it didn't. Well, he would worry about that later. He had to stay alive and protect Alex until they could find help.

"Come on," he said, trying to sound reassuring. "I know where we can go." He took her hand and led her into the complete darkness of the woods.

Jacob Diamont walked through the remnants of the tattered house. Bullet holes riddled the walls, and large chunks of paneling dangled from the ceiling, cut into shreds by automatic fire. Entire sections of the house had been blown out. To his left, water spouted from the cracked sink. Jacob looked up and watched curiously as a corner of the second floor sagged. This building was no longer structurally sound. His team needed to act fast and sweep the house for clues before the entire thing collapsed on top of them.

Amazingly, the computer terminal next to the sink was untouched and still functioning. It would give his people a chance to pull whatever data they could from their systems. Currently, one of his men was working to bypass security. Jacob stepped over a fallen beam and hunched over a body. He rolled it onto its back and signaled for someone to carry it outside. The cleaning team was on its way, and all the bodies had to be moved before the scene could be wiped.

"Wrap it up in twenty minutes. Strip the scene and finish the upload."

"Adonis," his man said, shaking his head. "All their systems just went hard lockdown."

The information could be time sensitive. Get it to the techs' hands immediately.

"Yes, Chiyva."

"Find the data center and yank out the drives," he instructed. "I want these on their way to the loyalty haven for analysis within the hour."

He peered out of the building and saw the line of corpses being dragged out onto the lawn. Half his team was scavenging for intel, while the other half was running corpse recovering. They had found five bodies here, and a dozen more across three other buildings. This was a large operation, possibly even one of the Prophus command centers.

The betrayers had put up a good fight. He had lost seven of his men in this assault. He would have to beg Chiyva's forgiveness. Jacob mentally ran through his own resources; he had only seven men left to complete this mission. Though the losses had been non-blessed and expendable, he hesitated requesting more support. After all, he had failed in capturing his quarry.

Forgiveness is a human quality. An irrelevant one. Result and efficiency are the only metrics that matter.

Efficiency was the key. No, Jacob would not beg for more men. His men had died destroying a major cog in Prophus operations. There was no shame in that. He would complete the job with the seven he had. He would do so even if he was the last man remaining. His standing depended on it.

One of his agents came in and handed Jacob a burned photo. "We found this remnant in an incinerating lockbox.

Tao! It was a rare visceral reaction from his Holy One.

Jacob took the picture and stared; his chest clenched. For over ten years, he thought he had avenged his grandfather that day on the freighter, and had even proudly told Chiyva that when he was blessed with his Holy One. Now he must bear this shame until the wrong had been righted. There had been rumors of Roen Tan surviving: scattered reports and sightings, but nothing concrete. By that time though, Jacob had had more important things to worry about.

The blasted Prophus had revealed the Holy Ones to the world and everything was in an upheaval. Within a year, the Genjix had lost much of their influence across the world, and Quasiform had stalled. Combined with the Council Power Struggle, Jacob had all but forgotten about the man. Still, he should have been surer, confirmed it somehow.

The burned photo was missing its bottom half, but it clearly displayed the heads of a child and a woman. Roen's face was only half shown. He looked older than Jacob remembered, but there was no mistaking that face. His visage had been burned into Jacob's soul from when he was twelve.

And if that was Roen, then the woman could only be his infamous wife, Jill Tesser Tan. She had the honor of being the Genjix's most wanted vessel, even more than the Keeper. If Jacob could kill her as well as Roen…

Then you will have earned consideration on the High Council as well as fulfilled your revenge.

"It is fate, Chiyva."

Fate is created, not ordained.

"I will earn my place on the Council."

Finish up here. There is much to do.

Jacob focused on the task at hand. His people were sifting through the remains now, searching for any clues that could lead them to where the Prophus had fled. He walked through the bullet-riddled kitchen and into the pantry, where a stairwell led to a dark pit. This must be one of the fabled Underground Railroad operations the Genjix had heard so much about.

His people followed the retreating Prophus underground to the tunnels shortly after they secured the house. The betrayers had scattered across the varied tunnels like rats. Jacob's men had captured a few of them trying to escape east toward the mountains, but had not found anyone else, yet. The other two men he had sent into the western tunnels still had not reported back.

"Adonis," one of his agents said, coming down the stairs. "A message. We found it in one of the bedrooms upstairs." He handed Jacob a notebook. On the blank back page, near the bottom left corner was a small circle with a sun wheel inside. A Seal of Shamash, and a clue.

"Hand me the black light," Jacob said, putting the notebook flat on the counter. He hovered the small handheld UV light over the blank page and watched as markings appeared in Korean. Jacob read the message. His grasp of languages wasn't as strong as many other Adonis Vessels', but he compensated with other assets. Besides, his role wasn't to think; he was simply an extension of his Holy Ones' will.

The scientist is heading south. We are done here. Clean the premise. You now have dual targets. You will need to split your forces to follow both. Be aware that the IXTF activity in this region is higher than most.

Jacob grunted. Those fools from Interpol were beneath contempt. Even now, as the Genjix pushed the world toward war, the incompetent IXTF wasted their time hunting wayward Holy Ones in ones and twos. Little did they know that within a few years, almost all humans would become vessels, and then within a quarter century, there would be no more humans at all.

Jacob signaled for his forces to wrap things up. Ten minutes later, a series of explosions detonated what was left of the buildings, leveling everything. The base underneath the main house received similar treatment. A cleaning team would arrive next to retrieve the bodies and remove the debris. By this time tomorrow, it would be as if the Prophus had never been here.

CHAPTER TWENTY-ONE
A NEW PLAYER

Timestamp: 2813

The first couple of years after the Great Betrayal were the worst of my life, and that's saying something. Constantly hunted. Always looking over our shoulders. Sleeping with one hand clasped to my kid and the other on a gun. Not gonna lie; I learned to hate the IXTF. They were a relentless group of assholes who obviously had no sense of decent business hours.

My boy's earliest memories were of us stealing off in the middle of the night, pursued by masked men with guns, hounded by sirens, and hiding in ditches. Many times barely staying a step ahead of arrest and the secret alien detention centers. I had many friends in there. I probably still do.

The Woodchuck Chuck was Roen's kind of bar. It was rundown, and looked like it was built during the first gold rush. The counter was made to look like one big log with a flat top, and there were half a dozen stuffed woodchucks arranged throughout the establishment. Best of all, they served dollar draft beers all day every day. To save the effort of making multiple trips to the counter, Roen ordered four glasses and brought them to the table near the window, where he had a clear view of Saint Alphonsus Hospital across the street.

Marco, sitting opposite him at the small round table, grabbed one of the glasses and took a swig. "Heavens man, what sort of piss beer is this?"

"It's an American beer. I think it's called Pa —"

"Well good God, no wonder. Is there anything else? I'll even drink a French beer if I have to."

"Snob," Roen said, swiping the two glasses in front of Marco and moving them to his side of the table. "Fine, I'll keep these babies all to myself. There, there, lovelies," he purred, stroking the glasses. "The redcoat is just an asshole." He put his finger to his ear, looked out the window, and then back at Marco.

The Englishman nodded. "Got it." A smile broke out on both their faces and they gave each other high-fives. Marco took back one of the glasses and held it up. "You're a cretinous dolt, but every once in a while, you have moments of brilliance."

Roen didn't know what cretinous meant, but why ruin the celebratory mood by asking? He clinked glasses with Marco and they downed their beers, both eying the other's progress to make sure they didn't lose. Then, they paused and listened as Elias updated them again.

"Give Prie four days to rest before we bust him out?" Roen asked.

Marco shook his head. "Nah, I say we nab him after we finish the mission. Depending on logistics, we could wrap up here anywhere from a week to a month. The longer we let the man recover in the hospital, the better off he'll be. Besides, we swipe him early, and we'll be smack in the middle of a manhunt as we try to complete the mission."

"There's risk with that plan, though," Roen countered. "We'll need to have him watched constantly, either by one of us, or someone on the inside. If we're not ready when they move him, he could slip from our grasps."

"It's a risk we'll have to take. We retrieve him at the last minute when we finish, not a day sooner." Marco picked up another glass of beer from Roen's side of the table. It seemed the bad American beer wasn't so bad after all. "By the way, have you heard back from Jill yet?"

Roen shook his head. The line had gone dead during their meeting, and his cell phone bricked shortly afterward. That could only mean a few things. Either vulnerability in their network had been discovered, and it had to be shut down to prevent intrusion, or someone external had taken it down. Jill could have also locked the system out, but that was reserved for emergencies.

In any case, Roen wasn't going to panic yet. The Prophus's network wasn't exactly what anyone would call robust. With things going the way they had for the past decade, the old infrastructure had suffered more than its regular share of failures. If the system wasn't back in a few days, then he could start worrying.

For now, he had more pressing matters to keep him occupied. Currently, Roen and Marco were surveying the outside of the hospital while Elias and Helen pretended to be a couple going to the emergency room because she was suffering from abdominal pains. At this very moment, Helen was in one of the ER waiting rooms while Elias had wandered away and scouted the medical center for Prie.

A quick search and a few questions later, the team learned that his surgery had been successful, and he was now in stable condition. Unfortunately, due to the fact that he had suffered a gunshot wound, and that the doctors had Penetra scanned him, he was now on full lock-down. There was currently a policeman guarding his door.

Roen looked up from his beer. "Elias says he thinks it's just a small-town deputy. With that sort of security, we could bust him out with a slingshot during our lunch break."

"Let's not push our luck, Roen."

They were into their second hour of surveillance when their luck pushed back. There was a small commotion at the other end of the bar as a group of people walked into the Woodchuck Chuck and took the table at the far end. Roen, focused on counting the paths the ambulances tended to use, paid them no attention.

"Hi, could I get three pitchers of whatever you have on tap, and a glass of wine. White, please," a woman asked.

Roen perked up. That voice sounded familiar. He slowly swiveled his head as casually as he could and saw her back profile: stocky, a charcoal business suit, brown hair down just past her shoulders, low heels.

"No, nothing too sweet. How about a chardonnay?" she continued.

Again, that voice. So familiar. Roen signaled to Marco, who had noticed his interest, to stay seated. He got up and wandered nearer to her at the bar, stealing a glance her way. Late thirties, early forties. Very athletic, but oddly stout body. Possibly military. Sharp alert eyes – she had noticed him staring right away.

He tried to think of something witty to say. "White wine in this joint. Classy."

Oh stop talking. Insulting her is not going to get you anywhere.

At least that's what Tao would have said if he were here. Roen meant it as a joke. Damn it. He realized how the words sounded right as they left his mouth. The woman gave him a perplexed, irritated glance and then turned her back to him.

That should be your signal to stop.

That was what Tao would say next. Instead, Roen doubled down and tried to make up for his mistake. "No, that's not what I meant. I mean, you seem to know your wines, which is funny because I didn't think this place, this town even, would attract…" He stopped.

The woman shot him an insulted look and then pointed at the group of men in the corner staring back at them. "You see that table over there with the four big guys? They're with me, so I suggest you just fuck off."

Roen swiveled his head and saw what looked like the offensive line for the Oregon State football team. They all waved in unison, none of them looking particularly friendly. Immediately, two scenarios popped up into his head. One involved shooting everyone and running out the back, and the other leaving that offensive line crippled and The Woodchuck Chuck a busted-up mess. He'd also still have to run out the back. They probably would have to find a new surveillance place too; one that didn't serve cheap beer.

Roen grimaced and swallowed his pride. He waved back. "Sorry to bother you," he mumbled, beating a hasty retreat.

"What the devil was all that about?" Marco asked. "I know she's the only woman in the pub but you really are all sorts of rusty, aren't you?"

"Shut up," Roen said. It still bothered him. He didn't

recognize her face. Could she be a Genjix? He wished Tao was here right now so he could confirm through touch. He wished Tao was here right now for a lot of reasons. His old friend wouldn't have let him put his foot into his mouth so badly. Heck, if Tao were here, he would just find her in Roen's memory for him. Most of all, he just missed his friend, and it was times like this that reminded Roen of all the small things that Tao meant to him.

They stayed at the bar for another thirty minutes. It seemed Helen was having a hard time getting discharged. Damn hospitals always moved at a snail's pace. She and Elias could probably just run out, but it would look suspicions.

It was getting loud at The Woodchuck Chuck. More patrons had come in, two locals and a few more who joined that woman's group in the back. They were getting rowdy, as if an old, well-acquainted group. The decibels increased even more as the drinks continued to flow. One more thing Roen learned while here; never try to out-drink Marco. The Englishman was wiping the floor with him.

"Never try to keep up with an Englishman. It's practically our national pastime." Marco held up a glass of beer and a glass of cola in each hand. "See, it's all in the wrists and the combo. Slam one, then the other. Rinse. Repeat."

It hit Roen right after he finished his seventh beer. He was walking back from his fourth trip to the restroom when that crowd in the corner roared with laughter, and the woman spoke. "Daws, every family has a resident idiot, and you're ours. It's okay, though; you're my idiot, so I've got your back."

Roen stumbled. That voice again. That awkward fit

in her suit. She wasn't a stout woman; she was wearing armor. Then he realized who she was. Blood drained from his face as he sat back down at the table.

Marco gave him a quizzical look. "You all right there, Roen? You're looking a little shaky."

Roen motioned with his head back toward that group. "Get your stuff together. We should leave. Those guys back there are IXTF."

Marco angled a very obvious look their way. "Well, Ahngr and I had devised a plan to take them out earlier when you seemed to be within their cross-hairs. Seems we still might have to put it in action then."

"Take out the big one second from the right first?" Roen asked.

Marco nodded. "The strong looking bloke. How did you find out?"

"Her voice. I've taunted that woman mercilessly over the past three years. She's Special Agent Kallis, Regional Director of the IXTF. Supposedly, she's a big shot at Interpol."

Marco whistled. "Seems you do have a talent for pissing off the right people. Fancy meeting her at a place like this."

"Could only mean one thing. She's come for Prie."

The two watched out of the corners of their eyes as Kallis got up and went to the log counter again, presumably to order another round of pitchers.

"I think I'm going to talk to her right now," Marco said, standing up.

"Don't do it. It's too risky."

"Keep your enemies closer," the Brit grinned as he sauntered over to Kallis and struck up a conversation.

The only thing Roen heard was "sorry about my friend

over there" and then laughter. He scowled as Marco did that Marco-thing of his for the next fifteen minutes. Then, much to his chagrin, Marco brought Kallis back to the table.

"Ralphy, old boy," Marco said, mouth turned up from ear to ear. "I believe you've already met Special Agent Fran Kallis from the, I'm sorry, what was your MI6 American equivalent again?"

Kallis laughed and stuck out her hand. "IXTF, and we're not American. It's an international task force. Sorry about that rough introduction earlier. I see a lot of creeps in my line of work, so it's sort of an automatic defensive reaction."

Roen plastered a smile on his face as he shook her hand. "No, it's all right," he said in a gruff voice. "It was totally my bad."

"So Cornelius tells me you guys are business partners out here."

Roen almost spit out his beer.

"Yes," Marco butted in quickly. "Redwood lumber is highly sought after over in the UK."

"It's a long way to go to buy wood," Kallis said.

"Well, we like to cut out the middle man," Roen said, playing along, "and source from the um, source." That didn't come out as smoothly as he had hoped.

Fortunately, Kallis didn't dig deeper, and they moved the conversation back to her. It seemed Marco made a good call making contact with Kallis. She and her team had made the six-hour drive from their headquarters in Seattle to retrieve an injured fugitive at the hospital across the street. Once the guy stabilized, they were going to bring him back for interrogation.

"So how long will you be in town, then?" Marco asked, turning his flirt on.

"Whenever the doctors give us the green light," she said. "Probably a week. Until then, I'm putting my guys, those meatheads back there –" she gestured at the back table. They waved. "– on guard twenty-four-seven."

"What did the guy do?" Roen asked. "Is he dangerous?"

Kallis was understandably evasive in her response. "I really can't get into it, Ralphy." She paused. "You know, now that I think about it, there's something familiar about you."

Roen coughed and lowered his voice even more. "I think I was just mistaken."

"Anyway," Marco's laugh was a little forced. "We have to get to an appointment with the lumberjacks soon." He made a show of patting his pants. "I seemed to have forgotten my business cards. May I be honored with your mobile?"

Kallis was too tough to titter, but for a second, she looked like she almost did. Her face flushed a little red and she handed him a card. "You ever get up to Seattle, Cornelius?"

"Our next stop actually," he said. "I won't have to wait until next week, will I?"

Kallis looked around the bar. "Guess your company will help pass the time in this small town." She flashed him one last smile, finished her wine, and then walked back to her table.

Once they were alone, Roen leaned toward him. "Ralphy? I sort of hate you right now."

Marco, all grins, looked at Roen and winked. He picked up his glass and downed it. "That's nine beers."

"And Cornelius? What kind of dumb ass cover name is that?"

"Wanted to feed her stereotype. That's all. Regardless, we have good intel now and the access we need. I suggest we take advantage of this opportunity."

Roen nodded. "A week is a little shorter than we had planned, but if we play our cards right, she'll at the very least tell you when she's leaving town. We won't have to guess. You just need to work that relationship while we're here. Good job."

"Someone has to do the hard work," Marco smirked. Roen wanted to punch the smug look off his face.

Let it go. Marco has always been like this. He is purposely pushing your buttons. Do not fall for it.

Roen listened to his inner Tao and did his best to shrug it off. Marco and Roen drove off in the car, giving every impression of heading for their meeting, then parked up in a quiet layby and waited to hear from Helen and Elias, who called in a few minutes later. They had finally checked out of the emergency room and were heading to the station wagon.

Marco sniffed as they drove back to the hotel. "I'll never pass as a businessman to Fran in this infernal contraption. What do you think about driving down to Boise and picking up a real automobile for me?"

This time, Roen didn't listen to his inner Tao and thumped Marco on the shoulder.

CHAPTER TWENTY-TWO
CLEANSING

Certain groups within the once-unanimous collective insisted that if humanity was allowed to prosper, innovation would come as well. Every experience I have had with this species, from the stagnation of the Roman Empire to the world-cleansing fire of the Black Plague, showed me that was not the case.

Do I have regrets about the chaos and deaths caused by our nurturing? Does a farmer regret the devastation he inflicts on the land when he tills it? Does a builder regret carving a city out of the flesh of a mountain? It is easy to think that the Holy Ones want nothing but to wage endless war. That is far from the truth. What we do is for the greater good.

Zoras

Enzo raised his fist and signaled for a stop. They were two levels below the metro and moving deeper underground. By Zoras's calculations, they were near the final turn of the entry tunnel below Vinnick's base of operations in Moscow. It would be a brazen act, one the Russian would not expect, especially so soon after the recent turn of events. However, Enzo had no choice but to strike quickly.

You will trip the perimeter alarms in that final stretch. Belay until the last moment. Once the attack commences, there is no turning back. You know the price of failure.

"Yes, my Guardian. I have lived with that knowledge since I was first blessed with you. Have I not lived up to your expectations?"

When the risks you embrace are this high, only one punishment exists.

"Then I am fortunate not to fail. The risks I take have always paved the way to victory."

We shall see if that continues. It will catch up with you one day.

"Luck does swing both ways. What I accomplish has nothing to do with luck."

The last turn led to a steep hundred-meter upward incline. This was as far as they were going to get before making their move. He signaled for a stop and looked back at the nine men and women walking behind him single-file in the darkness of the Moscow sewer. These were the finest operatives he had; his Hatchery siblings and the highest of the non-blessed operatives who hoped to prove themselves today for the honor of being blessed with a Holy One. This group would serve as the Trojan Horse into Vinnick's Troy. If they failed, the odds against them would be high. However, while Vinnick's Epsilons were good, they were not at the level of those trained in the Hatchery.

Enzo looked over at Azumi, Matthew, and Akelatis. He wished he could have brought more of his brothers, but they were needed elsewhere. Jacob was still hunting for the rogue scientist, and Palos – not a true Hatchery product, but still reliable – was watching over their new convert Natalya and her Spetsnaz.

Converting her had been surprisingly simple. Slipping in a shade container with a newborn Quasing while she was in the sitting room had done the trick. After she recovered from the initial sickness and realized what she had become, her loyalty to her government immediately wavered. With the politics of this region, all vessels were pariahs, and without the support of the Genjix, it was practically a death sentence in Russia.

Her loyalty was further strengthened when she became overwhelmed by the non-sentient newborn's mewing, rendering her incapacitated until given the suppression medication. Once she found out that the Genjix were the only ones who could continue to provide her with the medication to stop the sounds in her head, the deal was sealed, and she embraced her new blessing willingly. Even now, Natalya was assisting Paolo in converting the rest of the Spetsnaz with more of the shade team.

Enzo believed that loyalty and faith were better tools than blackmail, but he was low on options, and patience, for that matter. The first of the four catalyst facilities in North America was nearly completed. He should be there overseeing those projects instead of playing political games here. This was a tremendous waste of time. However, Quasiform could not occur unless all the catalyst facilities worked in sync, and since five of the facilities were in Vinnick's domain, he would have to be dealt with before Enzo could proceed.

Remember the Council directives on your rules of engagement.
Those damn rules. Would Vinnick's people obey them? They hadn't back at the church. He had little faith

that they would in this situation. There always seemed to be another set of Council rules when it pertained to Enzo.

That is always the case. The envious always band together against the strong.

What they did was irrelevant. Enzo was a true believer and followed the Holy Ones; that was all that mattered. He turned to his people. "Kill all who stand against you. No incendiaries. Your life is forfeit if a Holy One perishes."

The group nodded and prepared for the attack, stripping their packs and loading their rifles. Enzo gave his people a few minutes to collect themselves. He took his most prized possession, the Honjo Masamune sword, and strapped it to his waist. The famous samurai sword, long thought lost after World War II, had been in Sean Diamont's care for years. Jacob had offered it to him as a pledge of his servitude when he first begged to be blessed with Chiyva.

When it was time, he intoned, "Praise to the Holy Ones."

"Praise to the Holy Ones," they echoed.

Enzo slung his rifle onto his back and walked up the steep set of stairs at the side of the sewage tunnel leading up to the basement of the Genjix Moscow headquarters. He heard the whirl of a detection device attached to the ceiling focus on him and the clicks of the thermal imager registering his heat signature. No doubt they were Penetra scanned as well, all procedural and nothing out-of-the-ordinary for a Genjix base.

Vinnick's forces should register them as friendly. This network of tunnels had been used by the Genjix for hundreds of years in this city. They wouldn't know that they were under attack until the first shots were fired. By then, it would be too late.

They reached the main entrance, a large metal door with a display embedded in stone. Enzo gestured to Lagunov, a non-blessed logistics operative with aspirations of bearing a Holy One. Buying him from Vinnick had been a simple affair. A promise of a Holy One, albeit of low standing, was all that he needed. The man just wanted to ensure a place in the loyalty havens once Quasiform began.

Such easily bought loyalty means it can be easily sold again.

"And will reflect on his new standing."

Lagunov punched a code into a small terminal, and the door hissed open. Enzo kept his face down as his group entered a long corridor with a window to a security room on the left side. He should be the only one these common soldiers could recognize. No vessel or Epsilon would work security, after all.

The guard at the other end spoke to Lagunov over the speaker, and he placed a set of forged documents into a tray, much as if they were running a transaction through a bank drive-through. The conversation continued for a few seconds and rose in volume as the guard was unable to corroborate the forged documents.

Enzo, keeping his back to the window, leaned into Lagunov. "I thought you had this end secured."

"Apologies, Father," he stammered. "I will work through this shortly."

There were metal doors at both ends of the corridor. If Vinnick's security forces caught on right now, Enzo's people would be trapped. He watched out of the corner of his eye as Lagunov struggled to convince the security guard to just open the door. That damn Vinnick ran an operation with so much red tape. Eventually, Enzo ran out of patience.

Enzo turned and faced the guard. "Do you know who I am?" The man nodded, the blood draining from his face. "Good, brother," he smiled. "We have pressing matters. Open the door."

The guard fumbled with the intercom. "I'll clear this upstairs immediately, Father."

"You will do no such thing," Enzo remarked. "Open the door if you value your life. The Holy One demands it. The survival of the Genjix depends on this, and you will be rewarded for making the right decision." The security guard hesitated before pushing a series of buttons. The inner door of the corridor clicked and slid open.

"Take him out now," Enzo murmured to Matthew as he passed. He had no use for such gullible fools.

The fireworks began right as he walked through the door. His well-trained team spread out and moved efficiently through the lower level tunnel foyer. Matthew went to the security room door and shot the foolish guard. He looked back at Enzo and nodded. "We have the floor, Father."

"Lock it down. Bring in the main group," Enzo barked, hoisting a rifle and taking position watching one of the four doors leading out of the room. A few seconds later, the outer door to the sewers swung open, and a small army of his loyal units flooded the building. They separated into kill teams, each led by one of his Hatchery siblings, and spread out through the complex. Akelatis led two units toward the garage, while Matthew took three units to secure the front entrance. That left Enzo to take care of

Vinnick somewhere in the upper levels of the building. He signaled for Azumi and her units to fall in line.

You should retreat to safety and allow your siblings to take it from here.

"You know me better than that, Zoras. I lead by example. That is why my people are so loyal."

The source of your fanatical support will also be the source of your downfall. Either way, make sure the objective is reached.

Zoras had long abandoned trying to dissuade Enzo from some of his more foolhardy habits, such as insisting on leading attacks. He had come to recognize that Enzo was a different sort of vessel. He wasn't like Devin, who parceled out orders behind the safety of a desk. He was a lion who needed to hunt in order to stay sharp. It was the one vice his Holy One allowed, and for that, Enzo was grateful.

Azumi's group exited the basement room and made its way out to the main hallways, shooting indiscriminately. This was the heart of the billionaire's operation in Moscow. All the personnel here were his through and through. Enzo had given them one chance when he first arrived to show their loyalty to the true Genjix. That time had passed. Divine justice was at hand.

Footsteps to the right. Six sets.

Azumi was already on it, moving along the right side of the hallway while Enzo took the left. The security forces coming through were caught in crossfire and mowed down. A few seconds later, alarms rang through the facility, but Enzo was already leading his team to the second floor. He gestured for his rear operative to hold this stairwell as he began to clear the hallway. All through the building, he heard the rumbles of battle increase, shattering windows, cracking wood, and blowing chunks of concrete apart.

These old buildings were complicated mazes, filled with side entrances and doors. The enemy could be anywhere. A guard opened fire from a hidden spot in one of the rooms. Enzo ducked to the side just in time and cut him down. Two more appeared from an opposite doorway.

You are too much in the open.

"Secure this," he told Azumi, then stepped into the room. The security guard, using an overturned desk as a makeshift barricade, pulled out a pistol. Enzo, staring at the angle of the gun barrel, twisted and ducked the first two shots, and then walked casually toward the guard. The guard fired twice more, and each time Enzo, watching the trigger finger, dodged the bullet, even though he was only a few meters away.

"You might get one more shot off." He took another step closer. "Decide now."

The soldier, hands trembling, lowered his gun and fell to one knee. "Apologies, Father. Please guide me."

Enzo took the pistol out of his hand. "Prove your dedication."

The soldier nodded and, arms raised, ran out to the hallway right into the middle of the firefight between his people and the security forces. "Lay down your weapons," he screamed. "You are committing sacrilege against the Holy Ones. Come out and show your faith."

There was a slight lull in the fighting as both sides watched the spectacle. A few of the soldiers stood up out of their cover. One even laid his rifle down. Enzo strolled out of the room and stopped behind the still screaming soldier . Without warning, Enzo drew a pistol and shot four of the security soldiers in quick succession. The rest returned fire, killing the poor fool still waving his hands in the air.

Enzo used his body as a shield and pushed forward until he moved past their firing line. He threw the body aside, drew his Hanjo Masamune and began to butcher these unworthy traitors. He took out three more of Vinnick's guards before the rest of them had a chance to react.

As the soldiers turned to engage him, Azumi and the rest of his men finished them off. Without saying a word, they continued clearing room after room, killing soldiers and civilians indiscriminately. There were no rules of engagements when it came to betrayal.

Once they finished the second floor, they continued up to the next level. They met their first group of black-suited Epsilons at the top of the stairs. Enzo could always tell the Epsilons by their uniforms, which were essentially always black three-piece suits. They accompanied Vinnick wherever he went, and he was proud of how impeccably dressed his elite guards always were.

It was a contingent of five that ambushed Enzo at the top of the stairs. One of his unblessed died on the spot from a bullet to the throat. Azumi took a ricocheting bullet to the leg and dropped to one knee. Enzo tried to scramble to the other side of the hallway across the stairs, but their suppressive fire kept him pinned down. He leaned over the edge of the corner and almost took a bullet to the eye for his efforts.

He signaled to Azumi. "Can you move?" She nodded. Of course she could. He looked over at the remaining unblessed. They had done well so far. However, as regular humans, they were here exclusively to serve his purpose. "Prove your worth."

Without hesitation, one of them dove into the hallway, sliding toward the opposite wall head-first. Enzo saw at least two bullets strike her leg and chest. The other unblessed followed suit, charging forward. He made it three steps before falling to a barrage. This gave Enzo and Azumi just the opening they needed.

The two of them were able to lay enough suppressive fire to force the Epsilons back and charged the enemy's fortified position. One of the five Epsilons fell to a point blank shot to the chest, another from the Emei piercer attached to Azumi's wrist. Then it turned to melee, as Enzo and Azumi fought the three remaining Epsilons hand-to-hand, with the suited men wielding their trademark bayoneted pistols.

A slash to Enzo's chest right above his armor drew blood. He ducked the second slash and moved into the Epsilon's guard. He kicked the inside of the Epsilon's knee just enough to throw him off-balance, and then he threw an upward punch that sent the man's nose up into his skull. He was dead before he hit the ground. Enzo spun around and drew Hanjo Masamune, cutting the second Epsilon clean through from navel to neck.

Enzo turned and saw Azumi struggling with the last Epsilon. He was a massive man easily twice her size. He had both his hands around her throat and was squeezing. Her face was red, and veins bulged from her forehead. She was slashing at his sides with the sharp point of her piercer, but most of her blows were ineffectual against his armor. The left side of his face was bleeding from several large gashes.

Enzo wondered if he should help her, but Azumi usually hated being interfered with. He leaned against the wall and coughed, lazily waving at the Epsilon when he glanced Enzo's way. That earned him a glare from his sister. That slight hesitation proved costly for the Epsilon. She took advantage of his momentary lapse of focus, swung her legs up and wrapped them around one of his arms. She twisted downward and flung him face first into the ground. Azumi finished him off with a piercer to his throat.

Enzo offered a hand and pulled her up from the ground. "Well done."

"Your assistance was unnecessary, brother," she said.

"None was given."

He handed her a rifle and they continued up the stairs, taking out three more Epsilons along the way. However, other than that, resistance on the upper levels was surprisingly light.

Vinnick would not have so few of his Epsilons guarding him. He must not be here.

Enzo cursed. Was he too late? Had he delayed too long? Well, no matter. As long as he showed the Russian government who controlled the Genjix and who they should be dealing with, that was all that mattered. Sometimes, a show of strength was the best form of diplomacy, even if it was technically against his own people. Especially if it was against his own people. The Russians could only imagine how he would treat them if he treated other Genjix who crossed him in this way.

He put his ear to the comm. "Report status."

"Front gates secured," Matthew said.

"Epsilon group at rear exit. We have them pinned down," Akelatis added.

Enzo leaned into his comm. "The Epsilons are useless to me. Leave no survivors."

He looked at Azumi, who nodded and left the room. The operation here was almost completed. All they needed to do now was round up Vinnick's surviving intermediaries to the Federal Assembly and show these bought politicians how little their bribes were actually worth.

CHAPTER TWENTY-THREE
GENJIX FACILITY

Timestamp: 2944

Eventually, we learned to game the system and stay below the radar. At first, my family and I tried to live a normal life as the entire Prophus network entrenched and reinvented itself. We enrolled Cameron in grade school. Jill joined a small law practice and I... um... I ran a black market for firearms. Hey, let me know if you guys need some real guns. Ha ha, okay you're right. It's not funny.

We could never stay in one place for long, though. Those damn Penetra nets kept popping up all over the place, and the government was making scanners increasingly smaller and more efficient. If either Jill or my son got caught in just one of those nets, the damn IXTF swooped in, and then we'd have to move.

It was rare to have Marco at a complete loss for words. He stared through the monocular and stuttered. "That... that is supposed to be a reclamation plant? What the bloody hell do you boys recycle there? Plutonium?"

He handed the monocular to Roen, who whistled. "That's no moon."

"Pardon?" Marco asked.

"Never mind. You suck."

Elias, lying on his stomach next to Roen, rolled onto his back and checked their surroundings. He gestured at Chase to make a round on the perimeter. Then he pulled out a small map of the area. "Like I said, this joint is nigh impenetrable."

Marco pointed at the double layers of fences around a two-story concrete wall. "It's like bloody Fort Knox over there." He turned to Roen. "You Americans must take your recycling very seriously."

Roen scanned the perimeter. The two rows of fences, barbed wired on the top, spanned the entire length of the facility and made a ninety-degree turn directly into a steep mountain wall. The wall itself seemed to have been artificially carved so that it cupped the back of the facility like a lid. The front central gatehouse, nestled between double-layered fences, guarded a dirt road just wide enough for a small car. How did the Genjix move supplies in and out? Then Roen noticed something else.

"Oh come on," he muttered. "That fence is electrified."

"Splendid," Marco said. He pointed at several tubes protruding out along the far corner. "Any idea what those are? Exhausts? Waste expulsion?"

Roen moved his sights to two clusters of pipes along each end of the building. He watched as two birds flitted around it. "Can't be. Intake." He continued to study the perimeter, growing more uneasy by the second. "What the… I think that's a machine gun nest. And if I didn't know any better, I'd think those were murder holes."

"Did the Genjix use Henry Yeverley to design this place?" Marco mused. "All they're missing is a drawbridge."

Roen counted the number of searchlights that lined the perimeter along the top of the walls at intervals of a few meters. With almost two hundred meters of clearance from the tree line, a frontal assault would be impossible, and given how the facility was nestled in a mountain, that was really the only way to hit it, unless they went in from above, which would pose a different set of problems.

"How did Prie get in before?" Roen asked.

"Come with me," Elias said.

The small group made a wide circle around the perimeter just outside the tree line. A side entrance was bored directly into the mountain a little ways up the base of a steep hill, with a partially hidden tunnel just wide enough for two trucks side by side. If Roen hadn't been looking carefully, he would have missed the entrance entirely.

Elias pointed into the dark tunnel with the dim fluorescent lights on the ceiling. "This is where all their supplies are off-loaded. Prie waited four days for a supply convoy and snuck in with it. He was able to grab a couple of samples before he was discovered. Based on how he described the interior, we believe the real facility goes far deeper into the mountain. The buildings that we see up front are just the entrance. The Genjix probably excavated deep into the rock to mask their real operation."

Roen and his team spent another two hours surveying the Genjix base from every angle before making the hour-long trek back to the station wagon, which they had hidden off the side of the road. The group was palpably gloomy as they trudged through the foliage back to the car. Roen had seen his fair share of battles, and while modern warfare was a far cry from the often trench- and battle-lined firefights of the twentieth century, attacking this facility would be the equivalent of landing on Omaha Beach. If the defenses of the base were as strong as they looked, any attacking force would be charging into a wood chipper.

"I don't know about you, but Ahngr thinks we're proper fucked," said Marco.

Roen grunted. "I didn't need a Quasing to tell me that."

Chase, manning point, dropped to one knee and raised a fist. The group flattened to the ground and froze. He crept forward a few paces and then signaled back at them. He pointed at his eyes, held up four fingers, then pointed west. Roen listened for anything out of the ordinary. At first, it was nearly imperceptible, but he soon detected a steady pattern of footsteps on leaves and low conversations coming from that direction.

Their group was too close together. If discovered, they would be easy targets for whoever was out there. Marco fell back, signaling for Roen to move forward and for Elias to pull left. Roen swung his rifle forward and kept it close to his body. They held their position.

Chase returned a few seconds later and drew on his hands with his fingers. A dot and a line that passed very close to it. The cracking sound got louder. Roen pulled Chase with him and they retreated into the brush. A few seconds later, a patrol of five soldiers wearing full camo gear passed through where they had just been. He immediately saw the Penetra scanner on one of the men and prayed Marco was far enough away to avoid detection.

Roen, being in the middle of his group, motioned to each: Elias lead. Chase two. Then he set his sights on the third in the group, trailing after them as they passed by. Time slowed. The group, walking single-file, was as relaxed as a pack of wolves on the prowl. Judging by the way they moved, they were professionals. They looked well-armored and -geared too.

Chase put his finger on the trigger and looked to him for confirmation. Roen shook his head. Their team was unarmored. In a firefight, even with surprise on their side, they would be at a disadvantage. Armor technology had far outpaced weapons technology in recent years. Even at their distance of forty meters, unless they got a head shot, these might not be killing blows.

The team held their position for another ten minutes, until well after the patrol had gone. Then Marco motioned for the others to gather. Roen exhaled, feeling the adrenaline dump pass through his body. Even after a hundred battles, this experience wasn't something he could get used to.

"What's our location?" Marco asked.

Elias checked the map and the GPS. "We're eight klicks out of the facility."

Roen whistled. For the Genjix to have a patrol eight kilometers away from their base made their job exponentially more difficult. That meant any ground force that wanted to attack would have to gather over an hour away by foot before moving in. They would be detected long before they got within sight of the facility.

"This just gets better and better," Marco grimaced. "Come on, let's get back to base."

An hour later, the deflated group wandered into Roen and Marco's motel room. The team now occupied three adjacent rooms on the top level, with Elias and Helen in one, and Sheck and Chase in the other.

Sheck, the team's tech, had set up the operations center in his room, while Helen had turned theirs into the supply quarter. That left Roen and Marco's room for all of their meetings and meals, which was something Roen had an issue with. The team was all career soldiers and rarely stayed in one place for long. Because of that, they all tended to be slobs. Roen, on the other hand, had long outgrown his slob days. He had spent the past few years living planted in a home, so he valued his space and privacy, which was now at a rare premium.

He wrinkled his nose when he came in and saw Helen and Sheck lounging with their feet up on the table – the same one that they ate on, by the way – while playing cards. Roen grimaced and gave them the stink eye. He had told them time and time again to act like adults. He caught himself just now. When had he turned forty going on sixty?

My, how the tables have turned, Tao would probably say.

"Guy's gotta get through puberty eventually," Roen would probably have answered. "The wrong side of forty sounds like the right time to do that."

Age means nothing. Sean was in his sixties when he kicked your ass.

"And Jacob was something like seventeen. At least that shows that age has nothing to do with who kicks my ass."

"All right," Marco said, gathering everyone around. "Sheck, get the Keeper on right away. We need to have a little chat regarding this bloody impregnable fortress the Genjix have over in the hills. Helen, how's our situation in the hospital?"

Sheck nodded and left the room. The damn catalyst facility was so well-fortified, Roen wasn't sure if the US military could have busted through. It seemed, however, that the Keeper was keen on planning an all-out attack on this facility no matter what, as it was the only one of its kind not stationed in a firmly Genjix zone of control.

"I bribed a janitor for his keys and identification," Helen said, pulling a silver key and ID badge out of her pocket and placing it on the table. "Bought some scrubs at the local thrift shop and spent the entire day wandering the medical center. The entire building has awful security, but there's a three-man guard at Prie's door at all times."

"Any news on our boy?" Roen asked.

"All second-hand gossip from the nurses, but it seems Prie's something of a celebrity there. He regained consciousness today. Those IXTF cruds tried to interrogate him while he was still groggy. Thank goodness Pri was there to keep his head straight. Then they put him into an induced coma." Helen looked angry. "Sir, we have to get him out of there!"

Marco nodded. "Not until our mission is complete or they try to move him. I'm not feeling comfortable relying on the word of a federal agent I picked up at a bar. Think we can get one of the scout team's bugs in the room?"

"It'll be tough, and those things have a battery life window of maybe four days. Turning it on remotely and hearing anything useful will be a crap shoot." Helen hesitated. "There's one more thing. I was found out. One of the nurses caught me lurking and asked for my ID."

"What did you do?" Chase asked.

She shrugged. "What did you expect me to do? I bolted for the nearest door. Pretty sure I'm compromised at this point."

"We'll have someone else take your place." He looked at Elias.

Elias, who had a thick Brazilian accent, held his hands up. "Don't look at me. I'll stick out like a sore thumb the second I open my mouth. Besides, I'm a jarhead, not some thespian. You go then, sir."

Marco made a face. "And I wouldn't stand out? Tell me, how many Brits do you think pass through here every year?"

"Yeah," Elias said. "I can't understand half the words coming out of your mouth sometimes. It's like a whole different language."

"Yes, it's called English. From Eng-land."

"I'll go," Roen said, throwing up his hands. He took the keys from Helen. "Will those scrubs fit me?"

She eyed him and then pointed to her drastically smaller frame. "Do you think they would?"

"I'll just get some myself," he grumbled.

Sheck walked into the room. "Keeper says she'll give you ten minutes, starting forty seconds ago."

Roen and Marco dashed out of the room. Grabbing a conference on the same day with her was like trying to arrange for the pope to attend a Bar Mitzvah. If they didn't take advantage of this meeting now, they might not be able to reach her again for days. They sprinted to Sheck's room and jumped on the secure channel.

"It's one in the morning," was the first thing out of her mouth.

"Apologies, Keeper," Marco said respectfully. "My surveillance team has made a full appraisal of the target facility."

"That's great. Now put it in a report and send it to me so I can read it at a more godly hour. Your next objective is to propose an incursion plan as soon as possible. I want this facility out of play."

"Well, you see, Keeper," Marco continued, "my team and I have concerns –"

"Resolve them. Unconcern them and –"

"It's a death trap, Meredith," Roen cut in. "Everyone you send in won't make it past the third defensive barrier. And in case you're wondering, there are five. We can't go in from the air, since it's US airspace, and we can't go in from the ground. The Genjix have at minimum an eight-kilometer defensive patrol perimeter, and you can be damn sure that thing is bottlenecked all to hell inside. It can't be done with the resources we have available. Period."

The Keeper looked at Marco. "Well?"

He nodded. "I'm afraid so, madam. The Genjix must be well aware of our operating limitations in this country and have planned for them thoroughly."

There was a period of silence before the Keeper fixed an eye on Roen and acknowledged him for the first time. Then she grimaced. "Find a way."

"I don't think you understand –" Roen began.

"No, you don't understand," she said. "This is our only viable way of stopping Quasiform. We know that Quasiform requires a number of their facilities to kick-start the catalyst at the same time in order to initiate the chain reaction. Of all the locations we're aware of, this facility is the only one within striking distance. I don't care if it's a bad tactical option. It's our *only* option, so when I say find a way, I damn well mean find a way. Is that clear?"

Roen and Marco exchanged glances and nodded. "Yes, Keeper," they said in unison.

"Very well, then. I look forward to your report in the morning. So if you will excuse me, gentlemen, good night."

"Wait, Keeper," Roen said. "Have you spoken to my wife? I haven't been able to get ahold of her since our meeting, and my phone tripped the security cut. We've had outages like this in the past, but never this long."

The Keeper looked over at Marco. "Your commander didn't tell you? It was part of his morning status report."

"Tell me what?" he said, now alarmed.

"The Genjix attacked Jill's base of operations two days ago. The entire operation went dark."

Roen lost feeling in his fingers. "And you guys didn't fucking tell me?"

"Look," Marco said. "It's too early to jump to conclusions. Command got in touch with Hite. He'll grab a visual. It could be anything. Jill's my friend too, but we have a mission to complete and I can't have distracted –"

He never finished the sentence, because Roen clocked him in the face. "That's my family, you bastard!"

Marco came back a second later with one of his own, followed by a Judo throw that put Roen on his back. Roen managed to get two quick kicks on Marco's face as he got turned upside down. A few seconds later, the two had destroyed Helen's bed and managed to punch several new holes in the drywall.

The Keeper, watching them roll around through the screen, yawned. "Goodnight, gentlemen." Then she smiled, and the screen went black.

CHAPTER TWENTY-FOUR
SHOW MUST GO ON

A dark time began for all Quasing as thousands of hosts on both sides were either rooted out and imprisoned, or were forced to flee. It was interesting that it took a massive alien conspiracy to unite the world against a common foe. The nations of the world banded together and created the Interpol Extraterrestrial Task Force.

A new player in our hundreds-year-long war emerged, and they were ruthless. The IXTF hunted us down, confiscated our assets, and destroyed networks that had taken hundreds of years to build.

Baji

As the submarine sliced just under the surface of the Pacific Ocean, the atmosphere was somber. The retreat through the tunnels from the farmhouse had been frantic. Jill's group had barely gotten their supplies together and made it a hundred meters before the Genjix cut through the trap door.

Immediately, they heard sounds of fighting. She didn't know if the other team got to safety or not. Jill knew that Harry and Garrett had decided to stay behind in order to distract the pursuers. They knew that Jill, with the older Rin and Ohr in her group, would need every small advantage she could get.

Even then, two of the Genjix had caught up with them halfway into the steep and uneven tunnels before they could escape into the submarine. Fortunately, Jill, Freeni, and Vladimir were able to lay a trap and take them out.

"Jill," Freeni said, looking at the console. "We can't squeeze anything more out of her. We need to break toward shore now."

We are still far from the next station. You will have to finish the journey on land.

They would have to disembark and continue on foot. Jill glanced back at the sad-looking group sitting in the rear of the sub. "This bunch can't handle a long trek."

Then locate the nearest safe house, establish communications, and have Faust pick us up.

Jill steered the sub toward the coast. Their ride was an old commercial tourist sub Roen had won from a junkyard dealer playing darts. They had retrofitted the sub, removing all the benches and turning the vessel into a short-range transport for supply runs. Jill had conserved as much fuel as possible, but the submersible wasn't built for long hauls and the fuel was almost exhausted.

She looked behind her at the small, quiet group. The Russian was a complete mess, face contorted with grief and eyes bloodshot. Jill didn't blame him. The poor guy had lost his wife and child within a span of weeks. His entire life was in tatters. She felt his pain. At least she had gotten word that Roen was all right before the attack. Otherwise, she would be thinking that she had lost both her husband and child as well and would probably be in worse shape than Vladimir.

Ohr and Rin were in only slightly better shape mentally, though not physically. Neither of them had ever been players in this sort of game. Ohr was a political heavyweight, and Rin was a scientist. Neither had ever had to spend a night on the run before the past few weeks. This experience had to be quite a shock to them. They were learning the hard lesson of what their world was, now. Well, that was the life of a secret society operative. Inevitably, one's hands had to get dirty.

When the sub couldn't get any closer to shore, Jill stood up and motioned for everyone to follow. "Here's where we get off, folks. We're going to make landfall about three klicks north of Fort Bragg. From there, we go on foot. I have a safe house on the south end of Noyo Bay. We can rest there for the night."

She swung the packs and gear that she was able to salvage – all of her worldly possessions – onto her back and picked up the bundled rifles stowed in a sleeping bag. Between the five of them, they would have to share two rifles and two pistols. She nudged Vladimir on the shoulder. "Come on. Get up." He didn't budge. Everyone else began climbing up the ladder to the hatch. Jill looked back at him still sitting in his seat. "Vladimir, get your ass up. Now."

He just stayed there, staring at the floor, eyes glazed over. For a second, Jill wasn't sure if he was going to get up. The guy had suffered a lot. Every person had his limit; maybe he had reached his. Maybe his soul couldn't take any more grief, and there was nothing left for it to do but die. She had seen it happen on the battlefield before, to friends and enemies alike. Letting him end his pain could be the kindest thing she could do for him.

Jill gritted her teeth. Screw that. She stomped over to him, grabbed his elbows, and pulled. "We need to go, Vladimir."

"I have nothing," he said, the words barely audible. "Marta, Alex. Nothing. Just leave me."

We do not have time for this.

"Alex is probably with Cameron. He knows what to do. They are probably heading toward us as we speak," Jill said, pulling more insistently this time. "Get your ass up."

"My daughter is probably dead. Your damn son killed her!" he snarled, pushing Jill away. "If it wasn't for him, she would be here right now."

Either snap him out of it or drown him.

"I am not leaving anyone behind, Baji."

An imaged flashed into Jill's head of an ancient fishing boat slowly sinking. She saw one of the sailors with his leg trapped underneath a wooden beam. As hard as she tried, she could not pull him free. The boat capsized, trapping Jill underneath it as it sunk. Everything became blinding white, and then she blinked and saw the world in an entirely new way through the eyes of a fish.

"Point taken."

Jill gave Vladimir one measured look, swung her arm back with an open palm, then thought better of it. Instead, she closed her hand into a fist and clocked him across the jaw. Vladimir dropped onto his side like a sack of potatoes. He tried to retaliate, but Jill got past his weakly flailing arms easily. She pulled out her pistol and jammed it into his temple. "That's my son, you shit. He's out there, too, so don't even start with me, because the only thing that's keeping me going right now is the fact that I know he's well-trained and competent. I know that if he is alive, he will find me, and if your daughter is alive, he will bring her to us." She cocked the pistol. "Do you understand, or would you like me to end you right here?"

Vladimir nodded.

Slowly, Jill pulled back and holstered her pistol. She offered her hand, which he accepted, and hauled the guy to his feet. She tossed the heaviest pack at him. "You get to be the pack mule."

Vladimir rubbed his already purplish cheek and wiggled his jaw left and right. Then, surprisingly, he grinned. "Marta would have liked you, Jill Tan. Even if you are a betrayer. Sometimes, Vladimir just needs a reminder."

"Happy to oblige," Jill said, returning the smile. "And don't do that again."

"I won't. I trust your word that my daughter is safe."

"I wasn't talking about that. Don't refer to yourself in the third person. It annoys the hell out of me." Jill pointed at the metal ladder. "Come on, it's getting dark, and the temperature is dropping."

Once topside, the group had to wait until Freeni got the emergency raft inflated before paddling toward shore. Jill looked back at the submarine bobbing on the ocean's surface and pushed a small button on a remote. A few seconds later, smoke began to billow out of the open hatch. Several loud cracking noises followed, and then the sub tilted. In a matter of minutes, the ocean had claimed its latest wreck. It was a damn shame to lose such an asset, but the wrong hands – Genjix or IXTF – could get a lot from its salvage.

The small group stood at the beach, unsure of what to do next. Jill pointed to the wooden ramp up the beach. Just past it was a highway traveling north and south. "Let's move. No stragglers. We're wet, and the temperature drops at night."

It took the small group a little over three hours walking along the highway to reach their destination. The safe house at Fort Bragg ranked pretty low on the luxury scale of Prophus safe houses. It was an old trailer nestled in the back of an RV park held up by stacks of cinderblocks. Fortunately, it was a frequently-used facility, so it was relatively well-maintained and clean.

Check the emergency exit plan.

Jill watched the other four exhausted refugees march into the rusty chrome Twinkie-shaped trailer. She walked to the cliff at the back of the park overlooking Noyo Harbor and peered over the steep drop to the beach below while the others lugged the gear into the trailer. It had been over a year since she was last at this safe house. Down at the base of the cliff, hidden in the thick foliage, should be an emergency pack. Every safe house had a designated exit plan. Jumping off the cliff and tumbling down to the beach was the designated one for this trailer. It wasn't much of an escape route, but it was better than nothing. Not much better though.

The two dummies in her life – her child and her man-child – thought it would be great fun to test it out when they had first set up the trailer. Both jumped and tumbled down the cliff enthusiastically. Roen badly sprained his ankle, and Cameron earned a gash along his arm that needed stitches.

Like father, like son.

"Let's just hope we'll never have to use it."

It took Jill a few minutes to identify the marker where the pack was supposed to be hidden. Satisfied, she went back to the trailer and joined the others. The inside was cramped for five, with just enough room in the hallway for one person to walk through at a time. Ohr opened the fridge and pulled out a six-pack of beer and half a bottle of vodka.

"Any food?" Rin asked, looking over his shoulder.

He held up a bottle of Sriracha. "Ketchup, mustard, barbecue sauce, and this. At least you have the important stuff. How do you have a fridge full of condiments and no food?"

"The trailer wasn't expecting company for another two weeks." Jill made a mental note to get ahold of Faust, who ran the operations south of hers, right away. Just because her operation went dark didn't mean it was now defunct. There were still refugees who needed help. The Patels were still scheduled to move in two days. If they missed their transport, it'd be another three weeks before they could try again. Then there was the issue of the six outlier outposts operating in her region. Most had backup protocols, but she didn't know how thorough her cleanup operation was, or how pervasive the enemy. More of her people could be in danger. She sighed. There was so much to do. So many people depended on her.

Jill pointed to the sleeping quarters in the back. "Two to the back. One on the couch. Freeni, first watch. I'll take second. Then Rin, Ohr, and Vladimir. Freeni, hold the fort. I'll be back."

She left the RV and made her way through the darkness toward the office building up front. It was a moonless night, but the sky was full of stars. She hadn't slept in over thirty-six hours and was starting to feel the effects. She wasn't a law school student able to pull off all-nighters anymore. She wasn't even a policy director working in Washington DC. Jill was a tired woman on the lam trying to save a bunch of Genjix refugees while her son was somewhere out there. Possibly injured. Possibly dead. She shook her head and pushed those thoughts out of her mind. Cameron was well-trained. He was smart and able. He would find her. She believed it; she had to. She had no other choice.

"Get it together, girl," she growled. "People are depending on you."

It took a few seconds for her to find the relic she was looking for. The sad-looking pay phone attached to the side of the office building had seen better days. The ground under it was overgrown with weeds, and the paint had long flaked off. Jill half-feared the line would be dead when she picked up the receiver. With her cell phone bricked, she had few other options. Luckily, there was a dial tone. She looked around to make sure she was alone, and dialed the emergency number.

"Twenty-four-hour wake up service. We wake up to wake you up. Can I help you?"

"Identification Baji."

"Voice recognition matches Jill Tesser Tan. Current condition: Unknown. Base binary code required."

"Binary code zero, zero, one, zero, one, one, one, zero, zero, one, one, zero."

Silence.

"Baji, it's good to hear from you. We thought we lost you when the hard line tripped."

"Hey, Datlow. It was a Genjix raid. A full-blown assault. Vessel-led. Well-armed and coordinated." Jill leaned against the aluminum siding and looked up at the night sky. She closed her eyes. "Did any of my people report in?"

"Six of your outposts reported in after they received the alert. Two of your occupied safe houses as well. No one from your base of operations called in. I am sorry."

Rage welled up in Jill, not just at the Genjix, but also at everything else. At these refugees she was chaperoning. At Cameron for being missing; at Roen for not being here; at the government for not seeing things more clearly. Most of all, though, she was mad at herself for letting her people down.

Stop it. There was nothing you could do.

"I don't subscribe to that. There is always something that can be done."

As the infinitely wiser being, I am a better judge.

"Pulling rank on me? You haven't done that in a while."

I might not have the military mind of many other Quasing, but I have at the very least occupied three generals, one of them even deserving of the rank, so cut it out. You do not have time for this nonsense.

"Jill?" Datlow's voice came across the line. "Are you there? What is your status?"

"I still have passengers embedded on the Underground Railroad. The Patel group needs to catch their ship. Put all regional stations on comm lockdown. The attack was too well-coordinated. They knew exactly how to hit us."

"Will do. We have your manifest on file already. Hearne in Vancouver has already stepped in to assist and has rerouted the Patels through Seattle. All western stations are now on alert. Is there anything else?"

"I need a new crypto key authorized to continue operations from this location. Some of the work might have to route through Faust's operation to complete deliverables."

"Your base was just attacked, Jill. Surely, you can put that on hold until the situation stabilizes."

"No. There are too many lives at stake. Get that crypto key patched via Safe House CAFB49. I need to be on-line and working as soon as possible."

"It'll take an hour to route."

"One last thing. My son is missing. He might try to call in. Please let him know that I'm all right and set up a rendezvous for this location. I will try to check in every day or two."

"Of course. Our thoughts are with you."

"Thank you, Datlow." Jill stayed on the call for another five minutes, tying up every loose thread she could recall. It was at the same time cathartic and guilt-inducing. She was a compromised station in the Underground Railroad, a vital cog that was now broken. After she hung up the phone, Jill made the lonely walk through the darkness back toward the trailer, her usually busy multi-tasking mind strangely clear and empty. There was still much to do, but she had a hard time caring at this very moment.

Get some rest. Worry about resupplying in the morning. I would recommend moving further south if possible.

"I don't want to get too far away. Cameron could be trying to make his way here as well."

I guess this safe house is as fine a base of operations as any. Better than most, considering you are protected from two sides. Stay alert, however. We do not know how much of your network the Genjix uncovered.

She found Freeni and Vladimir sitting on lawn chairs on top of the trailer. They were chatting amiably and sharing beers. They both raised their cans as she approached.

"You up for cold one?" Freeni asked, holding up the

six-pack with two beers left. "A few months' expired, but bearable."

Jill grinned and climbed up the ladder. She was soon sitting next to Vladimir, cracking open a can. The beer was room-temperature, stale, and frankly tasted like syrup. However, it was the very thing she needed at this exact moment. She slouched in her chair and held her can up to toast the Russian.

Vladimir leaned in. "I want to thank you for earlier."

"For punching you in the face? Do you always thank people for that?"

"For snapping me out of my depression." He touched the purple blossom on his cheek and winced. "You punch like a Siberian railway worker."

"I will take that as a compliment, and you're welcome."

They clinked cans. The small group sat in exhausted silence as they drank and stared at the sky. For those few minutes, Jill allowed herself to clear her mind and not think about anything else. She just breathed in and out deeply, feeling her body finally settle down. She had been on this path for so long, she could hardly remember life before the Quasing War. What was the end game? How did this finish? She couldn't imagine that, either.

So much for clearing your mind and not thinking about things.

"Sorry. Can't help it."

Nothing to apologize for. You have succeeded far beyond my wildest hopes for you. I am infinitely proud and honored to call you my host.

"You know how to say all the right things to a girl."

I have had thousands of years of experience. That and I learned by watching Roen do it wrong all these years.

"That guy. I'm convinced his doing it wrong is what is so right about him."

A true idiot savant, then.

Jill's precious peace lasted until Vladimir opened his mouth and ruined the moment. "Do you really think we'll see our children again?" he asked.

Jill stood up, downed her beer and then crushed the can. "The Genjix better hope I do. Otherwise, I will spend the rest of my life hunting them down. Get some sleep, Vladimir. You have last watch."

She climbed back down into the trailer and rummaged through her bags until she found what she was looking for: a small gold bangle. She walked to the bedroom in the back, where Ohr was sleeping and Rin was reading a fashion magazine. That seemed to be the only thing she could find to read in the trailer. Jill made a mental note to restock her safe houses with better reading materials.

She gestured for Rin to come over and slid the bangle over the small Japanese woman's wrist. "I have something for you in case things go bad. This is very important, personally as well as operationally. I want you to keep it on you at all times."

Rin shook the bangle loosely around her wrist. "Not quite my style, but I appreciate the gesture. Anything else?" She held up the magazine. "I'm about to learn what was in fashion three years ago."

Jill pulled out her tablet and began to type on it. "Tell me everything you know about catalyst facilities, starting with that one just a few hours northeast of here."

Rin nodded. "Your people found it, then. You'd better get comfortable. This could take a while." She paused, looking at Jill intently. "Quasiform is a multi-phased approach to terraforming Earth, combining atmospheric, chemical, and seismic detonations coupled with the merging of acidic levels that would more or less, over the course of a few years, turn Earth's atmosphere into one not too far off from that of Quasar, the Quasing home world."

"We were aware of the atmospheric manipulation of the environment and the catalyst reaction rods."

"Quasiform can only do so much. The planet must also meet the process halfway. That is why for the past hundred or so years, the Genjix have been slowly increasing the average temperature of the planet. Chemically, the reaction rods, once heated to high temperatures, will release metastasizing catalysts into the atmosphere to create a chain reaction."

"Could you explain what you mean by seismic detonations?"

"You will find that over half the catalyst facilities, the one nearby included, are built over the beginning of a major seismic fault line. The process is meant to widen the faults with the intention of creating very large seismic shifts. Remember, Quasar's surface is completely liquid. To function optimally, Quasiform would raise water levels, while at the same time leveling large portions of the surface, so that Earth eventually becomes a completely submerged planet…"

Over the next three hours, Jill typed up everything Rin summarized about Quasiform and the catalyst facilities. The Genjix future sounded terrifying.

CHAPTER TWENTY-FIVE
FOUND

Timestamp: 3012

Eventually, we realized that it was no longer possible to live in large cities. Penetra nets were at too many stinking intersections. Regional IXTF offices popped up all over the place like coffee shops. It became untenable to live within a hundred miles of any major metropolitan area. We once had to move four times in a month.

The straw that broke the camel's back was when they started putting Penetra nets in the schools in Washington DC. Cameron got caught, and we had to yank him out and get out of town, barely staying ahead of the IXTF. Who was the bright genius who decided to put a damn scanner in a grade school? I want to punch him in the face. Oh, the president? Never mind. I'm not voting for him next year.

An argument erupted in room 224 of their motel. It wasn't a couple fighting, though, it was Roen and Marco trying to figure out what the hell they were going to do next. Their quarreling got so bad that Helen and Sheck, who were having breakfast on the balcony, stuck both their heads in to investigate. Elias would tell them later on that he could hear the ruckus all the way from the parking lot.

"And as always, Roen, you don't have the authority to make that call," Marco growled, his body still dripping wet, a towel wrapped around his waist. This probably wasn't the best time for them to quarrel, but he had just gotten out of a shower and was irritated with Roen, who had cooked the entire batch of bacon and was feasting on the stack while lying in bed. The Brit had recently developed a fascination with American bacon, and the two of them were single-handedly causing a bacon shortage in Ontario.

"You and that hag are going to get everyone killed," Roen snapped back.

"That's not your call. There is a command structure, Roen, and you are nowhere near the top. In fact, you're more like down here." Marco gestured at his knees. "We have our orders, and our team, you included, will follow them to the best of our abilities. That attack force is coming whether you like it or not."

"Damn it, Marco. Think for yourself, man. What does your pea brain tell you? Hell, what does Ahngr say about it? Why would you even consider following through with an attack when you know that," he held up a finger, "we don't have the firepower to take it, and," he held up two fingers, "they know we're coming. We have no chance. It's suicide. If we're going to do our mission right, we should be doing everything in our power to convince the Keeper not to go through with this."

"See. That's always been your problem. You decide something, and then everyone else can piss off if they don't agree with you." Marco stomped forward, shaking a finger, the towel flirting with disaster as the knot around his waist held on for dear life. "That's why you can't play nice, and no one likes you."

"Thank you, you didactic asshole," Roen said, purposely chewing through the plate of bacon as fast as he could. That fact wasn't lost on Marco, who looked like he was seconds away from diving onto the bed to snatch the plate away. Thank God he didn't, because Elias burst into the room a second later. With only a towel around Marco's waist, that would have been awkward.

To his credit, Elias didn't bat an eye. "We've got a problem." He closed the door behind him and looked out the window.

Roen sat up in bed and put the plate aside. He wiped his hands and joined Elias at the window. "Crap," he exclaimed.

Two white vans had pulled into the parking lot. The top of one of the vans had the familiar shark fins of the IXTF Penetra vans. Twelve fully-geared men stepped out. One of them walked into the office, and another took position at the driveway out to the street. The rest spread out and disappeared from view. At least two of the agents carried portable Penetra scanners.

"Rouse the men," Marco ordered, running for some clothes. "I want us packed in three and ready to move."

Roen went next door and kicked the napping Chase awake. "Got agents canvasing the motel. Get moving."

Like all good soldiers, Chase was up and throwing on his shirt five seconds later. Within a minute, he was dressed and loading a magazine into his pistol. Within two, the both of them were fully packed and ready to go. In another minute, the entire team was ready to move. Roen looked out of the window and watched as the six or seven agents made a beeline toward their end of the balcony hall.

Roen took a quick inventory from the window and spoke into his comm. "Multiple armed moving toward us. One at the driveway. One on the far edge of the lot. I have sights on him. Remember people, these are federal agents. Lethal force only if necessary."

Marco added. "They must have detected me in the room. We'll use that knowledge to our advantage. Take them out after they've passed Elias's door. Hoods over your heads, people. Helen, get the car. Everyone else, move the gear down. Roen, clear the lot."

Roen looked to his right, where the lone agent stood guard at the driveway. The safe option would just be to riddle him with bullets, but Roen preferred not to, if possible. That left one option. The next few seconds were anxious as the agents walking down the balcony got closer and closer.

"Opening in three, two, one…" Roen heard through the comm.

All three of their doors opened at the same time, and the team charged the federal agents from all directions. Roen, aiming through the window, plugged the guy at the far end of the parking lot twice in the shoulder. He ran out of the room and sped to the end of the balcony hall. He caught sight of the guard in the driveway below him and aimed low, shooting him in both legs. The guard fell to the ground, writhing. As the rest of his team disarmed the surprised federal agents, Roen jumped off the balcony and landed heavily on the ground.

He grunted as he rolled to his feet, tweaking his left foot in the process. He was definitely not a young buck anymore. That drop was a five at best. Roen limped just a little as he ran to the downed agent, who was still writhing in pain. Roen kicked his rifle away from him and pinned him down to the ground. The poor kid must have been eighteen; he looked like he belonged more in the chess club in high school than he did in a SWAT uniform. To be fair, though, everyone younger than Roen looked eighteen to him these days.

"Sorry, son," he muttered as he brought the butt of his rifle down on the kid's head.

He turned around and saw another agent charging from the back of the motel. He rolled to his left just as the guy opened fire. Landing flat on his stomach, Roen hit him in the thigh and once more in his side, spinning him around. This guy was going to be seriously injured. His armor had saved his life, but he probably had some broken ribs from the slug in the chest. Again, he felt guilty, but there was little he could do.

Roen picked himself up and ran to the body. The agent, also looking like a teenager, was clutching his thigh and rolling around in agony. He grabbed the rifle before the guy could reach it and flung it into the parking lot next door. He took one look at the bloody injury and thought better than to knock him unconscious. If he did, the kid was going to bleed out.

He pulled out a cord he always kept on him – usually reserved for strangling someone – and tossed it to him. "Put that around your injury and squeeze it tight."

Roen sprinted back to the parking lot and saw the rest of his team moving their gear down the stairs to the station wagon. He rushed back to them and kept watch as they loaded it up. "One more still loose," he said, scanning the perimeter. They were sitting ducks out here.

He caught sight of the guy creeping around the corner.

He ran forward and put one hand on the agent's rifle barrel and the other under his armpit. Then Roen lowered his weight and twisted, driving him into the ground. The agent tried to reach for his pistol.

"Don't even think about it," Roen said.

The stubborn fool continued to draw.

Roen put his foot on the guy's wrist. "Seriously? What part of 'don't' do you not understand?"

Still the kid squirmed. He just didn't know when to give up, which, while usually an admirable trait, was exceptionally stupid when someone had a rifle inches from your face while stepping on you. For a second, he considered whacking him alongside the head to teach him a lesson, but decided on a gentler approach.

"You got a girlfriend, kid?"

The agent, surprised by this line of questioning, stopped squirming and nodded.

"You want to see her again, right?"

He nodded again.

"I want you to, too but that's not going to happen if you move another inch. Got it?"

Third nod.

Roen heard a honk behind him and nudged the kid in the face with the rifle's muzzle. "Stay still. Live another day. The most important lesson you can ever learn is when to know you've lost. Don't make this mistake again, pal." He flung the rifle off to the side and ran to the waiting station wagon. They pulled out and were cruising toward highway 84 within seconds.

"How did they find us?" he asked.

"Random patrol?" said Elias. "Or they would have come down harder."

"Most likely they've been getting blips of me over the past few days and finally decided to do a sweep," Marco said. "Happens quite a bit back in London. They probably have a few scanners stationed at intersections, and we've been tripping them just enough for them to isolate this location."

"Where to, boss?" Helen asked.

"Crap," Roen growled, pointing at a Penetra van near the on-ramp in the distance. They made a U-turn and headed north down Olds-Ferry Ontario Highway, running into another van at the intersection of 201. Fortunately, this one was parked with no one inside.

"We have to get off the road," Roen said as they made another U-turn. "Someone's bound to notice us and get suspicious."

Marco sighed. "Guess we'll have to make use of the B location."

Everyone groaned. They had desperately hoped to not ever have to use that backup site. It was a small shed west of the river. Chase had found this place during one of his scouting trips when they had first arrived. It was an awful place to live, but it would serve its purpose until they could join the main Prophus force.

A few minutes later, they pulled off the road to the abandoned factory and drove around back to a small shack tucked in the corner of the factory's work yard. While Roen hid the station wagon in the main building, the rest of the team lugged their gear into the storage shed, the floor of which hid the door to the B location. The good thing about this safe house was it was buried several meters underground, so it would guard them against random Penetra scans. The bad news was that they would be underground without running water, central air, or beds.

Chase pulled open the floor panel and led them down a steep set of stairs. Roen sighed when he saw the living area. And he had thought the motel was a dump. The place was an old pump room that had been converted into a storage room and then forgotten once the factory shut down. Fortunately, there was still power, though little else. Other than four large columns symmetrically placed to hold up the ceiling, their new home was essentially one concrete square, filled with piles of junk one would expect to see in a mechanic's shop. The dust down here was thick enough that Roen couldn't see what color the walls or floors actually were. The lone light source at the base of the stairs was barely strong enough for them to see the far wall.

The ceiling in the living area was low enough that it made Roen feel claustrophobic, though unlike Marco and Elias, he didn't have to bend over to avoid banging his head on the pipes and beams zig-zagging around the ceiling. All in all, this place was a shithole. However, it would prevent detection. That would be especially important once they retrieved Prie. Who knew what condition he would be in once they snatched him out of the IXTF's grasp?

The team broke their gear down and set up shop. Marco took charge as each of them claimed a sleeping spot, ordering Sheck to get their comm system back and up and Elias to take inventory of their stocks. Helen and Chase were sent out to restock whatever supplies they had had to leave at the motel.

Roen ended up taking first watch, which was fine with him. He couldn't take more than a few minutes in that pit anyway. He found a small alcove in the third story of the factory overlooking the two roads to and from the location and settled in. His mind wandered back to what they had discovered at the catalyst facility. He adamantly believed that he was right. Somehow, he had to convince Marco. The guy was battle-hardened; he should know better.

It was times like this he wished Tao were here to advise him. To be honest, there was no time when he didn't wish Tao was with him. He would know what to do. His friend and mentor was good at more than just appraising tactical situations. He would make them see the light. Well, Tao wasn't here, so it was now all up to Roen.

"We are so screwed," he muttered, tossing a pebble at an oil drum in the yard below. He missed it by about five meters. "So screwed."

CHAPTER TWENTY-SIX
ON THEIR OWN

The Quasing on this planet were unable to identify a unified objective because, unlike our merged consciousness on Quasar, we were all singular beings on Earth, isolated from each other in our individual hosts. This was a new experience for us, being alone with our own thoughts. Over time, our individual ideas deviated from the collective. Because of this, we experienced dissension in our ranks and eventually fractured.

Tao

The last couple of days in the forest had been rough. At least for Alex they had been. For Cameron, it was just another camping trip. Unsure of the extent of the attack, Tao had recommended they hide and stay low until things had calmed down. After all, if the Genjix were based out of Eureka, which was probable, wandering into town would play right into the enemy's hands.

That suited Cameron just fine; he had been camping in the wilds with Roen for years. One of his fondest early memories was playing hide and seek with his father. Roen would use a Penetra scanner and try to find him while

Cameron did everything and anything he could to stay hidden. Since the scanner could continually track Tao, it was inevitable that he'd lose the game, but its limitation was that it could only provide directional proximity. By being clever, and with a lot of help from Tao, he was surprised at how well he could keep from being "tagged."

Alexandra Mengsk, the princess of Siberia, had toughed it out the first night, and they huddled together in the brush in the lone sleeping bag Cameron had in his emergency pack. Two nights, it seemed, was all she could take. When he told her on the morning of the third day that they weren't going to head into town yet, her composure went downhill fast. When they ran out of dried rations at lunch time and had to go without dinner, she threw a fit.

Remember the time you asked why your parents had to spend some time apart every once in a while? Well, here you go.

"Is this what married life is like?"

Sometimes. There is good and bad. You just hope for mostly good.

Cameron harrumphed, and looked over at Alex. The two hadn't talked since their last fight. She was sitting with her arms wrapped around her knees, staring at the ground. It had rained earlier, which only exasperated the situation. Still, Cameron thought Alex would have handled the situation a little better. She was a host, after all. Shouldn't she be prepared for this?

You should be more sympathetic to her. Alex was not raised to enjoy the wilderness like you.

"I'd think all hosts would be."

Not all agents were trained as I trained you and your father.

"Isn't survival a basic necessity?"

There are many ways to survive. All hosts are different,

*especially ones raised from infancy. Alex was meant to follow in
her father's footsteps, to one day control his financial empire and
become a player in Russian government. Tabs has played politics
in that region for over a thousand years.*

"That's true. I would suck if I tried to do her job."

*Well, first of all, you are very much like your father in that you
are not adept at languages, and politics bore you. You can barely
speak English, let alone Russian. You also make a poor chess
player, which in my opinion, is key in understanding political
dynamics.*

"Chess is boring, and hard."

*I rest my case. It will be cold tonight. Maybe it is time to head
into town. Find a roof over your head. Go talk to her. Apologize.*

"For what?!"

*You have a lot to learn, Cameron. Just trust me on this.
Apologize. Repeat after me.*

"Hey," Cameron dragged his feet as he walked up to
her.

"What," she replied, not bothering to look up.

"I'm really sorry you have to put up with this." He
repeated Tao's words verbatim, though not his inflection.

Damn it, Cameron. Say it like you mean it.

Cameron tried again. The words came out reluctantly
as Tao hammered in each word. "It's been rough out here
and I know I haven't been listening to you. I'm sorry."

Alex looked up at him. "Are you sorry?"

"I… I just said I was," he stammered.

*Do not extemporize. Just apologize again and offer a solution
to her misery.*

"I am totally sorry and I think you're right," he said,
trying very hard not to grit his teeth. "It's time we head
into town and find some shelter."

It took a little more cajoling before she finally acquiesced to leaving the campsite and heading into Eureka. It was actually very mysterious to Cameron how it came about that he had to beg her to do what she wanted to do all along.

The two packed up camp and headed toward Eureka. They had been camping on the fringes of it already, just staying out of view. It didn't take them long before they saw signs of civilization. They passed a few scattered houses, farms and warehouses. Cameron had considered breaking into one of these places for the night, but Tao had other ideas. If they were going to abandon the safety of the forest, they might as well go all the way.

As they walked, Cameron took out his cell phone and tried to get a signal. He had hoped that the outage was just from being deep in the woods. However, his phone still wasn't working. That meant his mom had ordered a complete shutdown. He and Alex were truly cut off from the rest of the network.

I have a way of getting in touch with them. For now, just take care of your basic needs.

"I'm worried Mom didn't get out in time. Dad's still missing too."

If Jill had time to initiate a lock down, she had time to escape. Your mother is very competent. Operate under the assumption that she is safe and looking for you as we speak.

The weather finally caught up with them, and they began feeling a few drops of rain. Cameron and Alex picked up their pace, continuing west until they reached the town's limits and hit Myrtle Avenue. Tao pressed them closer into the residential area. By now, it was night, and Alex had gone from complaining of being wet and hungry to complaining of being tired of walking. Cameron didn't blame her. His feet hurt, too. He reminded himself that she was only fourteen. As the oldest here, it was his job to keep them going.

All right, gramps.

To Alex's surprise, since they hadn't been on the friendliest terms of late, he grabbed her hand and held it as they walked, telling her that they were almost there, though he wasn't exactly sure where *there* was. He soon realized where when Tao had him turn onto Harrison Street. There was a tiny hamburger place where some of the high school kids liked to hang out. The hamburgers were better than average, but more importantly, it was in a wooden building in a less-trafficked part of town. The two went around back and studied the door. It was an older deadbolt with a flimsy frame. He rapped the door; it felt hollow. If he gave it a hard kick, he doubted the frame would hold up.

Or you can just pick it.

"Lock picking is hard."

You are just not good at it. Like someone else I know. Try first.

Grumbling, Cameron took out the set he kept in his pack and went to work. Tao had tried to train him before, and it had taken him weeks to successfully pick his first padlock. It still sometimes took him an hour to undo the most basic lock. Now, he had the added pressure of attempting it under Alex's expectant gaze. It didn't matter though. This door was the only thing standing between them and food, and as his father liked to say, "Nothing stands between a Tan and his food."

Five minutes into his attempt, after fumbling a dozen times and snapping two picks, he began to sweat. The rain didn't let up. Alex began to give him tips on what he was doing wrong. Twenty minutes into his attempt to pick the back door of a run-down burger joint, Cameron had had enough of this crap. With a frustrated guttural cry, he slammed the stinking lock picks on the ground, took a step back, and attempted to kick the door in half.

"Stop," Alex said, moving in his way. She rolled her eyes. "Boys." She picked up the picks and went to work on the door. Within three minutes, the door was open.

Like I said, different skillsets.

"Why didn't you just tell me you were a master thief?" he complained. "You stood there laughing at me for over twenty minutes."

"You were trying so hard. I didn't want to ruin your confidence. It was adorable." She patted him on the cheek. "Besides, I assumed a Prophus agent would know how to perform such a simple task. I guess I was mistaken." With a tinkling laugh, she walked inside.

"We can't be good at everything!" he called after her.

The hamburger joint consisted of nothing more than a tiny dining area, a range in the back, and a large walk-in fridge, all divided by a center counter with a register. The two made a beeline for the goods inside the fridge and promptly hauled out a dozen patties and packages of lettuce, onions and tomatoes. They added to their ill-gotten booty a bag of frozen French fries and several bags of chips. They dug into the chips while they figured out how to operate the industrial range and deep fryer.

Alex held up the bag of frozen patties and frowned. "It says grass-fed cows. What else would you feed them?"

Cameron shrugged. "Corn?"

Alex looked at him as if he was crazy. "Why don't you

eat the corn and give the cow grass that people can't eat?"

That stumped him. "Because, um, that would make a lot of sense, wouldn't it?"

It is a little more complicated than that, but she wins the point.

Alex turned on the lights once the fryer and grill were heated. Cameron rushed over and turned them off. "They'll see us," he said, much to her disapproval. It seemed she got cross whenever he contradicted her, no matter how right he was.

It took a few overcooked patties and batches of fries, but before long, they were dining on poorly-constructed burgers, chips, and fries. Cameron and Alex settled down for dinner, sitting cross-legged on the floor behind the counter. By candlelight, no less. It was the most romantic thing – the only romantic thing really – Cameron had ever experienced.

I obviously have been sorely remiss in your education.

At least the food was good. The two hungry kids scarfed down the burgers and chips within minutes and were contently nibbling down the mound of fries as they huddled closer together in the darkness. Outside, the rain came down harder. Now Cameron was glad they had decided to leave the forest. It would have been miserable out there. However, still in their wet clothes, and now without the warmth of the sleeping bag, they shivered as they edged closer to the small bundle of candles they had found in storage.

Cameron looked at Alex's face in the dark, the flickering light reflecting off her pale skin and blonde hair, matted down against her head. She caught his gaze and they both looked away. Cameron could feel his ears burning so hot they felt numb.

She reached out and touched his left brow. "Your cut is festering."

The fight with the Genjix sentry had left him with an ugly bruise just above the eye, but it had left a small gash as well. After two days out in the wilderness, it had become infected and hurt like crazy any time Cameron moved his face.

"It's nothing," he said, trying to smile, though that only made him wince.

"No, we should take care of that before it gets worse and infects your entire face. Would be such a pity."

Cameron's brain short-circuited a little as his heartbeat became the only noise he could hear. Beads of sweat or water – he couldn't tell anymore – dribbled down the side of his face. He felt like someone had grabbed the ends of his guts and wrung them like wet rags. It felt strangely sickening and wonderful.

All right, Marc Antony, you are starting to make me sick, which is supposed to be impossible. You and Cleopatra better cool it before you lose Egypt. Remember, she is a Genjix.

She was so close to him. He could feel her breath lightly touch his skin, and the slight shiver of her body. He noticed for the first time that they were both shaking. "We have to stay warm," he said.

Alex nodded. She looked at the rain splattering the windows outside, now coming hard at almost a horizontal angle. Then she reached out and felt his wet shirt. "We should get out of our wet clothes." She began to strip her jacket off.

Now I know Tabs is screwing with me.

Cameron didn't need any more encouragement. In a minute, they were in their undershirts huddling closer together for warmth. Alex shivered as she nuzzled against him. Awkwardly, Cameron put his arms around her shoulder and pulled the dry layers of their clothes over them like a blanket.

"You are so warm," she said, poking her cold nose against his skin.

Cameron, please consider the situation. You know who Alex is and where she is going. Do not get too attached. Once we find your mother, Alex will be leaving you.

Tao said please. Tao almost never said please. In another time, that word coming from his Quasing would have given Cameron pause. This time, though, the words went right through him.

All Cameron could think of was how nice it was, and wished he could somehow make time stay still. She was supposed to go with Vladimir to South America. What if he had died during that attack? Could she stay with him then? Would his mom and dad allow it? She'd be an orphan. How could they say no?

Of course it was a terrible thing to think about. It wasn't like he wished for Alex's father to die, but Cameron didn't know what he would do right now if Alex left. For now, he just wanted to keep her safe.

Puberty. I hate it. In the thousands of years using humans as hosts, you idiots have never evolved out of the worst of human conditions.

"What, Tao? Sorry, I wasn't paying attention."

Exactly my point. Do not worry about it. For now, get some rest. I will wake you in the morning before dawn. You need to clean up and be out of here before the store opens.

"What are we going to do then?"

Alex is right about one thing. Your cut is badly infected. We need to take care of that before it gets worse.

"How?"

Why, by keeping your perfect attendance perfect. You are going to school.

Tao waited an hour after both Cameron and Alex were deep asleep. Then he slowly untangled himself from her body. Control over the sleeping boy was awkward again as he got up and walked toward the back office. The experiments he had been doing with Cameron and the conscious control had been pretty cutting-edge. Now, without being able to use Cameron's consciousness as a conduit, Tao was once again feeling all the inefficiencies of unconscious control.

Tao looked back at the sleeping Alex. Now was a time for some secrecy. With luck, Tabs wasn't focused on what was happening outside of Alex's body. Still, he had better do this fast. He found the phone in the back office and dialed the emergency line.

"Twenty-four-hour wake up service. We wake up to wake you up. Can I help you?"

"Identification Tao."

"Voice recognition matches Cameron Tan. Current condition: Unknown. Base binary code required."

"Binary code one, one, zero, zero, one, zero, one, one, zero, zero, zero, one."

Silence.

"Tao, it has been days since the reported attack. We had feared you were lost, either your host or to the Eternal Sea."

"My host and Alexandra Mengsk survived the attack. This is the first I have been able to report in. What about the others?"

"Jill Tesser Tan survived and is currently at the safe house in Fort Bragg with the scientist. Can you rendezvous with them?"

Tao did some quick calculations in his head. "It's not an easy trip for two teenagers. Cameron has funds hidden in an emergency pack at school. We can try to retrieve it tomorrow, though public transportation poses a risk if the Genjix are watching."

"Steal an automobile then."

Tao grunted. He had hoped to hold off a little longer before starting Cameron's criminal career. Well, it was their best option until he could think of something better. He spent the next five minutes filling in as much information as he could about the attack, including the military-issued gear the sentry wore. In the end, it narrowed down which Genjix faction had attacked them, though Tao had a pretty good guess it was either the Chinese or the Russians, so either Enzo's rabid Quasiform group or a remnant of Vinnick's trying to either reclaim their assets – of which Rin was a valuable piece – or someone there trying to clean up loose ends.

In either case, it seemed more an unfortunate incident that Jill's operation was found, as opposed to a personal vendetta, several of which Tao knew he might be the target of. It shouldn't have made him feel better that he was probably not the cause of the attack, but it did.

He thought back to his old host Edward and his wife Kathy. It was as if history was repeating itself. In the end, what trail of tragedies and chaos would he leave this family? Probably the same as he had left the previous one, and the one before. Every time he tried to break this cycle, the hundreds of times, no matter what time period, where he moved or what he tried to do, the results were always the same. Maybe it wasn't the war that was evil, maybe it was him.

"Tao, are you there?"

"Yes, Datlow. By the way, have you heard from Roen Tan lately? He was missing-in-action last I heard."

There was a pause. "Records show he reported in a few days back with a Mountain North Region crypto key."

Relief flooded through Tao. Not knowing what had happened to Roen had weighed heavily on both him and Cameron. Tao had put on an optimistic face for the boy, but had feared the worst. The boy would be thrilled to learn that his father was all right.

"Thank you. I will figure out the logistics for getting to the Fort Bragg safe house. Inform Jill we are on our way and should be there in a few days."

"Will do, Tao. Be safe. I hope it will be a long time before I see you in the Eternal Sea."

"Likewise, my friend."

Tao hung up the phone and made his way back toward the corner where Cameron and Alex had passed out. It would be another couple of hours before they would have to wake. They would have to make a short trip to the school and then start making their way south. Best to steal the automobile outside of town limits, which meant...

Tao stopped as he turned around the corner into the kitchen and saw Alex standing there, arms crossed and leaning against the walk-in freezer. He noticed the knife in her hand and took a step back. Immediately, he considered three ways to disarm her, one of which might not injure her.

It would also depend on whether he was fighting Alex or Tabs. If it was the Quasing in control, he was fairly confident it wouldn't come to that. Tabs had only had a few months with Alex, while Tao had spent almost all of Cameron's life with him. His control should easily outclass Tab's. However, if it was the girl, he could be in trouble.

"Tao," the girl said, "you were on the phone."

"Tabs," Tao replied. "What is it to you, and what is with the knife?"

Tabs looked down at the knife and sheathed it. "Apologies. Never can be too careful, especially these days." She looked up. "You made contact. Where to next?"

Tao studied her. Could he trust Tabs, especially after what had happened over the past few days? "I think I prefer to keep that private for now, all things considered."

She gave him a flat stare. "After everything we have had to deal with together, I think I have earned a modicum of trust."

"Things are need-to-know, especially for you. I do not trust you."

"You still do not trust my loyalties, even after Alex and I helped you and your boy kill that Genjix soldier? Yes, I know you knew it was a Genjix. You lied about it being IXTF. You talk about how I am untrustworthy; you are one to talk."

Tao was silent for a while. Finally, he nodded. "You are right. Trust needs to begin somewhere, and since both of our hosts are in this together, I will bridge that gap. The good news is that Jill, Vladimir, and Rin are all well. They are holed up in a safe house south of us. We will head out tomorrow, right after we stop for supplies."

"Alex will be pleased," Tabs said. She held out her hand. "Come, let the children rest then. They have a long journey ahead."

Tao took her hand and together, they walked back to the corner behind the front counter, where for the rest of the night, they once again huddled to stay warm and to prepare for the long day ahead.

CHAPTER TWENTY-SEVEN
VOTER TAMPERING

It was not until the Industrial Revolution that our many centuries of work on the humans began to pay off. Before then, humanity had evolved at a meandering pace. The wars we pushed, while driving innovation, had taxed the species heavily. We considered abandoning them several times, but, by then, we were already too committed.

The arrival of the Industrial Revolution changed everything. Humans finally began to fulfill the potential we saw in them.

Zoras

"The joint meeting between the State Duma and Federation Council is in session, Father," Azumi said. "President Putyatin is on his way to the main floor as we speak."

Wait until he is in position before securing the exits. The interior chambers should have eight security, and two at the central podium.

Enzo looked over at Natalya. "Are the Spetsnaz in place?"

She nodded. "On your order... um, Father."

Most of the Spetsnaz Natalya and Akelatis had converted

were pragmatic; only two had tried to reject their destiny and had had to be put down. The loyalty of these new vessels was still suspect, though, which was why, without their knowledge, Enzo had small explosive detonators attached to the rear interiors of their helmets. After all, they were blessed with a Holy One now. It was Enzo's duty to see to their safety.

You are using the shade teams too freely. The rest of the Council will disapprove. Several already insist on banning this practice.

"The final battle is near, my Guardian. Sacrifices are needed."

It is distasteful. However, as long as you produce results, some compromises are acceptable.

"Once again, the rest of the council has proven not to have the fortitude to do what needs to be done. The Genjix have fallen soft and play down to the level of the Prophus. Perhaps after Quasiform begins, it will be time to consider disbanding the Council in favor of more centralized leadership?"

Dangerous thoughts, vessel. Keep them to yourself. For now.

Enzo held position behind the ornate door leading to the Federal Building main hall. Behind him, thirty of his operatives and ten of the former Spetsnaz stood ready.

After taking control of Genjix headquarters in Moscow, all that was left was to show the rulers of this country which Genjix was in control, and who they should really be aligning with.

"They're all in place, Father," Azumi nodded.

Enzo kicked the door open and strolled into the main hall, where the bulk of the Federal Assembly was in session. To either side of him, his people spread out to cover all the doors. Several of the politicians stood up in their seats, either looking for their security or trying to flee the room. To his left, Palos incapacitated one of the guards with a punch to the gut. Further down the hall, Azumi stabbed another in the leg with one of her Emei piercers. Seconds later, his people had secured the chambers and had trapped everyone inside. Enzo, hands on the hilt of Hanjo Masamune, casually strolled to the center of the hall and nodded to Putyatin, whose glare followed him defiantly all the way to the podium. His facade broke and he cowered when Enzo got close.

"Mr President," he bowed.

"You should have left Russia by now," Putyatin hissed. "You risk war between our two countries. I will have you imprisoned for this."

Enzo put a hand on the president's shoulder and shoved him aside. "I don't think so." He turned to the full assembly. "A few days ago, you held a vote regarding the relationship Russia would have with the Genjix. It has come to my attention that some in this esteemed council were inappropriately influenced by Vinnick's people. For that, you have the apologies of the Genjix. Those who committed the fraud have been brought to justice." He nodded at Palos in the back, who opened the door. Matthew and Akelatis dragged Vinnick's surviving intermediaries in single-file and forced them onto their knees in front of the entire chamber.

"Consider all of their promises void," Enzo said. He pulled out his pistol and shot one. The rest of his people inside followed suit as a thousand rounds fired from everywhere in the chamber pierced the dozen bodies. The weak-willed politicians screamed as smoke and loud bangs filled the air. He waited a few seconds for the chaos to subside before continuing. "Vinnick has fled Moscow. My people are searching for him as we speak. I intend to bring him to justice. For now, the Genjix call for a new vote. An honest one without the corrupted influence of my predecessor. As a last gesture of the sincerity of our intentions to be one with Russia, I offer you one last gift."

Enzo nodded toward Palos again. He opened the door once more and several agents carrying large black containers entered the room. They then locked the doors behind them and opened the lids. Dozens of sparkling lights drifted into the air and swirled around the ceiling of the chamber. Then, driven by instinct and survival, one of the lights moved into one of the Duma members. The man screamed. Another scream joined with his as another member was blessed with a shade. Then even more followed. Soon, the entire chamber of the Federation Council was filled with a chorus of terror and pain.

Enzo turned to a huddled Putyatin curled up and shaking on the floor next to him. He offered his hand. "Welcome to the family, brother." Enzo smiled as the horrified Putyatin recoiled backward. No matter. This would be the last time Enzo ever offered him his hand. The next time, the president of Russia would bend a knee.

He stepped off the podium and watched as hundreds of Russia's top officials reacted to being forcibly blessed by Quasing shades. Most were already on the ground retching, crying, or groaning in pain. It brought Enzo back to his own ascension, when Zoras had first blessed him. There were still a few Holy Ones in the air, searching for vessels. There must still be some members here who had escaped.

He continued to scan the room and saw a terrified older woman make a break for one of the doors. A Spetsnaz blocked her path. She screamed at him to let her pass. A moment later, the sparkling white light of a Holy One shot into her back, felling her.

"Father," Amanda's voice in his ear crackled. "We have an update on Councilman Vinnick."

"Hang on. I can't hear you over these blessings." Enzo walked toward one of the exits, turning back at the door one last time to witness his political masterpiece. He stepped out and closed the door behind him. "Continue."

"We extracted the travel records from one of his administrators during interrogation. The councilman took his entire entourage to North Korea."

Sung controls North Korea. He has always been unpredictable, but has never catered to either faction.

Enzo frowned. Sung was one of those shadowy Holy Ones who never played on the world stage. His control of his small fiefdom was near-absolute, and he held one of the only familial Quasing dynasties. His only responsibilities at this moment were production and storage of the catalysts. North Korea was currently one of five catalyst production facilities. Their production was minuscule compared to the others. China itself produced seventy percent of the catalysts. However, China sent all their manufactured catalysts to North Korea for storage.

"Get Sung on the comm immediately," he barked to Amanda. "Verify our catalyst stockpile levels."

"Stand by, Father." Amanda clicked over.

"He wouldn't move them. He risks everything we have built if he does."

It would be a desperate move for Vinnick to try to ransom the catalysts for his control. He would turn the rest of the Council against him.

Enzo paced the room for several excruciating minutes. He had nowhere to go! Surely he wouldn't destroy years of work and irreplaceable resources for petty politics. The Earth was a planet of abundance, with resources, alive and dead, that were near infinite. However, the particular minerals and radioactive iridium derivatives for catalyst production were extraordinarily rare.

"Father," Sung's voice clicked over the comm.

Already, Enzo knew the news was bad. He could hear the fear in the weak-minded vessel's voice. "How much of the stockpile did he take?"

"Sixteen tons. Forty percent of our storage capacity."

Enzo raged. That was enough to initiate Quasiform processes at nine catalyst facilities. "How could you allow Vinnick to take them?"

The fear in Sung's vessel's voice grew. "Apologies, Father, but Councilman Vinnick is on the Council and Flua is on the Grand Council. I dare not disobey."

That much was true. Enzo could not fault Sung for being loyal. "Where did he go?"

"He said he was going to relocate his operations to North America in order to personally oversee catalyst distribution over the hemisphere. I arranged for the transport."

A surprising choice. The United States was a wasteland for all Quasing, Prophus and Genjix alike. Vinnick must be in one of the many bases hidden on the continent, though only a few were large enough to store that much catalyst. That meant it would have to be either a catalyst facility or a loyalty haven.

There are four catalyst facilities in the United States, one in Mexico, one in Brazil and one in Peru. Only one in the United States has completed construction and is ready to go on-line. The facilities in Kentucky and Oregon are the largest, situated over fault lines on the continent.

There are three loyalty havens in the hemisphere: northern Canada, the Caribbean, and the Archipelago. They are likelier candidates, since all are under his direct control.

Enzo clicked over to Amanda. "I want you to pull up all the loyalty havens and catalyst facilities in the Western hemisphere. Send envoys on the ground and demand a full audit on my authority. Whichever one refuses is the one Vinnick is hiding in. Arrange for transport. We're just about done in Russia. I will be there in person to grind that old man under my boot."

CHAPTER TWENTY-EIGHT
SCHOOL DAY

The friction between the Prophus and Genjix is an unusual occurrence for our kind. We have almost always acted as a collective, having our merged ideas debated and agreed upon until we functioned as one focused being, a combined singularity, if you will. That is our true disconnect on this planet, something the Genjix had hoped to overcome with their recent invention of ProGenesis.

Tao

Cameron felt like crap the next day as he and Alex walked to school. His back was stiff, his clothes were still soggy, and he was exhausted. Tao and Tabs had woken them both up before dawn to clean up the mess they had made at the burger joint. His mood brightened a hundredfold when he learned that both his mother and father were all right, and it made Tao ordering him to mop the kitchen and wipe down the grill much more bearable.

An hour later, their Quasing had ordered them both to head off to school. He looked over at Alex walking beside him down Harrison Street. Strangely, her walking beside him holding his hand, coupled with finding out that his parents were all right, could very well have made this the best day of his life.

He began to whistle as they turned onto the block of his high school. With luck, he could swipe the survival pack and get fixed up by the nurse's office before classes started. Once they did, the entire high school would get locked down and that would make leaving much more difficult. The walk wasn't too far and soon they were crossing the football field into the main building. With the luck he'd had this morning, he might be able to see Mom by dinnertime.

"Look," he chirped cheerfully, pointing at a small grove of trees across the street. "Why don't you hang out there until I get back?"

Alex looked over at the park benches and shook her head. "No way, mister. I'm coming."

"It's an unnecessary risk," he said. "I can grab my stuff and be back in thirty minutes. Hour tops."

"Fine," she said. "You go get your bag of money and that cut taken care of. I am going to the locker room to take a nice long shower."

That is a really good idea. You two have been on the run and have not showered for days.

Cameron sniffed his shoulder. He did smell a bit pungent, though to him, it felt completely natural. He smelled like the forest.

Oh please. I have been in dinosaurs that smelled better than you two. As hard as I have tried, you somehow still follow in many of your father's footsteps.

"I should probably take one, too," he said grudgingly.

You also would attract a lot of the wrong attention in your current state, and it is doubtful they would let you onto a bus, either.

"It's settled then," she said. "I bet I can find a change of clothing, too."

Cameron looked at the shirt he was wearing. It looked like it was hanging onto his body by its last threads. On top of being smeared with dirt, grass stains, and hot oil, it had a dozen holes in it, as if someone had shot him full of arrows, courtesy of the many sharp brambles and thorns in the forest.

Another good point.

"Boy, you're really on her side today, aren't you?"

Logic over loyalty. Sorry.

"I'll remember that one day, Tao. You'll regret putting me second to reasoning."

Just like you will regret putting me second to a girl.

"I do not!"

It is all right. Reasoning dictates that at your age, you are too dumb to know better.

"I hate you."

The two teenagers joined the light stream of students walking into Eureka High School. It was half past seven, so classes wouldn't begin for about an hour. Most of the students here either had to be dropped off by their parents early, were here for projects, or making up a delinquency. Most ignored them, though a few glanced curiously at their tattered clothing. Almost every single guy outright stared at Alex.

In a school as small as Eureka High, strangers were big news, and a pretty girl was the biggest. For the guys, it was someone new to scope out, while the girls were already figuring out where she fit into the social hierarchy. Cameron was pretty sure Alex being seen with him was already knocking her status down a few rungs.

She leaned in and whispered. "What is wrong with everyone?"

"We need to get out of these clothes," he said.

They took the most direct route to the gym locker room and parted ways. Alex looked positively giddy in anticipation of a hot shower. She turned back to him as she went in. "How will we meet up again?"

Cameron frowned. "I'll hop in the shower too. Meet you in ten minutes?"

She made a face. "Yeah, no. I haven't bathed in days. Just go. I'll find you."

Before he could say anything else, she disappeared past the double doors. Cameron stood there, dumbfounded. Did she actually expect him to just stand out there and wait for her? They had to get out of here before class started. What was she thinking?

Worry about it later. You only have an hour. Get to the janitor's supply locker now.

"Shouldn't I shower first?"

Retrieve it while foot traffic is light. Besides, you need that change of clothing in it, unless you would rather wear your gym clothes.

"Yeah, right. Good idea. That would be embarrassing."

Cameron hurried out of the gym and sped at a half jog down the hallway toward the center of the high school. The janitor's supply locker was next to the cafeteria in a less-traveled side hallway. The door to the room was in an older part of school and had one of those old-school skeleton key locks. Even Cameron with his pedestrian skill at lock-picking had little problem with those. He slowed down as he crossed the cafeteria. Again, more looks. This time, one of the looks was from Mr Hunt, the teacher watching over the room.

Slow down. Act natural.

Cameron took a deep breath and recalled the tricks Tao had taught him to blend in. Move with purpose. Act like you belong. Relax.

"Cameron." Mr Hunt moved to intercept him.

You cannot allow him to detain you. There are too many eyes about. Draw him into the hallway before you disable him. Hunt is a heavyset man and favors his right. A hard kick to the side of his knee should do the trick.

"Are you serious? He's my math teacher!"

Lives are at stake.

"Yes, Mr Hunt?" he said, looking at him with what he hoped was the proper balance of respect and deference without looking like he was hiding something.

If you are trying to look innocent, you are not succeeding.

"Where's the fire?" Hunt asked.

"I'm sorry," Cameron said, gesturing at his torn and dirty shirt. "Fell on the way to school. Need to get a change of clothes."

Hunt looked him up and down, and then at the angry red cut over his eye. "Did you fall or did you get into a fight with a lynx? You'd better stop by the nurse's office."

"Yes, sir," Cameron replied, touching his brow and backing up. "It stings. I'll get it checked right away."

Ease up. Always underact, not over.

"It does hurt though."

"Get going, and stop running in the halls," Hunt said.

Putting on what he hoped was an appropriately chastised expression, Cameron retreated into the hallway. A few seconds later, he reached the janitor's supply room and stood dumbfounded by the padlocked handle and latch that had replaced the old skeleton lock.

Some kids must have broken the old door. Well, get lock picking.

Cameron scowled. This was the last thing he needed. He pulled the lock picks out of his pack and got to work. Padlocks were not too hard, but still a pain for a complete neophyte like Cameron. He was fortunate that this hallway was rarely used, because if caught, his only option would be to flee the school. A few students walked by, but most didn't give him a second glance. One even gave him a thumbs up. Ten minutes later, he was still working at it.

"I can't get this, Tao."

You have to keep your left hand steadier. Move your right in small increments.

"It's too hard. I'm just going to smash the door in."

You do not think that will cause a lot of noise? Here, find the calm and let me try to help.

Cameron felt the control of his body loosen slightly, as if an invisible hand was helping steady his left arm. Then, that same unseen force slowed down his small adjustments just by a smidgeon as the lock pick worked through its puzzle. A minute later, he heard a click.

"Wow, Tao. That was awesome. Tao?"

I need to rest a bit. That was more draining than I realized.

His mentor became silent. Cameron pushed his worry for his Quasing into the back of his mind as he walked into the janitor's supply locker and closed the door. It was a small room with two rows of shelves in the center and against the walls. The locker was filled with cleaning supplies, vacuums, mops, and everything else needed to keep the school tidy.

He ran to the back corner to a metal vent near the ground. It only took him a few seconds to unscrew the vent, reach in around the corner, and retrieve the pack.

Everything looked as he had left it. He opened the pack and pulled out the change of clothing from last year. Cameron quickly threw it on. He checked the envelope of cash and cursed. It only had sixty dollars. He had forgotten he had used some of the emergency cash this year to buy a couple of video games behind his parent's back and forgot to replenish it. Tao had warned him about that, too. Now, when he really needed the money, he might not have enough.

"You're always right, Tao," he muttered as he consolidated everything into one bag. He checked the time as he hurried back: 8.00am. He was running low on time. It had been over twenty minutes since he had left Alex. Was she waiting for him? He had better get back to her before she got in trouble. Cameron slung the pack over his back and hurried out of the room.

The hallways were now crowded with students, and he had to navigate the flow of traffic. He had hoped that his change of clothing would help attract less attention, but it seemed to have done the opposite. Even more kids now glanced his way, though this time their looks were accompanied with snickers. Well, nothing he could do about it now. He sighed and pressed on, passing the cafeteria back toward the gym. It felt like it took an eternity just to push through the crowds to get to the gym.

Cameron reached the locker room entrances and looked around; Alex was nowhere to be seen. His worse fears leaped to mind. Had one of the teachers found her? Was she sitting there wondering where he was? No time to worry about that now, he ran into the boy's locker room and hopped into the shower.

He originally had intended to only take a very quick

shower and hurry out, but once the hot water hit him, he felt himself melt as days of grime and travel washed off his weary body and loosened his tired muscles. All his worries evaporated and time seemed to tick by slowly. He caught himself, but it was still 8.10 by the time he got out.

"Oh crap!" he yelled as he hurriedly got dressed. When he looked up at the mirror, Cameron couldn't help but gasp. He looked ridiculous. Everything he wore looked two sizes too small. He had had quite a growth spurt since last year, having gained a few inches and some weight. His ankles and wrists were completely exposed, and that tightness around his pants… He felt his face turn crimson. Tao had told him to swap clothes more often, but he had been too lazy. Well, now he was going to pay the price.

I hope those video games were worth it.

"I swear to God, Tao. If you say I told you so…"

Would I do that?

"All the frigging time. By the way, are you all right? You sounded bad after you picked the lock."

You picked the lock, Cameron. I just helped a little. And yes, I am all right. It was just draining. You should get into your gym clothes. You can't move in pants this tight.

"There's no time."

Then do it quickly.

Cameron ran to his gym locker and threw on the much larger t-shirt and shorts he had stored there. They still smelled, but at least not as badly as what he had been wearing before. And they were both completely intact, and the right size. He hurried out of the locker room with the thin hope that Alex would be there. She wasn't. Deflated and unsure of what to do, he lugged his pack along the floor out into the hallway. It was so late by now that the hall monitors would be in place. He probably couldn't even sneak out of the school now if he wanted to. He hadn't even gotten to go to the nurse's office to get something for his cut. On top of that, he had lost Alex. How had everything gone so wrong so quickly? And it wasn't even 9.00am yet!

"I suck at this. I'm an awful strategist," he said, shaking his head and dragging his feet. He looked to his left, where a monitor was manning an exit.

Stop it. You know, very few of Napoleon's plans ever went as planned.

"I thought he was an incredible general."

He was. What made him great was his ability to adapt to battlefield conditions.

"I thought you hated his guts."

Oh, I do. Complimenting him just now made me want to leap from your body and commit suicide, but it is the truth.

The pep talk didn't help Cameron's mood as he walked into the crowded cafeteria. Part of him told him that he should be looking for Alex. Another part told him that she could be anywhere, and that the best thing to do was to finish his checklist and stop by the nurse's office for some peroxide. The cut on his head wasn't going to get any better. The problem was, the longer he wasn't looking for her, the more trouble she could get into. What if she wasn't in the building anymore? What if she thought he had abandoned her? He never got to tell her his true feelings.

Oh lord. Shut up. Get over yourself.

"Hey, Cameron."

He looked over to his left and, to his utter shock, saw Alex sitting at one of the benches. With Heather, of all people. They were at a table where most of the popular girls at school sat. Cameron blanched. How the hell had she gotten there already? He had been attending school for over a year and actually had a habit of avoiding walking near that table. Now, Alex was sitting in the middle of that gaggle of girls looking not only like she belonged, but was the center of the group.

Then he noticed her physical appearance. Now that she had showered and had a change of clothing, she looked fantastic. Where did she get the nice clothes she was wearing? Cameron found himself very self-conscious.

For a second, his heart forgot to beat and he found his breath caught in his throat as she got up and bounded to him. "I was worried about you," she said, putting her arm through his and leading him to the table.

"I found your exchange student in the locker room after my cross-country practice," Heather said. "She asked to borrow my phone to check her social network and was looking for a change of clothes. Gave her a set of my spares. You really lucked out on the exchange program, Tan." The girls around the table giggled. Cameron's ears burned.

"How did Alex already get in with that crowd? Why can't you teach me stuff like this?"

Sorry. I thought learning to hide and fight were more important assets to have than being popular in high school.

Cameron was in awe as he listened to Alex artfully ingratiate and embed herself with this group of girls. At first, he thought she'd try to fit in. Instead, though, he noticed her accent became just a tiny bit thicker, her mannerisms a little more graceful and aristocratic, yet her deference to the queen bees in the group obvious. Within just a few minutes, she had neatly placed herself in the social hierarchy of the Eureka High School cool kids' club, something Cameron couldn't get within a thousand feet of.

I have to admit: Tabs and Alex are very good.

The five minute bell rang before class and the cafeteria dispersed. Cameron watched as the entire gaggle of girls at the bench hugged Alex before they each went off their separate ways. She turned around and flashed him an innocent smile. "Just getting what I needed at the time."

That is why I tell you to be careful with this one. You might be able to survive in the woods and live off the land, but this is her world, and you could not touch her in this arena.

"Are we done here?" she asked.

Cameron pointed at his brow. "Nurse's office next, then we can bolt."

The two moved at a brisk pace toward the nurse's office, located next door to the library. In his head, Cameron planned his escape path out of the high school. Disabling the monitors – usually teachers – shouldn't be a problem, but he would really prefer not to do that. His English teacher, eighty year-old Ms Hannigan, usually took a spot during first period at the main entrance. Knocking her over just to escape felt decidedly wrong. He could run around her as well, but again, he could already see the disappointment in her eyes if he did that. She was his favorite teacher.

Priorities, Cameron.

"I'm just debating my options. What about the gym doors?"

Wannsik has class, but he is usually pretty busy. You might be able to leave without attracting attention.

"That'll be the plan, then."

Nurse Steff Sheung was twenty-five, and this was her first year at Eureka High School. She was at the same time extraordinarily sweet and completely vapid. She spent half of her time at school staring at her cell phone and the other half staring at herself. In between, she found a little time to direct kids with headaches to the cots and to bandage minor scrapes and cuts. Half the guys in the school had crushes on her, Cameron included. Though with Alex at his side, he wasn't feeling quite the same nervousness that he usually felt when coming here, which, to be honest, was pretty often.

"Cameron. Again?" Sheung said, looking up from her phone. She saw the cut and shook her head. Then she saw Alex next to him. "Who is your friend?"

Alex introduced herself as the exchange student and Cameron saw her behavior transform right before his eyes. Before, she was interesting and stood out, and the popular girls at the cafeteria swarmed around her. Now, she appeared shy and unsure, like a wallflower. In a few seconds, she seemed to have blended into the background while Nurse Sheung worked on Cameron's cut.

"It's infected," she frowned, dabbing him with the peroxide, "and a couple of days old. You should have had this checked."

He glanced over behind her shoulder at Alex, who was stealthily raiding the medicine cabinet. The girl was like a master thief, tip-toeing across the room and rummaging through all the drawers and cabinets. They made eye contact and she shook her head.

"Ow," Cameron said, pulling back a bit.

"Hold still," Sheung said. He fidgeted as she continued dabbing his cut. "Let me get a Band-Aid."

"Wait," Cameron said quickly. "I think I have a cut in my hair as well."

Sheung began to poke through his hair. "Is everything all right at home, Cameron? If you need anyone to talk to, I'm always here to lend an ear."

Cameron tried not to scoff. If one more adult asked him this question, he was going to scream. The only time Roen ever hurt him was when Cameron missed a block.

Well, there was the one time he almost dislocated your arm trying to show you how to fa jin.

"Okay, that."

And the other when he bruised your rib demonstrating Muay Thai strikes.

"Hmm, maybe my parents are abusive."

Well, you did stab him with a sword last week, and there was the time you broke his wrist with that aikido throw.

"We'll call it a draw then. In my defense, you were both telling me the throw wouldn't work unless I put everything I had into it."

We will just lay that blame on Roen then. No need to get your mother involved.

Nurse Sheung finished up with Cameron a minute later. By that time, Alex had stolen a dozen small bottles and packages from the office. The two fled the office as fast as possible. Sheung might be unobservant, but she definitely would notice all the stuff missing once she opened a cabinet. Their packs on their backs, they burst through the double-doors to the gym. He pointed at the metal doors on the far end of the room across the basketball court.

"Hey, Cameron," Wannsik said. "Going somewhere?"

Unfortunately, the coach's first period gym class was in session, and it contained the entire varsity football team.

The coach liked to put all his guys into first period so they could merge their morning workout directly with class. That gave them an entire day to recover before practice after school.

Cameron grabbed Alex's wrist and pulled her along. "Run. Stop at nothing!"

The two ran through the class, hoping that they could just barrel their way out the door before anyone was the wiser.

"Hey! Where do you think you're going?" Wannsik yelled.

"Where do you think you're going?" Bill, the varsity quarterback, repeated, getting in his way. Half of the school's varsity athletes followed suit and blocked their path to the exit.

No other choice now. Angle left. Do not let Alex out of your sight. Do not get surrounded. Try not to hurt anyone. Go!

Cameron let go of Alex and attacked, flowing through the motions, sliding in between students, using an open hand to grapple and body-check those in his way. He knew all the kids here, and most weren't bullies like some of the guys on the football team. However, they were blocking his way, so he had to take them down.

Hands grabbed at him, pulling at his shirt and arms. Someone smacked him in the face. Cameron spun and dodged, slicing between people, sweeping out with his feet and tripping them when he could, knocking others off-balance with his arms when he had to. He felt graceful and in-control. These kids stood little chance as he spun a guy around and pushed him into two others. He sidestepped a tackle and tripped another. Before he knew it, he had worked his way through a dozen bodies, half of which were now groaning on the floor. He also was pretty sure he hadn't seriously injured anyone.

Well done.

Cameron looked for Alex and gasped. Tabs obviously had not given her the same instruction about not hurting any of his classmates. Alex was laying waste to the soccer team. He saw three students on the ground unconscious and at least two puddles of blood. He watched, fascinated and horrified as she shattered Bill's nose with her fist, exploding bright blood all over the floor.

In a second, she moved in on the starting third baseman and broke his wrist when he grabbed for her. Then, before any of the now-terrified kids could run away, she actually pounced on one of the football linesmen and elbowed him on the back of the head. He collapsed like a ton of rocks onto the floor.

Get her out of here before she kills someone.

Cameron ran and grabbed her before she could cause any more damage. She almost seemed to be in a feral trance as he pulled her back. "We need to go." He wrapped his arms around her waist as she struggled against him.

Right as they stepped out the door, she became perfectly calm again. "Let's go," she said, and took off, leaving Cameron dumbfounded with nothing left to do but follow her.

CHAPTER TWENTY-NINE
HOSPITAL VISIT

Timestamp: 3133

The next few years were a blur. Small town Appalachia gave way to small town Midwest to small town Rockies. We even did a stint in Canada. Way too cold. By then, we had learned how to avoid the IXTF. The Genjix were dealing with their own consolidation and had largely forgotten about us, and the Prophus network was too much in tatters to mount any sort of steady operation. It was actually a nice time in our lives.

That all changed when the Keeper made a personal visit to our home.

Roen wasn't a big fan of hospitals. He usually visited them as a patient and was there for gunshot wounds, broken limbs, or some form of blunt force trauma. That kind of stuff he was fine with. He recognized that he would have been dead a dozen times over if it weren't for hospitals. That wasn't what bugged him about them. He just didn't like the smell.

There was something about that sterile smell that drove him nuts. Roen guessed it would be better than the stink of death, but every time he was in a hospital, it brought him back to that fateful day when he had to bust Edward's brother, Gregory, out of the long-term care facility. He ended up killing his first person that day, and then euthanizing Gregory that evening in order to free Yol. No matter how many times Roen had killed since, that day haunted him, and every time he stepped foot into a hospital and smelled the sterile hospital smell, he relived those moments.

Stepping into Saint Alphonsus was no different, though this time he was actually breaking into the building, as opposed to being a patient. His plan was simple. Find an exterior door in a less-traveled area without a surveillance camera. Once someone passes through, jump out of a hiding place and follow inside. In a small-town facility like Oregon, it should be a cakewalk.

Unfortunately, Roen picked too quiet a spot. He found a door near the far end of the loading dock that had a small garden for patients to sit in. It was a foggy morning, so finding a good hiding spot around the corner behind a thick bush proved relatively easy. He planted himself there and waited. And waited. And waited some more.

It was twenty minutes before someone used that door. Unfortunately for Roen, his attention had wandered by then, and he was a second too late in grabbing for the door before it closed. It was another fifteen minutes before someone else came out for a smoke. This time, he was ready and leaped to the handle before the door closed all the way. Once he got through the front outer door, all he had to do was act like someone who was supposed to be there.

Helen's scrubs had looked like a skin suit on him when

he had tried them on. Instead, for the first time since the desk job Tao had found him in, he wore a shirt and tie, and sported a pair of khakis. These he had picked up from the local department store down the street. Selections were pretty limited, so he was relegated to a baby-blue short-sleeve button down and a decidedly non-matching tie. He could imagine what Tao would say right now if he saw Roen.

Short sleeve button-downs are an abomination.

"Six bucks a shirt, man. Six bucks."

Marco and Helen had a field day poking fun at him when he tried them on. He wasn't sure that's what doctors were supposed to wear, but it seemed about right. The tie also wasn't hanging quite straight; the double-Windsor was one of those skills he had never gotten around to mastering, and he was too embarrassed to ask Marco for help. Jill was the one who usually took care of that for him.

It only took Roen a few minutes to sneak into the main hallway and blend in with his fake badge. That was the one nice thing about small towns; security was usually pretty lax. Now, all Roen had to do was act liked he belonged. That was really half the battle when it came to infiltrating any place. It was admittedly one of his weaker skillsets, but it wasn't like he was busting into Fort Knox here.

A few of the nurses and doctors threw looks his way, but most ignored him after he gave them a friendly smile and pretended to be busy. It took a little sleuthing and some flirting with some of the nurses – he really wasn't as incompetent as Jill and Marco made him out to be – before he found his way to the third floor recovery rooms.

No sooner had he rounded the corner, than he saw

two men guarding one of the doors in the middle of the hallway. Roen palmed the listening bug in his hand and pretended to ignore them as he tried to pass by the room.

Predictably, the two men stood up and one of them blocked his path. "Sorry, sir, this is a restricted area."

Roen acted confused. "I'm just trying to get across." He caught a glimpse inside the room. Prie was awake and propped up on the bed, talking to someone to his left. The commotion in the hallway must have caught his attention, because he turned to face Roen, and their eyes met. Pri must have told him something, because Roen received a slight nod.

Security was too tight. There was no way he could step foot into the room to plant the bug. Perhaps if he broke in at night, but Roen was willing to bet there were guards here around the clock. He had to be careful not to spook the IXTF folks, or they might just move Prie prematurely.

The one blocking his path became more insistent while the other guard in the back reached for his firearm. The person inside turned around and followed Prie's gaze toward him. Roen quickly turned away, taking the identification clip off his shirt and putting it into his pocket.

"Ralphy?"

Crap. She had noticed him. Roen stopped, turned around, and smiled. "Special Agent Kallis. What a surprise to see you here."

"Official business. You?"

Roen motioned toward his left elbow. "Was looking at some rot on a pile of wood. Fell off. Thought I broke an arm. Got it checked to be on the safe side. Trying to get out of here now. Kind of got my way twisted around."

"Good to hear you're all right." Kallis looked back in

the room and then at her two men. "Hey, Charles, I'll be right back."

The agent on the left nodded. "Take your time, Ma'am. Fritz should be here any minute, anyway."

She turned back to Roen. "I'll walk you out."

"Uh," he stammered. Without a good excuse, he sighed and allowed her to lead him out the hospital that he had just spent the entire morning trying to get into.

The two of them stepped out through the emergency room exit and into the cool dewy afternoon air. It had rained the previous night, and a low-hanging mist had fallen over the town. Roen stared longingly back at the hospital. He'd have to do this all over again.

"Well, Ralphy," Kallis waved, and paused. "Ralphy's not your real name, is it?"

For a second, Roen thought he had blown his cover, then he realized what she meant and shook his head. "Nah, only…" he had to take another second to pull up the stupid name Marco gave himself, "…Cornelius calls me that. My real name is…" To be honest, Roen didn't like Ralph either. He went with the first thing that came to mind. "…Rutherford." That wasn't much better. Mentally, Roen imagined himself palming his own face. He could see Tao doing it too, if Tao had hands. He could hear his friend berating him.

What did I tell you about not complicating your lies? Stick with Ralphy and keep things simple, dumbass!

"Okay, Rutherford," Kallis grinned. "I'll see you later."

"Hey," Roen called after her, not sure what he was doing. "You, um, want to grab some lunch?"

Kallis stopped, looked at Roen, then back at the hospital, and then shrugged. "Sure, why not? Not a big fan of these places anyway."

"I'm right there with you," Roen agreed. "Every time I truck through here, I get the chills."

Kallis frowned playfully. "Are you that big of a klutz?"

Roen realized his mistake a second too late and tried to play it off. "Ulcers. Comes with being Cornelius's business partner."

In his head, he began to tally all the lies he was stacking on top of each other. At this rate, if Kallis ever ran into Marco again, Roen would have to give him a complete dossier on his new secret identity. For now, he was just going to have to keep track of everything.

Keep it simple, stupid.

The two walked across the street back to the Woodchuck Chuck. It was here or the run-down pizza joint, the even more run-down burger place, or the fake Mexican fast-food place down the street. Not that Woodchuck Chuck had much better food, but at least they served alcohol, and that basically clinched their choice.

Pretty soon, the two were picking at mediocre fish and chips over a pitcher of crappy beer, commiserating on their shared hatred of hospitals. Roen had to do a little more creative alibi-building as she questioned him about the redwood lumber business. It became pretty clear five minutes into their chat that she was primarily interested in Marco.

After the initial generic questions about him, the conversation shifted to all Marco all the time. She asked about how they met, how they got into business, and what sort of guy he was. She delved a little deeper into why he was single at his age, if he was ever married, and whether he had children. And of course, Roen had to talk Marco up, which was one of the most painful things he'd had to do in recent memory.

It was bad enough he had to work for the guy, now he had to say nice things about him. Yes, Marco is nice and considerate. Yes, Marco is witty and a good friend. No, Marco isn't a player or have gambling or alcohol problems. It really couldn't get much worse. Eventually, though, he had lied enough to satisfy her curiosity about the Brit, and even got a few digs in, like telling her Marco loved to recite poetry and was once a junior champion river dancer.

"You should ask him to show you," Roen said. "He's fantastic. His nickname in prep school was Tapping Fairy."

Then it was his turn. Roen asked Kallis about how she got to her position and what she was doing in IXTF. He had much of this information already. The Prophus still had some access to certain federal personnel files. He had researched bios thoroughly when her name began to pop up more frequently during his jobs for the Underground Railroad.

She had risen through the CIA and was assigned to the IXTF during the agency's inception. Since then, she had been a fast riser within Interpol, but had been passed up for the directorship of the North America region twice. After her latest failure, when she was assigned to the Pacific Northwest, she thought her career had stalled. However, she found that she was enjoying this assignment much more than when she was operating out of New York.

"Part of it's the wilderness, and you'd be surprised, but part of it's the action," she said. "I can't get into details, but there is a lot of heavy traffic coming in from Canada south toward Mexico."

"Like drug smuggling?" Roen asked, playing dumb.

Kallis shook her head. "People smuggling, and lots of it. For some reason, a lot of aliens are running from something."

"Are these aliens really bad?" Roen asked. "I hear that they've been around for longer than we were. Doesn't that give them a better claim to the planet?"

She made a face. "That argument might have held water if they hadn't spent their entire existence screwing us. We can't trust them."

"Well, they did come clean," he said.

"Only after supposedly one side lost. At the end of the day, humans should be in control of our own destiny. They even admitted to purposely causing wars in order to advance technology. How messed up is that?"

Roen had to be careful here. It was a fine line between acting stupid and defending his cause. "I thought there were two sides to the aliens. Mind you, I'm only getting this from the news and the Internet. You're the expert here."

Kallis thought it over. "Well, there has been some evidence of two differing groups of Quasing. But we don't know if they're just playing us again. At the end of the day, it seems they need us more than we need them. They need to come clean and tell us everything."

Roen grunted. Fat chance of that. Kallis thought she knew what was going on, but if she only knew how deep the rabbit hole went. There would be no hope for reconciliation then. However, she did prove to him that she was somewhat open-minded about things, which was a far cry from the times he had spoken to her as the Rayban Ghost.

After their meal, he walked her to her car in the hospital parking lot. She smiled, a genuine one now, and held out her hand. "Hey, it was fun. Really. I'm glad we had this opportunity to chat."

Roen accepted it. He sincerely thought so as well. "Hey, um, I'm about to go see Cornelius. Did you want me to tell him hi? We've been running around busy over the past few days, but I'm sure he'd love to see you."

Kallis smiled. "Thank you, Rutherford. I'd like that. Cornelius has a really good friend."

Roen kept that smile plastered on his face until she turned away. He almost felt bad for using her, but it was important he and Marco nurture this relationship. Prie's life could depend on it. Still, Roen couldn't help liking Special Agent Kallis. She was the enemy, no doubt about it, but in another world, they could have been friends.

He watched as she disappeared into the hospital and turned a corner, and gave himself a mental pat on the back. He had used her in more than one way. His con job was a little sloppy, but the bug he had planted on the bottom of her shoe right in front of the heel should hold. Both the sole and the bug were black, so with just a little luck, she'd never notice the small attachment. He grinned as he hurried back to the hotel.

CHAPTER THIRTY
THE WAY SOUTH

ProGenesis, the modified artificial Quasing atmosphere, is a breakthrough because it not only allows us to reproduce, but also allows us to reconnect our thoughts. However, for many of the Quasing who call Earth home, it has a price that we are not willing to pay. There is a secret regarding my people that very few humans will ever be aware of, one that will change the way humanity views the Quasing forever.

Tao

Cameron and Alex scoped out the local bus station from across the street. There were seven cars parked in the lot and two buses with their engines on. The bus on the left would take them south to Fort Bragg. The question was, how would they get on it? Was it safe to even try? Cameron studied the faces of each person who walked to and from the station. He recognized some of them; it was hard not to when you lived in a small town. However, he wasn't prepared to make a trip across the street to buy a ticket, especially after what had happened at the school the day before. There was only one bus station in town, so it made coming here especially perilous. There was a high likelihood of either the Genjix or the police waiting for them. Or both.

Police car a hundred meters up the street. There is someone sitting in the blue sedan on the right. He has been there for thirty-five minutes.

"We'll never learn anything by just sitting here," Alex said. "Besides, the police are not going to watch the station just because a few kids got beat up."

"You don't know small towns, then," he said. "This is probably the biggest thing to happen to Eureka in years." He turned to her. "Besides, you didn't just beat them up; you brutalized them. We're just lucky you didn't kill anyone."

She rolled her eyes. "That is the Hatchery way. If you show compassion to your enemy, you only invite them to return twice as determined. Those kids will never try to stop us again."

She also got every parent and cop in this small town on alert for a blonde psychopath.

"You didn't have to do that," Cameron muttered. "It's made our escape much more difficult with everyone looking for us."

Unfortunately, Cameron's words probably weren't too far off. News in the small town had spread like wildfire that a bunch of students at the local high school got their asses kicked by a Russian teenager. As they are wont to do in a place as small as Eureka, the rumors had taken a life of their own. Right now, half the population probably thought there was a vixen serial killer in their midst, while the other probably thought they were being invaded by the Red Army, and were forming up as if they were in the movie *Red Dawn*.

Technically, there hasn't been a Red Army since World War II.

"Not very helpful right now, Tao."

Alex, who was wearing a beanie to hide her now-very-publicized blonde hair, stood up from their hiding spot. "We're not going to figure anything out hiding behind this garbage can. Go buy bus tickets. I'll meet you at the south end of the parking lot. We can hide in the crowd."

That sounded as good a plan as any. They weren't going to get any closer to Jill by staying here. He couldn't wait any longer, anyway. The bus was leaving in twenty minutes. If they wanted to be on it, he had to go now. He pulled his cap down on his head and shouldered his pack.

Get a contingency plan in place first.

Cameron pointed to an alley down the street. "If things go wrong, rendezvous there."

She nodded, and they split up. She circled around the back while Cameron braved the bus station. They had just enough to buy one-way tickets, though not enough for lunch. Cameron cursed those two video games. Food would have been nice. Or another set of clothing, or even a couple of bottles of water. One of the damn games wasn't even any good either.

I will not say I told you so.

"About spending the money or buying that game?"

Both. I mean, you already had the previous version of that game. Is it that much different?

"It had new decals to download."

You, somehow, have the greatest potential of all my hosts, and are one of the dumbest, at the same time.

"Gee, thanks for the confidence booster."

On the contrary, it is brave stupid people who change the world. The smart ones are usually too smart to even try.

Cameron made it three quarters of the way across the lot when he was accosted by Officer Underwood. Cameron groaned, partially because he had naively hoped that it might actually be that easy to get away, but mostly because he knew Underwood. The man lived a couple of farms down from the Tans and had once sheltered him when he got caught in a rainstorm biking home. Underwood even fed him dinner while they waited for his dad to pick him up.

Sometimes, we have to do unpleasant things. Be ready.

"Hello, Cameron," Underwood said, extending his hand out.

Crap. Underwood was shaking his hand. What did his dad say about men shaking hands? Something about how it's wrong to fight someone who shakes your hand, or some sort of man-code that has to be followed. He couldn't quite remember. Roen often spouted wisdoms that Cameron found wisest to ignore. For some reason, this one came back to him as he shook the policeman's hand.

"Hi, Mr Underwood," he said.

"Listen, son," Underwood said. "A lot of kids got hurt yesterday. I'm afraid I'm going to have to ask you to come with me to the station to explain a few things. Also, I need to ask you if you know what happened to your family's house."

"What happened to my house?" Cameron asked, stunned.

Underwood looked concerned, which just made Cameron feel even guiltier. "You don't know? The house is gone. Bulldozed over. Yours and three others in your area. Everyone's baffled by how it could have happened."

Genjix cleaning team. You need to get out of here. Now!

Cameron stood frozen while the words sunk in. Everything was gone. For some reason, he had assumed that once he found Mom, everything would go back to normal. Now, he realized there was no going back. The Genjix had come and wiped away his entire life in a matter of days. He slowly backed away.

"Come on, son," Underwood said, putting a hand on his elbow. He tugged, but Cameron wouldn't move, the shock numbing his entire body. Underwood tugged again. This time, Cameron tried to snatch his arm out of his grasp. The police officer reached into his side pouch for his handcuffs.

Cameron. Snap out of it. Remember, your parents are still alive. Everything else is just stuff. You need to get moving if you want to see your mother again. I cannot move you on my own. Your mind is not opened to me. Get moving!

"I'm… I'm sorry, Mr Underwood," Cameron said as the officer tried to cuff his wrist. He twisted away until he had reversed Underwood's grip on his elbow. Cameron snatched the handcuffs from Underwood and cuffed the officer's left wrist. Then he yanked down on the chain until the older man bent over. Then Cameron cuffed the officer's right ankle with the other end of the handcuff. Underwood hopped comically, twisted around like a pretzel, his right arm waving wildly around for balance. He considered taking Underwood's handgun. After all, they only had the assault rifle and the pistol. They could use another. The rifle was too unwieldy.

Leave it. No one knows you are armed at the moment. If you take Underwood's firearm, then they will list you as armed and dangerous. Leave the scene now. Head in the opposite direction and then circle around.

In one smooth motion, Cameron unhooked the deputy's belt and tossed it to the side. "I'm sorry," he said again and fled the scene. He sprinted north, knocking people over as he crossed the used car dealership's lot, around the back of the pizzeria, and then turned left down California Street. He ran halfway down the block before jumping over a wooden fence.

Cameron wasn't sure if anyone was in pursuit, but he didn't look back to find out. Now, as he hopped fences, benches, and hurdled over picnic tables, he was grateful for all the free-running practices his mom had put him through. He was putting them to good use crossing yard after yard until he reached the alley he had told Alex to hide in. Cameron spun around the deserted street, looking between garages as he continued jogging.

"Alex," he called in a whisper, "it's me."

She jumped out from behind a car inside a garage, pistol in hand, just as he passed. She looked to both sides and then pulled him toward her. Their bodies bumped together in the narrow pathway between the car and the wall. He felt his heart beat faster as she slipped her arm around his waist and pushed him into the car.

They lay down across the two front seats of an old Mustang. Cameron had his back toward the backrest while Alex lay with hers toward the steering wheel. The stick shift stuck up between them. She had to grab onto his arm in order to not fall off the leather seats.

A few seconds later, they heard the chirp of sirens as a police car drove through the alley. The low rumble of a car passed by, the tires crackled on the rough uneven road. All he could hear was his heart slamming against his chest as he pulled Alex closer. He felt her breath next to his. She turned her head to look up, and strands of her hair whipped against his face gently.

To be honest, after a humid day of hiding out in the alleys, she didn't smell that great. Heck, neither did he, for that matter. Coupled with the musty old scent from the leather chairs and their sweat in such a close space, it was actually pretty rank, but to Cameron that very moment, it was the most intoxicating feeling in the world.

Good grief.

She looked back at him, and Cameron could have sworn for a brief moment, their lips brushed against each other. He inhaled again. Then she lifted her head up past the back of the seat and stared out the back.

"I think they're gone," she said, sitting up.

Cameron followed suit, kicking himself a little for not being brave enough to actually just stick his lips out and complete the motion. Funny how he had experienced firefights, but couldn't work up the courage to kiss a girl.

"I've been working on this car," she said, pointing at the wires sticking out from below the steering wheel. "I haven't had a lot of practice with this."

"Let me," he said. "Trade me places."

He hopped into the driver's side as she moved across the seats. Again, their bodies brushed against each other. Her closeness distracted him as he began to work on jump starting the car.

Can I tell you that puberty is my most hated stage in humans?

"I thought dying was."

Sometimes, it is a relief.

"Come on, what would you do without me?"

Maybe have a host who does not blow a fuse every time a female gets within his airspace?

"I don't know, Tao. I think I'm in –"

I swear by the Eternal Sea, if you say "love," I will sleepwalk you off a cliff. Now focus on hot-wiring that car. You are all thumbs right now.

While he worked, another squad car drove by. Cameron was already lying on his side, but Alex had to lie on top of him again to avoid being seen. Again, he felt his heart thud in his chest as her hair draped over him.

"The humans will never stop hunting us," she said, raising her head again once the noise had passed. "Why do the Prophus still work so hard to protect them?"

"Because it's the right thing to do. Because the Quasing are the aliens on this planet. The least we all can do is try to live together in peace. Besides, if the Genjix succeed in Quasiform, it will lead to the extinction of humanity." Cameron talked through Tao's words, though he found himself having trouble understanding that logic sometimes as well.

No matter what, you are a human first, a host second.

"But I will never be just human again. I will be a host until I die."

Say that to your father.

"What if there's a way to live as a vessel," she said suddenly. Urgently even. "We have loyalty havens all over the world. The closest one is not too far, by Great Slave Lake. You can come with me. My father is very important. I'm sure he can arrange for all of us to survive there during the Great Quasiforming."

"Quasiform isn't going to happen," Cameron said. "The Prophus won't let it."

Alex shook her head. "You don't understand. It will happen no matter what the Prophus or the humans do. Once the Genjix finish all the catalyst facilities, it will happen. This is the last step. No one can stop them. The least you can do is survive. With me."

It was tempting. Cameron could think of many worse

ways to experience the end of the world than with Alex, but if they could actually survive it...

I cannot believe you are even entertaining this.

"I'm just thinking out loud, Tao!"

Thinking of turning your back on billions of people just because you are crushing on a girl.

"All right, thought police. Sheesh. Sorry for thinking."

The car rumbled to life. Alex squealed in delight and clapped her hands. Cameron wore a wide grin as he smacked the steering wheel, as proud as if he had just slayed a dragon. He wasn't a hundred percent sure he could hotwire the car; he had only done it twice before. He fiddled with the manual shift and put his seatbelt on. It was a good thing Roen had taught him how to drive a car in their open field when he was eight years old.

Alex threw her arms around his neck and planted a kiss on his mouth. "About what we talked about. Just think it over, all right?"

Cameron froze and suppressed the urge to dance.

No. No we are not thinking it over.

He nodded. "Sure thing. Come on, buckle up. Let's go see our parents."

He pulled the Mustang out of the garage into the alley and headed south toward the main street.

It should be a few hours to Fort Bragg. I want you to drive slow and not attract attention.

"Come on, let's go fast!" Alex said, putting her legs up on the dashboard of their stolen car.

Cameron punched the accelerator.

CHAPTER THIRTY-ONE
DATE NIGHT

Timestamp: 3201

I, at one point, thought we had escaped the Prophus's clutches, that we were finally free. If it had just been me, I'm sure no one would have cared, especially now that I'm not even a host anymore. However, I was naive; my family had two Quasing of high value. Jill was asked by the Keeper personally to lead a high-traffic cell in the growing Underground Railroad. My wife, always the responsible one in the family, accepted.

We moved to the Pacific Northwest and started over once more. We asked my in-laws to care for Cameron while we built the entire operation from scratch. It wasn't the best time and place to raise a teenager. I swore this would be the last time we'd be separated as a family.

"Nothing is impossible, Roen Tan," the Keeper scoffed. She used his full name. For some reason, both the Keeper and Tao, and sometimes Jill, now that he thought about it, felt that using his full name would get their point across to him more effectively, as if somehow the facts of the situation changed when attaching a surname.

Roen rubbed his temples as he leaned back in the chair and put his feet up on the table. "Keeper, I've been to this place four times in the past two days, examining it from every angle. Security is as tight in the middle of the night as it is in broad daylight. I'm telling you; it can't be done. This attack is suicide."

"I never had you pegged for a quitter, Mr Tan. You might be many things, but I had always considered you brave, if impulsive and stupid."

Adding mister, or calling him stupid, for that matter, wasn't going to change the facts, either. "Well, if my impulsive and stupid ass thinks attacking this facility is too risky, then think about how bad it must actually be."

The Keeper shook her head. "There are no other viable alternative objectives, Roen. This is it."

"And I'm telling you this isn't a viable objective, either. We'll have to find another catalyst facility to attack."

"You think we haven't tried?"

That threw Roen for a loop, given he hadn't been up to date with Prophus operations the past three years. It wasn't like there was a Prophus newsletter that got published every month. "We've tried already? Which ones?"

"The first four catalyst facilities we discovered, we attacked. All unmitigated disasters."

"And this one will be, too," Roen emphasized, slamming his fist on the table. "Look, we might not have seen eye to eye on a lot of things. You know, with our history and all."

"Are you referring to getting my nephew killed? Please. Go on."

Roen sighed. "Meredith, let's not do this again."

"Address me as Keeper. I believe I have earned the title."

"Why? Jill calls you Meredith all the time."

"That's different; I like Jill. Bottom line, this is the only catalyst facility that we've found that isn't in a region under Genjix control. We believe there should be another five or so in this hemisphere, but this is the first we've found, so it's our only viable target. We will not get another chance. We're going to hit it with everything we have. You say it's impossible, fine. Make the impossible possible then. Are we clear?"

Roen rubbed his face with his hands. "Yes, ma'am."

"Good, then if there's nothing else." The screen went dark.

His burner phone began to vibrate violently on the table, squirming its way off. On the old-school digital display were the numbers 911. The text was from Marco, who was supposed to be on a date with Kallis right now at the local steak house. What could the emergency be? Was he discovered? Roen sprinted out of his motel room, jumped into the station wagon and sent his response, giving his ETA and asking for a sit-rep.

The reply from Marco was, "Need extraction ASAP!!!!!!!!!"

"Guess Mr Charming Pants isn't so charming after all," said Roen, thinking the use of a 911 text on a bad date was a serious abuse of protocol on the Brit's part. He felt smug for a whole five minutes until he pulled up to the restaurant. Parked in the center of the parking lot was a Penetra van.

Roen cursed and reached for the pistol in the glove compartment. If Marco had been found out, he was willing to bet security on Prie would triple overnight. This could compromise their entire operation. That was assuming

Roen could even bust Marco out right now.

Roen stuck his pistol on the inside of his jacket and tried to act casual as he walked into the steak house. Either he was walking into the middle of a fight, or they had already captured Marco. In either case, the element of surprise would be key. He crept forward hunched over, his right hand inside his jacket as he opened the door and peered around the corner.

He was met by a bald, rotund older man with barbecue sauce on his shirt. The guy was looking at Roen as if he had gone a little mental. Behind him, his wife and three kids leaned over and joined in on the staring. Roen abruptly stood up and got out of the way. The mother put her arms around her kids and ushered them out. On the way out, Roen heard the dad mutter something about meth and scrambled eggs.

Roen craned his head to the right and saw what looked like a typical restaurant on a Thursday night. The tables were about half occupied, and Vivaldi was piping through the music system. Roen chuckled. Tao hated that guy with a passion. Well, more like Tao hated the entire Baroque period.

He clicked his pistol's safety back on as he wandered across the dining area. To his left, at a large ten-person round table, he noticed a group of people who looked distinctively military. Then he noticed the backpacks resembling Ghostbusters proton packs on the floor next to their chairs: portable Penetra scanners. No wonder Marco was spooked. All one of these guys had to do was turn a pack on, and he was a goner.

Roen scanned each table. Finally, he noticed Marco sitting in the far right corner, leaning intimately close to

Kallis. He didn't look like he was in trouble. In fact, he looked like he was having a pretty damn good time. Roen assumed a friendly face and walked toward them.

"Ralphy," Marco said, acting surprised and a little overly friendly. "What a surprise to see you here. What can I do for you, man?"

Kallis, wearing a more casual shirt and pants, brightened in surprise. She looked genuinely pleased to see him. "Hey, can't I get your business partner to myself for one night?"

Roen coughed. "Um, sorry to interrupt your date, uh, Cornelius, but we have a little situation that requires your attention."

"Oh?" Marco said, making a show of concern. He looked over at Kallis. "Excuse me, my dear."

He stood up and walked with Roen off to the side. "Act concerned, like something is urgent," Marco said.

"I am concerned," Roen snapped. "You nine-one-one'd me."

"Behind your right shoulder. Those are Kallis's people."

"I'm not blind, Marco."

"Well, seems those louts thought it'd be funny to crash her date, so they all decided to have dinner here tonight. They drove up in the Penetra van and walked in here with their bloody packs."

Roen stole a glance at Kallis, who was shooting her underlings a dirty look. "What about your date?"

"Nothing we can do about that now," said Marco. "Need you to be my alibi."

"Why didn't you just tell her instead of calling me here?" Roen asked.

Marco grinned. "This makes it much more realistic. Otherwise, it would look like I just buggered out on a date."

Together the two walked back to the table. Marco made sure to look very angry as he berated Roen about his incompetence in his mishandling of export documentation. Roen bit his lip as Marco laid into him. One day, this guy was going to get what was coming to him. He grimaced and bore it, though, looking properly chastised.

"I'm sorry, my dear," Marco said to Kallis. "I will have to make it up to you. A small crisis beckons." He shot Roen another look.

Kallis looked puzzled. "Can it wait a little bit? Our steaks are coming any second now. I can't eat both by myself. Or Rutherford, would you care to join me?"

"Well," Marco said. "I guess I could take it to-go."

"Well, since you're already dressed up, no reason to waste the evening," Roen said. "Thanks for the invite." He looked over at Marco. "It's a burden I'll have to live with. Eating your steak that is. I hope you got it medium rare. You'd better get going, boss."

Marco looked like he was about to object, but then he nodded. "Very well. Allow me to make it up to you, my dear," he said to Kallis. He paused in front of Roen with a forlorn look, and then departed. Roen turned to Kallis and sat down. He had been planning on having a ham sandwich for dinner, as that was all they had back at the shed. This was much better.

Roen and Kallis watched as Marco exited the restaurant. She turned and stuck a finger in his face. "Tell me the truth. Was it that bad of a date he had to call you in to bail him out?"

Roen held his hands up in an 'I surrender' posture. "You got us. This was all an elaborate ploy so Marco could get away right before the steak came, because he's secretly a vegetarian. And I accepted his invitation to take his place because as my business partner, he doesn't allow me to eat meat either back at the office."

"Really?"

"No, not really."

"You wouldn't tell me anyway, would you?"

Roen motioned at her group of people sitting at the other side of the restaurant. "Would you cover for your guys?"

"Good point," she chuckled. "That's my family there. God, country, family, and that group of assholes who crashed the first date I've had in months." The group at the round table all looked their way and raised their beer glasses.

"I find that hard to believe," Roen said. He meant it too. Kallis looked in her late thirties or early forties, and attractive. She had a no-nonsense demeanor that probably scared some people away, but she also seemed to have a good sense of humor. Right now, she was shaking her finger and playing with her guys. In many ways, Kallis reminded him of Jill.

"Hey, you want to take the party over there?" Roen asked.

"You sure?" she said. "I mean, those guys are kind of a handful. They'll eat you alive."

"I'll have you there to protect me, or to egg them on."

"Let's eat first. If we bring red meat to those savages, they'll devour everything." Kallis grinned. "You know, Rutherford, you're all right. I have a good nose for guys, and Cornelius is a little too smooth to be real, but you're an okay guy." She picked up her glass of wine and toasted him. Roen grinned, taking over Marco's scotch and doing the same.

A few minutes later, their steaks came, and the two enjoyed a couple of twenty-four ounce New York strips. Afterward, they joined the rest of Kallis's team at the table, and Roen got to know a few of her people.

Most were ex-military, so he identified with many of their experiences and stories, though he had to hide that from them. Roen did his best to not have to make up any more about himself by keeping the discussion focused on them. By the end of the night, after a couple of rounds of drinks, he had trouble keeping track of what was the truth, and what he had had to make up.

It really didn't matter anymore, anyway. In a couple of weeks, whenever the hospital released Prie, these IXTF agents would try to transfer him up to Seattle while Roen and his guys would try to stop them. That was probably the last time he would see any of these people, so he might as well make stuff up to fit in while he was here.

The group around the table ended up closing the restaurant. By then, the scotch had gotten to Roen, and he felt weird driving back to the base not totally sober with so many federal agents in the parking lot. Now that he thought about it, they didn't have a designated driver, either. In fact, the entire team all downed their beers before heading out, insisting they couldn't waste alcohol. Roen found himself liking these guys, even if they were the enemy. In another lifetime, perhaps, things could have been different.

"Hey, Rutherford," Kallis stuck out her hand as her group hopped into the Penetra van, "thanks for saving the evening."

Roen shook her hand. "It was my pleasure. Sorry about crashing your date. I'm sure Cornelius will make it up to you."

"No, I don't think I would have had a better time than the one I did. I'm sure it worked out for the best." The Penetra van's horn honked twice. Kallis looked over and gave it the bird, and then turned back. "You know, Cornelius is a smooth talker and probably the face of your company, but he's lucky to have you."

Roen shrugged. "Old Cornelius is a burden I have to live with."

"I bet it's a real heavy burden," she grinned. "But really. I know who the heart of the business is."

There was an awkward pause as Roen froze. It was times like this when he wished Tao were here. A guy his age should know how to handle these situations by now, but for some reason, it was a big hole in his education he had never filled.

"Thanks," was all that came out of his mouth, leaving an awkward pause hanging in the air before he was able to recover. "Why don't we all hang out again soon?"

Kallis hesitated. "Not sure if I'm going to be able to. You ever up in Seattle?"

Roen paused for only a split second, glancing down on the ground before nodding. "Sure. I'll look you up." He watched as the Penetra van pulled out of the lot. Once it was out of sight, he dialed the base. "Sheck, turn that bug on. I think IXTF is on the move."

CHAPTER THIRTY-TWO
FINISHING THE GAME

The technology that arose from the Industrial Revolution gave us new hope for this species. It not only allowed humans to experience massive population growth, it also allowed them to expand rapidly in their never-ending hunger for resources. This, in turn, allowed the Genjix to push the boundaries of our Conflict Doctrine even further. For the first time in history, we began to see them as not unlike ourselves.

Zoras

Ever since Baji's Great Betrayal, the United States had been the most vigilant in the ill-conceived war against all Quasing and had set up the world's most effective Penetra net on their borders. All flights, sea routes, and border checkpoints were continually scanned. It made leaving the blasted country difficult, and entering near impossible, at least without extraordinary effort and cost. Unfortunately, Canada had extended to the United States the right to watch their borders in a similar fashion. Therefore, any movement to the entire North American continent was expensive and risky, and had to be carefully planned.

Unless you were on the Council, then extraordinary cost be damned.

The trip from Moscow had been physically draining, and had taken much longer than necessary. Enzo had left the same night as the Genjix takeover of the Federal Assembly, routing to North Korea first, and then flying overseas to an ocean-bound freighter. Due to the stringent security of the IXTF, especially across the western coast of North America, the Genjix had to be airdropped a day out of Vancouver. Then it took another two slow days for the damn ship's cargo to offload into Port Metro.

Fortunately, the IXTF watched the ports in Canada much less stringently than they did the ports in the United States, and all the two hundred Genjix had to do was stroll out of their containers in the middle of the night and board the six transport helicopters waiting to ferry them over. Enzo scanned the landscape below him as his little armada passed from land to water over Great Slave Lake.

It was little surprise that Vinnick had chosen this location for the loyalty haven: heavily wooded area, large body of water, isolated, mountainous landscape. The perfect location for a hidden base to survive the apocalypse. North America was the only continent lagging in these facilities, the inherent government difficulties slowing construction. Because of all these heightened restrictions, building costs for haven facilities were four times what they were anywhere else in the world. Well, except for maybe in Japan and southern Britain. The real estate prices in those regions were out of control. It was all a colossal waste of money in his opinion.

Enzo scanned the vast body of water as they neared the center of Great Slave Lake. Nothing; just calm waters. He turned to Amanda. "Is our man in place?"

She raised a finger to him as she spoke into a comm. He allowed this indiscretion, if barely. Sometimes, when she was busy or stressed, she forgot her place. She nodded a few times, and then looked up at him. "He is, Father. Stand by."

A few seconds later, four large metal towers rose up from the depths of the lake. The gray structures, shedding water as they grew, were large cylinders with domed tops. They reached approximately twenty meters above the surface and stopped, then four square wings hanging inside the space between the towers swung up until they formed a giant platform.

"First three transports, prepare to airdrop," Enzo instructed. "Second grouping lands once we secure the area."

Have your people secure the area. You do not need to be the first to land.

"Very well."

It was a common wisdom Zoras often needed to instill in him. Even after all these years, Enzo had to fight the urge to be the first in every battle. It wasn't a surprise that Protesilaus ranked as one of his favorite childhood heroes. Now that he commanded the fate of the world, his wise guardian had to be heeded. Still, he felt his toes and hands itch as he saw the units from the three transports rappel down onto the platform. Within seconds, they had secured it and waited for the other three transports to land.

He tapped his foot impatiently as his transport moved into place, deciding to leap as it hovered two meters above the ground. He landed with a loud clank against the metal floor and was instantly surrounded by the units already there, taking defensive positions around him.

What are the odds of Vinnick lowering this platform while we are here?

"I was assured by our contact on the inside that it won't happen."

There was a grinding sound from the northeast tower, followed by a hiss of air pressure releasing. The door opened, and three men walked out. His men moved in to disarm and disable them.

Enzo raised a hand. "Hold."

Obviously, they hadn't come up here to fight. He recognized two of the men. One was Sergii, Vinnick's heir, and the other was Gates, his handpicked commander for this haven. Interesting choices. The third seemed just a bodyguard, a foolish and wasted security measure.

Sergii is a highly-trained Sambo practitioner and trained in savate in France. Gates is the cousin of a Dutch politician, and earned his Holy One while they were playing golf and the politician suffered a stroke. The third is an unknown.

"The commander and his future. This is his surrender."

Be wary. We saw this before at the Church of the Disposition of the Robe.

Enzo watched as the sea of his black-garbed units parted, and the three approached. The Adonis appeared relaxed, but Enzo could detect tension around his eyes, the slightly forced casualness of his movements. By all accounts, he was very well-trained, even though Enzo didn't consider him a real Hatchery brother. Vinnick would have accepted nothing less. At one point, the two of them were competitors, spoken of equally highly as potential vessels and discussed in the same breath. Maybe it was time to test that.

Gates, on the other hand, looked like he was about to soil himself. He was a vessel barely worth mentioning. Highly valued vessels did not become commanders of backwater bases whose only purpose was to keep insecure believers alive during the greatest elevation of the species.

He bowed a little lower than Sergii did when they reached Enzo. "Father. This is an unexpected honor. We did not anticipate your arrival."

"He means he does not know why the platform was brought up."

Indeed.

Gates wasn't used to conflict and the power struggle within the council. Enzo could see desperation in his eyes as he looked at the group of armed men. Enzo didn't blame him; the two most powerful Genjix Council members were quarreling in his front yard. He'd be forced to choose sides shortly. Before he could say another word, Enzo walked past him toward the entrance. Akelatis fell in line to his right. Azumi to his left. She signaled for the rest of their people to follow.

"Father, a moment," Gates called, running up beside him. "Due to the sensitive nature of the facility, I'm afraid the inner sanctum of the catalyst facility needs to be locked down."

Enzo ignored him and continued to the door leading down to the haven. He was well aware of Sergii trailing to his left, as well as the guard keeping pace to his right. He knew that Azumi had her eyes on the Adonis Vessel. He was the real danger here.

Gates continued to plead with Enzo until they reached the door. The fool actually had the audacity to jump in front to block his path. "Father, please. I serve the Holy

Ones, but this is an untenable situation and a risk to this very important Genjix operation. There are issues that must be resolved by both sides, I understand. However, I must insist that this conflict be resolved elsewhere. The Council Power Struggle has no place in a loyalty haven."

Enzo gave him a flat stare and watched Gates shrink before him. Then, without looking, he pulled out his sidearm and shot Gates's guard in the neck.

"You have an objection?"

Gates's face turned a shade of purple, and the sounds coming out of his mouth became half-stutters and squeaks. Akelatis walked up and clubbed the man on the side of the head with the butt of his rifle. Enzo continued walking down the stairs of the metal tower into the base. Once on the main level, he was met by quite a few black rifle muzzles.

Sixteen Epsilons, forty standard security. No vessels among them.

Gates staggered up from behind. His eyes were still unfocused, but he seemed to have learned his place.

"Zoras, what do you know about his Holy One?"

Jara is a scientist and has focused on technological evolutions since the early Mesopotamian period. He is credited with the invention of the chariot and later notable inventions such as bleeding, the axle wheel, and condoms. He is best known for several high-profile failed inventions.

"Like what?"

He once tried to create a courier system using trebuchets.

"Not a bad idea, actually."

I thought so, too, until the system started accidently killing people.

"So he is a scientist and not a warrior."

You will have to treat him delicately, since his reactions can be unpredictable.

Sergii appeared next to Enzo and bowed deeply. "Father, Councilman Vinnick also has a large stockpile of the catalyst reaction rods. As you know, they are invaluable to Quasiform operations, and this underwater base is extraordinarily delicate. Please see the wisdom in parlaying first to insure that holy relics are not put at risk."

Interesting. He just called you stupid and threatened you with the catalysts' destruction. If Vinnick has brought the stolen stockpile here, then Sergii is right. It is far too valuable to risk destroying.

Enzo looked at the sixteen Epsilons behind the barricade and considered his options. Violence in this space would be messy. Any invading force would have to fight through modular rooms. The defenders would have several bottlenecks to keep them contained. He glanced up at the ceilings. Any rupture of these facilities would probably doom them all as well, which ruled out explosives.

As always, your habit of embracing risk will be your downfall. Seek another option.

"It hasn't yet, my Guardian. Recommendation?"

Parlay first. Turn the tide in your favor before striking. The current odds are against you. The base defenders alongside the Epsilons vastly outnumber your forces. They also hold the tactically superior position. This is a test. Prove you are able.

"Your will, Zoras. However, I cannot tolerate the way that worm continues to bargain with me."

Hold him accountable, but do not endanger the catalyst reaction rods. That is strong leverage.

Enzo grimaced. The past few weeks in Russia had showed that if there was one thing Vinnick could beat him at again and again, it was duplicitous diplomacy. It was time Enzo stopped playing this game and leveled the playing field. There was more than one way to play at diplomacy.

It had always been his experience that if you removed someone's choices, they would more often than not do what they were ordered. In the case of Gates, Enzo planned to do just that. Show authority, and the followers would be more than happy to just follow.

He looked at Gates. "Commander, have your security forces arrest the Epsilons."

Gates blanched, and his security forces balked at the command. However, before he could respond, Enzo had turned to the Adonis Vessel. "Sergii, my son. You have a choice now: whether you wish to be a Genjix or dead. You are an Adonis Vessel, and I understand your loyalty to Vinnick, regardless of how misplaced it is. You are also an asset to the Holy Ones and the Genjix. Do not make the mistake of following a vessel and not the Holy One. Flua is still yours if you wish, but you must follow the true Genjix."

Sergii was not a fool; all Adonises were highly-educated and trained. He understood the situation before him. It didn't matter that Sergii and Enzo were approximately the same age, for Enzo to have a Holy One and Sergii to still be waiting for that blessing placed them worlds apart. Enzo read the man's eyes and forced his hands to stay relaxed by his sides. He just had to trust that either Sergii would make the right choice, or Enzo would outdraw him. In either case, Enzo depended on the Adonis's desperation for a long-overdue blessing. Enzo offered it to him now. Surely that was more valuable than clinging to an out-of-favor human.

"Father," Sergii struggled to choke the words out as he fell to a knee. "There is no need for more conflict. I can handle the Epsilons."

This is a dangerous proposition. Sergii with Flua makes him Vinnick's true heir and a strong threat to your supremacy on the Council.

"Even if I am the one to offer it to him?"

You legitimize him.

"Prove your loyalty," Enzo said. He took a step back as Vinnick's heir, now Enzo's lapdog, waved his hands at the Epsilons.

"We are all Genjix and serve the Holy Ones," he said. "Lay down your arms. Boris, Vadim, Yegor, put your rifles down."

The one called Yegor, a gruff long-bearded soldier, scowled. "He was like a father to you, traitor." He aimed his rifle at Sergii. The Adonis dodged the shot, but it was too late. All hell broke loose, because Enzo's agents opened fire. The rest of the Epsilons fired back. A three-way firefight broke out. All the while, Sergii tried in vain to reestablish the peace. Enzo pulled out his pistol and shot him in the back.

"Problem solved. Wasn't so difficult, was it?"

Find Vinnick and finish this. We have a new world to birth.

Word spread quickly as the security forces and the Epsilons turned on each other. Small firefights broke out in the hallways and rooms. Enzo's units joined forces and swept through the vast segmented base that was spread out along the lake floor like a spider web. It was tedious and slow work, but he didn't mind. In the end, wiping out all the Epsilons was the right decision, regardless of the body count. The Epsilons were loyal to Vinnick first and the Genjix second, so they were useless to him.

The final surrender came six hours later in the medical module of the haven. The twenty remaining Epsilons had erected barricades and dared Enzo and his men to attack their fortification. At first, they had tried to send an envoy, offering fairly generous terms just for those twenty souls to walk out of the room. All they wanted was their freedom to walk away from the Genjix and a transport under their own control to go wherever they wished.

Enzo had considered just jettisoning the entire module off the base. Instead, he shot the envoy and sent in the entire haven's security force. It was a bloody massacre. He had thought the Epsilons would surrender after they ran out of bullets, but to their credit, they armed themselves with their bayonets and dared Enzo to send in more men. He was more than happy to oblige.

In the end, the twenty Epsilons took out three times their number before finally succumbing to the haven's security. Fortunately, it was isolated to the medical module. Enzo walked around the ruins of the medical bay after it was all over. It would be weeks before this place could be used again. In a module meant to hold thirty people, there was almost three times the number of bodies strewn about. Some of the corpses were piled so high, Enzo had to order them removed before he could continue deeper.

He found what he was looking for in the far back of the bay. Vinnick's body lay still. By the looks of it, he had taken his own life moments before the medical module fell. Enzo stared at the empty husk that was once his hated enemy. This wrinkled bag of bones and skin was the foil that had delayed the Genjix from achieving their final objectives. Now, he was gone, and all Enzo could think about was next task at hand. For some reason, he thought he would feel something else.

In Vinnick's still-warm hand was a note addressed to Enzo. He picked it up and unfolded it.

"You might have won, but you will never get Flua, you bastard. May the Holy Ones have mercy on this Earth."

Enzo growled and crumpled the note in his hands. "He has robbed me of my moment."

The victory is all that matters.

"It is a Pyrrhic one, nevertheless."

Enzo turned to Gates. "Clean this mess up."

Jacob made one pass around the perimeter of the school before he walked inside to the crime scene. He motioned to the *Seattle Times* press pass when one of the local law enforcement officers stopped him at the front door. Jacob noted the pistol at his side, holstered with the strap locked in place. No armor either. He would be easy to take out.

The officer waved him through, and he joined a gaggle of reporters speaking with the principal and gym teacher of the school regarding the incident that had left a dozen students in the hospital, two of them critically injured. He stood at the back of the group and listened to a retelling of the morning's events.

Jacob raised his hand when the questions had come to a lull. "Excuse me, Hamilton Foster, *Seattle Times*," he said with a Midwestern accent. "Could you tell us about the injuries that the children sustained?"

The principal stepped in front of the gym teacher and read off a list of broken bones, ruptured spleens, and torn joints, emphasizing that all the students were expected to make a full recovery and that the school was taking steps to ensure that something like this would never happen again.

I would be interested in what sort of precautions the human could implement to stop a Hatchery-trained vessel.

If these children were trying to stay under the radar, they were doing a piss-poor job of it. Or maybe that was the point. Who were they trying to alert, though, the Prophus or the Genjix? Which vessel was leaving these breadcrumbs?

By their description, the injuries are consistent with the girl's style.

"Especially the focal point of her attacks. Solid Sambo techniques."

Jacob felt his body flex involuntarily. His revenge, long thought completed, was now overdue with interest. Roen Tan's family would be the perfect form of payment. The itch that he had thought long scratched was now painful, keeping him up at night. Jacob was eager to settle. His grandfather's soul needed peace.

"Adonis," another of Jacob's men called in. "We just received a report over the police band of an assault a few hours ago at the local bus station by a boy fitting the description of our mark."

"Moving," Jacob replied. "Meet me down the block."

Find out which buses were readying for departure in that time frame.

"Trying to board a bus out of town? Do we know to where?"

He spent another thirty minutes interviewing several of the school staff. They were all aware of this Cameron Tan, who seemed by all indications a quiet boy who rarely spoke and never made problems. The teachers were shocked he was involved.

"Adonis," one of his men reported. "Report of a submersible off the beach two hundred klicks south. Locals found a burning wreck and hauled it to shore. Timestamps match the events and paint a relatively clear scenario."

Jacob spoke into his ear piece. "Confirmed. Get a body south immediately to search the wreckage. I want a black light on it immediately. Report back if you find a Seal of Shamesh. Let's move."

CHAPTER THIRTY-THREE
FREE PRIE

Timestamp: 3333

The passage through the western coast of the United States down to Mexico is one of the most-traveled in the Underground Railroad. What I initially thought was a cake job became one of the more difficult operations I'd ever had to work on for the Prophus. It was also one of the most rewarding.

At first, the stream of tired, desperate refugees from Asia was a deluge. So much so that it attracted the attention of the IXTF and became one of the Prophus's most active regions. It was there I earned superhero status as the Rayban Ghost.

The farmhouse was gone. The entire damn thing. Gone. Roen stared at the satellite pictures, then back at the surveillance shots Hite took on the ground. There was nothing there; his entire life, as if it had never existed. The only thing in the now-empty field that even resembled any sign of his life was the buildings' rough outlines, now filled with upturned earth and rubble. Tears flowed freely down his face. The life he had built, the first in a decade that had felt stable, safe, and happy, was now reduced to a mound of black soil.

Roen knew this had been par for the course ever since he became involved in this Quasing war. Even worse, he still had not spoken to his family. He had finally got ahold of Datlow and coaxed the truth out of her. Once she'd sent over the images, he realized it was worse than he had feared.

His only solace was that his family was all right. Jill had contacted Datlow early in the week and Cameron a few days later. If they were still missing, he would have hopped into the station wagon, wooden panels and all, and made a beeline back toward home, Prie and the Prophus and this catalyst facility be damned. If either of them had been injured or worse, he would have never forgiven himself.

He had sworn to stay by their side and to protect them forever, no matter what. It seemed no matter how hard he tried, he just couldn't keep that promise. This was the first time in years he had been away from his family for this long, and some Genjix asshole demolished their house. Roen curled his fingers into fists and crushed the images in his hand.

Marco, sitting next to him, looked at the crumpled image. "You all right, mate?"

Roen shook his head. "Genjix attacked the farmhouse."

Marco paled. "Your family?"

"They made it out, thank God, but everything else is gone."

"Well, that's all that's bloody important. I need your head with you, man." Marco held up a fist. Roen tapped it with his. He appreciated Marco's concern. The two were operating much better together than last time in Egypt, partially because both of them were getting too damn old to fight over ego. More importantly, Marco seemed to have become less of an asshole as he got older. Two dust-ups were considered light for them.

"By the way, Roen," Marco added. "If the operation goes wrong, I want you close to Prie. You're taking Pri as a last resort."

"Uh, no," Roen made a face. "What am I, some sort of surrogate incubator? I've already done my tour of duty."

Marco looked surprised. "I thought you would want it. You know, become a host and be somebody again."

Be somebody again? Scratch that. Marco was still the biggest asshole ever.

"They've arrived at the hospital," Sheck said. "Chase says convoy of three vehicles, including the Penetra van. Helen reporting an ambulance standing by as well."

"Move out," Marco said as the rest of the team ran through final preparations.

The chatter about Prie's extraction began immediately after the team activated the bug under Kallis's shoe. Against the advice of doctors, the team had decided to transport him as soon as possible, though he was barely well enough to be moved. Because of his delicate state, there were concerns that the long drive to Seattle would be too dangerous. Instead, they had arranged for a small plane to arrive at Ontario Airport, where he would be transferred by air to the regional IXTF headquarters in Seattle.

The team had originally thought the IXTF was going to move him down highway 84 by convoy and had planned accordingly. Activating the bug had saved them. It gave them just enough time to scramble and adjust their rescue plan. Now, they had a distance just over three klicks from the hospital to the plane to work with. It left very little room for them to maneuver. The only saving grace was that they knew the exact route the IXTF team was taking to the airport. Roen had to give it to Kallis; she left little to the imagination when it came to detailing their plans. Roen's team had stayed up all night to implement a contingency plan, stealing a Plymouth Voyager minivan, an old pickup truck, and jerry-rigging a series of low-grade IEDs.

They buried the IEDs on the only stretch of gravel road and now the team was in position waiting for the convoy to arrive. Chase and Helen would tail the convoy in the minivan while Elias manned the pickup truck hidden behind the gas tanks a little off to the side. The rest of them had to hide in a barn way off from the ambush point, just far enough away from the Penetra van's range.

Marco, Sheck and Roen waited just inside the door for their signal. While they had elected to be covered from head to toe in their standard-issue combat gear, Roen wore his typical hood and Rayban glasses, preferring to armor only his vital organs. He was also designated the tactical lead during this operation, simply because everyone else had an accent, which would give them away in a heartbeat. Well, everyone except for Chase, who was from Dallas, but that guy couldn't lead children to an ice cream truck, let alone a last-minute multi-faceted ambush.

"They're pulling onto 33rd now," Sheck said.

Marco pulled the ski mask down over his head while Roen knotted his hoodie tight to his face. He adjusted the Rayban sunglasses and shouldered his rifle. He caught Marco staring at him.

"What?" he asked.

"You look like the bloody Unabomber," said Marco.

"That was kind of the point," Roen said. "I think I look cool."

"Look a bloody fool more like it."

There was a long pause.

"You're the fool," Roen retorted lamely.

There was a sound of a crash, which was their cue. The three of them charged out of the barn, sprinting across the field. Elias had rammed the lead Penetra van with the pickup truck, effectively blocking the ambulance's path. The IEDs, buried on the left side of the street, went off on the two rear vehicles. The trick more or less worked. One car was flipped onto its side, but the explosion missed the back car. Helen resolved that a second later by ramming the minivan into it.

"Try not to kill anyone," Roen yelled through the comm, knowing he sounded like a broken record. He had told the team half a dozen times today already, but he especially meant it this time, because he had just met most of these IXTF guys a few days ago. He had shaken hands and drank beers with them. Killing them felt wrong.

It didn't stop him from doing his job, though. He clocked the first IXTF agent who climbed out of the rear car – Martin the vegetarian – in the face, hopefully knocking the guy out. The next guy, a perpetually chuckling older gentleman named Nate, raised his pistol at Roen before Marco clubbed him with the butt of his rifle.

On his left, Roen saw Sheck run up to the Penetra van and the ambulance and shoot out the tires on both. Marco charged over to the overturned car in the middle as another of the IXTF agents tried to crawl out of the driver's side window. He hauled the man out – Valentine, the rookie of Kallis's team – and threw him on the ground, knocking him out with a punch to the temple.

To his left he heard a gunshot and then another. Roen saw Kallis standing there, blood streaming down the side of her face. She was aiming somewhere behind Roen. He looked back and saw Chase fall. Cursing, Roen charged her, covering the distance between them as she turned her attention to him. One shot went high left; the second missed his face by sheer luck when he lowered his head and tackled her. He felt the bullet scorch the air as they collided.

Roen had thought he could take out the smaller woman easily, but Kallis was no slouch. She hooked her arms around his waist and twisted left upon impact. Both of them fell and rolled on the ground. Roen got to his feet just in time for her to kick at his face. She missed and nailed him in the neck instead. He felt his throat constrict as he stumbled backward.

Kallis scrambled for her pistol, which had fallen to the side. Knowing he wasn't going to beat her there, he dove forward and tripped her as she ran. The two exchanged blows. He could tell right away she had a Marine Corps Martial Arts Program background. Back and forth they went as she pressed. Roen defended as he examined what was going on in the rest of the fight. His team had secured all of the IXTF's vehicles by now. Elias and Helen were opening the ambulance doors. Marco was approaching Roen and Kallis, rifle drawn.

"No," Roen yelled, shaking his head. The momentary distraction earned him a kick to the groin that doubled him over, then a combination of punches and kicks to his head and body. He ate the first few strikes and backpedaled, studying her cadence. He had to admit; she was good.

Better than he gave her credit for. But not good enough.

He slipped outside her guard and tried to force her to the ground with an elbow lock. Kallis escaped and rewarded his efforts to peacefully incapacitate her by flurrying his face with punches, causing his head to bounce forward and backward like a speed bag. Finally, fed up, he growled, palmed her face and chopped her legs from under her.

"You just don't know when to give up, do you?" He spat blood from his mouth onto the floor. "Stay down." Then he felt the adrenaline dump, and the pain in his groin made its presence felt. He hunched forward and clenched his body. He wasn't going to walk right for a few days. She thrashed at him while he kept her pinned down.

Marco had the rifle trained on her face a moment later. Kallis froze, and Roen let his grip on her face slacken. He stood up and limped backward, gasping. "Holy cow, that hurts."

She took one look at his sunglasses and hoodie, and spat on the ground. "You must be the Rayban Ghost. I knew your greasy fingers would show up here. My men…"

"…are all still alive," he said, "which is more than I can say for one of mine. Now stay down before I even the score. On your stomach!" He tried to keep his voice low and guttural, but he knew he was walking a fine line. He took out sets of plastic binds and tied her arms behind her back. She squirmed as she glared at him. The rest of the IXTF agents were bound in a similar fashion.

He turned to Marco. "Did we secure the package?"

Marco nodded, pulled out a pistol and handed it to Roen. Roen took it and pointed it at Kallis. "How's Chase?"

Marco shook his head and Roen swore. "Get ready for

transport then," he said, his eyes never moving away from Kallis.

The death was on Roen; he knew that. He was the one who had pleaded with the team to try to avoid casualties. It still hurt every time Roen lost a guy. It felt personal this time, because he had tried to accomplish Prophus goals without injuring good people. Now, Chase had paid the price. Tao would have called him an idiot for being so soft.

You should have focused on your people and your objective first.

That's what Tao would have said, and he would have been one hundred percent correct.

It seemed his noble efforts weren't lost on Kallis either. "Rayban Ghost, you held back there. Why?"

"You noticed?"

"Been in enough fights to recognize when a man is pulling his punches."

Roen knelt over her and tapped the ground with the pistol. "By the way, you owe the Eureka Animal Shelter another ten grand for the lives of your men."

He looked over at the ambulance and saw his guys wheel Prie around the corner. Then Marco and Sheck came back to retrieve Chase. He grimaced as they picked up his limp body and took him away.

"We're all saddled up," Marco said through the comm. "On our way back to base."

"Giving you guys a five-minute head start," Roen replied. "Use it wisely." He checked the time. Pretty soon, someone was going to notice this mess on the airfield. He needed to make sure his guys were as far away from here as possible. He looked over at Kallis squirming her way to her side. With a grunt, she bent her knees forward and wormed her way so she faced him lying down sideways.

"So, Rayban," she said. "Are any of my guys hurt?"

"Not my concern." He checked the time again. In the distance, he heard the faint howling of sirens. He had to get moving.

"You're a bastard, you know that, Rayban Ghost," Kallis called. "I'm going to hunt you for the rest of your God damned life."

"Oh no, not that." He shrugged, scanning the perimeter. "Guess it's a burden I'll have to live with."

Her eyes widened. "A heavy burden?"

Roen gave a start and realized his mistake too late. He took off at a sprint, heading the opposite direction of the sirens.

"Hey, come back here, Rayban!" he heard her scream. "Rutherford!"

Roen stumbled, cursing himself for making such an idiotic mistake. In his self-loathing for losing Chase, he had turned one mistake into two. This one could have serious consequences as well, not just for this mission, but for a long time.

Well, no matter, it had happened. Roen had to move on. Even if he had accidentally given himself away, what's the worst she could do? They had Prie now. The attack on the catalyst facility would happen in a couple of days, and by week's end, he'd be out of her reach forever.

CHAPTER THIRTY-FOUR
REUNITED

As honorable as the Prophus's intentions seem, the truth about the Quasing is much less so. The reality is that the Genjix really are the real Quasing. You see, if I was to equate our species to any on Earth, I would say we are locusts. We are a swarm of trillions of creatures moving as a giant organism from solar system to solar system, consuming resources and mutating planets to our will.

Tao

What should barely have been a three-hour drive from Eureka to Fort Bragg took Cameron and Alex over a day. It seems there had been a reason that Mustang was in a garage. After they got through the stop-and-go traffic out of Eureka, which sorely tested Cameron's ability to shift manually and the poor car's transmission, they discovered a painful high-pitched grinding any time they went over thirty miles per hour, no matter what gear Cameron tried for. Five hours later, they were still forty miles away from Fort Bragg when their next misfortune hit: the frail muscle car ran out of gas. The two teens decided to camp one last night under the stars and finish the trek the next day.

Dusk was approaching by the time they finally reached Fort Bragg. Both of them were exhausted. Alex in particular was in a bad mood. She looked preoccupied and even nervous as they crossed the bridge over the Noyo River. Cameron, on the other hand, was getting excited. He could see the RV park on the cliff overlooking the bay to his right.

His eyes automatically wandered over to the steep drop down to the bay, and he reflexively touched the scar on his left arm. He shuddered. The first time he ever got stitches was because he was an idiot and thought it'd be fun to roll down that cliff. Mom had had to stitch him up herself without anesthesia. He still had nightmares about that pain every once in a while. He wasn't afraid of heights before he pulled that stunt, but he was a little now. That's what he got for trying to show off to his parents.

I told you that was a bad idea.

"Remind me to always listen to you when I act dumb."

You should listen to me all the time then.

"Pfft. Whatever."

Cameron looked away from the cliff and searched for the trailer. He had come here with Roen on resupply runs often, so he knew exactly where the trailer was parked. In fact, if he looked closely, he could see someone sitting on top of the silver bullet-shaped housing at the far back. Could that be Mom? It was getting dark, so he couldn't quite make out the figures. Half of the sun was already submerged below the western edge of the ocean. He figured they might have about fifteen minutes before night fell.

"Come on," he said, picking up the pace. "We're almost there."

"Wait," Alex said, pulling back. "Enjoy the last few moments we have together."

"What do you mean?" he asked.

"Once we're back with our parents, it won't be just us anymore. Maybe never again. After all, you're staying here, and I'm leaving for South America."

Those words cut through Cameron's heart like a dagger. He held her hand and slowed his pace to a crawl as they walked the final couple of hundred meters to the trailer. He didn't know how, but somehow, she had turned this moment of joy into a death walk.

Cameron, Alex will be under the protection of the Prophus. You will see her again. Sooner than you think.

"I can always visit," he said.

She moved in close and wrapped an arm around his waist. Not sure what he was supposed to do next, Cameron hesitantly put his arm around her shoulder. Alex squeezed herself closer. They reached the end of the bridge and turned right into the lot, walking even slower. Every step toward his mother and Vladimir was one closer to them being torn apart. For a split second, he entertained the idea of running off.

Do not be stupid. No, too late. You are being stupid. Cut it out.

Alex stepped in front of him, forcing him to stop. She threw her arms around his neck and kissed him on the mouth. At first, Cameron had no idea what to do. He froze as she moved herself close to him, her lips locked onto his in quiet, nervous desperation. He put his hands on her waist and squeezed. This was his first real kiss, and as far as he cared, the only thing in the world right now that mattered.

Be careful, Cameron. You are setting yourself up for a bad Greek tragedy.

The two of them seemed to have become one for what felt like an eternity. There he was, a hundred meters from reuniting with his family, and all he wanted to do was stay standing here for the rest of his life. For the rest of their lives. Now that he thought about it, he didn't know if he could live without her. Panic set in.

Good grief. I do not suppose you would listen to any advice right now?

"Shut up and leave me alone, Tao."

I kind of figured.

By the time they broke their embrace, the sun had fully set, and their lips were chapped. The only reason they even broke it at all was because a grimy, fuzz-ridden old man in suspenders was leaning against a trailer leering at them.

"Come on, we should go," Cameron said reluctantly, moving toward the trailer again.

"There's a way we can be together," she said, planting her feet. "If I go with my father and you stay here, we might never see each other again, or it could be years before we're together. Let's go to the loyalty haven instead. We can be together right away. I can talk to them. We can work things out. Stay apart from this stupid war between the Holy Ones and the Prophus."

Wait a minute. This sounds dangerous. I think we need to have a talk right now and reconsider a few things, Cameron.

"Can we talk about this later, Tao?"

The girl just told you to defect to the Genjix. Besides the fact that it is completely out of the question because they will kill you to get to me before you step foot into their base, do you think this is someone you really want to be with?

"Yes. Well. No. Well, I don't know. I think she's just

confused. I know I sure the hell am. Oh forget it, let's just go find Mom."

That is another thing. I am no longer sure taking her to the safe house is a good idea. Maybe we should lead her to a safe hiding spot first. Something is really wrong here.

"Stop right there." It was too late. The teens froze in place as two armed figures appeared out of the darkness. Cameron pulled Alex behind him.

"Let me see your hands," the other figure said. Reluctantly, Cameron put his hands up as several lights from all around shone directly upon them.

"The Patels aren't happy with the accommodations. What a surprise. I don't care if he needs to turn sideways to enter his quarters. It's a research vessel, not a cruise ship. You tell that pampered son of a bitch that if he isn't happy with his quarters, he can jump off the ship." Jill clicked over to the next channel. "Sorry about that. It's my favorite hotel guests. Look, it's all gone bad. Suspend transactions with all supply lines…"

The door to the trailer swung open, and Freeni popped her head in. "Perimeter breach. Two figures."

Find Rin and make sure she is safe.

"I'll have to get back to you, Hite." She tore the comm piece off her ear and drew her pistol. She jumped out of silver bullet and, crouching, trailed after Freeni.

A second later, she heard Ohr shout out "stop right there" and saw the light he was shining at the clearing on the other side of the field. She huddled against the wall of the trailer and squinted at the two figures further up the gravel road. Her hopes flared when she saw them from afar, though she kept her excitement in check. Ever since the Keeper had told her that her son was alive and on his way, she had seen him everywhere she looked.

He is the right height for Cameron. The smaller figure matches Alexandra Mengsk.

They were the right size and didn't look armored, but so did those other kids who were cutting across the grounds heading to the beach the other day, and that couple who wanted privacy the night before. Every time it hadn't been Cameron, it had eaten Jill up a little more. It was all she could do to not head north looking for him.

This time, though, after Ohr shone the light and she saw Cameron's face, a huge weight lifted off her. She took off running toward him, the flashlight in her hand dancing all over as she pumped her arms. Her patience had paid off. There was her boy, alive, standing right there. Hell, he looked better than they did. Thank God for Roen spending all those hours training him. Thank God for Tao guiding him. Thank God!

She barreled into him and wrapped her arms around her son. She cried from the sheer pain of her happiness. God, she could barely see right now. All her fears and anxieties washed away. The past few days had been tense. Tao had called in, and then nothing. Hite had reported the farmhouse was no longer there. Roen was alive and up against the IXTF. The Keeper had ordered a massive attack on a Genjix. The local news had a blurb about an assault at Cameron's high school. All these grim things were happening all around her. She had despaired. However, her son was now here, and she had faith that everything was going to be all right.

He has grown and proven himself. You have raised a fine son.

"Let me look at you," she said, pulling back and looking

him over. She immediately noticed his forehead. The infection was wider than the bandage on the cut, and she could see the angry purple and red bruises under the skin. She pulled the bandage back and made a tsk sound. It was ugly, but he'd had much worse before.

Cameron winced and pulled back. "I'm fine, Mom. Both of us are." He looked behind him at Alex standing there, waiting quietly. Jill knew right away something had happened between them. That girl was looking at her the same way Roen used to look at Jill's dad. Well, it was bound to happen. They were already getting close before the attack. The two traipsing all this distance could only have brought them closer.

Tao must be fuming that his host has fallen for a Genjix girl.

"She's an ex-Genjix now."

That remains to be seen. Tabs falls closer to the fanatical end of the spectrum.

"Come," Jill said, reaching for the girl. "Your father has been worried sick."

"Is he here?" Alex said in a small voice.

Jill nodded and gave the girl a hug.

"Is Papa all right?" the girl asked. "And the others? Rin? Mr Ohr?"

"Come," Jill said, putting her arms around the two children. "Let's go surprise them."

Freeni beamed at Cameron, and he enthusiastically waved back. She disappeared and returned a few seconds later with the rest of the people inside the trailer.

Vladimir burst into tears as he fell to his knees and opened his arms. "My little girl."

Alex left Jill's side and ran into his embrace. If anything, the Russian's reaction was even more extreme than her own. He sobbed big, shoulder-wracking sobs and began to talk so fast in Russian Jill couldn't make out what he was saying. Jill sympathized with the pain he must have felt over the past week. It wasn't that Alex meant more to Vladimir than Cameron to Jill, but Alex was all he had left in his life.

She gave Cameron one more squeeze and leaned in. "I'm proud of you, son. You did it. I'm sure Tao helped, but it was you who took responsibility and got both of you here safely."

His face fell a little. "I'm sorry, Mom, but we might not be able to go back to Eureka anymore. There was an incident at the school. Alex and I had to beat up a few kids."

"That's so Tao," Jill laughed, not really caring about anything else right now. "It's all right. Our house isn't there anymore anyway. Don't worry. We'll find a new place to call home. You're going to have to tell me all about your grand adventure over dinner."

"What about South America?" he asked. "Maybe it's time we leave the country. Go someplace more friendly to us."

Jill followed his gaze to Alex. That girl must have really gotten to him if he was talking about leaving the country. Jill worried. Cameron seemed to have caught the bug hard.

It is probably better he gets his heart broken now than later in life. Teenage love, while annoying and dramatic, is rarely as fatal and permanent as it can be with adults.

"That's because you're not a mother, Baji."

Technically, I am more qualified than you. I have been a mother thousands of times.

Alex was whispering something to her father, who glanced over at Cameron and Jill first with concern, then with shock. He stood up abruptly.

Oh there they go. Daddy is now going to get a shotgun to protect his little girl.

"He'll have to get through me first. I wonder how many times I have to beat him up before he stops threatening my son."

The blood had drained from Vladimir's face. He said something Jill couldn't quite make out. He looked like he was about to faint.

"Are you all right?" Jill asked.

"We need to leave here right now," he said. "Now, before it's too late."

"Unfortunately, it already is too late," a new voice said from off to the side.

Before Jill knew what was happening, five figures emerged from the darkness. Each were armed, hooded, and in armor. She recognized the silhouette of their guns and immediately drew her pistol. Freeni did the same. However, they were outnumbered, outgunned, and her son was right in the middle of it.

"Put the gun down, Jill Tan," the lead voice said. It was male, deep, and exact. In fact, his cadence was so neutral, he was either a television anchor or an Adonis Vessel. He also knew who she was. Her heart sank as the man walked up to her.

The hooded and masked figure looked at her and then at Cameron. She tried to pull her son behind her, but he shook his head. "Let go of the boy." She reluctantly did, and watched in terror as he took off his gloves and cupped Cameron's jaws with his hand. "Tao." The name came out of his mouth in a growl. Then he reached over and touched Jill's face.

Chiyva! How is this possible?

The man threw his hood back and pulled off his mask. "My name is Jacob Diamont, and tonight I pay back a long-overdue debt."

CHAPTER THIRTY-FIVE
JACOB HUNTING

As has happened many times in the past, humanity required course adjustments. That was what The Great War was; just another reset and correction. As they had in the lead-up to the Black Plague before it, the humans themselves had created a false safety net with a network of ill-advised treaties in an attempt to maintain prolonged peace. The Genjix merely snapped that peace and pushed the dominoes forward by murdering a petty Archduke of Prussia, one Franz Ferdinand, who happened to be host to the Prophus Baji.

Zoras

It didn't take long for Jacob and his men to secure the betrayers. After all, they had arrived into Fort Bragg earlier that morning and had spent the entire day waiting for the boy and the girl to lead them to the Prophus safe house. He had found the Sign of Shamash in an alley next to the bus stop, and the instructions written in invisible ink on the wall told him to watch the main highway going through the town. Jacob was surprised when he found the two children walking down it instead of driving. That just made his job easier.

Jacob had to admit; the wait was longer than anticipated, and he was getting restless. Alex should have brought the boy down yesterday, and he had almost called off their reconnaissance of the street. However, Chiyva's wisdom had prevailed.

The betrayers are in no rush to leave. We should not be in one to move in.

His guardian was correct, and now, after all these years, justice was at hand, and Jacob's vengeance was almost complete. He looked at the woman and the boy. Roen Tan's wife and offspring, and in the boy, the Prophus Tao, who had been with Roen when Grandfather was murdered. It was only fitting that Jacob was now Chiyva's vessel. Fate had come full circle.

The priority is the scientist.

"Of course, Holy One."

Rin was on her knees, arms bound behind her back. She was the only one they really needed. The others, Ohr and Vladimir, in many ways more despised than the Prophus, were Genjix in name only. These weak-willed, selfish moderates had only used the Holy Ones and the Genjix to enrich themselves without ever fighting for the cause. They were parasites that sapped the strength of the true believers. Then there was the girl, Alexandra, the one who had led Jacob here. She was standing next to her father, looking nervous. It was time to test her loyalty as well.

"How did you find us?" Jill asked.

He backhanded her casually, knocking her to the ground. The boy looked ready to pounce on him. Jacob smirked; he would welcome that. The group waited in silence until the last member of Jacob's team returned from the trailer.

"It is clear, Adonis," he said.

Jacob checked the time. The helicopter would be arriving shortly. There were five on his team, including him. Seven with Rin and Alex. That left room for one.

Baji is the logical candidate to bring back. She is a logistics expert, and her vessel is highly ranked. Tao is a rabid wolf, and the two from Vinnick have no value.

"Your will, Chiyva."

Jacob pulled out his pistol and screwed on the silencer, then casually scanned the faces of the prisoners before shooting Ohr. He watched as Ohr's Holy One left his slumped body and disappeared into the air. He had pondered using a flame on Ohr's Holy One, but that was outside his authority. These were technically Genjix Holy Ones after all.

"Come here, girl," he beckoned to Alexandra, and handed her the pistol. "Show me your worth as a Genjix. Do what must be done."

She squeezed her eyes shut and nodded. For a second, Jacob thought she was going to refuse, and that he would have to kill her after all. Instead, she inhaled, opened her eyes and pointed the pistol at her father. "I'm sorry, Papa. You and Ladm betrayed the Holy Ones, an unforgivable sin. I will forgive you one day, and may we see each other in the Eternal Sea."

"Alexandra, my precious girl," Vladimir said in Russian. "Papa loves –"

She pulled the trigger, and he collapsed onto the ground, blood flowing from his a hole in his chest. She had given him a clean death, at least. She handed the pistol back to Jacob, her face devoid of emotion. He put a hand on her shoulder. He was sympathetic to what she had just had to do. How could he not be? It would have been difficult, even for a weaker Adonis Vessel. The Hatchery in Russia was a pale comparison to the real one in Costa Rica, but he still considered them brothers and sisters, though lesser ones. Now all that was left was the offspring of Roen Tan.

You do not have much time. Make it quick. Your justice and revenge are well deserved, but time need not be wasted. The transport is landing in five minutes.

"Your will, my guardian."

"I need him to know," Jacob said aloud, his voice barely louder than a whisper. "I need Roen Tan to know what his treachery and his cowardice have cost him, and he needs to know who exacted justice."

The two women and the boy exchanged glances, then Jill took a step forward. "I am the one in command. Take me and let the others go. Freeni is just a foot soldier and knows nothing. The boy is just a boy."

Jacob chuckled. "Not just a boy, woman."

"Take me and be done with it, Genjix."

Jacob smacked her again. "Be quiet, betrayer. You are coming with us, but by my say-so." He looked to his left at Freeni and then shot her in the knee. She howled as she collapsed. Freeni would live, though she would never walk right again. "You will be the messenger to Roen Tan." He turned to Cameron and holstered his sidearm.

"What do you want?" The boy was wide-eyed, looking enraged and panicked at the same time. His eyes darted back and forth like a caged animal's. The man holding his arms pushed him forward.

Jacob could see the terror in his eyes as the boy looked at him, and then to his mother, and then surprisingly to the girl. Interesting. Jacob took several steps forward, and the boy retreated. "You remember Taiwan, Tao? I thought twice justice was served, and you eluded me both times. Now we will see the son pay for the sins of the father."

Before Cameron could open his mouth, Jacob launched himself forward and punched him in the gut, doubling him over. He followed up with a right cross that sent the boy sprawling onto the grass. Behind him, Jill screamed.

"Shut her up," Jacob ordered.

One of his men came from behind and struck her on the back of the head. When she tried to take a step forward, he chopped her legs from behind and forced her to her knees. Then he grabbed her hair to lift her face up, so she had to see what Jacob was about to do to her son.

"Please, don't," she moaned.

Jacob moved casually toward Cameron. "Your first vessel was no match for me, Tao. Let me see how your second fares."

Cameron picked himself off the ground and attacked. Jacob recognized the same movements that Roen had utilized over ten years ago. The same footwork; similar angled movements. Palming guards, chambered fighting lines; all the same. Those memories were still fresh in his mind. Every second. He had relived and relished them for years after they had happened.

The boy attacked, coming at Jacob from the side: palm strike, swing, side step, low kick, throw. Jacob dodged them all with ease and with a sudden change of direction, slapped the boy across the face with an open palm. The boy fell to the side, rolling on the ground clutching his cheeks.

Do not spend too long playing with him.

He had talent; Jacob gave him that. He was already

almost as good as his father was in his prime, though if Roen had stood no chance back then, the boy stood even less of one now. In ten years, once he had grown into his body and had had his fill of battle, he might be formidable, but for now, he was too raw. Too much potential; not enough experience.

Tao's vessel attacked several more times, throwing combinations, switching up tactics, even once trying to bite Jacob. Every time, the man toyed with the boy, emphasizing how superior he was to Tao's host.

Jacob didn't want to seriously injure him. It would be a pity to ruin his fun if Roen's offspring was to die on him right away. He didn't know how tough the kid was. No, Jacob wanted to break the boy's spirit and humiliate Tao as much as possible before killing them both. Every time he slapped the boy and knocked him down, he forced Cameron to get up to try to attack him again. This happened a dozen times until finally, Cameron flinched and hesitated. He stayed down on the ground instead of picking himself up. That was when Jacob knew the boy had no more fight in him.

"Get up," he smirked. "I haven't even broken a sweat yet. Get up, or I will finish the beating on your mother."

The boy got up once more, looking skittish, his legs noodly. His face was purple and swollen from the repeated slaps. Blood dripped down his nose, and he had a cut lip. Other than that, the boy was hardly physically injured. Mentally however, he could see in Cameron's eyes that he had shattered the boy's spirit. Jacob lifted his hands and Cameron recoiled in fear. Jacob relished the moment and took a mental picture. It was one he would revisit for years to come.

Then, something peculiar happened. Cameron's eyes glazed over slightly, and he seemed to have relaxed and gained a second wind. When he approached Jacob again, it wasn't with the same near-desperate jerking motion of his previous attempts. He seemed more assured and in-control.

The transport is within sight. Finish this now.

"Your will, Chiyva."

"Get the flamethrower out," he ordered one of his men.

In the distance, he also heard the faint peal of police sirens. Someone must have seen what was happening and called it in. Jacob glanced up at the approaching black speck in the sky. His team would be long gone before the police arrived. Still, it was time to end the charade.

Jacob turned to Jill, who was still on her knees. Tears were streaming down her face. "Say goodbye to your offspring, betrayer."

He saw a flicker out of the corner of his eye and raised his guard just in time to block a strike from the boy. Strange, this time he had covered ground faster than before. A flurry of strikes followed: high kick, low punch, spin, sidestep, trip, high punch. All the movements happened in a blur. The last strike hit Jacob on the bridge of the nose, causing it to bend sideways. He felt a sharp pain momentarily as he stumbled backward. How was this possible?

Something is different. He is moving much faster and hitting harder than before. His movements are more fluid as well. It is as if you are fighting another person entirely.

"I still owe you for Rianno, Chiyva, you bastard," Cameron snarled.

Is that Tao speaking? How is that possible?

The boy attacked again, hitting Jacob from all sides,

no longer moving as predictably as before. It took Jacob several seconds to adjust to this new speed and movement, but he was a veteran of thousands of fights. No matter what new trick Tao and his vessel had somehow pulled over him, it wasn't enough. Cameron managed to hit him a few more times, once even cracking Jacob's rib, but in the end, experience and age won out.

Jacob got Cameron trapped in a vice and grinned as he torqued the boy's head. "Hell waits for you, betrayer!"

Before he could complete his motion, Jacob was blindsided from the back and knocked to the ground. He looked up in time to see Jill half-carrying, half-dragging her son toward the ocean.

"No!" Jacob screamed, drawing his pistol and firing.

It was too late. The two betrayers reached the cliff and tumbled over.

Jacob scrambled to his feet and ran to the edge. He could hear them crashing through the foliage, but he saw nothing in the darkness. It was a steep drop, thick with vegetation that hid their whereabouts. They could have fallen anywhere. Jacob took a step forward and began to climb down.

"No, Adonis," one of his men said, grabbing his arm. "The transport is here, and the police are arriving. We have to leave now!"

He is right. The scientist is the priority. Vengeance can wait.

"No!" Jacob screamed, throwing his head back to roar at the sky. The fates were testing his patience yet again. He looked back over the cliff one last time, desperately searching for any signs of his prey as his men dragged him toward the helicopter waiting on the grass by the trailer. Then, he looked at his man picking himself up off the ground. The woman must have overpowered him. With a dismissive scowl, Jacob pulled out his pistol and shot him in the face. That was the price of failure.

"It isn't over, Tao," he said as he got into the helicopter. "The inevitable comes."

CHAPTER THIRTY-SIX
BACKUP

Timestamp: 3389

Eventually, Cameron joined us, and we were a whole family once more. I would like to say that it was because he missed his parents, but it's really because he was heartbroken over the death of Eva, his grandparents's dog. Still, he was getting older and rapidly becoming the one thing I'd dread he'd become. There was nothing I could do to stop him. It had been inevitable from the day Tao had entered his body.

I decided then to just embrace the inevitable. Instead of trying to prevent my child from becoming a Prophus, which he would anyway, with or without my blessing, I decided to make him the best damn agent possible. Together with Tao, I began to teach him everything I knew.

The Frenchman Prie was a relatively poor patient, which was in line with Roen's experience when it came to babysitting guys like him. He was demanding, obnoxious, arrogant, and was so high-maintenance that they had to allocate him a full-time nurse. Everyone except Marco drew straws; Elias lost. Actually, Sheck and Helen had rigged the straw-pulling so that Elias would lose. Fortunately, he was the most laid-back of the group and took the job in his stride.

The team had spent half the night burying Chase under a tree along the Malheur River. Roen had insisted on doing the majority of the digging. Now, Chase's empty bed was a constant reminder to Roen of his poor decision-making and the price that came with his mistake.

None of the guys blamed him; they were too good people for that. They all agreed that things happen in the midst of combat that were outside anyone's control, but he felt their judging eyes when they looked his way. Was he too careful with the enemy? Had his directive inadvertently caused Chase's death? That thought weighed heavily on his conscience.

When they returned to base, against all their protests, Roen insisted on taking watch for the rest of the night. He grabbed a six-pack from the mini-fridge they had bought for the hole-in-the-ground and was walking toward the guard point before any of them could stop him. For the first hour, he stewed in his own guilt.

He sat down on the lawn chair in the factory alcove overlooking the roads and raised his can of beer. "Rest in peace, Chase Hoffman." He downed the entire can and threw it at the oil drum in the yard below, missing by a mile. He scowled. "Tao wouldn't have made that mistake."

Your people come first; your objective comes second. Everything else is crap.

That's what Tao would have said. He would have scolded Roen for caring too much about the safety of the enemy and not his own people. And he would have been right. Roen exhaled and picked up a second can of crappy beer. He rotated his shoulder, massaging the muscles up and down his arm and back.

"I'm such a screw-up," he muttered, downing the second beer and chucking the can at a crate in the corner. He missed. Not surprising. He had been bad at ball sports ever since he tried to put the round peg into the triangle hole as a kid.

A short while later, he heard the clanging of footsteps on metal grating. Marco came up the stairs and pulled a lawn chair next to him. Roen took a can of beer from the cooler and handed it over. Marco clinked cans and chugged half of it before resting it on the ground next to his chair. He threw his head back and sighed, looking at the slowly-fading stars dotting the sky.

"You should get some rest, Roen," Marco said.

"I told you I have the rest of the night covered. That dank hole creeps me out."

"Well, I'm taking this watch now. That's an order. You can chill out here with me if you'd like."

Roen acknowledged Marco with a slight nod. He had realized over the past few days that he had the guy figured out all wrong. Under the ego was a man who cared as much for the Prophus, and in a way, for Roen's family, as Roen did. He had heard gossip from the guys about Marco, just snippets here and there. There were very few hosts who had sacrificed as much for the Prophus as Marco's family had. He owed the guy probably more than a few thanks and apologies. Maybe it was time to finally bury the hatchet. Roen yawned as they continued to sit in silence.

"Get some sleep, Roen," Marco said. "God knows your mug needs the beauty rest."

The sun was just coming up from the east, its burned

orange rays splashing across the darkened factory yard. Roen caught himself dozing off again and slapped himself awake by putting the now only-cool can of beer to his cheek. He remembered the first time he had had to do one of these exercises. Tao had him watch a patch of water on Lake Michigan for hours. It was pretty soul-crushing. Like all things, though, he got better at it over time. For Roen, the trick was to keep alert with your eyes while forcing your mind to sprint over things that bothered you.

In this case, his mind wandered back to Chase, his now-flattened house, and his family. Doubt crept into him about every decision he had made over the past week. Hell, his entire life. There were only a few times in his life when he had felt self-assured. Not coincidentally, it was when he was with Tao.

He wondered where Jill and Cameron were right now. He should have been with them, he shouldn't have come on this job. He questioned being here even now. Marco had pleaded with him to stay and finish the mission, and out of a sense of duty, Roen had agreed. Again, was that the right decision? He didn't know. Everything just felt so wrong.

You are being delusional and have gone over the edge. Cut it out.

That's what Tao would say, but when Roen tried to repeat those words to himself, they felt hollow and useless. It was because he just didn't believe it. The guilt gnawed at him. What if he had watched out for his men more than for the IXTF? What if he had insisted on staying at home with his wife and son instead of coming here with Marco? What if he had not listened to Tao and stayed with Jill when Cameron was small? What if he had not gone to that

Decennial? Sonya would still be alive then. All those what ifs, these decisions that all led to his life now. Was he doing the right thing? Most undoubtedly. Would he have made the same choices? Undoubtedly not.

"How's our patient?" Roen asked finally, breaking the silence. He could only take so much of his own pity party before he started to annoy even himself.

"Irritated and demanding we rob a pharmacy for painkillers."

"One of his more reasonable moods, then."

Marco agreed. "He told me he wants crepes for breakfast."

"What are you going to feed him?"

"I dunno. I told him I was going to check our stock and be right back, and then I came up here and hung out with you."

Roen chuckled and they clinked cans again. The mission should be almost over, and he would soon be reunited with his family. That *was* the right thing to do. He could hang tight a little longer. The Prophus forces would be en route within the next few days. They would attack the catalyst facility in the middle of the night through two identified points of weakness. One was the supply tunnel, and the other was a sewage exhaust that Helen had determined only functioned during daylight hours. It would be an awful mission, and he predicted minimum fifty percent attrition, and at best, a twenty-five percent chance of success, but these were numbers the Keeper was comfortable with.

"Damn witch," he muttered. If he were one of those lucky enough to survive the attack, he would finally get to see his family. He finished his can of beer. "I shouldn't have gone clubbing that night."

"Pardon?" Marco asked.

"It's nothing. One fateful decision to go out the night I met Tao. I was actually thinking about staying home and watching the unabridged version of *Metropolis*..."

"Roen," Elias called from the first floor. "You there?"

Roen looked away from the window, feeling a little sheepish that Elias had gotten the jump on both of them. "Up here."

"You have a call in the shed."

"For the two of us?"

"Just you."

Could it be? Roen forced himself to stay calm, though for a second, he considered diving over the railing and rappelling down the rusty chain hanging from the ceiling. At the very last second, he reconsidered. It would be an awfully embarrassing way to die. He took the extra minute to scramble down the stairs and jogged into the shed, almost tripping and falling down the steep stairs.

Sheck was fidgeting with the comm station and had pulled up the local news on his computer. The team was huddled around it, watching as the local anchor relayed a breaking story about the arrival of the National Guard and how Ontario was now under martial law. There was now an evening curfew, cars weren't allowed on the roads after midnight, and all citizens were required to carry identification on them at all times. Anyone caught breaking these stringent rules would be subject to arrest.

"That IXTF woman really wants you back," Helen said to Prie as she changed his bandages.

He shrugged and held his palms up. "I would, too, if I were her and I had lost me. Even unconscious, we Frenchmen are just too irresistible."

Helen yanked the bandage off suddenly and Prie howled.

"Careful," he snapped. "You are going to rip the stitches and I will bleed out all over you and then one of you undeserving fools will have to take Pri."

"Should have left him with the IXTF," Marco chuckled, following Roen down the stairs.

"I heard that, Marco," Prie snapped. "Pri still remembers that time Ahngr left him to die against that horde of Zulu warriors."

"Hey," Roen added. "Ahngr left Tao to die during the Great War."

"Once an asshole," Prie said.

"Always one," Roen agreed.

"Sir," Sheck interrupted the conversation. "Got someone on channel three who wants to talk to you."

Roen pushed his way through the small crowd of people and snatched the headset out of Sheck's hands, shooing everyone away. He changed the channel to three. "Yes?"

"Roen! Thank God it's you."

He felt a pain in his chest probably not unlike a heart attack and for a moment, nearly fainted with relief. He began to sniffle in a most unmanly way.

"Are you all right, honey?" she asked.

"You're all right," he sobbed. "I saw the pictures of the house. You were missing for so long. I wanted to come look for you. I couldn't, though. They told me you made contact but that was it."

"I'm all right. Alive at least."

Roen exhaled and tried to keep himself from falling apart. "Where are you? Is Cameron with you?"

"I'm with Faust's cell right now. Some of his people picked us up this morning. Roen, I told you to put a crypto key in the submarine."

"I forgot," he said sheepishly. "So you're all safe? Hang tight at Faust's base. I'll have things wrapped up here in a few days, and then after the attack I'm heading straight to you."

"Actually," she said, "I'm not staying."

"What do you mean?" he asked.

Then she told him everything, starting with the attack on the farmhouse to their escape to the submarine. She explained how she had to run their operation from the trailer, and how they decided to stay put until Cameron arrived. She finished with their reunion and Jacob showing up.

Roen's blood froze in his veins at the mention of the Adonis Vessel. His heart stopped and his fists tightened at hearing Jacob's name. His mind turned to rage when he heard about Cameron's fight with Jacob. "Cam was…" he asked.

Jill was sniffling by this time too. "He got beaten up a little, but he'll be all right. It looks much worse than it is. His pride suffered the worst beating. Roen, you should have seen him. He's grown up so much."

"So where are you going now?"

"We need to get Rin back. I placed a tracking device, the bangle, on her. It went dark somewhere in Northern Canada, then Cameron remembered Alex talking about a loyalty haven. The Keeper moved a satellite to the vicinity, and we picked up the beacon again. I'm taking Faust's entire team with me. We attack in three days." There was a long pause. "Roen, Cameron wants to come."

"Over my dead body!" Roen thundered.

"I can't stop him," Jill said. "Tao says we need every able body for this mission, and he's right. The Keeper has already approved it."

"Fuck the Keeper!"

Roen collapsed over the table in despair. She was right. His wife and child were attacking a Genjix base, and here he was on a stupid suicide mission. He buried his face in his hands. He should be with them. He had to be with them. Then, something occurred to him.

"Hang tight, Jill. Don't leave until you hear back from me."

"Don't do anything stupid, Roen. You can't abandon your mission."

"I'm not, but just wait. Please."

He took the headset off and beckoned to Sheck. "Schedule a call with the Keeper for this evening. All hands." He looked over at a puzzled Marco. "I'll be back. There's going to be a change of plans."

Marco frowned. "What do you have in mind?"

"I'm going to recruit some backup," Roen said, strapping on his holster and heading back up the stairs.

It took Roen six hours to find the right moment. He passed the time changing hiding spots – basic surveillance 101: locals tend to get suspicious if someone stays in one place for too long – and pretending to debate Tao on the effects of the Japanese Meiji period on the modern world stage. In the end, Roen basically ended up blaming Commodore Matthew Perry for the United States' involvement in World War II and eventually the rise of the Communist government. Of course, imaginary Tao was in agreement, mostly because Perry was not a host, so Tao could lay that blame completely at humanity's feet. Tao was biased that way.

Roen found the right moment shortly after two in the afternoon. Kallis and four of her team walked into the

Woodchuck Chuck for lunch. An hour later, the four
guys walked out. Roen waited until they were out of sight
before he crossed the street from the parking garage he was
lounging in. He made one circle around the bar, checking
the back door to see if it was unlocked – it was – and then
he peered through the window. She was facing the west
wall, seemingly focused on the tablet in her hands. The
burger and fries on her plate were half-eaten, and the glass
of beer was mostly empty. From the times he had hung out
with her and her team, he knew that Kallis's people never
left beer unfinished.

He opened the door to the bar as softly as he could, and
then sped across the length of the room. The barkeep gave
him a puzzled look, but he had seen him around enough
over the past week to not give him any trouble. Kallis had
her side to him. All she had to do was look to her right,
and one of them was dead. Fortunately, whatever was on
the tablet was more entertaining than her surroundings.
Well, Roen was about to fix that.

"Hi," he said, and immediately regretted his opening.
There were probably twenty things he could have said
to diffuse the situation. Tao probably would have done it
right. Oh well, Roen was stuck with Roen, so he was just
going to roll with it. "Please don't reach for your sidearm,
Kallis. This is like that Han Solo with Greedo scene." He
tapped his pistol on the underside of the table.

She froze and slowly placed her hands on the table.
"Thanks for removing all doubt, Rayban Ghost."

"I kind of figured my cover was blown when you called
in the armed forces this morning. I'm still waiting for the
paratroopers."

"What do you want, Rutherford, if that's actually your

name, or Ralphy, or whatever?"

Roen shook his head. "Do you know how hellish my childhood would have been if I had been a Rutherford?"

"Do you know how hellish I'm going to make your life after today? There's no way I'm letting you out of this town. Dead or alive, you're mine, Rayban. Your best bet is to just shoot me now. Waller just got out of surgery. We were up all night seeing if he'd pull through."

"I hope he's all right." Roen remembered Waller. He was the older agent who shared pictures of his four children. Then the guy tried to get him to drink a line of tequila shots. Roen liked him.

"I'm sure he'll love to hear that from you in person," she snapped.

Roen sighed. This wasn't going as well as he had hoped, though in truth, what sort of reaction did he expect from her? "Like I said a dozen times before, Special Agent Kallis, we're the good guys."

"Like hell you are. You put half my team in the hospital."

"Well, you killed one of mine."

Kallis ran her fingers through her hair with her left hand while moving her right toward the edge of the table. "Guess I win the big-dick contest, Rayban. So unless you have something else to say, why don't we just get on with it now?"

This approach wasn't working. Roen had to remind himself that he needed Kallis, probably more than she needed him right now. The problem was, she had every reason not to trust him or the Prophus. After all, he did just jump her guys the other day, not to mention all the lies he had told her over the past week. She must also be kicking herself for hanging out with the same aliens she was trying to catch. Hell, she went on a date with one.

Roen decided to take a risk, hedging a bet that if he made the first move, she might be decent enough to follow. That, and he gave himself a fifty-fifty chance of beating her to the punch. "Obviously, we have some trust issues to work through." He looked over at the barkeep. "Hey, Lou, can we get a couple of beers? Whatever is on tap." Then to her surprise, he slowly raised his hands from underneath the table and placed them flat where she could see them. "No threats. I just want to talk."

Roen thought this was a bold gesture, a show of really extending the olive branch. He couldn't think of anything else to do to sway her opinion. He just hoped that she couldn't hear the desperation in his voice. However, for some reason, he had a flashback of Sonya shaking her head saying, "Well that was dumb."

Kallis stood up and drew her firearm. Roen kneed his side of the table, flipping it toward her and sidestepped as she opened fire, the bullet narrowly missing his chest as it plunked into the wall. The table momentarily distracted her as he lunged forward and tried to knock the gun out of her hand. Unfortunately, she was ready for it and held on. Then, she swung it across his jaw, almost knocking him out.

Strangely, the Sonya in his thoughts continued to shake her head. "You never learn do you?"

Roen's training kicked in, Tao and Master Lin's words echoing in his head. Combat was like kissing. He moved close into her guard so she couldn't point her pistol at him. A body should react like sand. He kept his body relaxed as Kallis tried to push him away. She only succeeded in throwing herself off balance. Control is lucid; be even more so. Roen hooked his arms around her wrist, and with a chopping motion, flicked the pistol out of her hand and into his. He bent her over and wrapped his legs around her arm, then he dropped to his knee, trapping her underneath him. He looked up just in time to see Lou standing open-mouthed in the middle of the bar with two glasses of beer in his hands.

"Thanks, my good man." Roen pointed the pistol at him and motioned at the table with his head. "Put them right there. And if you would be so good as to close shop for a bit, shut the curtains, and lock the door, I'd appreciate it."

Kallis growled and struggled underneath him as Roen kept his pistol trained on the barkeep. When Lou had done as he was ordered, Roen motioned to the table right behind the one they were sitting at. "Now pour yourself a beer and have a seat." He relaxed his grip on Kallis's arm and slowly let her up. He took her pistol, pulled the magazine out, and tossed it to the other side of the room.

"Have a seat."

Kallis scowled as she sat back in her original chair. Behind her, Lou, hands shaking, downed his beer.

"Go help yourself to another one." Roen waited until Lou returned with a fresh brew before he righted the table. He sat down again and shoved the pistol to the center of the table. "Here's the deal. There's one bullet in the chamber. You're going to listen to what I'm going to say. Afterward, it's up to you if you want to shoot me or let me go."

She looked down at the gun just within reach of her hands. "I can always just –"

"Sorry, arresting me isn't an option. Shoot me or let me go. After I say my piece. Deal?"

Kallis nodded.

Roen reached into his bag and pulled out a manila envelope. He slid it forward. Her eyes followed his motion, but Kallis didn't move. "Go ahead, open it." He watched her face while she pulled out a series of satellite images as well as all the detailed notes that Roen's scout team had gathered over the past month.

She looked up. "That's why your people are here. You guys are planning on attacking it. Why?"

"It's not a recycling plant," Roen said. "That facility is sitting on top of the beginning of a major fault line that spans down to Mexico. The Quasing who built it are planning on using it to detonate a series of cascading explosive effects that will change the entire world."

He could read the disbelief in her eyes as she looked at the image again. "How can one building do that?"

"It's not one," he admitted. "They have several all over the world, including at least a couple in the United States."

She looked up. "You are part of the Prophus?"

He nodded.

"And the ones who own this facility are the Genjix?"

Roen waited patiently as Kallis continued reading the notes. He saw the blood drain from her face right about the time she got to the part about the nuclear reaction generators, and then even more when she read the summary of their assessment of the facility defenses. Finally, hand trembling, she put all the files back in the envelope and pushed it forward toward him. "Why are you showing this to me?"

He pushed it back toward her. "Keep it."

"Why?"

"You want to chase and capture bad guy aliens? Well, they're right there."

"How do I know it's not a trap?"

"It could be inside," he admitted. "But I guarantee you'll find Quasing in there. Just look at the evidence. Check it out, but please be careful and bring bigger guns when you do."

He stood up and put a couple of bills on the table. "Drinks are on me." He leaned forward. "I'm going to walk out the door. This is your chance to shoot me." He waved at the barkeep. "Sorry for pointing a gun at you, Lou." The barkeep waved, still stunned and unsure what to do.

"Wait," she called after him as he headed toward the door. "What if I have more questions?"

Roen exhaled. If she was going to shoot him, that would have been the time. He reached the front door and turned back to face her. "Just ask for me. We're always listening."

"Why are you telling me all this, Rutherford?"

"Because believe it or not, Special Agent Francesca Kallis, we want the same things. My people aren't strong enough to stop the Genjix from destroying the world, but you are. You're the only one who can stop them." He paused and looked back. "Please call off your dogs. I need to get out of here and visit my family." Then, without looking back, he walked out of the Woodchuck Chuck.

CHAPTER THIRTY-SEVEN
MOVING PIECES

There is irony at play here. The assassination of Baji's vessel Franz Ferdinand created a cascading effect of destruction that the world had never seen before. It was soon followed by an even greater war, birthed by the aftershocks of the first. With those conflicts came the advent of the atomic bomb, as well as the foundations of space travel. This is the Conflict Doctrine gloriously at work.

However, just as Baji's vessel's death helped usher the Genjix closer to victory, her current host, Jill Tesser Tan, committed the Great Betrayal, which has brought us closer to defeat.

Zoras

Enzo turned a slow circle in the center of the pitch dark landing platform. It was so black outside, he couldn't see the four towers just meters away. He closed his eyes and listened. It was quiet, too, except for the soft whistle of wind and the lazy sounds of waves striking the metal structures. It was cold as well. His exposed hands and face felt the chill seep in almost immediately. He didn't let it bother him.

A few minutes later, he heard the soft whupping sound he was waiting for and saw a single blinking light coming from the southwest. Eventually, he made out the shape of a transport as it came to hover over the platform and landed on the edge. The wind swirled around him. The force of its blades coupled with the Arctic air cut Enzo's face like razors.

The temperature had dropped precipitously over the past few days as a cold front moved in from the north. The planet was still far too cold for the Holy Ones. Quasiform would resolve that. Between the catalyst kicking off and burning the ozone layer, the controlled seismic detonations of major planar fractures, and the chemical reactions purifying the ocean and air, the Heaven of the distant stars would soon exist on Earth.

Enzo had studied all of the major religions of the world. Almost all had prophecies of eschatology, be it the Rapture or Ragnarok or even that passive-aggressive Buddhist seven suns. Every religion ended humanity, usually citing divine will. That was the one thing that Enzo agreed with them on, except that in this case, it was his divine will that would end the Earth and give birth to the new Holy home world. Right now, though, it was just too damn cold.

There is no need to show strength to a landing helicopter. Your body probably will appreciate the shivering.

"I will not show weakness, even to myself."

Still, he was grateful when Jacob finally got out of the helicopter and kneeled. "Father, I return, having fulfilled the task you bestowed upon me."

Enzo glanced behind Jacob's shoulder and saw Rin step out of the helicopter. He noted that her arms and legs weren't bound.

"Whom does our scientist serve?" he asked.

"She says the Genjix," Jacob replied. "Rin claims to

have been swept up by traitors and unable to make contact for rescue."

"So she wasn't the one who initiated contact? Who, then?"

Enzo noticed a second smaller figure climb out of the helicopter, again without binds. She was nothing more than a girl, looking around the platform nervously. She spied Enzo and their eyes met. Recognition filled her face and she ran forward and fell to one knee next to Jacob. "Father," she breathed, face down to the floor while she held her left hand up.

Enzo touched it. "Tabs."

"Praise to the Holy Ones."

Jacob nodded at her. "Tabs was the one who made contact with our emergency channel and left notes for us to follow in the house. She contacted us again a few days later and led us to Rin. She has proven herself worthy."

She is Vladimir Mengsk's daughter. He was high in Vinnick's circle.

Enzo beckoned the girl to stand. "Alexandra? Vladimir's daughter, if I remember correctly. So young, yet so dedicated. An Adonis as well, if I remember your vessel," The girl's face flushed red. Enzo put a finger under her chin and lifted it up toward him. "Your standing is raised, Alexandra Mengsk. When we return, your Adonis training will continue."

"Thank you, Father."

Next came Rin. The scientist approached Enzo and fell to her knee as well. "Praise to the Holy Ones."

Enzo and Jacob exchanged glances, and then Enzo had her stand. "I am told you were kidnapped and held against your will."

Rin nodded. "Brother Jacob and Chiyva were heroic in returning me so that I may finish my work for the Holy Ones."

"Welcome, then, sister, and fulfill your destiny." Enzo motioned toward the door and watched as the girl and the scientist were led to the elevator.

Enzo put a hand on Jacob's elbow. "Put them both in surveyed rooms. I want them under watch twenty-four hours a day. Have you spoken directly with Rin's Holy One?"

Jacob shook his head. "I have not had the opportunity."

"See to it tonight. Make sure the Holy One and the vessel are aligned. If not, kill her and give Chisq a new vessel."

"Your will, Father."

Enzo watched Jacob depart just as Coen, the new commander of this loyalty haven, came up from below. "Father, you asked to be informed as soon as possible. It will require five more days before the lift mechanism can be repaired."

Enzo nodded absently as he stared out over the calm icy waters of Great Slave Lake. He had made a point to plant one of his operatives in each of the loyalty havens during their construction and administration. Coen was his operative at Great Slave Lake. He was the man on the inside who had raised the platform for him and damaged the lift mechanism in order to make sure the platform could not be lowered while Enzo's forces were disembarking. For his service, Coen was blessed with a Holy One, the one who had occupied Gates.

It seemed that Coen had done too good a job sabotaging this base, though. Now, the towers were stuck above water until repair crews could get the mechanisms running again. Until then, the haven was exposed and vulnerable. Luckily, they were in the center of a lake in the middle of the wilderness not too far from the Arctic Circle. Civilization was sparse, and unless someone explicitly knew to search this area, the threat of discovery was minimal. In any case, ending the Russian's reign was well worth the risk.

This haven may end up serving as the command point for North American operations. See that it is ready.

"Yes, my Guardian."

Enzo turned to Coen and put a hand on his shoulder.

"This haven is yours. The proximity of this facility makes it a key staging point in the upcoming war. There are a few additions that will be needed. Are you prepared?"

Coen dropped to a knee in reverence.

Enzo beckoned him to follow. They took the elevator from the tower down to the main section of the base. Maintenance crews were still cleaning up the battle of the previous day. Supposedly, a few of the Epsilons still hid within the nooks and crevices, waiting to exact revenge for Vinnick. Poor foolish misguided fanatics, not only had they placed their faith in a false believer, they were now fighting for a lost cause. Their willful foolishness made them unworthy of the Genjix.

This loyalty haven was the largest in the world. It was built more like an underwater city than a base. Designed for up to three thousand inhabitants, the haven was a series of large rectangular layered modules connected to a central vertical shaft known as the spine. The top of the spine was a series of massive hydraulics that moved the four towers twenty meters into the air when in use, and underwater when not needed.

Enzo and Coen walked into the command module on the second layer just off the first radius of the spine. An electronic blueprint of the base on one screen illuminated the delicate balance of the underwater base. From the side, the haven looked like a squat Christmas tree with a pole through its center. A series of green lights displayed the condition of each section, from its operating parameters, to the air levels, to how many living souls were operating in each module.

The modules spread across the lake's floor like a spider web, crisscrossing intersections at different layered points, dividing the haven into sections, each with a specifically assigned function. The hydroponics farm was engineered to sustain the entire population of the base, while the advanced underwater hydroelectric cylinder could keep the haven powered indefinitely. With only three hundred permanent command staff, a hundred and fifty security forces with overlapping duties, and a hundred of Enzo's operatives, the entire base was sparsely inhabited. Large sections of the haven earmarked for housing still lay closed off and dormant. Enzo could think of better uses for the space than idiotic dorms for weak-willed vessels.

"Sections six through fourteen and nineteen through twenty-three, and all their adjacent vertical platforms." Enzo switch the display to highlight the ones he was referring to on the eastern side of the lake. "Convert these facilities to hangars. Vertical takeoff platforms."

"What about housing, Father?"

Enzo ignored him and continued. From setting up a permanent nerve center for surveillance and clandestine operations, to a resupply depot for land units, to a launching point for bombings, Enzo intended this to be a military base ready for when the war began.

There was currently only one functioning catalyst facility in operation, and three more under construction. There would need to be eight within the hemisphere before the reaction could begin. However, this continent had proven to be the most resistant to the Genjix's infiltrations. The United States would be the most difficult country to subjugate. Unfortunately for the Genjix, the last battlefield for Quasiform's success would be here.

Akelatis ran up to him and bowed. "Father, urgent message from the catalyst facility in the northwest United States. It is currently under attack.

Enzo grunted. "By the Prophus? I highly doubt they can–"

"By the IXTF, Father."

Enzo looked at the messenger, alarmed.

We cannot allow that facility to fall. Work the political channels to suppress the IXTF. Handle their units on the ground by force. The truth of the facility must be buried.

Enzo quickly relayed the instructions, ordering their political resources to suppress and delay any warrants the IXTF might have. The quickest solution would be to wipe out the IXTF forces and then buy government and media silence. It was a risky move, but there were few other options. The fledging multi-government agency had finally grown some claws and was becoming an increasingly annoying thorn in the Genjix's side.

"Father," Akelatis said, relaying the message. "The facility begs for support. They do not have enough men to securely wipe out the entire enemy force."

The cleaning team must be thorough. All IXTF personnel on the ground will have to be eliminated to a man. There can be no survivors. Any leaks, especially when it comes to the deaths of federal agents in this particular government are difficult to wipe.

Enzo quickly considered his options. Pulling in resources from Asia would take too long, not to mention the difficulty of moving large numbers of men through border security. However, losing the facility would be a disaster. Losing that stockpile of catalyst agents was not an option. There was only one way to be sure his interests were secured.

"Send half of my personal guard," Enzo instructed. "Delay if you can through political channels to buy time for them to arrive. I want the IXTF wiped out."

Akelatis bowed. "Your will, Father."

It was risky sending his forces over to defend the facility. However, they would be put to better use there than rotting here at the bottom of this lake. Enzo would have gone himself if he could, but the United States was too volatile for someone of his stature. Soon though, once the war began, he would personally lead his forces and invade the Western hemisphere. Then, once the world was in enough chaos and all the catalyst facilities were ready, Quasiform would begin. By the time humanity figured out what was happening, it would be too late.

CHAPTER THIRTY-EIGHT
REUNION

The Prophus took on a new role in the years after what is now known as the Great Betrayal. For more than five hundred years, we had struggled to beat the Genjix. Now, our new directive was to provide safe passage to everyone who was persecuted by either the Genjix or humanity. That was how the Quasing Underground Railroad was born.

A series of safe houses and checkpoints was created to funnel fugitives toward the few countries in the world that had lax security when it came to alien detection. The survival of our species became the Prophus's new primary objective.

Baji

Jill made a mental note that if she ever got her operation running again, not to spend a nickel on this three-dimensional display Faust was using for the briefing. A notorious early adopter within the commander ranks, Faust always spent a good chunk of his budget on these bleeding-edge toys. Some ended up proving to be extremely useful, but most were crap.

Right now, she was looking at the latter and trying to

figure out what it was trying to show. The projection was supposed to be a three-dimensional rendering of the Great Slave Lake in the Northwest Territories, but in its attempt to be detailed, it looked so messy that it reminded her of one of her baking experiments gone wrong.

Faust pointed at the display. "Here's an image of the center of Great Slave Lake during a routine satellite pass seventy-two days ago." All she could see was what looked like a large mass of water. "Now, here's an image of this exact same spot four days ago, when the Keeper gave us clearance to move the satellite over the region," Faust continued, snapping a picture of the lake and zooming in. It looked exactly the same as the previous image, but now there was a small group of structures rising out of the water. "Based on Tao's intel and Cameron's talks with the girl, we're looking at a Genjix loyalty haven. We left the satellite in place and saw this over the next few days."

"Is it a giant sub?" she asked. "And if it is, what would it be doing in a lake?"

It is a landing platform. Chinese design. Used on their newest submersibles.

"That's what we thought at first," Faust continued. He clicked on a remote in his hand. "However, the structures never move."

The fast forwarding continued. A few days later, a lone signature flew in from the southwest. There was one heat signature on the structure waiting for it. Then several people departed from the flying signature. Then the group of people on the platform walked into two of the corner columns.

Faust clicked off the display. "That platform hasn't moved since that incident two days ago. Yesterday, five more transports came by and picked up what looks like a large group, perhaps a hundred heads, and then they all headed southwest. We're not sure where, but their trajectory seems to have them headed somewhere in the Pacific Northwest territory."

"The platform hasn't submerged since?" Jill asked, not quite able to shake off a strange feeling about that. Something didn't seem right.

Foolish to keep a platform raised if they are trying to hide it. Something must be wrong down there. Best to strike as soon as possible.

Faust shook his head. "Still sticking out like a sore thumb. Maybe they have a lot of traffic coming in and out. Conserving energy by staying above water."

Jill tapped her finger on her chin. "Would be silly to build a secret underwater lair and then have something like that stick out. Something must be preventing them from lowering it."

"Regardless," Faust said. "Here's our advantage. We're pretty sure that was Rin they took there. The timestamps are about right. With that large group of people leaving, this might be our only chance to sneak in and get her back."

Jill nodded. "We infiltrate with a team of nine, find Rin, and sneak out before those five transports return. I wonder where they went."

"I might be able to answer that," a familiar voice said from behind her. "And instead of sneaking in, let's just throw the kitchen sink at it."

Jill turned around and stared, shocked. In a split second, she launched herself out of her chair and barreled into Roen's arms. He grunted from the impact as her momentum pushed him back into the wall, but he held onto her just as hard. She kissed his lips, wrapped her arms around his neck, and then kissed him some more. It probably was unprofessional to do so right here in Faust's command room, but she didn't care. Neither did Roen, it seemed. The two stood alone in the world for what seemed like hours as they tried to catch up on soothing the pain and fear and worry they had felt for each other. Eventually, someone had to ruin it for them and coughed.

Perhaps it would be wise to adjourn the meeting. First, ask Roen what he meant and why he is here. He is supposed to be assisting the attack on the catalyst facility, which is supposed to commence tonight.

Jill was tempted to just ignore Baji and keep on kissing her husband, but the sooner she got the answers Baji needed, the sooner everyone would leave her and Roen alone. She broke their embrace and pulled back. "You're supposed to be blowing up a catalyst facility right now. Tell me you did not go AWOL, or by God…"

Roen grinned that beautiful goofy boyish grin. He squeezed her arms. "Change of plans. We suckered someone else into doing the dirty work for us, so we're all going to join your party instead."

For the first time, Jill noticed Marco and a group of guys standing at the door. He gave a lazy wave and winked. She went up to him and gave him a hug. "Thanks for bringing the lug back to me in one piece."

Faust walked to the table and gave Roen what Jill called their bro-hug. The two grown men would throw their arms around each other, but instead of a real hug, they would do this silly chest-bump-single-pat-on-the-back, as if too much physical contact was frowned upon. The two went back a long way and had been scuba diving buddies. Roen was on Faust's fantasy football league, and Faust came up to the farmhouse for Thanksgiving every year. In fact, it was because of Roen's prodding that Jill got Faust the promotion to this region.

"You're not supposed to be here," Faust said. "Jill's right. If you've disobeyed a direct order again, I'm going to have to arrest you this time. I can't tell the Keeper 'no' twice."

Roen rolled his eyes. "Why does no one believe me when I say I'm on the level?"

"Because you never are," Faust grinned. "So what's going on?"

Roen explained the situation with the IXTF, and how right at this very moment, the federal government was pitching an old-fashioned siege of the Genjix. As predicted, the Genjix facility was heavily defended, and the IXTF were getting their butts kicked, but it was only a matter of time before they took it, whether within the next few days or the next few months. At the end of the day, not even the Genjix could match the United States government in a heavyweight fight, especially when the government had home-field advantage.

Jill didn't quite seem convinced. "Don't you think the Genjix can buy their way out of this one, like they always do?"

"I know the woman in charge," Roen said. "She'll get the job done."

"What would prevent them from coming after us next?" Faust asked.

"Nothing," Roen admitted, "but at least it's not our guys dying trying to break in there. The Keeper is going to reallocate the forces meant for the catalyst facility to busting out Rin. So there you have it, Jill. Use us wisely. Most of the squad commanders won't get here in time, so we'll have to relay the plan remotely, but I believe everyone is on board for first thing tomorrow."

This changes everything. The attack will have to change from a small-team infiltration to a fully-staged assault.

The group in Faust's tactical command center spent the rest of the evening devising a new plan. They broke for a late dinner and reconvened to coordinate their plans with the commander of the attack force flying in from Greenland.

"At best, the rest of the attack force will rendezvous with us in the air," Faust said, as they worked through the times.

"Who's leading the attack?" asked Jill.

Faust looked down at his tablet and blinked in surprise. "Seems our favorite Aussie colonel." He looked up and grinned. "I thought the bloody bastard retired."

"What?" she exclaimed. "Who dusted the mothballs off him? Shouldn't he be on a beach drinking Mai-Tais and failing to hit on local girls?"

"He should be. I attended his retirement party." Roen frowned, shaking his head. "Old bastard can't let go. If he's un-retiring, I want that set of golf clubs I gave him back."

Marco shook his head. "Seems the old bugger is intent on coming back on his shield."

Dylan had retired from active operations two years ago, and no one had heard from him since. Supposedly, he was living out his golden years hunting poachers in the outback.

I do not know how wise it is pulling another host into this operation, especially at Dylan's age.

"Baji, I am not telling Dylan 'no.' Besides, he's probably still spry and strong as a bear."

On that we agree.

At this point, Roen checked the time and excused himself, pulling her with him as he left the room. Jill led him to the upstairs balcony, where they snuggled on a hammock while looking up at the sky. A stead wind blew in from the ocean, just cool enough to make shared body warmth necessary, but not uncomfortable. The sky looked heavy, filled with large puffy clouds that blocked any sign of the moon or the stars. A breeze swept in from the ocean, and Roen could smell the salt in the air. For a few beautiful moments, they just lay there together, basking in the night. Roen gently put his hand on her face, turned it toward him, and kissed her. He pulled her in closer and she wrapped a hand around the back of his neck. There was a desperation in them, a feeling of relief mixed with a sense of dread.

After all, they had each thought they had lost the other over the past few days. And now that they were together again, they were going off on another dangerous mission. The moment they shared right now was all they had. Tomorrow would be another day when this blasted war would threaten to take everything that meant anything in their world. They'd both lost so much already.

Roen's looked on the edge of tears.

Jill stroked his chin. "Hey you, what's going on inside that thick noggin of yours?"

His voice broke as he spoke. "I'm sorry. I failed. Again. I should have been there. For you and Cameron. I let the Prophus lure me away again on an inane mission, and

I wasn't there to protect my family when you were in danger."

Jill could tell he was being harder on himself than usual. Ever since Tao had left him, he had been trying to overcompensate by being husband, father, and Prophus agent all at the same time. It was an impossible task. She hit him on the chest harder than she meant to. "Nonsense. I sent you away."

"I should have said no."

"You did say no. I ordered you to go."

It is times like this I like your husband. Seems he finally got through puberty after half a century.

"Hush, Baji."

Roen shifted in hammock, swinging it precariously. Jill was pretty sure this thing wasn't made to hold both their weights. "Don't do it again. Please. In fact, after this, I'm done. I quit." He paused. "Is that okay?"

I love how he asks for permission.

"Oh, Roen. Why don't you hold off retirement plans until after this mission?" She kissed him again. "We should probably head back. They're probably looking for us."

He grunted, which was his way of giving a lukewarm affirmative. "I'm going to skip the rest of the meeting and let you brainiacs figure stuff out." He paused. "I should have asked earlier. How's Cameron?"

Jill had hoped to delay his seeing their son as long as possible. She knew it was cruel not to tell him right away that Cameron was here, but she knew how he was going to react once he saw him, and she wanted calm Roen for just a little while. "He's here, Roen. Sleeping. Look, he got kind of beaten up. It looks much worse than it is. Please don't blow your top and freak out."

Roen sat up, almost dumping them both off the hammock. "What! Here? Why didn't you tell me?"

"I know what your priorities are in life. I mean it, though. Don't freak out when you see him."

That just made him tenser. "I'll keep that in mind, but it doesn't mean I won't freak out."

She led him to the other side of the warehouse, to the sleeping quarters. Faust's cover was an old theater prop warehouse, so there were many nooks and turns. Jill had put Cameron in a small guest room on the top level. She led Roen to the door and opened it slightly.

The light fell on her sleeping son's face as they crept in. Jill had to prepare her husband for what he was about to see. She put her arms around his waist and hugged him tightly. Roen gasped when he saw Cameron's bruised face, and his body stiffened, all his muscles tightening.

"Remember, it looks a lot worse than it is."

She led him to the edge of the bed. Roen fell to his knees and brushed the hair away from Cameron's face. She could sense the struggle raging inside him. He balled his hands into fists.

She leaned over him and kissed him on the cheek. "You need some time alone with him?"

He nodded. "Please."

She caressed his face and kissed him on the lips. "I'll be back at the meeting. Let him rest if you can. And if it's Tao, tell him to let Cameron rest as well."

CHAPTER THIRTY-NINE
FATHER AND SON

Timestamp: 3422

As good as Tao and I are at what we do, I don't think either of us are prepared for how good Cameron is becoming. I haven't been prouder and more terrified for his future than on the day I realized that he could kick my ass. With this new technique he and Tao have developed, he truly is becoming something more than human.

Here is where I realized my mistake. I've helped mold him into a Prophus Adonis, but this will only drive him into more and more dangerous situations. In trying to keep him safe, I've doomed him to this life of danger, and there's nothing I can do about it.

Roen knelt next to Cameron's bed and held his son's hand. His mind raced, bouncing between his own self-loathing for not being there to protect his child and his burning rage at that son-of-a-bitch Jacob Diamont. The two factions traditionally had an agreement about not touching families. Sure, Cam was a host, but he was a kid still and would always be that small baby in his arms. The longer Roen thought about it, the angrier he got.

One of Cameron's eyes opened, then the other. "I know you are beating yourself up something fierce right now. It is at the same time endearing and pointless, so cut it out."

"Tao," Roen began, and stopped. He wasn't sure if he should apologize to Tao or berate him for putting his son in this predicament. In the end, he took the easy route and let his ire show. "How could you let this happen to him?"

Tao turned to his side and frowned. "Excuse me? What exactly did you expect me to do? The farmhouse was attacked by Genjix, and I pulled your son to safety. Do not misdirect your anger because of your guilt."

Damn, that alien knew him too well. Roen admitted to himself that his fury was completely misplaced, and that he was yelling just so he could yell at something. He was certain Tao had probably saved Cameron's life. Still, the cuts and bruises on his son's face were more than Roen could handle. Without an outlet for his raw emotions, his body did the only thing it could think of; he began to cry.

"Oh come on," Tao began.

Right now, Roen didn't care what his stinking stupid alien mentor thought. With shoulder-wracking sobs, he hugged his son and cried more tears than he had since Sonya died. The thought of the consequences of every decision he had made putting his son in danger hit too close to home. He wanted to grab his wife and son, and steal them as far away from all of this as possible. Enough was enough. His family had paid the price for his sins for too long.

"I'm sorry," he sobbed.

Tao frowned. "I forgive you, Roen."

"Not to you, damn it. To my son. I'm his father. I should

have been there to protect him. I let the Prophus lead me away from the people I love again. I've failed as a father and as a husband."

Tao, actually looking awkward, put his arms around Roen's shoulder and patted him on the back. "There, there. Things are going to be all right."

"Shut up, Tao," Roen snapped. "Things aren't going to be all right. I've cursed my wife and child to a lifetime of this stupid war."

"You think being ignorant of the realities of our war would make this all go away? You of all people should know better than that, Roen."

"It's all right to punish me. I'm a man. I can take it. Cameron's just a kid."

"Roen," Tao said, sitting up. "He got slapped in the face a few times. He's had worse in training. Remember that summer when you sent him to Lin?"

"That's because Lin's a grumpy bastard."

"He's young. He heals quickly. He'll be fine. By tomorrow, when we head to that loyalty haven –"

Roen reared back. "No fucking way! When we go, not you. Cameron is not going within a thousand miles of that place."

"It's not your choice, Roen. Cameron's a host. I'm his Quasing. We make the call, and I say he's ready."

Roen quivered with rage as he towered over Tao. "Over my dead body. You think he's ready? He barely made it out alive last time. He's obviously not ready."

Tao slapped himself in the face. Cameron yawned and blinked several times. Then he saw Roen and brightened. "Dad!" He jumped out of bed and threw his arms around him.

"Hey, son," Roen clasped him happily. "What did I tell you about running into trees?"

"Ha ha. This time, that tree hit back really hard. Have I got a story for you?" His voice trailed off and then he furrowed his brow. Then he looked up, renewed intent in his eyes. "Dad, I'm going with you."

Damn that Tao.

"Look, Cam, I know you want to help, but you're just not ready. Not this time. You have a whole lifetime to join this war. This isn't your fight yet."

Cameron shook his head and pointed at his face. "Sorry, Dad, like it or not, I'm involved now. Besides, Temujin fought in pitch battles when he was ten."

Roen threw up his arms. "Always fucking Genghis Khan. Do you know how many times he's pulled that card on me? You know what? Tao's Holy Grail of manliness was also a pretty shitty human being. Did he tell you that?" He leaned in. "Give it up, Tao. It's ancient history."

Cameron stood up and tried to intimidate Roen. "I'm ready, Dad."

Roen folded his arms in front of him and harrumphed. "I would rather let that scientist die than send my son to attack a Genjix base."

"Dad, Jacob is there."

"All the more reason to stay a million miles away."

"If we don't take care of him now, he'll spend the rest of his life hunting us. You know he won't rest until he kills all of us. We'll always be looking over our shoulders."

"Then I'll take care of that bastard."

"No, you can't. He's gotten better. Stronger. Faster. You couldn't beat him back then, you're no match for him now."

Roen snorted. "Right, and you are. You're no match for me, so what makes you think you can shake a stick at that asshole?"

Cameron folded his arms. "If you leave me behind, I'll be on a transport within an hour heading north. You can't stop me from going."

"You're staying, and that's it," Roen bristled. "Even if I have to lock you in a cell until we get back."

"You know that won't work. I'm a host. I'll outrank everyone guarding me. Heck, I outrank you, Dad."

Roen realized how few options he really had. There really was nothing he could do to stop his son from going, so he used the last card he had in his deck; he tried bribery. "Look, son, just wait until your seventeenth birthday, and I'll personally add you to the network. We'll go to Mexico together to that gunsmith you've always wanted to meet. We'll get your own handmade pistol." It almost sounded like he was pleading.

Cameron rolled his eyes. "How about this, Dad? I'll make you a bet. Hand-to-hand combat. You win, I stay. No complaints. I win, and that's that."

Roen had to stop himself from laughing at his son's brashness. "You spend a week by yourself, and suddenly you think you're a tough cookie, eh? Fine, you're on."

Cameron walked to the door. "Come with me."

"What?! You mean right now? Get outta here. You should be in the intensive care unit, not on the sparring floor. Come on, get back to bed. This is ridiculous. Your mom is going to kill us."

"Come with me," his son repeated and walked out of the room, giving Roen no choice but to follow. The two went up a flight of stairs and out to the roof through a metal door. They walked across the tarp roof down the length of the warehouse, past a row of generators and pipes to an area with a flat surface. Cameron scanned for protrusions on the ground and then turned to face Roen.

Cameron held up his guard. "Attack me, Dad."

"Look, Cam –"

Before Roen could say another word, Cameron attacked, covering the ground between them faster than he thought possible. Before he knew what was happening, his body reacted as the air near his face popped from one of Cameron's punches. Roen threw his hands up and blocked three subsequent strikes, each one knocking him backward.

"What the devil?"

Then he noticed the throbbing pain in his forearm. Those hits hurt. In fact, Roen couldn't remember being hit this hard since when he used to train with Lin. When had his kid turned into this? He barely had a chance to say anything as Cameron launched another flurry. His fists were blinding, swinging high and low, at the same time moving laterally outside Roen's guard.

Cameron was still fighting with Tao's style, but he was doing it as if he was on steroids. Blinding speed mixed with expert positioning drove Roen back. He ducked when he could, blocked when he had to, and gave up ground faster than the French in World War II. Within seconds, he felt the railing on the edge of the warehouse hit his lower back. Then Cameron got a punch to the side of his head that flipped his entire body over onto the ground.

"Ow," was all he was able to get out as he gasped for breath.

His son appeared and held his hand up. "Things are

different now, Dad. You don't have to protect me. In fact, you need me."

Roen picked himself off the floor and studied his son. This wasn't the same son he had left a little over a week ago. He was different, more assured and hardened. What happened to him, and why did he want to go so badly? And most importantly, how did he get so damn good?

"Tao," he asked. "What did you do to my boy?"

"I'm still here, Dad."

"No one gets this good just like that." He snapped his finger. "As far as I know, no pharmaceutical has invented a Kung-Fu pill yet. What gives?"

Cameron hesitated. "Tao and I made a discovery. We're more symbiotic than ever now."

The words sunk in, and Roen sputtered. "Wait, it's Tao moving? That's impossible."

"It's still me. I can take over any time, but in spurts, he can take over without any loss of control."

Then Cameron explained to Roen how the two of them were able to combine the t'ai chi and meditation, and how Tao's strong bond with Cameron enabled this ability. It was at the same time uncanny, evolutionary, and downright frightening. Roen hated it.

"Is Tao controlling you now?" he asked.

Cameron shook his head. "He's sleeping. That minute of fighting we just did wore him out. It'll be a little while before he comes around."

"Really?" Roen threw a jab at Cameron. His son blocked it, but the superhuman speed was gone. They threw a few exchanges and as Cameron said, he was a regular human again.

"It works in spurts," Cameron explained. "But Tao

being in control will be the only way any of us can beat an Adonis Vessel."

"I don't know, son. What you're showing me is –"

"What are you two idiots doing?" Jill yelled from across the roof.

The two of them gave a start as she stormed in between them. She grabbed Cameron by the ear and pulled him away. "You should be in bed." She turned to Roen, furious, and smacked him on the shoulder. "He should be in bed!"

Roen held up his hands in a shrug. "I know! That's what I was telling him. He dragged me up here."

"Dragged you? You're his father." If anything, she looked even more pissed off. She turned to Cameron. "You're grounded."

"Yeah, you're grounded," Roen echoed.

She turned back to him. "You're grounded too."

"What? You can't ground me. I'm your husband."

She fixed him an eye and dared him to say another word.

Roen shrank back. "For how long?"

"For life. Or until I say so. And you, Cameron, you aren't to leave this warehouse until after we get back from the –"

Cameron went up to his mother and cut her off by giving her a hug. He then patted Roen on the shoulder. "I'll let you explain to Mom. Have fun." Grinning, his ingrate of a son fled the roof, leaving a bewildered Jill.

"What did he mean by that, Roen?" she asked.

Roen took a deep breath and prayed he was going to survive this conversation.

CHAPTER FORTY
INSERTION POINT

The Prophus are aware of the consequences of Quasiform, because we know our nature. We are fighting against our instincts, which are to consume a planet and mold it into our own image. That is our truth.

Earth is a unique circumstance. It took a long time, but many of us have learned to respect and love the indigenous species of this world, something that has taken millions of years to cultivate. Therefore, this time, we must fight our nature.

Tao

Get closer to the meeting. I need to hear what the plan is.

Cameron, sitting in the far back of the transport, was looking out the rear porthole. He glanced over at the front, where all the adults were hanging out. Marco was going over last-minute tactics with them as the Chinook sped toward the Genjix loyalty haven. He caught sight of his mother and shrank inside his armor like a turtle retreating into his shell.

First thing we do when we get out of sight is get rid of this outer jacket.

"Thank God. I can't even put my arms down wearing all this stuff."

Once Roen had decided that he couldn't stop Cameron from going, his father had cocooned him in a triple layer of armor, as if bundling him up for a blizzard. Now, Cameron looked like one of those kids swaddled by their overly-protective parents for their first day of school. With all this gear, he wasn't sure he could roll himself back to his feet if he fell down.

When Jill found out about Roen losing the bet to Cameron, and that she couldn't do anything to stop him from going, she blew her top and went on a complete tear, threatening to lock him in the warehouse basement until he turned twenty-one. When he pointed out that the warehouse didn't have a basement, the conversation went even further downhill. At one point, she threatened to shoot him in the leg to prevent him from going.

You probably should not have said it was my idea.

"It was though!"

And bringing up Vercingetorix was a mistake, considering he died pretty young.

"That was your idea, too! Man, Tao, you're getting me in trouble."

I admit I did not handle this situation well. At least you're going, though.

At least there was that. For some reason, Cameron knew he had to be on this mission. Maybe because he knew his dad couldn't beat Jacob without him, or maybe it was to prove to his father that he was a man. Maybe he felt like he had to redeem himself for what that asshole Jacob did to him and Mom. Or maybe it was because he felt so betrayed by Alex. That last thought particularly stung.

He gripped his rifle tightly and pulled it close to his body. Well, he deserved answers, and he was going to get them if he had to attack the damn Genjix base to get them. He wouldn't admit it to anyone, but Alex had hurt him so badly he cried. Thank God no one saw that.

I saw it.

"You don't count."

I tried to warn you about her.

"You're not helping."

But nope, teenage humans. The worst, most ill-conceived creatures in the universe.

"Other than turkeys, right?"

Yes, nothing beats those morons. Some of the worst hosts on Earth. But seriously, get up to the front so I can hear what's going on.

"I don't want to. I need to hide from Mom until we leave the helicopter. She might still find some way to chain me to a railing."

Tao flashed an image of a vast desert inside Cameron's head. It was midday, and the sun felt like it was roasting his skin. The outer metal of the tank he was perched on scalded him as the tank rumbled and whirled up and down sand dunes. He covered his eyes with his hands and looked into the distance, then he looked back at where he had come from. Nothing but pristine dunes. Even the tank tracks he had made were already covered with more sand.

The sun hammering down on his back was unbearable, so he climbed into the hatch. The solace of darkness lasted only a few seconds as the oven that was the inside of the tank made it hard to breathe. A few minutes later, he had to climb back out for air. This back and forth happened a dozen more times, and then the tank ran out of gas.

One of my previous hosts decided that he would let his tank commander take care of all the plans while he napped. Tank commander got shot through the eye. Host made a wrong turn during the retreat. Get my drift?

"Wow, that sucked. Don't show me stuff like that again, especially before we go into a situation where I might die."

Trust me. Any death you might suffer here is far better than getting baked to death.

"Not making me feel better, Tao."

Just get your ass up to the front.

With only a slight pout, Cameron dragged himself closer to where all the grown-ups were huddled, avoiding Jill's glare. He settled into a seat behind Faust and looked out the port window again at the vast Canadian forests.

Faust interrupted Marco during the summary. "Are we really only going in one way? With only one entrance, it'll be a death trap."

Marco nodded. "It won't be easy. Based on the satellite footage, there's four ways down: three stairs, one elevator. The ones taking the elevator will have to rappel down. The good news with that setup is that once we get down to the main base, they can't trap us in a corner, since we're coming in from all four sides. The other good news is, because we're in an underwater facility with pressurized air, I think it's pretty safe to say neither side will use explosives."

"We've been far dumber before," Roen piped in.

The entire group chuckled, except for Jill. She looked

his way, and her already-stern face darkened even more.
Cameron knew when to tread carefully when his mom was
this way. Unfortunately for Roen – er, Dad, he reminded
himself – he sometimes was too much of a blockhead. She
already wasn't talking to either of them.

Technically, you outrank Roen anyway.

"Well, don't make me give him orders. He won't take
it well."

*Oh, we will never play that card. He is much more easily
cajoled into doing what needs to be done than ordered.*

The meeting went on for another twenty minutes.
The most recent satellite images were beamed over to
the transport, faint structural imaging of the underwater
base. It was much larger than initially estimated, and
Marco worried that they were biting off more than
they could chew. The attack force could be severely
outnumbered.

Minutes later, two more Chinooks pulled up to their
starboard side, and the three of them moved into formation
to speed over the Great Slave Lake. Cameron's stomach
began to churn, and he felt the urge to throw up. He
clenched his hands to keep them from shaking and tried
to stay calm. He had never felt these sorts of butterflies
before. What made this mission any different than the
ones he had run with his father over the past year?

*There is a big difference. You might not have known this, but
you were in absolutely zero danger during all those jobs. Roen
saw to that. This is an entirely different beast.*

"You aren't making me feel better."

*Throw up if you'd like. I told you not to have all those pancakes
for breakfast.*

"Everyone else did."

Did you see anyone else go for thirds?

"Well, Uncle Marco, Faust, and Dad had some scotch before they got on the transport. I'm guessing that's probably not very good for them."

That is a different story.

The platform came into view a few minutes later. Four grayish metal beams were sticking out of the center of the lake, making up the corners of a large metal platform. The three transports circled the metal towers a few times, closing in until they were following each other in a tight triangular formation, with each front of one transport pointing at the tail of another. Then, synchronously, they lowered and came to a rest on the platform. All the agents jumped out into the middle, using the three transports as a barrier.

Cameron stepped out onto the platform and was hit with a blast of Arctic wind. He inhaled the chilly air into his lungs, shaking himself out of his numb stupor. This was the real deal. He was going to go fight the Genjix, not just tag along, hide in the woods, and snipe at federal agents with a hard-shell tranquilizer rifle.

He watched as his dad greeted a chubby red-faced old man. It took him a few moments to realize it was Uncle Dylan. It had only been two years since he had last seen Uncle Dylan, and retirement did not suit him at all. He had gained some weight, and his face was an unhealthy shade of red and purple. He carried a limp, and waddled almost as if he were pregnant.

"What the hell are you doing here?" Roen cried, throwing his arms around Dylan, giving the big man a rough embrace. Dylan, now well into his sixties, was Roen's only surviving mentor. The others – Sonya, Stephen, Paula

– had long fallen in battle. Each of their deaths had hurt Roen very badly, and he had been particularly happy when Dylan had announced his retirement.

Dylan tousled Roen's hair. His father would never allow anyone else to tousle his hair like that. "Meredith gave me access to mission updates. Saw you were going on a batshit suicide mission. Couldn't let my boy do that alone, could I? Pulled in a ton of favors and got smuggled back into the States. Had to fly across the Pacific on a cargo plane and everything. By the time I got here, the whole fiasco was called off, thank God. Was an awful plan to begin with. Anyway, then I caught wind of this little operation, so I thought, hell, I'm already here, might as well." He spread his arms out and beamed at Jill. "My girl, you look finer with every passing year. I'm still gobsmacked this guy landed you." He gave her a bear hug, lifting her off the ground and twirling her. He turned, and his wide grin brightened even more when he saw Cameron. "Well fuck a duck, Cameron!" Dylan exclaimed holding his arms out. He wrapped Cameron up as well. "I can't believe your ma let you come."

"She didn't," Jill said, her eyes darkening. "And I'd appreciate you watching your language around my son."

"The whole damn crew off to see an old mate on his last hurrah, eh?"

"It's not always about you, Dylan, no matter how much you wish it were," Marco said.

Dylan nodded and shook his hand. "And always a stuffy one to ruin the festivities."

A heavily-armored agent – one of several from Dylan's transport carrying riot shields – approached. "Insertion points are ready, Colonel. All the doors are cut open. Even if these columns could lower, the Genjix wouldn't dare anymore. Ready on your go."

Dylan nodded. "Split into your teams. Coordinate through all the hosts. Operation Saeftinghe is a go."

Cameron looked at his mother; she and Marco were team leaders. Dad was probably going to be with her as well. For a second, he considered asking if he could go with Dylan instead. His mother probably would put him in the far back. He hadn't come this far not to see any action after all.

You have so much to learn.

Roen came up to him from behind and put a hand on his shoulder. "Listen, pal, I have an important job for you. We need to make sure our exit points are secure and open at all times. The squad assigned to guard the transports is a little short-handed. I want you to shore up their ranks."

Cameron's heart sank. He wouldn't be allowed to participate in the attack after all. He wasn't even going to make it down into the base. Might as well have just stayed at home. "Dad," he pleaded. "Come on. Let me prove to you I can do this."

"You already have, son. I'm tremendously proud of you." Roen's voice caught a little. "Being a soldier requires being on the front line and also taking care of the rear. I need you up here. It's an important job."

"But the Adonis…" Cameron stammered, trying to weasel any excuse to join the main attack.

"I will call for you if we encounter Adonis Vessels," Roen said.

"Tao, do something! Order him to let me go down with the others. You know he's not going to let me do anything."

He is right. This is a lesson I had to teach your father as well.

Guarding the escape point for the entire mission is as important as any job.

"What happened to all that big talk about me being ready?"

This is all part of the experience. I agree with your father sliding you softly into these roles, especially with your recent distractions.

Cameron swallowed the retort he was about to throw at both his father and Tao. "Fine, Dad."

Roen put his hand on Cameron's shoulder. "I couldn't wish for a better kid. I can't say it enough. Keep your ears on the comms. If things go poorly, get out of here and live to fight another day. Got it?"

Cameron bit his lip and nodded. Roen pulled him in and squeezed tightly before walking away. Just then, his mother blindsided him with her own hug, her face moist with tears.

"You are so grounded when we get back, but I love you, Cam. Listen to Gwenda. Do whatever she says. I'll see you topside in a few."

Cameron watched as, one by one, the Prophus agents entered the four metal columns. The bulk of the teams went down the three sets of stairs while a smaller team rappelled down the elevator door they forced open. In a few moments, he was alone with the pilots and the squad of three agents guarding the helicopter.

"Commander," Gwenda approached, bowing. "It's an honor to meet you and Tao, sir."

"Uh, thanks?"

A host is always a commander. Act your rank.

"I'm stationing you at the elevator doors, sir. Keep on comm channel nine, and please follow my orders at all times."

Cameron nodded and watched as she left him to relay instructions to the pilots.

"Some commander I turned out to be."

One day, you will learn that assignments like this usually are the best. Let us just hope that today is not that day.

CHAPTER FORTY-ONE
THE ATTACK

The Quasing have always been able to predict the future. Time is cyclical, and for thousands of years, events have regularly repeated themselves. As much as humanity has changed, it has for the most part stayed the same. The way we treat humans now is similar to how we treated them when they first discovered fire. The power struggles, strategies, and manipulations we ran during the Mesopotamian era were similar to the ones we ran during World War II. That has always been the key; humans were always a constant.

This is no longer the case. Now they know us. The pattern has been broken.

Zoras

Enzo watched the red blip approach from the south on an intercept course toward the Four Towers, which was what the base workers called the landing pad. It was soon joined by two additional dots heading from the east. Soon, the three dots moved into formation and closed in on the loyalty haven. Enzo was willing to wager that it was the Prophus.

He didn't know how they had found this base, but it couldn't have been a coincidence that a Prophus attack force appeared shortly after the bulk of his operatives left to reinforce the catalyst facility, especially since Jacob had just delivered the scientist here. It could be the Canadian military, though the last time he had had a strength analysis done on North America, Canada's armed forces ranked just slightly below the New York City Police Department. In any case, shooting these invaders down over the water would be a simple task. Far easier to destroy and cover up than bury knowledge of the haven's location.

"Coen," he said carelessly, not looking away from the screen. "Get men up to the platform with shoulder-mounted missiles and blow them out of my sky."

"Uh, Father?" Coen replied.

"Have a diving unit prepped as well. I want bodies pulled and identified. See who we're dealing with."

"Um, I'm sorry, Father, but we don't have any missiles. In fact, we don't even have any grenades. It's a haven directive from Councilman Vinnick. None of the underwater havens are allowed any explosives, not even a self-destruct."

That would make sense, though probably inopportune at this time. In hindsight, maybe sabotaging the platform was short-sighted.

Enzo frowned and turned to the Coen. "Nothing?"

"Not even C_4."

"Well then," Enzo said, gesturing to Azumi and walking briskly toward the armory. "We do it the old-fashion way. Sound the alarm. I want all personnel armed; my people first."

Coen hurried after him. "I'll send security up to the

platform to keep them at bay."

Enzo turned on him. "What do you think will happen when you send forces up to the platform with no cover, armed with only small arms, with the wind howling, in total darkness? They won't see the enemy; they won't hear the enemy. They'll be cut down like target practice. So no, you will not give that order. In fact, you will not relay any order unless I expressly give it. Do you understand?"

Coen bowed in submission. "Yes, Father. Apologies."

"Good. Have your security forces ready to move on my command. Lock down the command center with a kill switch on my order." Enzo turned and walked toward his quarters.

With the speed of the three incoming bogies, he had less than twenty minutes to organize what was left of his people. Who knew how many of the enemy was coming? Who knew which enemy it was? It didn't matter. Neither the Prophus nor the IXTF, nor the Canadian military, for that matter – he chuckled at the thought – had Adonis Vessels. It was the Goths trying to match swords with the Roman legions all over again. Enzo was looking forward to this.

This is a distraction we can do without. Do not underestimate our enemies. They have defeated you before.

"I do not register temporary setbacks as defeats. I can count on one hand how many of these setbacks I've had, anyway."

All it takes is one more to unravel you.

"It will not be today, my Guardian."

Amanda and Azumi fell in beside him as the alert broadcasted across the entire base. "Amanda, lock down our network and data integrity. Move all important noncombatant vessels to the escape pods for holding." The entire base became a hive of activity as Enzo's people, the security unit, and the civilians within the haven readied defensive positions.

"And the non-blessed and civilians?"

"Expendable, save for ranking and important personnel. Total strength count?"

"Five Adonis, twelve standard combat vessels and seventy-seven agents. Haven defense force of eight-three. Ninety-one civilians. The six emergency pods can only fit one hundred forty-four, Father."

"Make a list. Shoot anyone else who tries to board."

Enzo felt the tingle of the thrill of battle as he mentally organized the resources he had at his fingertips. For him, it was all about control. He was the chess player, and all his forces were pieces executing his will. He didn't just want to defend the haven, he wanted to obliterate the enemy in the most emphatic way possible, with the highest attrition, and he wanted to do it up-close and personal. Optimally, Enzo should be coordinating all the attacks at the command center. Unfortunately, that room was right next to the spine, and would be one of the first places the enemy attacked. Vinnick's fool architect did not design the haven to repel enemy attacks, instead relying on their radar cloaks to just keep it hidden.

Enzo quickly ran through several scenarios. "Coen will lead the security forces and expendable civilians at the insertion point. He will then pull back and hold the command center for as long as he can. Divide the remaining security personnel into units led by vessels. Palos will hold the communication center and Jacob the catalyst stores. Akelatis on life support and Matthew to secure the escape pod routes. Amanda, coordinate the evacuation. Everything goes through me. Have them prepared to move on my mark. Azumi, take one unit and capture the platform. I want their extraction point negated after the initial insertion point is lost. We lure them deeper into the base and then trap them."

"Your will, Father," she nodded.

This tactic is a risk. The safest course of action would be to block the point of entry.

"That gives them a chance to escape. It will be much easier to cover up if there are no survivors."

Amanda and Azumi got to work relaying the orders while Enzo returned to his quarters. He took his time strapping on his customized armor and loading his weapon magazines, rifle, pistol, and assorted knives. For him, preparing for battle was a divine ritual, a blessing and sacrifice to the Holy Ones. He intended to show his devotion by expunging as many of the enemy as he could. Finally, he strapped on the Honjo Masamune sword.

When he was ready, Enzo stood up and admired his reflection in the mirror. Before him stood an emperor and prophet, ready to pass final judgment on the unholy Earth and usher forth a new paradise. His standing would be unmatched by any vessel, equal to that of the Gods, and he would stand for eternity alongside the Holy Ones once they ruled over Earth. But first, he had enemies to slaughter.

He was notified a few minutes later by Coen, running operations from the command center, that the enemy had breached the entrance. In the distance, Enzo could hear the sounds of battle begin to bounce along the metal walls of the haven. He checked himself in the mirror one more time. "Praise to the Holy Ones."

It was time for him to wield his will and strength against the enemy.

"Adonis." Harlen, one of the vessels, approached him, bowing. "The warehouse module is secured. Two exits, one each through the front and rear, each covered by a unit. Third unit holding behind cover right next to the stockpile."

Jacob nodded and continued to watch the monitor as the evil Prophus attacked the loyalty haven through the Four Towers. First, several large canisters rolled out from the three main stairwells, then plumes of smoke exploded, rolling through the hallway like an encroaching storm. Then, the silent screen flashed sparks of lightning bursting within clouds of heavy smoke.

He switched the views, cycling to a camera behind the makeshift barricade that Coen had ordered set up. The fool had tried to encircle the entire four-column entranceway instead of fortifying one side. Now within the heavy smoke, his lines were too thin, and the odds of hitting their own people were as high as hitting the enemy. Jacob continued to watch as several large rectangular riot shields emerged from the thick clouds, moving forward together like Roman legion shields of old.

Hela's experience in the military was always more on the supply side. The new commander, Coen, seems to have little experience in handling such situations.

"I should be there at the front, not back here on guard duty." Jacob scowled at the pallets of catalyst containers. It would probably be hours before the Prophus reached these warehouses in the far western end of the haven, assuming they even got this far, which he doubted. And while he realized the importance of these stockpiles, he felt his presence here was beneath his standing as an Adonis.

Nothing is more important than these catalysts. Have them prepared to be moved in case the conflict worsens.

"Your will, Chiyva."

Jacob gave orders to have all the pallets placed on wheels, then settled in to wait. He could hear the fight far off, the sound of gunfire rattling through the base. If anything, the noise seemed to be getting further away, not closer. Out of boredom, he occupied himself with the monitors, changing channels and searching for the enemy. The Prophus were destroying the cameras they passed, so he was met with static on several views, and most of the ones that were still functioning were either clouded with smoke or quiet. Then he switched over to the command center and saw a phalanx of shielded men batter through the glass walls of the room.

"Glass walls are a poor choice for the heart of the haven. The placement of the command center near the central hub was poorly conceived as well."

Vinnick must have used the same architect who put New York's Emergency Command Center in the World Trade Center.

It made for relatively poor television. The Prophus forces took the center easily, which at best was a symbolic victory. Within seconds of the center falling, Enzo had given the order to cut power to the module. Jacob watched through the still-active security camera as the enemy milled around, trying to get any of the systems to work. Then he sat up and ran to the screen. At first, he thought he had hallucinated.

I saw it too. It is him.

Jacob couldn't believe his luck. He had despaired that

he wouldn't ever be able to find Roen Tan again, especially after his wife and child had escaped Jacob's grasp, and now the man had decided to come to him. Roen, looking just like Jacob last remembered, was speaking with several of the Prophus. Then something happened off-screen, and he ran out of the room.

It was pretty transparent to Jacob what Enzo was doing, having used the low-standing security forces and non-essential civilians to soak up the initial Prophus attack at the center point of conflict. That would be where the enemy would expend most of their efforts for the entry, and in such cramped quarters, would incur heavy collateral on both sides. If that was the case, the Genjix might as well sacrifice the rabble.

The way Enzo had organized the front lines, he had purposely drawn the enemy out in what seemed like an easy victory. Now, after they had expended energy and resources, it was time for the trap to close. And in the process, Jacob would have his revenge.

"Get me a tablet and patch me through to our security camera system," he said. "It's time we play a game."

Jacob signaled for some of his units to stay with the stockpile and the others to follow. He left the warehouse and made his way down one of the maintenance shafts. They'd have to go up two levels behind the enemy's line and hunt. The villain and his kin had escaped him long enough. For this fight, Jacob only had one objective. He intended to draw Roen Tan in and finish him off once and for all.

CHAPTER FORTY-TWO
THE COUNTER

For the Prophus, it seems there is no longer a path to victory. This is our twilight hour. We cannot defeat the Genjix. We cannot hold off the humans indefinitely. We are destined for extinction unless something drastic saves us. However, it seems we have burned all our bridges.

Baji

Jill felt uneasy combing through the wreckage of what looked like the enemy base's command center. Their attack had broken through the initial defenses too easily. Jill wasn't a master tactician, but even she felt like something was off. It could be that they had just been lucky. After all, they had caught the base in a moment of weakness, when the enemy had moved vast numbers away to defend the catalyst facility. Maybe the Prophus had finally caught a break. God knows they were long overdue one.

"Look at this," Marco said, tossing a book to her. "Loyalty Haven Operating Manual."

It only took a few seconds of flipping through the pages to figure out what this place was for. She tossed it over to Roen, who did the same. Jill looked down at all the powered-down systems and screens, and watched as one of the engineers tore open a side panel to look for hard drives to salvage. Everything was going according to plan. They had taken this center area, and the Genjix hadn't tried to mount a counterattack yet.

"Baji, what do you make of this? I am surprised the Genjix are taking such humane steps to ensure their vessels' survival during Quasiform."

Same. All the intelligence we have on their leader Enzo runs counter to what we're seeing with these loyalty havens. Perhaps not all Genjix are on board with Quasiform. It might be something we can exploit in the future.

"Teams two to six, report," Marco said.

A smattering of coordinates filtered through the short-range comm tablets all the commanders were using. It was the only way they could keep track of each other scattered around the underwater base. Currently, dozens of small squads were navigating the maze-like facility, pushing back the enemy while searching for Rin. Surprisingly, they'd encountered very little resistance. Hopefully, their luck would hold. She prayed it was just as quiet at the extraction point.

"Cameron, how's it looking topside?" Roen spoke, reading her mind. He held up seven fingers to her. She switched over to channel seven and stayed silent. She was still angry with both of them and knew that Cameron would hesitate to be honest if he knew she was listening in.

"It's boring up here, Dad. And cold, but mostly just boring."

"Welcome to the life of a secret agent, son." Roen

grinned. "Hurry up and wait and then get so damn bored you wish something would happen, until something does. Then you can only pray to be bored out of your mind again. I call it being perpetually unhappy."

"Yeah, yeah. Tao's already told me. He also told me about the time you fell asleep keeping watch at that grocery store and Mom just left you there."

"Well, you and Tao were supposed to wake me up."

"I was four and fell asleep. Tao didn't want to wake me."

Jill smiled as she listened to them. Roen and Cameron shared a bond that she could never understand, not that she really wanted to. Baji was more than enough for her, though their relationship was very different from the one Tao had with Roen and Cameron. It was moments like this that reminded her how good her family had had it over the past few years, and how bad things really had been before they had founded the operation at the farmhouse. Were they fated to go back to those dark times? She didn't know if she could handle it again.

"Well, Cam," Roen chuckled. "A good soldier always sleeps—"

In the background, Jill heard a smattering of gunfire on the channel. Alarmed, she switched to channel five and pulled up the platform commander. "Gwenda, report in. Gwenda!" There was no response. Jill's heart began to skip beats. Every fiber in her ordered her to charge up one of those towers and check on Cameron.

Roen appeared next to her. "I'll check on him."

"Hurry," she whispered. He kissed her and sped off.

All the channels lit up and the other leads – Faust, Dylan, Marco – began to bark out orders. She switched back to channel four and heard chaos as all of her teams were suddenly swarmed by Genjix. She checked their locations on her tablet. They were spread too far apart. Some of the teams manning areas already thought secured were under attack as well.

Jill exchanged looks with Dylan and Marco, and they began to flag hand signals while issuing orders in rapid succession on the comm, pulling the over-extended teams back and reinforcing others. However, the trap was sprung, and the Prophus attack force was besieged on all sides.

A hail of bullets ripped through the remnants of the glass wall, sending everyone scurrying behind the rows of consoles. Jill dove just under a stream of bullets, sliding along the floor next to Marco.

"Jill, I have a team pinned down from the northeast on the second level sixty meters directly south. Can you do anything for them?"

Jill nodded. "I can recall two groups. We'll hit them from both sides."

"Perfect, love. My boys appreciate it." He looked over the edge and returned fire. Then he broke into a grin. "Just like old times, eh?"

"You're one twisted bastard," she said, pulling up the GPS on the tablet. "Team nine, back forty meters left and help out team fourteen at junction. Seven, hold that intersection. We are entrenching. Two, you are over-extended. Sixteen, you're not moving. Sixteen?"

On the other side of the room, Jill saw Dylan creep closer along the wall toward the shattered windows. "Give them something pretty to look at," he yelled.

Marco stood up and strafed the opposite direction. With the enemy's attention focused on Marco, Dylan broke a window and sent down barrages with his combat shotgun. By the time he pulled back, enemy fire had noticeably lessened.

Faust dove by next to Jill and pulled her to her feet. "My guys east said they found a couple of civvies and maybe our scientist. And one of my teams in the south says there're at least three sets of shitheads heading this way. Come on, get going."

Marco and Dylan had finished off their attackers. The small group at the command center ran out and made its way east, their heavy footsteps clattering on the grating. The lime green hallways were a mess of bodies and lingering smoke. On the ceilings, the row of harsh fluorescent lights flickered and sparked over the double-wide main corridors.

"Jill, we have a concentration incoming from two levels below," Dylan said. "Pull support from the south side. My guys up there say it's still relatively quiet. Also, get word from the platform. We need to keep that egress route open."

"You got it," she answered. "Keep communications open while we move. Faust, I need a group to help squad nine flush out a nest at the intersection. Can you assist?"

The four of them headed down the hallway, continuing to direct their forces as best they could while on the run. Around them, Marco's scout team tried to keep them protected, but the entire operation had deteriorated into a deadly game of cat and mouse. Jill looked back at the four metal columns further west down the hall. That's where Roen and Cameron were. She prayed her family was all right.

The first half-hour guarding the platform was peaceful and boring. The agents guarding the Chinooks – Ms Gwenda's team of four, three pilots, and Cameron – were assigned two to each stair, one at the elevator, and one watching the skies. Cameron unfortunately had drawn the short straw and was watching the damn night sky and seeing nothing. It was pitch black outside. He took his job seriously, though, and walked a big circle around the triangle that the three helicopters formed.

"This job sucks ass, Tao. This isn't what I signed up for."

Oh, I am sorry. You were expecting to be entertained? Clandestine agent work is filled with a lot of tedium. Ask your father sometime. You should be used to this by now. The two of you have gone on missions several times already.

"That was different. Hunting or tracking isn't the same as guard duty. I never want to do this again."

Ha. Boy, did you pick the wrong profession. Next thing you know, you will tell me you think fighting is bad.

"Well, now that you mention it –"

I swear if you say the p-word, I will throw you over a balcony while you sleep just to get a new host.

"Punctual? Predictable? Pedagogical?"

Too bad you didn't embark on a career as a professional spelling bee competitor.

"Oh, lighten up. Come on, entertain me. Be my shiny bauble."

There was a long pause before Tao finally spoke. *Right there, you remind me so much of your father. I miss him. My time with him was far too short.*

"Well, if something happens to me, you guys can meet up and date again."

Hush. Do not say things like that.

"I'm just kidding."

I am not.

Roen calling temporarily broke up his boredom. He could hear the chatter in the background down wherever his father was, and it all sounded so much more interesting than what he was doing now. In typical Roen fashion, his dad began to spoon-feed him advice that Tao had already given him a hundred times before.

The sound of automatic fire on the southeast corner punctured the otherwise quiet and calming sound of waves breaking against the columns. One of the guards yelled something and more gunfire blended with the waves and screams into a cacophonic mess. Cameron got off the comm and ran to that corner, just in time to see four Genjix rush out of the stairwell. One of the guards was lying face-down, while the other was on his back, writhing in pain and trying to return fire.

"Spread out," Gwenda barked. "Flanking positions!" She looked over at Cameron. "Commander, inner triangle. Please."

"But I have no sights from there."

"Go!"

One of the most important rules is to follow orders.

"This is bullshit," Cameron grumbled as he climbed through an open door of the helicopter on one side and then out the other to the inner triangle. He kept his rifle against his shoulder as he swiveled back and forth through the opened doors, ready to shoot if the enemy came into his sights. The violence continued for a few more seconds before silence fell again.

Cameron heard a few calls of "clear" followed by a "stairwell clear."

He saw a shadow blur to his left through one of the helicopter doors, and before he could yell a warning, he heard a cry of pain followed by three gunshots. Jumping into action on pure instinct, he dove and slid under the nose of a Chinook to roll to the other side.

Cameron aimed his rifle at the new threat and stopped, mouth agape as he stared at the most incredible sight he'd ever seen in his life. Unfortunately, the incredible sight was busy killing the team guarding the platform. A small woman, wearing what looked like a full-blown armored ninja costume, was moving so fast she was almost a blur. She carried a strange, spear-like blade on both wrists and a pistol in her right hand. She moved with the grace of a dancer, slicing through the team like a shadow. The only time she was still was when she pulled the trigger, which to Cameron's horror, was aimed point-blank at Ms Gwenda's face. Within seconds, the bodies of the entire team were slumped on the ground, throats slit or gunshot wounds in their heads.

Get moving and shoot that bitch!

By the time Cameron snapped out of his trance, she was gone. He scrambled to his feet and ran to each of the bodies. Everyone was dead, killed cleanly and quickly. A new sort of terror gripped him as he looked around for this woman. This was vastly different than when he had had to fight Jacob. Then, he had been raging too hard to think. He just wanted to protect his mom. Now, he was alone, and the intense fear was overwhelming.

Keep it together, Cameron. Stop holding your breath. Exhale. You are dealing with an Adonis Vessel. It is nothing you cannot handle. You have already fought one before. In fact, she is not better than Lin, and you have sparred with him dozens of times.

"Well, Lin is eighty, and beat me while he was reading the newspaper."

He just likes to show off.

"What is a boy doing here?" the woman's voice said from somewhere in the air behind him. The wind was blowing so hard, it seemed to come from everywhere. "Are the Prophus that lacking for men?"

Cameron swiveled his body back and forth, staring into the darkness for any signs of movement. He thought he saw a shadow on his left and opened fire, cracking one of the Chinook's windows. Then, he thought he saw something else on his right and fired once more, again hitting nothing. She was toying with him.

"Such heavy equipment for one so young," her voice almost hummed as she spoke. "Logically, you must be a vessel. Which one, I wonder? Only one way to find out."

Though he was looking straight at her, Cameron didn't notice her until she was almost on him. She leaped out of the darkness, one of the blades on her wrist extended. It was all he could do to block her attack with the flat of his rifle, so her blade bounced off the metal body. She twisted her arm and his rifle slipped his grasp. He was barely able to dodge two more swings from her before she grabbed his wrist. A kick to the midsection tumbled him to the ground.

"Tao!" she hissed.

Szin. This must be Azumi. She is a top lieutenant to Enzo. I wonder what she is doing here. Be careful. Many of Szin's hosts have been ninjutsu practitioners.

"The Genjix were ninjas?"

The Genjix were everything.

Cameron scrambled to his feet, one hand clutching his stomach. The woman was studying him with a faint trace of a smile on her pale face. It was the only thing he could make out in the darkness.

"One of my brothers is very much looking forward to speaking with you at length, Tao," she spoke with a mocking tone. "I believe I will present you to him alive, as a gift."

She sheathed the two blades on her wrists and attacked. It was so dark outside, and her movements were so fast, that Cameron couldn't see what she was doing. He blocked a swing and a kick, and then found his legs swept from underneath him. He crashed on the hard metal surface and rolled to his feet, swinging wildly with his fists.

Azumi stayed just out of his reach and then suddenly darted in. Cameron was blindsided by a downward smack that doubled him over, followed by something he didn't even see that staggered him backward. He juked to the side and swung again, missing.

Before he knew what was happening or where she even was, he found himself caught in a chokehold. Immediately he felt himself losing consciousness. The first thing that crossed his mind was wondering how she had even gotten behind him. The second was how someone this small could be so strong.

Cameron clawed at her forearm and tried to pry her python grip loose. The best he could do was keep from passing out. Barely. The woman jumped on his back to get better leverage. She wrapped her legs around his waist in a body triangle and squeezed harder. Cameron felt himself blacking out. Desperate, he pulled out his pistol and tried to shoot behind him. She laughed and karate chopped it out of his hand, and somehow Cameron found himself not only getting choked, but also in an elbow lock. Now it was a race to see if this crazy tiny ninja was going to break his arm or choke him unconscious first.

Full charge backward, rotate right. Go!

Cameron moved without thinking; following Tao's directions was second nature to him by now. He charged backward and slammed into the metal wall of one of the towers, causing a low hollow bonging sound to echo across the structure and earning him a grunt from Azumi. Then he tried to twist out of her grip. He made the mistake, however, of twisting left instead of right, and went straight through the blown elevator doors into the open shaft.

Oh crap. Your other…

The two of them tumbled head over feet into the darkness. Azumi held on to him as they plummeted down what felt like several stories. He could feel her trying to twist around and roll on top of him. He flailed, desperately trying grab onto something.

Find the calm!

Right away, Tao took control. He shot his arms out to block Azumi and elbowed her in the gut. He grabbed her arms, and the two grappled for control of the fall. Mid-air, without being able to plant their feet against something solid for leverage, the stronger person won out, which in this case was Tao. He prevented Azumi from rolling on top of him and swung her around until she was positioned below.

Then they struck a hard surface with a thunderous echo of metal, and everything went black.

CHAPTER FORTY-THREE
DARK TIMES

Timestamp: 3475

In the end, I have to accept what I've done. Without my blundering, Jill and Cameron might have lived normal lives. Hell, I doubt I could've even landed Jill if it hadn't been for Tao. I'd be one of those chubby cubicle worker bees who clocked in nine to five jobs and woke up one day, retired, wondering what happened to my life. You know, there was a guy named Pete who once warned me about that. I wonder how he's doing now.

Anyway, if I had to choose all over again, I'm not sure if I would have done the same thing. I guess I'd have to, or Cameron would never have been born. See, screwed either way. Story of my life.

Roen's worst fears were realized when he finally reached the platform. He burst through the stairwell opening and didn't find a living soul. The guards should be up here. Something was wrong. There was no way Gwenda or the pilots would have abandoned their posts. Where could they have gone, anyway?

Roen peered inside one of the helicopter openings and

then moved to the other side. Nothing. He crouched and hugged the outer body of the Chinooks as he swept the outer perimeter of the platform. Still nothing. Where was the team?

He reached the last bend of the third helicopter and nearly tripped over a body. He turned it over and recognized one of the pilots, dead from a cut throat. He looked past the body and saw several more lying in assorted positions on the ground and against one of the columns. He checked them as well. While Roen wasn't a forensics expert, he had seen enough battle scenes to know what had happened.

A team of Genjix had assaulted the platform, taking out one or two of the guards. Gwenda's team had moved in quickly and contained them. None of the Genjix seemed to have gotten more than two meters away from the doorway. Then, they must have been attacked from behind. Surprised by someone with a blade. Some of the squad had died from knife wounds, others from single gunshots. The blade wounds were interesting. Two of the bodies were shanked, as if stabbed by a very thin spear. The other two had their throats cut, but they were shallowly done. Whoever did this was precise. An Adonis Vessel. Fortunately, none of these bodies were his son.

"Cameron, where are you?" Roen bellowed, his voice barely perceptible over the howling wind, a hundred possibilities running through his head. Could he have gotten away? Was his body thrown over the side into the lake? Did he run downstairs? Panic set in as he looked over the edges of the platform. It'd be impossible to see a body in the darkness, especially with the Prophus's black armor.

The thought of finding the body of his son crippled him.

The thought of not ever knowing, even more so. Despair hit Roen like a truck. The rifle clattered onto the ground, and he dropped to his knees. All this pain; all this violence. And now, his son another victim of this stupid war. What was left out there if he didn't have his boy? What did he have to live for? Vengeance? It felt hollow. Justice? There was no such thing.

Then Roen thought of Jill. She was still down there. Alive. He hadn't lost her yet. She was all he had left in the world. He had to protect her. Roen slapped himself in the face. No, he wasn't going to give up on Cameron either. He would never give up on his boy. Cameron was smart; he was able; he had Tao. Roen wasn't going to give up until he saw the body. He was going to assume that Cameron was alive and had fled down to the base somewhere. And his son needed him.

"God help the Genjix," he growled picking up his rifle. If his son and wife were dead, he would take that hollow vengeance and fill it with the bodies of their killers.

He sped down one of the other stairwells and then back up through the last stairwell. Then he looked down into the elevator shaft. The light wasn't strong at the bottom. The cut panel at the ceiling of the elevator offered very little illumination. He thought he maybe saw a figure down there, but he couldn't be sure. For all he knew, it could just be his imagination hoping against all hope. Still, Roen wasn't going to leave anything to chance. He would tear this entire damn base apart panel by panel if he had to, in order to find his son. He looked at the metal cables hanging in the middle of the shaft. He frigging hated heights.

Well, there was nothing he wouldn't do right now; he

was desperate enough to try. Roen slung his rifle across his back, took a deep breath, and hesitated. He took a few more deep breaths, and had two more false starts before he decided "to hell with it" and jumped across the gap. His first attempt on the cable missed, and his second rope-burned his hand, and he almost fell. His third desperate grab succeeded, and he found himself dangling precariously in the middle of the shaft. He laughed a little crazily in relief and began to rappel down. Roen was two-thirds down the cable when he saw two bodies, one of them in Prophus armor. His breath caught in his throat when he landed on the top of the elevator. It was Cameron! He felt the panic set in as he felt for a pulse and for injuries.

Cameron's eyes opened. "Roen, you found me."

"Hey, buddy," Roen choked the words out. "How are you feeling?"

Cameron sat up. "He is unconscious. I did not want to wake him yet. He might need rest. He has no broken bones or internal injuries. However, thank goodness he had a soft landing." He turned and saw the body.

Roen turned the body over. "Is she…"

"…dead. One of Enzo's Adonis lieutenants," Tao said. "I saw her Quasing Szin leave. Let us hope he does not find a host in time."

"Azumi is a big gun, and my son got her, huh?" Roen helped Tao to his feet. "Why don't you stay here until all of this is over? I think he's had enough."

Tao shook his head. "No. You left him alone once, and he ended up at the bottom of an elevator shaft. I would prefer he stay by your side. Hang on, let me try to wake him up."

Somehow, though Roen knew it was more dangerous

for Cameron to come with him, he couldn't find it in himself to object. He just couldn't stand letting his son out of his sight. Cameron's eyes became unfocused, and a few seconds later, his knees buckled and he groaned.

"Ow," he mumbled. "Why do I feel like I just went five rounds with Lin?"

"Well," Roen couldn't help but smile. "You went toe-to-toe with an elevator car."

"Did I win?"

"It didn't kill you."

"Makes me stronger?"

"Something like that. Can you stand?"

Roen helped Cameron to his feet and then checked the car below them, hanging upside down and looking at the hallway outside the half-opened elevator door. When he was sure it was clear, he dropped down and motioned for Cameron to follow. The two of them left the elevator and crept down the hallway. Roen noticed right away how Cameron fell in line, using the SWAT tactics he and Tao had drilled into him. His chest swelled with pride as they expertly scoped out each room and secured each intersection one by one.

They reached the entrance to the command center and found it a hulking mess. Roen motioned for Cameron to stay put while he peeked his head around the corner and scanned the interior. It was completely abandoned. He signaled for Cameron to follow as they checked inside. Bullet holes riddled everything, the walls, the consoles, the screens. A large battle had been waged here. Bodies from both sides were strewn across the floor, but none were Jill or the rest of the commanders.

"Dad," Cameron said. "There're people coming."

The two scrambled to the far back of the room and hid behind a row of consoles as four Genjix passed. Two of them paid the room only a cursory glance before moving on. That could only mean one thing; they were behind enemy lines. The Prophus forces must have been pushed away from the center point. That couldn't be good.

"Jill," Roen whispered into his comm. "What's your status?"

She clicked over, but the sounds of fighting in the background were so loud he could barely make out her words. "Roen!" Then it was garbled. Then he heard "east of" and "pinned" and then she was cut off. That was enough for him, though. He pulled on Cameron's sleeve.

"Where to?" he asked.

"We're going to save your mom."

Cameron's face scrunched up, and his exhausted and pained expression turned into determination as he caught his second wind. Roen saw true grit in his son's eyes and realized for the first time that Cameron really was ready. He was ready now, inside as well as out.

Roen patted his son on the back. "Let's rock this party."

The two of them headed east from the command center down the main hallway. Jill's message wasn't much to work from, and Roen usually wouldn't operate on such light information, but this was Jill, and he would go east until the end of the world for her.

They took out three Genjix, each roving by themselves, and avoided two full patrols of five. The sound of fighting intensified the further they moved away from the spine. Some of the enemy traffic became too heavy on this floor, so they went down a level to avoid patrols. They circumvented several blockades and continued generally east, sometimes going up or down a level when they hit an obstacle. Soon, they were completely lost.

Nonetheless, they continued moving in an easterly direction. Roen couldn't be sure, but he could swear they were being stalked. There were always shadows and noise coming from somewhere, giving them only one path to move as they ventured deeper away from the spine.

"Dad, do you know where we're going?" Cameron asked.

Roen shrugged. "I didn't think too far ahead, besides heading toward your mother."

His son rolled his eyes. "Tao says he can get us back to the command center. He also thinks we're being corralled somehow."

Roen frowned. "Why does he think that?"

"Something about how at every intersection, only one path seems open. Should we go back?"

"Screw it. We go east until we find your mom."

The two entered a dimly-lit portion of the base filled with large cavernous rooms. Their progress slowed as visibility worsened. The sounds of fighting had died as well. Part of Roen was screaming at him that he was heading the wrong way. However, he knew that Jill wasn't where he had just come from, so he continued to prod them forward, hoping to find a set of stairs back up to the higher levels. They had just passed a series of large empty rooms when Cameron stumbled upon a room with two dozen large pallets of containers about neck-height in the center.

"Dad..." Cameron whispered. He pointed at his eyes and then into the room.

Roen peeked inside and saw two men lounging among

the pallets. One was leaning against a stack, while the other was tilting back in a chair.

"Let's check it out," Roen whispered.

They waited until the two worst guards in the world were too distracted by their conversation to notice them. They crept inside, staying in the shadow behind one of the pallets. They positioned themselves near the wall and Roen motioned to Cameron to take out the guard on the right. Then he counted down from five.

Before he reached two, Cameron tapped him on the shoulder and pointed to the north wall at the far end. Wait, make that three of the world's worst guards. Another was having a cigarette, watching the door on the north side. Roen paused. If there was a guard watching that door, then there should have been one... A second later, his question was answered. One more guard came in from the south, where they had just entered. Now they were trapped.

One of the men in the center called to the new guard that just walked in. "Hey, Brent, see any of the Prophus while you were taking a piss?"

"Naw, I whipped it out and scared them away," he replied.

The rest of the guys laughed. "This is the sweetest gig," someone said. "Ain't no Prophus making it all the way down here."

"It's pointless," another said. "How else you ever going to earn yourself a Holy One pulling guard duty?"

"Not going to earn a Holy One dying in combat," Brent added.

"I agree with Emi. Vessels and higher ups have priority with the havens," the first one said. "What do you think'll happen to us scrubs if we haven't earned a Holy One by the time Quasiform starts?"

"I can't wait for it to begin," Emi continued. "A world rebuilt. Paradise on Earth, with us in control. I don't know why the rest of the world fights it. They should be helping us."

"Do you really believe everything the Holy Ones say about that paradise?" Brent asked.

The other guard nodded. "I didn't believe in aliens before either."

"Tell the truth," Brent said. "I signed on for the riches. Being a lord in Heaven is just an added perk."

"Watch your mouth," Emi snapped. "The Holy Ones will cut you from ear to ear for blasphemy."

Roen and Cameron exchanged glances, and he gave his son a series of hand signals. He didn't think Cam understood all the orders; it had taken Roen almost five years before he was able to communicate fluently with them, but he knew Tao would understand. Then he counted down from five.

On zero, Cameron leaned over the side and shot a grouping at the left guard in the center of the room, while Roen, feeling overly confident, sprinted and strafed his assigned target on the right on his way to the guard at the far end. He missed all his shots, but Cameron took the remaining guy in the center out for him. Roen dove and slid along the floor, making several shots at the surprised guard near the door at the north end. It took him three shots to knock the guy out. By the time he had picked himself up and gotten back to the center between all the stacks, Cameron had already handled both guys there and the guard at the door where they had come in.

"You're definitely my son, aren't you?" he grinned.

"Maybe not," Cameron answered. "I nailed both my targets, and cleaned up yours."

"Ooh, that cut deep."

"Tao told me to say it," Cameron admitted.

Roen pulled one of the containers off the pallets and opened it. He held it up for Cameron to see. "Catalyst reaction rod. A crap ton of them."

"I wonder why they're here," Cameron said. "You'd think they would keep these things in a Fort Knox sort of place, not relatively lightly guarded in the middle of enemy territory."

"I wonder that too." He put his arms around Cameron's shoulder. "Come on, let's go find your mother. We can lead the rest back here when this is all over."

As they made their way toward the exit, three figures emerged from the shadows and blocked their way. Roen pulled Cameron by the collar and ran toward the north door. Three more figures appeared. They were trapped. Roen and Cameron retreated back between the cover of the pallets.

"I spent the entire battle looking for you, Roen Tan," a familiar voice said. "Even in the middle of our base, you are difficult to track." The center figure walked under a light shining from the ceiling, and Roen's heart skipped a beat. The stuff of his nightmares was here.

Jacob Diamont had finally caught up with him.

CHAPTER FORTY-FOUR
AT ALL COSTS

Our relationship with the humans is no longer tenable. The Prophus saw to that. They had hoped to avert total defeat by revealing us to them, or perhaps they had hoped to find a new ally in humanity. It makes little difference. All the Prophus have done is ensure humanity's destruction. Their blood will be on the Prophus's hands.

Gods do not treat their children as equals.

Zoras

Enzo watched the console as his forces deteriorated before his eyes. The trap had at first been a resounding success. However, bit by bit, encounter by encounter, his units were beaten back. As much as he wanted to blame the weakness on the haven's security forces, that couldn't be the case. Those forces had long shattered. The Prophus were now pitted against Enzo's elite guard, and they were winning.

He couldn't lay the blame on his men – they were better-trained and better-armed. In fact, in every single small unit encounter, his squads came out victorious. Yet, as the battle across the haven raged on, he found fewer units at his disposal, with his options diminishing by the hour. One by one, his units were destroyed. Even his Adonis siblings. Matthew and Azumi were dead. Akelatis was captured. In his own damn chosen field of battle, no less. How was this possible?

Enzo was Hatchery-trained and had been learning from the best military minds since he was old enough to walk. His only purpose in life was to lead and to win wars. He would have been confident to match his war prowess against any military mind, be it George Patton, Napoleon Bonaparte, Tran Hung Dao, or even Sun Tzu. It physically pained him to be losing. It was inconceivable that the enemy had a leader who was capable of defeating Enzo in battle with an inferior force on terms of his choosing. Just who was the Prophus commander?

I would dearly love to know as well. However, that is irrelevant. You have failed gravely, Enzo, and your standing has lowered. Initiate an orderly retreat.

"Retreat? Impossible. The catalyst reaction stockpiles will be lost."

They can be replaced or reclaimed. I cannot. The odds of victory no longer offer acceptable risks.

"Zoras, I have never lost a battle before in my life. I will not lose one now."

Perhaps you have finally met your equal. Seems more than your equal actually. You only have one option. Act on it.

"Damn it, Zoras. I am the leader of the Genjix. I will not tolerate having the rest of the Council believe I have been routed."

As you often do, you forget yourself vessel.

A dozen scenarios ran through Enzo's head. He was playing a game of chess with roughly the same amount of pieces as his opponent, but he was cornered, boxed in from two sides, and his enemy was chipping away at his pawns. He thought five steps ahead, trying to move his pieces to claim any sort of advantage, but in most cases, he would lose his king, which was the catalyst reaction rods.

Unless he was bold. In this game of chess, he was the queen.

"Palos, pull back to my position," he barked over the comm. "Cover the escape pods. I'm taking two-thirds of the remaining forces and marking a new defensive perimeter."

"Your command, Father," Palos responded. "How long is the new line?"

"All the way down to lower level storage. We will hold until all the pallets with the catalyst reaction rods can be retrieved."

Amanda looked worried. "Father, escape pods one through three are in Prophus-held territory now," she stammered. "There isn't enough room in the pods for all the catalyst pallets, vessels, and high-valued Genjix."

"Then re-evaluate. The catalyst reaction rods have the highest priority."

"Father," Palos buzzed in urgently. "The enemy is pressing."

You are on the Council. In this situation, your place should be on the first pod to escape, not leading a last desperate attack.

"Jacob is still down there holding the room. If I do not cut a path for him, he will be trapped."

Chiyva is a hard sacrifice, but one we have lived with before. He will find his way back in time.

"I have already lost too many Hatchery siblings today. I will not lose another one."

Enzo rallied his units around him; he had twelve at full

strength and several at partial strengths at his disposal. Most of them would be sacrificed for the greater good as they punched their way to the loading area of the main freight shaft. He deployed his units in almost a wedge formation, as if utilizing old cavalry charge techniques. The point of the wedge would suffer high attrition for sure, but their sacrifice would give the flanks time to react to the enemy. Enzo and his personal guard put themselves just behind that vanguard unit as they charged forward.

The wedge smashed through the first two intersections guarded by the enemy, decimating them. He soon found himself mixed in with his vanguard forces, fighting on the front line, where he was most comfortable. With him leading the way, the Prophus melted against their onslaught. Within the first few minutes, Enzo's men were already halfway to the supply room. The gigantic freight elevator was in sight. If his forces could hold that area, assuming Jacob had handled the catalyst stockpile room, Enzo's gambit would have paid off.

"Amanda," he spoke into the comm, "have you been able to get ahold of Jacob?"

"He controls the room still, Father," she said. "He has Prophus trapped in there, but is taking care of the situation now."

Enzo continued to press. By this time, the enemy had formed a defensive barricade at the main intersection just before the freight elevator. He reassessed his options.

You can turn left and make a wide arc, but that is three times the distance to the elevator. If you head down a level, you can reach the cargo room by foot, but then you will still need to take the freight hallways by force in order to move the catalyst reaction rods to the escape pods.

"Then we go forward."

Enzo ordered his men armed with riot shields to the front and charged, creating a battering ram across the forty meters to the chest-level barricade. He lost a man on his left and one in front, but the momentum carried his team forward. Half of his point unit had fallen by the time they were within five meters of their goal.

Enzo attacked, grabbing a shield from one of the fallen soldiers and stepping on the back of the man in front of him. He leaped over the barricade and crashed into three of the enemy. Instantly, he was back on his feet, swinging the riot shield like a club, taking out swaths of the Prophus.

One of the enemy tried to shoot him point-blank in the chest. Enzo grabbed the barrel with his free hand just as the man opened fire. He spun out of the way and swept the foot of the shooter, bringing the top of his shield down on the man's head.

Left at your ten!

Another Prophus shot at him, this time nearly hitting Enzo in the face. He barely managed to cover up in time as automatic fire hammered his shield. He tucked his legs and pushed off, ramming into his enemy and knocking him down. Enzo stomped down on her neck. Within the ten seconds it took his men to climb the barricade, he had killed seven Prophus soldiers.

You have lost a step.

"Apologies, my guardian. I blame it on all the years of being a damned bureaucrat."

"Secure this point," Enzo commanded. "We will utilize the barricades against them."

He barked out a succession of orders. The gambit seemed to be paying off. He had sacrificed his secured position on the chess board and was now forcing the enemy to fight in an extended line. He checked his attrition rate. Forty percent less than he had deemed acceptable, no doubt from his decision to single-handedly take the barricade. His men could now reinforce the freight elevator and call workers to move the pallets. Maybe with the tide turning, he could just stay and beat the enemy outright.

You have impressed me once again, but you are overly confident. Do not let this temporary success blind you to our priorities. Retrieving the catalyst stockpile will be a victory at this point.

"Father," Palos said over the comm. "Scouts believe they've sighted the enemy's forward command post."

A blip appeared on his map of the facility. The location was just around the corner. Enzo moved over to the edge and peered around to see a mass of Prophus troops guarding a large intersection in one of the main hallways. He recognized a few of the figures: Dylan, a colonel in their forces. Marco, one of their higher-profile agents. Then he saw the woman, Jill Tesser Tan. Enzo's hands tightened into fists. She was the most wanted of all the Prophus, even more than the Keeper, and the most hated by all Genjix. Even Zoras hissed when he saw her.

This does not change our plans.

"Zoras, it's the Great Betrayer and the rest of their command. If they fall, their entire operation falls."

Possibly, but your units have established the support line for Jacob. The catalysts are still more important.

Enzo hesitated. The safe decision was to retreat with as many of the catalysts as they could recover. Quasiform would only be delayed slightly. However, that retreat would be his first defeat and reduce his standing among the Genjix. No, he could snatch this defeat and turn it into a victory with one bold stroke. He was an Adonis Vessel, after all, undefeated, the greatest of all vessels. He would impose his will and strength on the enemy and show them who truly was their better.

A guaranteed partial defeat, or risking everything for complete victory. This is a gamble, vessel.

"I can defeat them and end this in one blow, Zoras."

You will reap the rewards or consequences, in either case.

He repositioned his men for the attack and communicated his new orders. "Continue the retrieval. You will have less defensive support, but I will draw their attention to something more pressing. Palos, push your perimeter forward and meet me at the Prophus command post. Now!"

He waved his units forward and the wedge attack – riots shields in front – made a right turn directly into the teeth of the enemy's defense. The initial enemy barrage was deafening. At the same moment, Enzo experienced memories of one of Zoras's previous hosts, who had led a Forlorn Hope charge into San Sebastián.

The first line of his fighting force dropped before they had moved ten meters in. They were expendable, however. More took their place, locking their shields in as phalanxes of old. Others picked up the shields of the fallen and moved to the front. All they needed to do was get him close enough to wreak the vengeance of the Holy Ones upon these Prophus.

I see at minimum of four vessels. Be wary.

"None can match an Adonis."

Halfway down the hall, the Prophus line made the foolish decision of charging with its own shields. Two lines of them broke out of the barricade and charged. The sound of the sides colliding was immense. This time, instead of going over the top through the Prophus defenses, Enzo drew his Honjo Masamune. With his sword in his right hand, a pistol in his left, and the shield wrapped over his left forearm, he envisioned the glory days of war, when battles were fought the way they were meant to, through skill and strength of will, when the winner was the man who drew the blood of the most enemies with his own two hands.

The line for both sides bounced backward from the initial impact, giving Enzo just enough room to slip through his units and get to work. He swept low with the sword, cutting through boots and flesh alike, felling several of the enemy. Ducking behind his shield, he felt the impact of the bullets on its surface. A moment later, the line behind him caught up. More of his units charged, hitting the second layer of the Prophus, who were not armed with shields.

Enzo waded in, slashing indiscriminately, a walking god of war slaying both the enemy and those Genjix who were in his way. Collateral damage was always acceptable, as long as the goal justified his actions. And now, Enzo was going for the enemy's throat. It took him longer than he would have preferred. He had half a dozen bodies to wade through, after all.

Once he got into the interior though, he got to work, moving with a speed and grace only a Holy One-infused Adonis could. He felt the pace and beat and tension of the battle flow through him, knowing exactly when and how and where to strike at all times. Enzo was so attuned, he felt he could have waged this fight blindfolded.

Soon, the Honjo Masamune was coated in blood,

slippery to hold and weighed down by the slaughter. His shield was dented from the concentrated fire, and his pistol was down to three shots, but he pressed on, taking out the enemy's communication station, slicing through the guards of the commanders, and disrupting their entire operation.

"Elias," the one named Marco screamed as Enzo put his sword through a man's throat. Enzo pulled the Honjo Masamune out just in time to raise his shield against the three shots that hammered against it. Then, to his surprise, Marco rammed into his shield with his body, trying to knock it aside. He was soon joined by Dylan, their fat colonel. The other commanders had all stopped directing troops and were engaging him.

Except for that traitor woman. Jill continued to stand there and speak into her comm while the others did all the work. That coward. It pained him that she was still alive while his brothers and sisters had died in the field. The Betrayer was barely a candle to Azumi's bonfire.

Two of them hammered at him with bullets, trying to flank him for a shot. However, no two mortals, vessels or otherwise, could take him down by themselves. He blocked a grouping of bullets from Dylan, dodged Marco trying to club his head off with the rifle, and attacked. A quick dart forward speared Marco in the leg with the Honjo Masamune, and then he turned and knocked Dylan down with a bash of the shield to the head. He reversed his grip and rammed the sword down at the fat man's chest. The ugly colonel proved surprisingly fast and spun out of the way at the last second.

Right temple. Duck now!

"Burn in hell," a voice to the side of him said.

Enzo saw one of the commanders with a pistol aimed at his head a scant meter away. He twisted away just as the man pulled the trigger. He felt a sharp pain burn his cheek. He finished his spinning motion and swung his sword in an uppercut. The Honjo Masamune sliced his assailant from groin to neck. The man, a look of shock on his face, tried to open his mouth as blood poured out of the long wound. A sparkling light left the man's body and floated into the air.

"Faust!" the Betrayer screamed as his body fell backward. It seemed Enzo finally had her attention. She took aim at him and fired.

Left side chest. Now!

Enzo dodged with ease and the bullet hit one of her Prophus soldiers in the back. Realizing her error, she became more cautious and closed in, exactly what Enzo wanted.

The one named Marco, now limping, attacked with his rifle, still trying to knock Enzo's shield out of the way. Enzo parried with the Honjo Masamune and slid the blade low to take out the fool's other foot. Marco stumbled out of the way clumsily, narrowly avoiding losing his leg. He was off-balance, however, and slipped on the wet floor.

Enzo switched the angle of the Honjo Masamune and sliced the man's chest open. Marco screamed as a fountain of red exploded all over the ground. Just as Enzo lifted the blade for the killing blow, his chest exploded in pain. He was knocked onto his back. He saw Jill locking eyes with him as she aimed another shot. Enzo kept the shield close to his body as she bounced bullets off it. The woman was a pest. He would make her pay.

Up now! She has just pulled back to reload.

As he scrambled to his feet, Enzo took a punch to the face from the fat ugly colonel. Another punch caused him to stagger backward. As the third punch came, Enzo leaned to his left and countered with the hilt of his sword, punching it upward through the soft tissue where the neck met the head. The large man toppled over, clutching his throat.

Enzo, gasping from the exertion, watched as the Australian writhed on the ground, his mouth opening and closing as if a fish out of water. With a determined smirk, Enzo walked up to him and gave him a salute with his sword. "You fought well, betrayer. You almost beat me. But like the rest, you are not equal to Enzo, leader of the Genjix. Now, to the Eternal Sea with you." He reversed the grip of the Honjo Masamune and brought it straight down into Dylan's stomach. The old man shuddered and gripped the blade as it pierced him.

All that was left now was the woman. Enzo looked around for her, but she was nowhere in sight. He tried to pull the blade out of the enemy leader, but couldn't. He looked down and saw that Dylan had grabbed the sword's blade collar and guard with his hands, and was keeping it in place in his stomach. Enzo yanked again. Still, the blade wouldn't come out.

"She's a fine blade," Dylan rasped. "I'm keeping her."

"You are not worthy…" Enzo began. He tugged again, but the fat bastard would not let go.

"You think too highly of yourself, you fucking bastard," a woman's voice said from behind. Then Enzo felt several sharp pains in his back. He stumbled forward. He spun and lashed out with his shield, just missing the woman as she ducked underneath it. Then she fired again, this time plugging him three times in the stomach at close range.

Enzo flew backward and landed roughly on the floor. The pain was greater than anything he had ever felt before. He felt his vision blur as she calmly walked up to him. Instead of finishing him off like she should have, the fool bent over and checked on the Australian.

"Dylan," she sobbed as sparkling white lights of his Holy One danced into the air above them.

Enzo's vision darkened for a few moments, and when his eyes focused again, she was still there, this time, checking on Marco. Enzo tried to sit up.

Stay still. Your wounds are serious.

"I refuse to let the Great Betrayer defeat me."

The physical exertion was too much, and he lost consciousness again. This time, he wasn't sure for how long. When he managed to open his eyes one more time, he heard the rushing of water like a gigantic waterfall and saw bright yellow colors flashing above him. He could barely make out the woman's face as she shouted something imperceptible and shot her gun somewhere outside his field of vision. He couldn't make out what she was saying, but it felt desperate. Maybe victory was still his. After all, he had never lost before. Even injured, he was fated for this glory.

Enzo blacked out one more time. When he came to, he saw a friendly face. "Palos," he groaned. He was being moved. He could tell by the way the patterns on the ceiling ran behind Palo's head.

"I have you, Father," Palos said, leaning over him. "Rest. We're getting you out of here right now. The evacuation is commencing."

Then everything went black.

CHAPTER FORTY-FIVE
LAST MEET UP

Now you know our truth. We are not wise or caring beings. We are not a species that respects and honors other forms of life. We are an aggressive, engulfing, terrible force that consumes entire solar systems.

If the Genjix are successful, Earth as you know it will die and follow the fate of the many thousands of other planets the Quasing have colonized. The Prophus do not wish that fate upon Earth. We fight now, and we will do so until there are none of us left. Until the Eternal Sea.

Tao

"Lock the doors," Jacob ordered, his voice echoing off the high ceilings in the large room. "No one is leaving until we've come to a proper resolution, Roen Tan. And not just you; your betrayer as well." The room lit up as a stream of flames burst into the air. "We're settling this once and for all."

"Stand behind me, Cam," Roen said, hand on Cameron's chest, pushing him against one of the stacks of catalysts.

Cameron looked over at Jacob, the two men with him

on one side and the three on the other. "Dad, there's too many. You're going to need me."

"I got this, Cam."

Roen needs to get over himself if you two are going to get out of this alive.

"Tell me about it. Story of my life."

Take out the other guards first. Then with two versus one, you might have a fighting chance.

"Roen Tan," Jacob called from the doorway as it clicked shut behind him. "Remember me? You do, don't you? I can tell by the fear in your voice. Have I haunted your dreams all these years? Rest assured, this will be the last time we ever meet."

"I'm sorry," Roen yelled back. "My memory's a little fuzzy. Who are you again?"

"I was the boy who beat you to within an inch of your life. That was a long time ago, old man. I won't make that mistake again."

"Oh yeah, you're that punk with the grand-daddy issues. Well, come on then," Roen yelled. He turned to Cameron. "Watch the other doorways. Shoot anything that walks." Then he knelt down and whispered into the comm. "Jill, we have a situation. Might need you to bail us out. Jill?" He put both hands over his ears and concentrated. "I can't make out what she's saying. It's louder than Wembley Stadium on the other end. Something about a counterattack. We're on our own, buddy."

Blitz the northern end and run. That is your only chance.

Roen whispered into Cameron's ear. "Here's what I want you to do. Guard the center area and use the stacks for cover. I'll take out the enemy at the north end and then we sneak out."

What? That will never work. What a dumb plan.

"Dad," Cameron said. "You can't keep trying to coddle me. You need me."

"Roen Tan," Jacob barked again. "I have an offer for you. I'm walking in now."

Roen and Cameron both stuck their heads above the pallets like gophers out of the ground and watched as Jacob sauntered in. "You mean like last time, when we put our guns down and fought it out like we're no better than the animals?"

"Actually, Roen Tan," Jacob said, "you tried to shoot me when I offered."

"Oh yeah. I did, didn't I? Oops. That kind of dampens the trust in our relationship, then."

"I'm still willing to offer you a deal." Jacob had reached the first row of pallets, still looking relaxed. The two Genjix soldiers behind him stayed at the doorway.

"What do you have in mind?" Roen asked.

"First of all, Roen Tan, show me your hands. Both of you."

Roen raised the rifle until it rested on the pallet and aimed it at Jacob. "Okay, what next?"

For a man who had a rifle pointed at his head, Jacob was very relaxed. "Fair enough, Roen Tan. Here's my offer. Surrender your rifle and pistols – I know you must have two – and come out with your hands up. I beat you to death in front of your boy, and then he will be free to leave. I will even guarantee his safety out of this base."

That made Roen pause. "So my life for his? That's it? That sounds surprisingly… reasonable."

"He can't be serious!"

He is playing for time. I hope.

Cameron looked over at his father's face and could tell that his dad was actually considering it. He had the worst poker face in the world. "Dad," he hissed. "You're not actually considering this shit, are you?"

"Watch your mouth," Roen said absently, his eyes still locked on the Adonis. "So my son walks right out that door. I put my guns down and surrender, and then you do whatever the fuck your sadistic mind can think of. That's it?"

Jacob smirked. "No, he stays while I beat you to death. I want him to watch you die slowly and painfully while I break you bit by bit. I want the image of your death branded into his mind for the rest of his life. I want the face of his father's killer to haunt his every waking hour. Then perhaps he will know a little of the pain you caused me."

Cameron's blood turned to ice, and he felt a chill move through his body. This Jacob guy was completely unhinged. Even the thought of leaving his dad with him made Cameron want to throw up.

"Tao, do something!"

We need to see what your father decides. Unfortunately, that could be the best option. Otherwise, I doubt any of us will walk out of this room alive.

"You fucking suck sometimes, Tao."

Roen is right; when did you get such a mouth? I know your father, though. He is up to something. Be ready.

"You really didn't take my advice when I told you to date, did you?" Roen was saying. "That's probably a blessing for the girls. Look, Jacob, you have some serious issues."

Jacob shrugged and rolled his eyes. "Make up your –"

Roen pulled the trigger. A single shot echoed across the cavernous room. Unfortunately, Jacob was either expecting it, or all the rumors about Adonis Vessels being superhuman were true. He tilted his head just slightly to the left and the bullet whizzed by his head into one of the containers behind him. That's when the short-lived negotiations dissolved into a fracas.

"Get Cameron on the level, Tao," was all Roen shouted as he swung his rifle to the left and took out one of the Genjix guarding the doorway. Then he aimed upward and shot out the four giant warehouse lights directly above them. The center of the room went dark.

Opposite side now! Get some distance from your father. Hide between the pallets. Keep moving. Stay inside the black.

Cameron swung to his right and shot off three groupings, all missing. He ducked and moved down the aisle, finding moments to stick his head out and potshoot the men guarding the door. The Genjix there were at a severe disadvantage, standing in the light without cover. All Cameron had to do was wait until he had a good shot and get them from the shadows. Even then, he missed several more times before he finally nailed two of the guards at the north end of the wall. The last one, realizing his bad positioning, charged forward toward the pallets and disappeared around the corner.

Cameron pulled back and saw Roen and Jacob running around the square pallets and shooting at each other, the gunfire like a strobe light in the darkness. Every time Jacob turned in Cameron's direction, Roen would try to suppress him and draw him back. Cameron couldn't quite make out how the fight was going. He could only see the action unfold in the brief flashes of light.

Do not worry about your father. He can keep Jacob busy. It is up to you to take out the other Genjix.

Cameron moved his attention to the guards at the southern end. He scampered to the edge of the pallets on the other side and caught both guys right as they were creeping toward him. He took them out easily.

As he was making his way back to the northern wall, he accidentally walked into the remaining Genjix. The man must have crept up on the other side of the pallet. The two bumped into each other, startled, and then opened fire simultaneously.

Fortunately, Cameron got the first shot off and hit the guy in the face. Unfortunately, the Genjix got his off as well. The bullet struck Cameron's rifle and ricocheted into his chest. The impact was enough to knock him onto his back, skidding him several meters until his head bumped against one of the pallets. Luckily, the advanced body armor prevented the bullet from penetrating his body.

Not so lucky was the feeling that someone had just whacked him with a baseball bat. It hurt so badly, he momentarily blacked out. Writhing on the ground, his vision was blurred by hundreds of sparkling explosions. He actually thought for a moment he had died and that it was Tao floating above him.

Sorry, pal. I am still here.

To top it all off, the pain was so sharp, he felt a couple of tears dribble down his face. It took him a few seconds to pull himself together. He pushed himself into a sitting position and wiped his eyes with his sleeves. "Well, that was embarrassing."

It is all right. Thinking you lost me is worth crying over.

"I cried because it hurt so much."

Nice excuse. I plan to make fun of you for the rest of your life. For now, get yourself together and check on Roen.

Cameron found his rifle on the ground and picked it up. He tried to reload the magazine and struggled to pull it out. He finally yanked it out, and then found that the new one wouldn't go in. Flipping over the rifle, he found a large dent, probably where the Genjix's bullet had hit it.

Cameron reached for his pistol and found his holster empty. Crap, he had dropped it up at the platform when he was battling that crazy ninja woman. He ran to the body of the dead Genjix. The Genjix – a large heavyset man – was lying on top of his rifle. Cameron tried to roll him over, but struggled with the limp body. He looked and saw Jacob pinning Roen against a stack with his left elbow at Roen's neck, both struggling for the pistol that was in his right hand. Roen had both his hands on Jacob's wrist, trying desperately to keep the pistol from pointing at his head. He was slowly losing that battle.

Screw it. No time. Go help Roen!

Cameron charged at full speed and rammed Jacob in the side. The two of them flew into the air and skidded across the floor. Roen collapsed, choking and grasping his neck.

Roen seems to be injured. Take Jacob out before he recovers. This could be your only chance.

"While he's down?"

Images of a medieval battle flashed in his head. In it, the men-at-arms were stalking the field of bodies, using maces and clubs to finish off the remaining wounded enemy. It was a gruesome sight and more than a little uncomfortable. Part of Cameron objected to nailing a downed opponent in the back like that. Then he saw an image of one of the wounded surprising one of the careless man-at-arms, reaching up and stabbing the guy in the gut as he walked over to club him. The last thing he saw was Tao's host running over and stomping on the guy's head.

Screw battlefield ethics. This is war. Go stomp on his head!

"Okay. Point taken."

Cameron somehow managed to get up first, though Jacob wasn't far behind. The Adonis Vessel was on his hands and knees when Cameron ran at him again, trying to imitate that fading image of the head stomp. Jacob was fast, though. He caught Cameron's foot as it was coming down and flipped it aside. Then he swept Cameron's feet out from under him.

Before Cameron could recover, Jacob was towering over him. He picked Cameron up like a rag doll and punched him first in the gut, and then in the face. Cameron got flashbacks of the beating he had received earlier. He took a lazy swing that Jacob brushed aside. Then Jacob spun and threw Cameron head-first against a stack of boxes. Dazed, Cameron blinked and fell back down.

"You bastard," Roen said, rising unsteadily to his feet.

Cameron watched his father attack Jacob with a newfound fury. Having seen him in action before, Cameron knew how good Roen was. Only Lin and maybe Uncle Marco were better, but the difference in speed and skill between Roen and Jacob was noticeable, and not in a good way.

Get up. Get up! Roen is not going to last long.

It seemed Roen knew that as well. "Get out of here, Cam," Roen yelled while eating several punches to the face. "Hurry!"

"Screw that."

Cameron. Let me take control. You are too worked up right now. Relax.

As much as he tried, Cameron couldn't put his head in the right state for Tao to make that connection. The more he watched his father take a beating, the worse he became. Finally, unable to sit still anymore, he decided to jump in and help. With a roar, he charged Jacob from behind. This time, the Adonis Vessel was ready for him. He engaged Cameron effortlessly, even while he fought off Roen, making sure to keep moving so that they couldn't attack at the same time or flank him.

Watch his legs. Very high-level Shotokan. He will dart in and out.

Cameron tried to keep the spacing between them, but Jacob was just too fast. The guy had a way of closing the distance before he could react. He jabbed Cameron in the face and then got out of range before Cameron could retaliate. Slowly, the Adonis beat both Roen and Cameron's faces into bloody messes.

Cameron's legs were the first to give as a devastating kick caught him in the midsection and sent him tumbling to the ground. He gasped for air and tried to get up, but had trouble finding his bearing. He watched helplessly as Roen took the full brunt of Jacob's attention and was soon sent crashing to the ground. He could tell by the way his dad landed awkwardly on the floor that he had broken his arm.

Jacob stood over them and smirked. "Father and son. Both weak losers. I shall relish my final justice."

You have to find the calm, Cameron. It is our only chance.

"I'm trying, Tao. I can't."

Roen picked himself up again. Cameron was amazed

at how his dad could still be standing after taking such a beating. Jacob had done a number on his face, and with the way his arm hung at his side, there was no way he could protect himself, let alone attack an Adonis Vessel. Still, Cameron watched with amazement and worry as his father stumbled toward Jacob.

"Get out of here, Cam!" Roen cried, and attacked once more.

To Cameron's horror, the one-armed Roen whiffed on several left-handed swings only to take a couple more smacks to the face that staggered him. Then, to everyone's surprise, he lunged forward and clocked Jacob hard, hitting him with a really solid punch across the chin that knocked the Adonis to the ground. Instead of pressing his advantage, Roen stopped and looked Cameron's way.

Their eyes locked and Roen communicated volumes with his stare. As the blood dripped form his smashed nose and large gash on his brow, as it poured out of the side of his mouth, his father said goodbye. With that one look, he told Cameron that he loved tao. That his sacrifice had better not be in vain. He told Cameron to find his mother, to say goodbye for him. To tell her that he loved her. Finally, Roen told Cameron that he was proud of him, more than anything in the world. That he could die knowing how his son had grown up. Most of all though, Roen was telling Cameron to just get the hell out of there.

And then the look was gone, and Roen focused back on Jacob, who was still picking himself up off the ground. Roen growled, a low guttural snarl, ran forward and kicked Jacob in the ribs, eliciting a grunt from the Adonis Vessel. Then he punched down, clocking Jacob across the face, followed by another kick to the midsection. His dad continued to press, cutting Jacob's scalp open with his knuckles and hammering at Jacob's face with his one good arm. This turning of the tide was brief as Roen tired, and Jacob tossed up a spectacular kick out of nowhere that snapped Roen's head to the side. Roen stumbled a few steps more and collapsed in a heap.

I hate this, but your father is right. Better one survives than neither.

Using the side of the pallets for support, Cameron clawed his way back to his feet and dragged himself away from the scene. He looked back one more time at his father, probably the last time he ever would. Roen saw him leaving and actually smiled through the blood and swelling on his face. "You made the right choice, son," he was saying. Then a kick from Jacob flashed across his face, and he collapsed again. Cameron couldn't look anymore.

He rounded the corner of the stack, took two steps toward the door, and fell to his knees. It physically pained him to take another step and leave his father like this. It felt wrong and cowardly, and he knew that this decision would haunt him for the rest of his life. It didn't matter that damned Tao and his damned father both had told him to leave, that it was the right thing to do. He loved his father too much to do the *right* thing. Every fiber of his being told him that the price he'd pay wouldn't be worth it.

Cameron closed his eyes and breathed in. And out. Then he inhaled again, each successive breath longer and deeper and slower. It was one of the most difficult things he'd ever have to do, to attempt to find the calm in the midst of panic, to try to find that balance and peace when he knew his father was being beaten to death a few meters away. He knew that the more desperately he wanted it, the harder it'd be to grasp. So he breathed. In. Out. Instead of being a drowning man grasping for the surface of the water, he let go.

When he opened his eyes again, he felt a surge of energy. He was still there, conscious, and the control of his body was as simple as putting his hands on the steering wheel, but right now, Tao was in control, and this connection was stronger than it had ever been. Tao powered up his body and shot it around the corner and back at Jacob.

Jacob saw him coming and took a defensive stance as Cameron attacked. They clashed, and he threw a combination of elbows, leg kicks, and arm locks, all while sidestepping whatever the Adonis threw at him. Jacob's eyes widened as he realized that something was different here. The speed between their exchanges, the attacking and defending, the quick movements and tactics, was blinding.

Jacob proved stronger, but Tao was faster, and his movements were smoother. Tao took a few hard blows to the face and stomach, but in return he hacked at Jacob's left knee until it buckled. Their exchange continued for several minutes as both used the terrain to their advantage, playing a deadly form of tag. Cameron could feel both Tao and his body weakening, but he trusted Tao to pull through. However, nearly five minutes into their frantic fight, Tao finally gave out.

I cannot maintain control. This is too much.

And then Cameron felt his entire body sag as full control returned. He nearly fell on his ass. Jacob was hardly in better shape. Both men were exhausted as they broke their exchange and eyed each other warily.

Jacob, unsteady on his feet, smirked. "You put up a really good fight, boy. I didn't know you had it in you."

His beautiful Adonis face was a mass of purple putty, and by this time, he was dragging his useless feet along the ground. Cameron was even worse off, though, if that were possible. The entire left side of his body screamed from pain, and his left eye was so puffy, he couldn't see out of it. Jacob watched as Cameron straightened his back and readied for one more round in their fight.

Cameron was on his own now. No more Tao. No more master to guide him. The two stalked in a circle, each probing for the right time to attack. Cameron leaped in, but was easily repelled by Jacob dancing to the side and popping him once in the cheek for his troubles. Cameron got a kick to the side of Jacob's knee that nearly buckled him.

"What's the matter, boy?"

You can do this. Tao's voice was so weak he could barely hear it in his head. *He is as exhausted as you are. You are ready. Your parents and I believe in you. We are all with you.*

It heartened him that Tao was still there, and it reminded him that he was fighting not just for himself, but for his dad and for his Quasing. They depended on him. He couldn't fail them, but he knew he couldn't beat this guy. Jacob was stronger, more skilled, and faster. He held every advantage.

Then Master Lin popped into his mind. The wise old kung fu master was fond of saying that winning a fight was sixty percent aggression, twenty-five percent conditioning, and twenty percent skill. Cameron never had the heart to tell Lin that he sucked at math.

In this case, Cameron was outmatched on two of the

three, but that aggression he could manage. There was nothing more desperate for him than winning this fight. Right now, exhausted and outmatched, aggression was all he had left. He thought about his family and their destroyed house, then he saw the disgusting smirk on Jacob's face. Cameron dug deep; the only thing left was to charge, to just keep going until he was dead. He gave his unconscious father one last glance, then dug deeper and darker than he ever had, and with a snarl, focused his aggression on one thing.

The attack took Jacob by surprise. The Adonis's leg was too injured to dodge Cameron barreling into him. He managed to pop Cameron in the face once, and then the two were on the ground with Cameron on top. Blinded by fury and desperation, he attacked on instinct and left nothing back.

All he could see were the images of his family and loved ones, of his Prophus friends lost and of the life they had had to lead for all those years of being hunted by the Genjix. In addition, he saw an image of Edward Blair, of Zhu Yuanzhang, and of Rianno Cisneros. All the pain and grief Jacob, Chiyva, and the Genjix had inflicted upon Tao and Cameron, he repaid now.

The exchange last a few seconds or a few minutes or an hour, Cameron didn't know. In the end, he stopped only when his arms gave out and he saw a white sparkling glow leave Jacob's body. His eyes followed as the light moved and flitted in the air, first to the locked door on one side, and then all the way across to the other. It moved from the bodies of the dead Genjix, floating over each one by one. Then it moved into the center of the room as if trying to decide what to do next. Cameron looked to the side and saw his father lying unconscious a few meters away. The thought of the Genjix inhabiting Roen filled Cameron with abject terror.

Chiyva must have thought the same thing. Realizing that Roen could be the only host available in the room, the Quasing moved toward his father. Cameron searched desperately for a way to prevent the Genjix from inhabiting his father. He looked down at Jacob's belt and saw the handheld flamethrower. Quickly plucking it out of his harness, he stood over his father's body and shot a stream of flames into the air, keeping Chiyva at bay.

"Stay back, you bastard!" he screamed, the words coming out garbled in his blood-soaked mouth.

Chiyva darted left and right, trying to get around the flames, but Cameron followed the sparkling being's path, shooting bursts at the Quasing if it got too close. The two sparred for several minutes, until finally, in a fit of desperation, Chiyva went low and dove for Roen's body. Cameron stepped in front of his father and shot a full burst directly into the Quasing. He watched grimly as the flames consumed the sparkling white creature until pieces of it, like embers of a fire, floated up into the darkness.

When he was sure there was nothing left of Chiyva, Cameron fell onto his back next to Roen's body, too exhausted and hurt to move. He thought about passing out, thought about how nice it would be to sleep it off. Maybe never wake up again. It wouldn't be a bad way to go, would it? Then he thought about his father. Was Roen still alive? He opened his mouth and tried to call his dad's name. Nothing came out. It took him a few more tries before he could muster the syllables together and force them out of his mouth.

"Roen?"

There was a long pause and whatever worry Cameron's broken body could muster began to grow. Was he too late?

"What did I say about calling me Dad?" Roen's voice was weak, barely a whisper, but it came across clearly in the otherwise dead-silent room. "And when did you get such a filthy mouth?"

And just like that, the panic disappeared, replaced by a glowing sense of relief. "Are you alive?"

"I think so, but I kind of wish I was dead."

"Well, I'm glad you're not."

"That's why you're the only one who can sign the Do-Not-Resuscitate form, not your mom."

Cameron chuckled, and it hurt worse than he ever imagined. He thought about getting up, but decided he liked the floor here way too much. "We should probably get out of here. Mom's going to be worried."

Roen raised his head off the floor. "Is Jacob dead?"

"Yeah, Dad. I killed him. Got Chiyva too."

"Cool." He heard a shuffling to the side and then a groan. "Argh. I think I broke my arm." He heard more shuffling. "Damn it, I think I broke both arms. Cameron, you're going to need to help your old man up."

EPILOGUE

Timestamp: 3887

One thing that I do know, and this is irrefutable, the war will continue. The players will come and go. The names and faces will change, but there will always be a new host to take the place of fallen comrades. That's how it has always been since the beginning, and how it always will be after we're all dead and buried. This will continue until, as the Quasing like to say, we meet in the Eternal Sea.

All right, I think we're done here. I'm hungry. What's for dinner?

Enzo woke up in a stale white room. That buzzing. A fly? No, the harsh fluorescent light. A sharp white glow stung his eyes. He squeezed them shut, but the white still seeped through; he covered them with his hand and took several deep breaths. He felt some pain, a lot of discomfort, but mostly just numbness. They must have pumped a lot of drugs into him.

Everything was out of focus, from the sterile-colored walls, to the sound of chatter just outside the room, to his hazy memories. What happened? He thought he heard

Zoras speak, but couldn't quite make out the words. His Holy One's voice sounded more like an itch on the back of his brain than a divine God channeling wisdom into his head.

Enzo closed his eyes, squeezed them tight. Slowly, the world came into focus as his senses collected themselves. The chatter outside the room coalesced into words he understood: Mandarin. The color of the walls, the distinct sterility of this particular facility, the feel of the sheets. This was the 301 Military Hospital; he was back at home in Beijing. He had cheated death, though to his shame, had not pulled victory from the jaws of defeat. It was his first, and Enzo swore, his last.

Zoras was saying something, and bit by bit, the words became clear. His Holy One was telling him to rest, not to move, to push the remote near his right hand to fetch the nurse and inject more painkillers into his bloodstream. He decided to forgo both for now until he had a better grip of his surroundings. He tried to sit up in bed, and had to stop as pain surged up his body, which changed his mind on the painkillers. He pushed the button and felt the immediate effect of the morphine coursing through his body.

Gritting his teeth, Enzo tried to sit up again. After all, he was not only an Adonis, he was the leader of the Council. He would not hold court lying in bed. He forced himself into a seated position. For the first time, he noticed the tubes sticking into his arm, his chest, his nose. He reached up to yank them out.

Leave them. Your injuries are many and severe.

"How long have I been gone? What happened?"

It has been three days since you were evacuated from the loyalty haven. Two Chinese destroyers were deployed to the Beaufort Sea and a commando team extracted all the survivors. Palos saved your life.

"His standing has been raised. I will see to it."

Now there are other things you must attend to. The remnants of your Assembly are nearby.

"Amanda," Enzo said, the words coming out in a slur. "Amanda. Attend me."

His assistant popped her head in and gave a start. "Father," she said, walking in and bowing. "We did not expect you to wake for another day or two."

"Assemble."

"But, Father." She looked uneasy. "The doctors recommend rest."

"Assemble!" he snapped.

In a few minutes, the remnants of his inner circle were gathered. The absent faces spelled out which of his brothers and sisters had fallen. Only a few of his younger siblings were here, and none of the ones he had grown up with at the Hatchery.

There were a few new faces too, not from the Assembly. What were they doing here? That girl – Mengsk's daughter, no doubt trying to reclaim her position and ownership of her father's wealth. Well, those funds would be needed now to rebuild Genjix operations. There was another boy next to her, Hatchery-trained by the looks of him, possibly a new vessel, given the casualties they had sustained recently. Well, he would need good people around him to recover from this mess.

He looked each person over. "We will have to grow a new Assembly. There is too much work, and I have too few I trust." He looked over at Palos and acknowledged the grizzled vessel's contribution to saving his life. "How are our operations in Russia?"

"Unstable, Father. The remnants of Vinnick's operation have united and are allying themselves with the new vessels in the Federal Assembly. You left a vacuum in Russia before the situation stabilized, and they took advantage. Much of what you gained will need to be recaptured."

"And the North American continent?"

"The IXTF is now in control of both the catalyst facility and the loyalty haven," Amanda said, scanning her tablet. "Total casualties at the loyalty haven were eighty-seven percent. The catalyst facility…" she paused, "… fought to the last man. It was total attrition."

"More importantly, what of the catalyst reaction rods?" he asked.

"Between the two facilities, a total of twenty tons of the catalyst reaction rods are now in Interpol's hands."

Twenty. Tons.

That was half of their global stock. It would take ten years before they could replenish that amount. Damn Vinnick for stealing the rods. This delay had proven so costly. The others on the Council would use this against him.

Not just the others. All the Holy Ones feel that this catastrophe could have been avoided.

"My standing is lowered. I understand. Still, time is meaningless. We can rebuild."

There is something else. Ask Amanda to bring forth Weston.

Enzo complied, wondering who that was.

The young man at the back next to Alex came forth and fell to one knee. "Father," he said reverently.

"Who is this boy, Zoras?"

Stand up and greet him.

"Why?"

Do as I command, vessel.

Not quite understanding the order, he pulled the tubes and needles out of his body – the ones going up his nose in particular hurt – and tried to get out of bed, except when he twisted his waist to swing his legs over the edge, they didn't obey. Puzzled, he tried again. Nothing happened. Then he realized that he couldn't feel his toes or feet. He poked his thigh with his fingers. There was no sensation.

"It can't be," he muttered, more perplexed than anything. "I don't understand."

It is as I feared; you are paralyzed.

Enzo looked down at the body that had failed him, and then up at the circle of people standing around the bed. It must be awkward for them to stand over him like this. Well, they had better get used to it, then. His recovery could take a long time.

"It seems my injuries are more serious than I thought," he began. "I'll need more staff to assist me during the physical therapy."

No, Enzo.

"My Guardian?"

You have been a devout vessel, Enzo. However, your body betrays us. Your time is at an end. Weston is your replacement.

Enzo's hands froze and his body stiffened as Zoras's words sunk in. He was being replaced by a new Adonis Vessel, similarly to how he had once replaced Devin. How could that be possible? He was the leader of the Council, leader of all the Genjix. He was blessed above all others, his standing higher than any other to have ever walked on this planet. He was the one who was supposed to usher in Quasiform. This couldn't be how it ended!

"Zoras, my Guardian. My Holy One, we are so close to completing our goals. We must see this through. A transition at this crucial moment would be disastrous."

I am still close to achieving my goals. Your part of the journey has ended... You rarely heeded my wisdom, believing yourself an equal. It was tolerated as long as you saw success. However, the longer you walk along the edge, the higher the odds of your inevitable fall. I had warned you years ago to be careful of your place among the Genjix, Enzo. There is only one penalty for extreme failure on the Council.

"But Zoras..." Enzo found himself at a loss for words as his destiny – so assured a few days ago – was taken from under him. He felt true fear for the first time in his life – fear of failure, fear of unfulfilled fates, fear of this new reality. Mostly, he felt this new fear of dying. Throughout his life, he had thought himself not only special, but a prophet. Now, he knew the truth, and it killed him more than any physical death could.

As if given a hidden signal, Palos – the vessel with the unwavering loyalty, who had watched over him since the very first day Enzo had become a vessel – approached and fell to one knee next to Weston. He held up a tray in his hands. On it was a glass of water, a cyanide pill, and a serrated knife.

"Praise to the Holy Ones," those in the room chanted.

"Praise to..." Enzo began the prayer reflexively, but couldn't quite get himself to finish it.

The Edmonton Long-Term Veterinary Care Center was one of the nicest animal hospitals in all of Canada, except that it had only cared for four animals in its seventy-year history; three dogs and a cow that happened to have been hosts. It was also one of two remaining long-term medical facilities for the Prophus in North America, Canada being relatively ambivalent in their policies toward the Quasing, and Arizona being relatively ambivalent toward the policies of their government.

The cover for the hospital, a large unadorned brown building an hour north of Edmonton, was perfect for the constant stream of medical supplies that were drop-shipped in. The hospital's supplies were being strained this week, as over sixty injured Prophus agents now called the center their home, at least for the next few weeks, if not months.

Cameron Tan stared out the window while a nurse re-sewed a cut on his brow, courtesy of the beating that Jacob Diamont had given him. Twice now. He had gotten the cut during their first fight, and it seemed Jacob found joy in repeatedly bashing him in the same spot over and over again in their second. Maybe he was just an eyebrow hunter.

That is what I would do if I were Jacob.

"You're very brave to hold so still," said the nurse, an elderly woman. Cameron had never heard an accent like hers before and wondered which part of the world the Prophus had recruited her from. As for being brave, it was more because of the local anesthesia. He couldn't feel the top part of his face right now. She could be tattooing it for all he knew.

He had had another nightmare last night and had split the cut open when he woke up flailing and fell out of bed. This was the third consecutive night he had had dreams about the attack on the Genjix base four days ago. The first night, he was too exhausted to dream. Now, while he waited for the nurse to finish her work, his mind wandered back to the terrible events that had happened there.

So many people he knew were now gone, people he had grown up with. Uncle Dylan and Faust were almost family. No, they were family. Uncle Faust was Dad's best friend and Cameron saw him every holiday. Uncle Dylan was an important man, but he was also Cameron's godfather. Then there were all of Mom's people at the farmhouse. They were his babysitters, friends, and playmates. Everything that he had known, his entire life over the past few years was gone. Almost everyone he cared about was dead, and it hurt.

It is not an easy life. This war will claim many loved ones. I have lost more people I care about than I can count, hosts and Quasing alike.

Cameron's thoughts moved from the friends he had lost to the people he still had. Thank God Mom and Dad were still alive, though Dad was now more mummy than human. Both his arms were in monster casts with fiberglass going all the way past his shoulders. He wore a neck brace, had his chest wrapped in plaster, and one leg wrapped past his knee. The nurses in the hospital doted on him and called him the Golem. Dad loved the attention.

Uncle Marco was scheduled for another surgery tomorrow. This would be his third in five days. They were still hoping to save his leg, and he would have a terrible scar along his chest. Needless to say, he was probably retiring from active duty after this. Cameron had tried to see him a few times, but all he did was sleep. Medically-induced coma they said, and Ahngr, his Quasing, was ordered not to take control for fear of further injury to his frail body.

Rin, the scientist, was recovering alongside a handful of

other civilians caught during the Genjix evacuation when Jill's team was able to cut off their escape route. She had suffered a broken leg and was now recovering in the same hospital down the hallway from Dad.

That left Alex. Just the mention of her name made his chest contract just a little. Of course he wasn't going to see her at the base. In fact, he had forgotten all about her while he had been fighting there. Like they would send a fourteen year-old girl to fight anyhow. Well, Cameron had gone, but it was against the wishes of his parents.

He was being foolish; he knew that. It was stupid of him to have let her influence his going to the haven. What was he going to do, confront her? Ask her why she would stab him in the back like that? Ask if their time together – that one whole week – was even real, or just one big lie? Would he have just shot her or something? It was all just very immature of him; Cameron knew it and felt ashamed for being so selfish. Good people had died, and all he could think about was the girl.

No, Cameron. There is no shame. You were betrayed and have a right to be hurt. You know better now. Learn from it. Alex is the enemy. If you ever see her again, do not make the same mistake.

"I'm just so stupid, Tao."

It is an unfair burden to place on you. You are still young. Maybe it will be best if we pull you out of this for a while longer. You were robbed of a childhood. Perhaps we can give you some peace in your teenage years. Perhaps relocate you to Switzerland or England to finish school. Perhaps even go to college.

It was enticing, that thought of a normal life. Cameron almost agreed on the spot. The war should still be here when he was ready. He could just join and help the Prophus later, right? However, that would leave his parents and remaining loved ones fighting while he was gallivanting in safety. Could he live with himself? He knew the answer to that.

"There you go, dear," the nurse said. "The glue should hold better this time. Try not to split it again."

Cameron stood up and stared into the mirror at his bandaged head. Nurse Sheung at school would never believe he fell off a tree looking like this. He looked like, well, like he had just come out of a pitched battle. He thanked the nurse and headed to his father's room. They had placed him in a private room on one of the top floors, since he was pegged for long-term care. He found Roen awake and seemingly in a cheerful mood. Mom was sitting next to his bed, and they were laughing and holding hands. Both of them brightened even more when he walked in.

"The prodigal hero returns." Roen lifted a club arm and waved. "Ow."

"How's my little man doing?" Jill asked.

"Hey, guys," Cameron said, giving his mother a hug and high-fiving his dad on the part of his club arm where the hand should be, earning him another "ow."

"Pull up a seat, son." Roen tried unsuccessfully to gesture at a chair. Cameron pulled one up close to the bed and sat down next to his mother. She reached out and held his hand. Right then and there, he knew he had fallen into a trap.

"Listen, Cam, your mother and I have been talking. What do you think about studying overseas in the UK? The Keeper can pull some strings, and we can enroll you in school there, and possibly have you attend Oxford when you're old enough."

Cameron saw the expectant looks in his parents'

eyes and realized that they'd already conspired with his Quasing. "Tao, you totally went behind my back, didn't you?"

Maybe.

"I thought you were on my side."

I am on everyone's side.

Cameron stood up and crossed his arms. "No. I'm not leaving you guys. Forget it."

His father and mother exchanged glances. "Actually," Roen said. "I thought I'd come with you. I think I'm pretty much done. I'm officially retired the day these damn casts come off."

Cameron looked at Jill. "You, too?"

His mother shook her head. "Got offered a new job. Thinking about taking it."

"Is it in the UK as well?"

"No, but it's close."

"What's the job?"

"The Keeper's."

WHAT! Baji is the new fucking leader of the Prophus?

Cameron wasn't sure who was more shocked, him or Tao. Probably Tao. Still, the news left him speechless. That would mean...

"You're moving to Greenland?" he asked.

She nodded. "Kind of a requirement for the job. Meredith can't do it anymore, and her heir, the Keeper's new host-in-waiting, is too young to take the reins – thanks to your Dad, by the way – so she asked me to take interim command. Probably a five- to ten-year stint."

"Will Dad go with you?"

Roen grinned. "I'll be traveling between you both and living out my golden years in retirement while you attend school and your mom slaves away for the Prophus in the Arctic tundra."

Cameron's mind raced as he considered the relocation. In truth, he was used to it by now. He had been traveling most of his life, going from place to place. Sure, he'd be far from his grandparents, but it was probably for the best now that he was a Prophus agent. Wait, was he? Cameron had assumed that starting from the mission on the haven, he'd be a full-blown operative, but if he went to school, were they going to pull him from the front line?

"Am I still going to be an agent?" he asked.

His parents exchanged looks. "No," they said together.

"Then screw this." Cameron shook his head stubbornly. "You're not going to tuck me away while you guys risk your lives and the Genjix destroy the planet. I think I've proven myself enough."

"Look, Cam," Roen said. "You are a Prophus agent already. However, this damn war isn't the only important thing in the world. You need an education. You need friends. You need a life outside of the Quasing. That way, you know what you're fighting for."

They are right. It will just be for a few years. Get a degree. Figure out what is so beautiful about your species and your world.

"I... guess."

It took another thirty minutes of convincing, but in the end, Cameron accepted his parents' decision. Wasn't like he had much of a say in all this, especially with all three of his parents hammering him, but he realized in the end it was for the best, and it was the only way they could stay close together. At least for a little while longer. The family had come to a consensus and were about to hug it all out when Liesel, Jill's new assistant sent from Greenland, walked in.

"Ma'am," she said, saluting. "We have a situation. There's been an unusual chatter along several underground channels. We believe it's a message."

Jill switched gears and was all business. "For me? From the Genjix?"

"No, we believe for him." She pointed at Roen.

She frowned. "What does it say?"

Liesel looked down at her tablet. "Rayban Ghost. Let's talk."

Roen knew how ridiculous he looked when he got off the elevator onto the fourth floor of the IXTF regional headquarters in Seattle. The security guard at the entrance stared, mouth agape, as he hobbled into the hallway. The casts on his arms forced them up like Frankenstein's, and with most of his body in wraps, he must have looked like a walking punchline.

It also was pretty damn painful to make the trip here by himself from Edmonton. However, Kallis insisted this be done in person. Cognizant that this could just be a trap to haul him in, Roen insisted on going alone. The risk was high, but the possible payout was even greater. Besides, his wife, as the new leader of the Prophus, would bust him out, right? Well, at least he hoped so. Roen limped into the office like Quasimodo and waved at two of her guys he recognized from Ontario. Fortunately, they were far too shocked by his appearance to assault or arrest him.

"Wow, you look like absolute shit," a familiar voice said.

Roen did a complete body turn and saw Kallis, hands on her hip and facial expression somewhere between bemusement and surprise.

"A little help here?" he asked, eyes looking down at the messenger bag about to fall off his shoulder.

No one moved a muscle to help him. Roen should have figured. After all, not only did he work for the aliens, as a full human, he was actually betraying his own species. He was also the Rayban Ghost. They knew for a fact that he had not only injured, but probably gotten some of their brothers- and sisters-in-arms killed, though in Roen's defense, he had tried his damnedest to avoid that.

Most of all, though, they probably felt like he had completely betrayed their trust. He had sat at their table and broken bread with them. Well, had had drinks, which in this day and age was the same thing. For those in his line of work, it meant something. He had played them for fools and manipulated them. That was something that was difficult to forgive.

"Back to work. All of you," Kallis snapped. She gestured to Roen. "Come with me."

He hobbled after her into an interrogation room. The bright side was that none of the agents pounced and tried to cuff him. That was a good sign; it probably meant that he wasn't going to get arrested and thrown into prison. Well, the day wasn't over yet.

They went into a bland gray room with a table in the center, two chairs on each side, and a window at one end. On the desk were a pen and paper, and a video recorder, pretty stereotypical, like a bad cop procedural movie. Kallis took a seat at one end with the camera behind her, and Roen sat down on the other side. The camera was already on.

"Thanks for coming," Kallis began. "What happened to you, anyway?"

"Roller-blading accident." Roen shrugged. When she gave him a look, he decided to stop trying to be witty. He was never really good at it, not since Tao left him, anyway. "That underwater base your people captured and are trumpeting as a major coup against the aliens?"

She nodded.

"You're welcome."

Kallis looked back at the video recorder with the lights on and turned back to him. "Right. Well, over the past two weeks, we captured two alien bases and we saw some crazy shit in there. Our best guys have no idea what they're for. I bet you do."

He nodded. "Maybe."

"So instead of us trying to reinvent the wheel, I'd thought I'd just ask someone who already knew," said Kallis.

"What are you offering?"

"Immunity."

Roen shrugged. "And?"

Kallis leaned back and studied him for a few seconds. The silence was long and exhausting, but Roen knew this trick. He waited for her to shut the camera off, which she did a few seconds later. Of course there was another hidden camera behind that two-way mirror. Now the real negotiation began.

She pointed at the stack of papers in front of her. "Past couple of days, I went over all the operations pertaining to you over the past two years. You went out of your way to not kill my guys. Sure, some died, and others got hurt, but you tried to avoid casualties."

"Like I said." Roen tried to act as casually as he could. Did she want him to incriminate himself? "We're not the…"

"Bad guys," she finished. "I believe that now." She paused. "I want to work with you and your people."

"With the Prophus?" he said, surprised. Now he really did wish Tao was here.

"You specifically. I want you to be the liaison between the IXTF and the Prophus."

"Do you even have the authority for this?" he asked.

Kallis broke into a smile. "You're looking at the new North America Deputy Director of the IXTF, so yes. Capturing two huge alien bases in the span of a couple of days gets you all sort of accolades and promotions."

"Well," Roen said, "you're welcome again. So what are you offering?"

"Full immunity for all the Prophus," she pressed, "as long as we receive complete cooperation between IXTF and your... organization, with you as the intermediary. Only you. I don't trust anyone else."

Roen's mind raced. He was pretty sure he wasn't in a position to make a treaty with Interpol's Extraterrestrial Task Force. This discussion should really be between Kallis and Jill, not a guy like Roen, who was supposed to retire. Hell, he should be the last guy in the world to drive Prophus policy.

"Why me?" he asked. "We have diplomats who will work better with you. Heck, we have people working for us who are already part of the IXTF.

Kallis scowled; she didn't like hearing that. "Because these aliens inhabit people. They all have their own agendas. I'm sure you do as well, but you're the only person I trust right now on that side. Because I have a file this big on you, and the enemy you know is safer than the enemy you don't."

"That's it? I'm the least bad option?"

"That and we have no idea what we're up against. From what I can tell, something bad is going down, but our lab boys can't make heads or tails of what we found in that giant facility. Care to shed some light on it?"

Roen grimaced. "It's part of a giant terraforming operation that will remake Earth into a new Quasing home world, except that process will kill all life on the planet. We've been trying to stop it. There're a couple of these facilities hidden in the United States. We don't know where they are exactly, but we can help you find them."

Kallis sat across from him, looking stunned as he spoke. The blood had drained from her face and she sat very still, as if Medusa had turned her into stone. It took a while for his words to sink in. Finally, she coughed and cleared her throat. "That's some deep shit. So assuming it's all true, then I'd say our goals align. We both want humanity to continue breathing, so let's do it together. As long as IXTF leads the operation, I'd like you on board. What do you say?"

For the past few years, the Prophus had been teetering on the brink. Still, this was probably the greatest opportunity they had of turning the tide against the Genjix. Otherwise, this recent victory might have bought them a few years, maybe even ten, but the writing had been on the wall now for a long time. The Prophus weren't going to make it out of this century. By his estimation, the Earth wasn't going to, unless something extreme and drastic happened. Maybe this was it.

He swiveled to his left and aimed his right arm at Kallis. "Deal."

She shook his hand. "There's one more thing, Rutherford."

She accentuated that name. "I need the truth from you."

"My real name is Roen. Roen Tan."

"That's a start." Kallis looked toward the mirror and then back at him. "But I need to know everything. If this is to work, let's have a fresh start and be completely honest with each other."

"There's a lot to go through," he said. "We could be here for a while."

"I'll have coffee and Chinese food delivered."

"How about pizza?"

She smiled. "Pizza it is."

She turned the camera back on and spoke in a clear voice. "Let's get started. Timestamp: 0001. From the beginning, shall we?"

Roen made himself comfortable and looked directly at the camera. "My name is Roen Tan, and I am a Prophus operative. I used to be a host to a Quasing alien named Tao. 'Used to' because, well, let me start from the beginning. I first met Tao in Chicago…"

ACKNOWLEDGMENTS

I've pretty much thanked everyone under the sun in the first two books. From my loving wife Paula and my family, to my amazing fans, my agent Russ, and the countless booksellers carrying my books on their shelves, THANK YOU all for your support. I would have never made it without you. Yes, thank you as well, Eva the Airdale Terrier.

I'd like to take this chance to specially recognize a few people who sparked my writing career. Angry Robot Books in March 2011 decided to have a one month open submission. During those thirty-one days, 992 writers submitted queries, partials, and manuscripts to the robot overlords with hopes for being published. Over the course of the next year, through three levels of readers and rejections, twenty-five manuscripts made it to editorial phase. From there, five were chosen for publication, including *The Lives of Tao*. This moment changed my life. It opened a door to a new career and fulfilled a lifelong dream. After years of toiling, I was doing what I was meant to do on this world. And for that, no matter where I go from this point on, I will eternally be grateful to the people of Angry Robot Books who made my dream a reality.

So, to Amanda, my original reader, Lee, my editor, and Marco, my publisher, *thank you*. You will always have a special place in my heart. A special thanks also to Michael Underwood, Caroline Lambe, and the rest of the Angry Robot crew for being such awesome people.

To my buddies Roen and Tao, you two guys are more than characters created from the whims of my imagination. You're more to me than the words on the paper. You have been my friends and guides through my own adventure and I am blessed to have followed you through yours. I hope I did you two a service. I know it's not a happily-ever-after ending but come on, did you really think it'd end up that way? I'm sorry for putting you through hell but you sucked it up and I'm proud of to be linked with you both.

You two deserve a vacation, somewhere nice and sunny where no one is trying to kill you. Don't get too comfortable though. Stay in shape and don't eat too much pizza; I might need to call you guys back into service one of these days. Until then, I'll see you guys in the Eternal Sea.

Wesley Chu, Chicago, May 2015

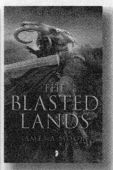

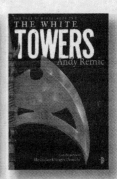

HEY, YOU!

- **Want more** of the best in SF, F, and WTF!?
- **Want the latest** news from your favorite Agitated Androids?
- **Want to be spared**, alone of all your kind, when the robotic armies spill over the world to conquer all weak, fleshy humans?

Well, sign yourself up for the Angry Robot Legion then!

You'll get sneak peaks at upcoming books, special previews, and exclusive giveaways for free Angry Robot books.

Go here, sign up, survive the imminent destruction of all mankind:

angryrobotbooks.com/legion